THE LANGUA

Sue Frost is a journalist and broadcaster. She has been the agony aunt at *Woman* magazine for the past nine years. Her first novel, *Redeem the Time*, is available in Arrow.

Also by Sue Frost

Redeem the Time

THE LANGUAGE OF NIGHTINGALES

SUE FROST

ARROW

Published by Arrow Books in 1998

1 3 5 7 9 10 8 6 4 2

Copyright © Sue Frost 1998

First published in the United Kingdom in 1998 by Hutchinson

Arrow Books Limited
20 Vauxhall Bridge Road, London SW1V 2SA

Random House Australia (Pty) Limited
20 Alfred Street, Milsons Point, Sydney,
New South Wales 2061, Australia

Random House New Zealand Limited
18 Poland Road, Glenfield, Auckland 10, New Zealand

Random House South Africa (Pty) Limited
Endulini, 5A Jubilee Road, Parktown 2193, South Africa

Random House UK Limited Reg. No. 954009

A CIP catalogue record for this book is available
from the British Library

Papers used by Random House UK Limited are natural,
recyclable products made from wood grown in sustainable forests.
The manufacturing processes conform to the environmental
regulations of the country of origin.

ISBN 0 09 924212 5

Typeset in Ehrhardt by
Palimpsest Book Production Limited,
Polmont, Stirlingshire
Printed and bound in Great Britain by
Bookmarque Ltd, Croydon, Surrey

In memory of Lynne Fletcher
1957–1997

'In the depth of winter, I finally learned
that within me lay an invincible summer.'

Albert Camus

Chapter One

She woke that day to a world in which everything seemed changed.

The bed was wider, strange in its emptiness, and the peep on the digital alarm sang sweeter, more tuneful than she remembered.

She opened her eyes reluctantly, fighting awareness. The light beyond the bedroom curtains was tinged with mauve, a pale radiance she'd never noticed before, and the photograph on her dressing table, a blurred enlargement of herself and Sean at some office party, jumped to life before her gaze, as though the glasses in their hands might suddenly rise up and clink. *I am losing all this.*

She got up and drew the curtains cautiously, afraid of what might lie beyond.

Outside, the avenue of spindly elms waved brilliant green and the early sun spun threads of silver on to the bleached flags of the street.

Laurie drew in her breath.

I am losing all this. I never knew I had it, and now I'm losing it all.

The joy of the known, the unspeakable loveliness of the utterly familiar . . . She trembled before it, feeling its fragility.

Then she walked into the kitchen.

In there, too, everything gleamed brighter. The steel saucepans shone like buffed silver, and the ceramic cups on their rack by the sink seemed plucked from some impressionist painting, cerise, cobalt blue and lemon.

She sat down at the breakfast bar, watching her limbs fold with a sense of wonder. How wonderfully functional the human body seemed, how exquisitely formed. Even her own breathing seemed more rhythmical than she'd ever experienced before, a precious flow of sound imparting shape to her movements.

She reached for a pitcher of milk inside the fridge, and poured steadily into a cup. She took a sip, then saw her fingers, white as the milk itself, clasped on the handle of the cup.

'*Nothing will ever be the same again.*'

This time she spoke aloud, and her voice, sounding out in the silent kitchen, seemed weak and uncertain, unfamiliar in the faint, panicky rise at the end of the sentence.

'*Quite possibly, I am going mad,*' she said, trying out the sounds without conscious recognition of their meaning, intending only to consider the effect and compare with what she'd known before.

'*I'm not who I used to be. I have crossed an invisible divide. I can never, ever return.*'

If her responses had been less sharp, then she might have thought herself tranquillized, or even drunk.

But instead she seemed to inhabit a previously unimagined state, as though a covering net of normality had been ripped from the window of her perception, leaving her shocked and raw, stunned by the terrible beauty of an ordinary day.

Then the doorbell rang, and the cup jerked out of her hand on to the kitchen floor where it smashed before her startled gaze.

And in a moment, the world resumed its old, haggard face.

'You've broken one of your lovely cups,' Gloria Davison said, stooping to pick the shards from the floor, 'what a shame.'

Laurie shrugged. Her earlier mood had vanished, giving way to a curious passivity.

'I've got five left,' she said.

'But you bought those cups with Sean! Spain, wasn't it? Never mind, when all this is over, you can take a long, relaxing holiday. Buy some more cups . . . Where is Sean, anyway? Don't tell me he's working today!'

Laurie shrugged again, a reflex that seemed appropriate to her passive state, yet nevertheless was unaccustomed to the self she had once been.

'Sean has gone,' she said carelessly.

Gloria dusted the kitchen floor and began to tidy the worktop.

'Well really, darling, I do think he might have taken the morning off . . . Just to wish you luck and say goodbye!'

Another shrug. 'He's already said goodbye,' Laurie replied.

Gloria tightened her lips in a familiar gesture of scorn.

'Men are simply useless in a crisis,' she said lightly, wishing Laurie to understand that this was no particular criticism, merely an observation on the natural state of things. 'Don't worry about Sean. I'm sure he'll be fine.'

Laurie nodded, forgoing the now habitual shrug.

'I'm sure he will . . . And in any case, it's no business of mine. Sean has gone. He isn't coming back.'

She hadn't meant to impart this news in quite so bald a fashion, so flat a tone, for she knew only too well that Gloria would think her grief-stricken, hiding her broken heart beneath a show of unconcern. But in truth, she *was* unconcerned. Her life with Sean, for so long the centre of all hopes and ambitions, now seemed a distant dream. She hardly cared if she saw him again, and if she did, well then, she would be gracious and polite. But essentially unconcerned.

I'm not who I used to be. I have crossed an invisible divide. I can never, ever return.

For a moment Gloria looked as though she might burst into tears, an event so unprecedented that Laurie almost took fright, briefly contemplating a hasty retraction.

But then Gloria rallied, doggedly asserting that things couldn't possibly be that bad, breezily dismissing all evidence that suggested anything contrary to her own inimitable conclusions.

'Sean will be back,' she said cheerily. 'We mustn't forget,

3

Laurie, that this whole thing is quite a trauma for him, too . . .'

At once Laurie was jerked from her passionless state.

'Don't talk to me about Sean's trauma,' she snapped. 'This one is all mine.'

Gloria smiled indulgently.

'I'm afraid that isn't true, darling. I'm your mother, remember! Nobody suffers like a mother . . .'

Laurie bent her head, willing herself to desist from this particular lamentation, and then, wondering why she shouldn't say exactly what she liked and finding no answer, gave up.

'Well, I shall never have a child now,' she burst out, 'so that's one little bit of suffering I won't have to endure!'

Gloria had forgotten the map, a curious oversight for one so well-organized and so committed to this particular journey, and a sure indication of unusual distress. But Laurie was immune to any but her own distress, and made her irritation plain.

'Sorry, darling . . . We'll just call in at the shop and pick up the directions . . . Won't take a minute . . . And then you can say goodbye to Shelley . . .'

Gloria was flustered, fumbling in her bag for the car keys, checking the glove compartment again for the letter from Norfolk, and finally pulling away without looking in her mirror, provoking an angry hoot from behind.

'So I made a mistake!' she shouted as the wronged driver overtook with a scornful glare. 'We're none of us perfect!'

This unlikely admission couldn't pass unnoticed, even by Laurie in her subdued state, and she raised one eyebrow. She mightn't choose to go to Norfolk, but she certainly wanted to arrive in one piece.

'What a brute!' she said lightly. 'Wonder what's eating him this morning?'

Gloria relaxed and blasted her own horn at a wobbling cyclist.

Laurie relaxed too. They were back on course.

4

The shop was open, much to Laurie's relief. It would have been just like Shelley to take an extra half-hour when the boss was away, but here she was, beaming behind the brazils and the barley, mashing the tofu for a lunchtime special, sorting out the old copies of *Veggie World*, supervising the waitress and the kitchen help, rearranging the vitamins.

She winked at Laurie.

'A nice cup of Miso before you go?' she inquired.

Gloria vanished in search of her maps, and Laurie sat down at the table where she'd consumed so many of her childhood suppers, lentils of every shade, greens and grains, nutburgers, soya sausages, and brown rice all the way . . .

At the New Leaf Wholefood Store and Cafe, very little had changed in twenty years, despite the challenge from health-conscious supermarkets and trendy delicatessens. There was still a demand for unbleached flour and unsulphured apricots, for Gloria's tempeh sandwiches and dried apple flapjacks. And there was a whole new market for exotic potions and pills.

But for all that, Gloria continued to fret about a change of name. New Leaf had seemed very clever at the time, but now it seemed . . . Well, rather *Old Hat*.

Sean had come up with some alternatives.

'How about Nuts to You? Or Beans R Us?'

Shelley had added a couple more.

'How about Pulse-Ate? Or Lentil Health?'

Laurie, to her surprise, had been offended, and realized that she wanted no change. The New Leaf, for all her vexed relationship with wholefoods and remedies, was nevertheless her family home. She'd grown up among the bags of chickpeas and the boxes of carob. Gloria should let it be.

Shelley sat down at the table.

'Shall I say I've got to be away at four? Or shall I tell her not to hurry back? It's up to you . . .'

Laurie smiled gratefully. Shelley had transformed herself to help out Gloria. No white make-up, no black-rimmed eyes, no spiky hair. She looked well scrubbed and whole-some, the sort of girl you'd be happy to have mashing your tofu. It was astonishing.

'Could you tell her she'll have to get back? By the way, you look amazing.'

'I feel naked as a baby's bum,' Shelley said, 'but never mind, what are friends for?'

Laurie felt her eyes smart.

'Thanks,' she whispered.

They drove away from the smart city suburbs, north, through dingy streets lined with dejected brown trees and half-hearted hydrangeas poking their scrubby heads above the confines of crumbling garden walls, then east, on to the motorway.

'I went to Norfolk once before,' Gloria remarked when they glimpsed the first sign for Norwich, 'with your father. It was very wet and very flat. A bit like him, really.'

Laurie did not want to discuss her father, nor to antici-pate his arrival which would be difficult enough when it happened, but Gloria seemed suddenly to consider that her customary brusqueness on the matter of her former husband might be misplaced in these new, unfortunate circumstances.

'He's terribly worried about you, darling,' she said has-tily. 'He'd really like you to fly out to Washington ... I don't suppose you'd rather do that ... Would you?'

I don't want to go to Washington. And I don't want to go to bloody Norfolk, either. I want both of you to leave me alone.

'I guess not,' Laurie said, unable to control another shrug.

'That's settled then,' Gloria murmured happily. 'I've done my duty. I told him I'd ask.'

Laurie's preference for Norfolk irrefutably confirmed, Gloria was now at ease, talking animatedly about plans for redesigning the New Leaf – which might shortly be renamed The Lemon Tree or The Juniper Berry – and turning the top floor into a consulting suite.

6

'I thought about aromatherapy . . . And reflexology. That girl from the yoga class is awfully good with feet. You should have your feet done, darling.'

'There's nothing wrong with my feet,' Laurie said.

'Well, it's not your feet, of course! By manipulating the feet, they can tell if you've got various things wrong with you . . .'

'I hardly think that's necessary. I know exactly what's wrong with me.'

'Sorry, darling. That was rather crass. I mean they can suggest different forms of treatment . . . Just by looking at your feet. She told me I needed Bryonia for my chest . . .'

Laurie drew a deep breath and clutched at the sides of her seat.

'Isn't it enough that I'm going to this ridiculous place in the middle of nowhere?' she demanded tightly. 'Can't you be satisfied with that?'

Gloria, chastened, turned to face her daughter and the car swerved to the centre of the road.

'It's not ridiculous,' she said distractedly, hauling at the driving wheel, 'I only want the best for you Laurie, and Doctor Mitchell has a fine reputation . . . Even your father has heard of him!'

Laurie, unnerved, said nothing, and they might have continued in tactful silence had Gloria not chosen this moment to state her case.

'If you'd listened to me before,' she said unhappily, 'this would never have happened. You don't look after yourself, Laurie. You've neglected your inner needs and your body has rebelled.'

'Stop the bloody car,' Laurie said suddenly. 'Stop it this moment! I want to get out.'

'Stop? Whatever for?'

'I'm listening to my body's needs. I'm hungry. See that cafe over there? I'm going right in to order egg and chips.'

'Egg and chips!' echoed Gloria, disbelieving. 'Laurie, please . . .'

'Cholesterol and carcinogens,' Laurie said grimly. 'And

7

why the hell not? It can't do me any more harm, can it?'

In the cafe she resisted egg and chips, for this would have been an affront too far. Instead they ate wholemeal sandwiches filled with carrot salad and cottage cheese, Laurie satisfying her rebellious spirits with a weak cappuccino.

'I don't suppose these carrots are organic,' Gloria said gloomily. 'They're probably thick with something terribly toxic . . . like DDT.'

'Hasn't DDT been banned?'

'Not in Third World countries,' Gloria replied.

'Well, these look like thoroughly British carrots to me.'

She was teasing now, gently indulging her mother in the way she'd learned over many tiresome years, enduring each new fad with long-suffering grace, accepting that some whims, like Gloria's energetic pursuit of organic produce, were reasonable enough, while others, like chanting yogic mantras for half an hour each morning before breakfast, were simply tedious.

But though Laurie might reserve her opinions and had even been known to mock when Gloria wasn't listening, a daughterly sense of duty always kept her from open refutation. She preferred to prevaricate, giving her mother the benefit of considerable doubt, arguing with Sean, among others, that Gloria did no harm, indeed, might do some good, and was therefore to be allowed her dietary foibles and her mystical fancies.

It was this habitual policy of tolerance that led to the final showdown with Sean.

'This is madness,' he'd shouted at Laurie when the Norfolk plan had been revealed. 'You're putting yourself in the hands of some quack because you haven't got the guts to contradict your mother!'

'It's not like that!' Laurie shouted back. 'I'm willing to try anything, so why not this?'

'Because it's bullshit, that's why! Like everything else your barmy mother comes up with! What will it be next week? Digging up mandrakes when the moon's full? Or has she tried that already?'

He was still shouting, and Laurie was both astonished and offended by his anger. She didn't understand it, and she didn't mean to endure it.

'This has nothing to do with you,' she said coldly. 'It's my decision. I've got time on my hands, after all.'

Sean made a visible effort to calm his temper.

'What about your father?' he'd asked at last. 'What does he say?'

'He's paying for it,' Laurie had replied.

Now, nibbling at her cottage cheese sandwich, her appetite predictably gone, she considered that this piece of news, delivered with all the panache of a punch line, had proved the ultimate blow for Sean. Her father, seemingly so rational, so measured and considerate in his opinions, so careful and diplomatic in his dealings with his ex-wife, had shown himself in thrall to Gloria, just like Laurie herself. Or so it must have seemed. The truth was rather more complex, an unspoken understanding between father and daughter, long-held and inviolate, that Gloria stood at the most vulnerable point of their skewed triangle and therefore needed protecting.

'Don't finish that stuff, darling,' Gloria commanded, breaking into her thoughts and indicating the cappuccino. 'Caffeine makes you tense.'

Laurie pushed her mug aside. 'Don't you think I'm tense already?'

'Yes, of course,' Gloria soothed, sweeping the half-eaten sandwiches into a litter bin and waving imperiously at a waitress. 'That's why nothing should be done to increase your agitation . . .'

She suddenly delved into her handbag and produced a slim glass phial.

'I think you need the Rescue Remedy,' she pronounced, waving the bottle under Laurie's nose. 'These flower concoctions are very effective . . . It'll have you feeling full of hope in no time . . . We'll just wait a few minutes until your sandwich goes down . . .'

Laurie stood up and walked out of the cafe.

'I don't need a rescue,' she said over her shoulder, 'I need a cure.'

The grandly titled and lavishly appointed Crompton Hall lay halfway between Norwich and the North Norfolk coast, the principal building in a hamlet of pink brick cottages proclaimed, in the brochure, as numbering among the finest examples of late-medieval agricultural dwellings in the country.

The Hall itself, in which Dr Dale Mitchell, late of the University of California and now director of the Movement for Regenerative Studies, had set his stall, was itself very fine, the epitome of an English country house at its most glorious moment.

Gleaming rose and bronze in the afternoon light, the house reared above a wooded loop of road as Gloria's car took the bend from the village, an elegant sprawl of windows, wings and turrets rising beyond an avenue of vivid limes.

'They filmed *Mansfield Park* here,' Gloria remarked.

Laurie said nothing, merely thrust her hands into her jacket pockets and clasped her fingers tight. Her fortitude had withered as they entered the village, and now, as the car swung between the unbending limes, it finally perished. She was frightened, confused and sick at heart.

'Looks more like Manderley than Mansfield Park,' said Gloria brightly as they drew up, 'and here comes Mrs Danvers!'

The woman who emerged from behind stout mahogany doors to escort them up a flight of sparkling stone steps did indeed look somewhat forbidding, an erect, bespectacled figure in a grey business suit.

But when she spoke, a soft Mediterranean lilt and gentle smile transformed the image.

'Laurie Davison,' she said warmly, 'welcome! I'm Ruth Christianos, the Centre manager, and I'm here to show you round . . .'

Still Laurie said nothing. She'd been seized by the urge to run, and her sense of panic, far from rendering her compliant or respectful, was fostering a growing hostility.

'Can we see the rooms?' Gloria asked eagerly, following Ruth into a pale panelled hall flagged with veined Italian marble. 'Tonight, when I'm back home, I want to visualize Laurie in her room so I can send a healing vibration . . .'

'Oh really!' snapped Laurie. 'If you're so good at healing vibrations, what on earth am I doing here?'

Ruth laughed.

'Maybe you're here,' she said, smiling directly at Laurie and avoiding Gloria's gaze, 'just to have a good time? Relax, unwind, chill out . . .'

'A week in Marbella would do that,' Laurie replied frostily, adding under her breath: 'and cheaper.'

Inside, the house stretched away into elegant splendour, long open salons leading off the marble hall and a fine alabaster balustrade winding up to a vaulted gallery.

Laurie listened dully as each room was entered and its purpose explained, her eyes drifting across empty brocade sofas and stuffed footstools. Visualization, meditation, relaxation, massage, art and music, counselling . . . Ruth Christianos detailed a smorgasbord of therapies, all for Laurie's benefit.

'But nothing is compulsory. You can simply sit and enjoy the surroundings. The only required session is a short daily interview with Doctor Mitchell . . . And in addition, he'll be asking you to keep a journal, a record of your thoughts as treatment progresses.'

'Where is Doctor Mitchell?' Gloria inquired squarely, enough time having been spent admiring fireplaces and ceiling decorations. 'Naturally we're extremely keen to meet him . . .'

Dale Mitchell, they were informed, was out walking in the woods, and most of the Centre's residents were with him. Laurie would meet him before supper.

'Is all your food vegetarian?' Gloria demanded, having fretted over the brochure's imprecision on this point. 'And is it organic?'

'We serve a variety of cuisines,' Ruth replied smoothly, 'all expertly prepared.'

'Using the highest quality ingredients, I suppose?' pursued Gloria unnecessarily, for it was hardly likely the Centre manager would admit to anything less, and Laurie, unable to control her contempt, emitted an audible snort.

'For goodness' sake,' she hissed at Gloria when Ruth moved briefly out of hearing, 'just let the woman say her piece. It hardly matters what they give me to eat. The bill's already been paid!' And Gloria, briefly silenced, followed her daughter up the staircase.

The bedrooms were large and luxurious, some still containing the solid Victorian washstands and chests which must have furnished the house in its country mansion days, and Laurie had been given a principal suite, three adjoining rooms hung with heavy flock wallpaper and rich velvet curtains, crimson, chocolate and gold, womb-like and faintly oppressive. But the suite faced south with a view across the grounds to a wooded area beyond, and in the distance Laurie could see a silver lake, bright as a mirror in the late afternoon light.

'The whole place is beautiful,' Gloria exclaimed, having temporarily suspended her inventory of ideas to admire the lavish tapestry counterpane on Laurie's bed. 'Just look at the work in this quilt! It's very therapeutic, of course, manual labour . . . I've often said Laurie ought to do something with her hands . . .'

Laurie's fingers twitched in her pockets.

'Maybe I'll try sign language,' she said abruptly. 'That might help me get my views across.'

Gloria was hurt.

'I was just thinking about Shelley, making her jewellery,' she muttered defensively. 'It's very creative. Good for the spirit. That's all I meant.'

Laurie was deeply irritated. On the strength of a one-day stint at the New Leaf, Shelley had been transformed in Gloria's estimation from wild child to wonderful human being. She only hoped Shelley would do something soon to redress the balance.

She sat down heavily on the bed, registering the presence on her pillow of a hefty silk-bound notebook, its peacock-blue cover elaborately decorated with a Chinese motif and fastened by a golden tassel. *No escaping Dr Dale's journal!*

Gloria moved to the window, staring out in anticipation.

'Is that Doctor Mitchell over there? Coming out of the woods?'

Ruth Christianos looked past her.

'Yes, that's him. He sometimes takes clients out to the summerhouse by the lake . . .'

'Clients?' Laurie said sharply. 'Is that what you call them?'

'Some people don't like to think of themselves as patients.'

Gloria beamed.

'That's just what I've been telling my daughter! The very idea of being a patient is terribly depressing. I'm sure it must have an enervating effect on the spirits . . . It's so important don't you think, to be positive? We're all ultimately responsible for our own health, both in body and mind. And the two are so intimately related . . .'

Ruth turned quickly to Laurie.

'Would you like to meet with Dale now? I think he'll want to see you right away . . . Mrs Davison, maybe you'd wait in the music room with a cup of tea?'

'Tea?' asked Gloria faintly.

'Fruit tea,' replied Ruth Christianos with a faint smile, 'made from our own organic elderberries.'

Laurie lay down on the tapestry quilt and closed her eyes against the opulence of the room.

A heavy hand seemed to have settled upon her, weighing her down into the softness of the bedclothes. Her limbs felt languid, as though movement required a great effort, and her heart was like lead, a solid ball inside her chest that shook her whole body with its remorseless beat.

All the exquisite sensations of the morning had vanished, so that now the rich bedroom hangings seemed sickly and the yellow light outside her bedroom window gaudy and harsh.

More discomfiting, Sean's objections to the Norfolk enterprise seemed cruelly intelligible now that she'd actually arrived. There was surely no good reason for her being here, except that Gloria had wanted it, indeed, had insisted upon it.

She was, Laurie reminded herself, in a weak and vulnerable condition. She was no match for Gloria, and felt unequal to the challenge posed by Dale Mitchell.

She had no doubt it would be a challenge, and of the most wearisome kind. The Centre's brochure had not been encouraging, offering woolly promises of 'treating the whole person' and promoting 'a spiritual journey of discovery'. It was just the kind of vague quasi-Eastern philosophy that Gloria favoured, and now it seemed to Laurie the very least appropriate thing to fit her for the trials that lay ahead.

Anticipation of those trials brought her suddenly to tears, terrifying, gasping sobs that jerked her frozen limbs to life so that she threshed and struggled on the enveloping bed. For several moments she wept, the ugly sounds muffled by the cloth of the bedspread, until a gentle voice outside her door informed her that Dr Mitchell was waiting.

'I'll be there,' Laurie said, sitting up and reaching for the man-size box of tissues ominously situated at the side of the bed right by the silk-bound journal. 'Just give me a moment.' And in a moment she had resumed her hostile pose.

He was waiting in a downstairs room she'd already been shown, the so-called counselling suite, quiet, airy quarters which had once housed the library.

The room was still lined with leather-bound books, and above the carved fireplace hung a portrait of two young women in Edwardian dress. In this place the spirit of Crompton Hall prevailed, and the Centre for Regenerative Studies seemed utterly foreign and remote.

Laurie had meant to remain similarly remote, detached

and polite in her responses to all questions, but something about Dale Mitchell provoked her immediate dislike, precipitating the collapse of any pretence at indifference.

'Laurie . . . Welcome . . . Come and sit here beside me.' He stood up from the sofa, a tall, tanned, golden-haired cowboy, dressed in blue denims and red-checked shirt, straight off the Range.

He grinned at her evident confusion.

'Excuse the informality . . . We've been walking in the woods. Maybe tomorrow you'll come with us?'

He gestured at the sofa, and Laurie summoned her defences.

'I prefer a chair,' she said coolly, 'and I shan't be going walking, if you don't mind.'

He smiled, displaying a perfect set of polished teeth, a good ten thousand dollars' worth, Laurie thought uncharitably.

'That's up to you, Laurie . . . But maybe you'd like to tell me why you're here? What you're hoping Crompton Hall can do for you?'

His eyes were focused upon her. The colour of pewter, they seemed to scan her every thought so that she faltered when she came to speak, imagining he saw all prevarication and detected each evasion.

'You know why I'm here,' she muttered.

'I know what's written in your file, but I'd like you to tell me in your own words . . .'

'The truth?'

'I'd find that most interesting.'

Laurie shuffled on her stiff, upright chair.

'I was given immediate leave from my job. I have some time to fill in . . .'

'And that's the whole truth?'

Laurie made her decision.

'I'm here,' she said, tilting her chin and staring straight into the pewter eyes, 'because my mother decreed it. My mother knows all about these things. She thinks I've made myself sick. She thinks I can make myself better by an act of will. She thinks you and your screwy ideas will encourage me to do it. She thinks you can bring about a regeneration.'

He considered this carefully, his face grave and calm.

'And what do you think, Laurie?' he inquired at last. She turned her eyes from him, fixing instead on the portrait of the two young women over the mantel.

'I have cancer,' she said steadily. 'I think I'm dying.'

Chapter Two

It was Sean who found the lump.

They had walked that day to the Portobello Road where Laurie bought a Victorian nightdress buttoned up the front and hemmed with blue ribbon, and Sean, raising an eyebrow and twirling an imaginary moustache, suggested they go home immediately so that she might try it on, and he might rip it off.

And afterwards, in a most un-Victorian post-coital exploration, he'd made contact with something new behind her left nipple.

'What's this, Laurie?'

'What's what?' she'd said dreamily, still thinking of the nightdress and the scenes it might have witnessed. There surely *was* such a thing as progress, even in the vexed arena of sexual relationships, and even when every move and counter-move toward commitment seemed depressingly familiar.

Sean propped himself up on one elbow, and looked down at her, his hand still clasped on her breast.

'There's a lump here. A hard lump.'

'That's because you're squeezing too tight. Let go, and it will disappear.'

He shifted his grip and began to prod beneath her nipple.

'It's solid,' he said. 'A solid lump. How long have you had that? I've never noticed it before . . .'

Laurie felt her skin chill, as though the door had suddenly swung open on the stifling bedroom to admit a wintry breeze. But the door was still closed, the afternoon unseasonably warm.

'It's nothing,' she muttered, pushing his hand away. 'I've had it checked out.'

'When?' he persisted, staring down with irritating intensity. 'When did you have it checked out?'

'I don't know . . . A year ago, maybe. It's benign.'

He lay back on the bed, his eyes closed, his limbs relaxed.

'That's all right then,' he said.

And with dread intuition, Laurie suddenly knew that it wasn't all right.

Slowly, gently, so she wouldn't alert him, she began to examine her left breast. Yes, there it was. A solid lump beneath the nipple, cunningly concealed so that no casual fumbling would find it. Was this the same lump her doctor had examined and pronounced harmless?

She got up and walked to her dressing table mirror, lifting the breast to peer beneath it. The skin seemed gathered, puckered like the rind of an orange, although the lump itself remained invisible.

'Hey, come back!' said Sean from the bed. 'I haven't finished.'

Laurie, struggling with rising panic, picked up her watch from the dressing table.

'It's after two,' she said curtly. 'Shouldn't you be going? Tina will be waiting at the door.'

'I said some time after three . . .'

It required nothing more than Tina's name to banish the afternoon's intimacy, and when Laurie went back to the bed, he moved away from her, reaching for his clothes.

She watched him dress, and thought, as she always did when he was here, in her flat, eating her food, fiddling with her computer or making love in her bed, that there had been no man she'd ever wanted more. It was inevitable, a given of the modern world, that he should have arrived in her life trailing a whole cartload of complications.

Gloria, of course, had anticipated just such a circumstance.

'If you wait as long as you have,' she'd said to Laurie on meeting Sean and later being delicately appraised of his marital difficulties, 'then it's obvious you won't get first pickings. You have to make do with some other woman's leftovers.'

'He left her,' Laurie objected, 'and before you ask, it was

nothing to do with me! He walked out months ago, and in any case, he'll soon be divorced.'

But more than a year later, Sean was still not divorced, and Saturday afternoons were given over to Megan and Mollie, golden-haired, blue-eyed daughters with Enid Blyton names over whose baby photographs Laurie had fretted and dreamed, and for whom she planned a beautiful half-sibling. Soon, when Sean and Tina finally aborted their ill-conceived marriage and he was free to marry again . . .

Now he leaned over the bed to kiss her goodbye, and Laurie, still seized with a burdensome presentiment of doom, was suddenly afraid of being alone.

'I'll drive you,' she said, 'I'll drop you off at the end of the street so Tina won't see me.'

He shook his head.

'If she gets the slightest inkling you're around, she won't let the girls out of the house . . . You know how it is, Laurie . . . I can't risk upsetting her.'

She watched him go with her heart banging out a signal of distress, nothing more, she told herself, than her usual pain at being so neatly and effectively exorcized from this vital aspect of Sean's life. She had never been allowed to meet his daughters, and as long as Tina prevailed, she never would.

But this time, the distress was something more.

'You okay?' he asked her dutifully, as he opened the front door, his jacket swinging from his shoulders, his collar undone and his blond hair still damp with sweat.

She fastened his collar and smoothed the wet strands from his face, although, when she considered it, she wouldn't at all mind Tina surmising that he'd just got out of bed.

'I'm okay,' she said brightly, 'but tomorrow, I think I'll go back to the doc and get that lump checked out again . . .'

There is never a good way to deliver bad news, but some ways are better than others.

'That's malignant,' Laurie's doctor said, washing his

19

hands at the surgery tap then adjusting his paisley cravat. 'You need an immediate appointment at the breast clinic. I imagine they'll want to operate straight away.'

Laurie blinked.

'Operate?'

'A mastectomy. Looks like it's spread to the lymph nodes, too. There's a little lump here under your arm . . .' He burrowed into her left armpit and wobbled his finger to demonstrate. 'You'll need scans to see if it's spread any further. Liver, lungs, bone . . .'

She blinked again, staring at his jovial face above the lurid cravat. She reminded herself why she'd chosen this doctor above the sort Gloria favoured, earnest ladies in floral dresses who practised homeopathy on the side and thought acupuncture more use to the human race than paracetamol.

Laurie's doctor was different. He considered beating around the bush akin to medical negligence. Patients were treated as intelligent grown-ups, able to take the facts on the chin, and if they didn't quite understand the facts, why then, to ask searching questions, or at least go away and look up the relevant terms in a medical dictionary.

Now Laurie closed her eyes, seized by a vision of Rock Hudson in some Fifties Hollywood comedy, the hypochondriac hero who overhears the other guy's diagnosis.

She opened her eyes. 'How long have I got, Doc?'

He laughed.

'Who knows? How long have any of us got? I don't mind telling you I drink too much, and I love bacon and eggs. I could keel over any moment.'

Laurie was not humoured by this reply, and suddenly glimpsed the divide she was about to cross. The mid-life heart attack was a potential calamity that might never strike. But cancer, eating away within, unseen, its parameters unknown, was a different kind of calamity, the ever-present spectre at the feast.

She buried her face in her hands, and when she looked up, it was to accuse.

'But you said it was benign! I came to you a year

ago, and you told me not to worry. How come I've got cancer?'

The doctor was momentarily flustered.

'Well, it certainly looked that way to me . . . Perhaps, in retrospect, I should have referred you . . . But of course, what starts out as benign can turn malignant. It's up to you to keep an eye on things and come back if you're worried.'

So then, Laurie thought distractedly, Your life in Your hands. This doctor, this high priest of orthodoxy, was in truth no different from Gloria. And she knew exactly what Gloria would say, albeit couched in the coy and careful terms of complementary medicine. It was all her own fault, her responsibility.

Her doctor was on the phone, talking quickly in hushed professional tones, fixing an appointment with the breast surgeon for the following day, all the while eyeing her carefully.

'You need someone with you,' he said when he'd finished his call. 'Can we contact your mother?'

God forbid!

'It's okay, thank you,' Laurie replied, dazed, 'I'll call my boyfriend. He's the one I need.'

She'd taken a full day off work, imagining that she might go shopping afterwards, or even meet Shelley in town for lunch. When Shelley wasn't tramping the malls trying to flog her jewellery, she was sitting in her kitchen, threading beads and charms on to bits of silver wire. It was a vivid contrast to Laurie's own working life, and she took every opportunity to home in on it.

But how absurd these plans now seemed. How foolish, how fruitless, was everything that smacked of normality.

She walked back to her flat in a blind agony of unknowing, registering nothing of the world around her and almost stepping under a car as she crossed the road outside her home.

What had she been expecting, for God's sake? To have the original benign diagnosis confirmed? No, not that. She

21

had feared the worst, and with sickening inevitability, the worst had come to pass.

And yet, she considered, there is surely something in us all that clings to hope, for if it weren't so, how would we live?

Then another voice whispered: *Hope or denial?*

Inside her home, everything was just as she'd left it, but subtly, almost imperceptibly, the atmosphere seemed to have changed, as though her desperation were pervading the very air around her.

She picked up the phone.

'Sean Youngman, please.'

'Is that Laurie? This is Jim . . . Thank God you called! We've got a real emergency here . . . Problems with the new system, I'm afraid . . . Any chance you could look in?'

Laurie stared into the phone, unable to recall any minor detail pertaining to her working life.

'I'm having a day off,' she muttered.

'But you installed the system! We've been trying to get hold of you. Sean said you'd be able to look in . . .'

She put out a hand to steady herself, clutching at the wall and hearing her fingernails scrape across the plaster.

'Can I speak to Sean?'

A muffled expletive followed, then suddenly she heard his voice, the familiar tones, although harassed, calming her immediate fear.

'Sorry about this,' he mumbled. 'The whole lot's gone down. I did say you were on a day off . . . But it would be very helpful if you could look in . . .'

Laurie leaned back against the wall, her legs trembling, her knuckles white as she clung to the receiver.

'There's no easy way to tell you this,' she said shakily, 'so I'll come right out with it. I've got cancer. I have to see the surgeon tomorrow. He'll probably operate right away.'

There was a long silence.

'Christ Almighty,' he said at last.

Another lengthy pause.

'Dear God,' he offered by way of apologetic after-thought.

22

Laurie felt she would surely faint.

'Please come, Sean. I need you here with me . . .'

This time the pause was momentary, but long enough to make her understand that his response was not instinctive.

'Yes,' he said quietly, 'of course you do. I'll be there just as soon as I can.'

She sobbed and shook and he held her close, stroking her hair and kissing her wet face.

'It'll be all right, won't it?' she begged. 'I mean, lots of people get cancer . . . And they don't all die, do they?'

She drew away from him, searching his face.

'As long as they catch it early,' she pleaded. 'It's really not that serious . . . Is it?'

His eyes flickered briefly into hers, then he gazed away into the room beyond her shoulder.

'Have they caught it early?' he asked.

Looks like it's spread to the lymph nodes, too. There's a little lump here under your arm . . . You'll need scans to see if it's spread any further. Liver, lungs, bone . . .

'Yes, of course they have! It's only a year since I first went to the doctor . . .'

'You ought to sue that bastard,' Sean said.

She was weeping loudly when the doorbell rang, and only registered the intrusion when he got up to answer it.

'Whoever it is, get rid them! I don't want to see anyone!'

He crouched down beside her and took her hand.

'It's Shelley,' he said gently, 'I asked her to come.'

She stared at him, disbelieving, and he looked away.

'Shelley?'

'She's your best friend, isn't she? I thought you'd want her here.'

A vision of Shelley rose before her, matt black hair teased into evil spikes, eyes like some demented badger, pools of jet sunk in chalky white, chains clanking, leathers flowing, crazy jewellery swinging from every orifice and lobe . . . Shelley, her oldest, her dearest, friend . . . Yes, of course she wanted Shelley!

Laurie sank her head to her knees and howled.

'I wanted you,' she gasped to Sean as the doorbell rang again. 'I only wanted you . . .'

Shelley burst into the flat like Superwoman on speed, face set in a smile of determined encouragement.

'Booze,' she demanded, taking one look at Laurie. 'Where's the booze? We all need it.'

And in a moment Laurie was staring at a perfect gin and tonic, ice fizzing and lemon bobbing. She took a sip, and as Shelley sat down beside her, felt her panic begin to subside.

'Tell me everything!' Shelley said throwing an arm around her shoulders. 'Tell me who you've seen, what they said, and what happens next.'

In the doorway, Sean drained his glass then set it aside.

'I'll leave you to it, if that's okay,' he said, grinning nervously at Laurie. 'Sorry, but I really must get back . . . Like I said, the whole damn show went down.'

Shelley was of the opinion, frequently voiced when among her friends, that men could be neatly divided into three categories, Creeps, Turds and All-Out Bastards.

But for Sean, she made an exception.

'He's a mutant. Combination of all three.'

Laurie shook her head.

'He's just a little boy,' she said tightly. 'I'll let him run off and play with his computers. When he comes back, I'll pretend all the nasty things have gone away and tuck him up in bed . . .'

But, soothed and temporarily restored by the gin, she revised this analysis, not least because she could imagine exactly what Shelley might say if encouraged to elaborate. And in any case, it wasn't true. Sean was not a man to dodge his responsibilities. This was what had most impressed her, right from the beginning. She would normally run a mile from married men, but Sean was different. Sean had left his wife, but he certainly hadn't abandoned his daughters. He wouldn't abandon her either.

And indeed, that evening, after a day punctuated by alternate bouts of hysterical tears and periods of gloomy introspection, frantic if cursory research into breast cancer treatments and statistics, more tears and, finally, a descent into stupefaction, Laurie's faith was rewarded. Sean came back.

'Okay kids,' said Shelley, eyeing Sean meaningfully, 'I'm leaving you alone . . .'

At the front door she hugged Laurie and cast a worried glance back at the sitting room. 'Call me,' she muttered fiercely. 'If he so much as puts a foot wrong . . .'

It was unclear what Shelley expected, and Laurie hardly knew what she expected herself. But she knew what she needed, and she willed him to provide it.

He smiled uncertainly as she sat down beside him, taking her hand in his.

'How are you feeling?' he inquired cautiously, an elementary mistake for little more was required to compound Laurie's distress.

'Oh, fine!' Her voice was a strained falsetto, unfamiliar to them both: 'How do you think I feel? I've just been told I'm dying!'

He shot her a startled glance.

'Is that what he said? The doctor, I mean . . . Did he really say that?'

Laurie said nothing, fighting her emotion.

'Surely he didn't?' Sean ventured nervously, 'I mean, they never say things like that . . .'

'They do,' Laurie contradicted grimly, and with a certain morbid satisfaction. 'This one did. He told me he didn't know how long I'd got.'

Sean's eyes widened briefly, then he hung his head.

'I don't know what to say,' he whispered, squeezing Laurie's hand, 'except that I'm sure everything possible will be done . . .'

In other circumstances this tepid reassurance might have served, for when nothing positive can be said, the choice of trite generality over silence is most often received with forbearance. But in this case it merely provoked Laurie's ire.

'Well, if you think so,' she said sarcastically, 'then that's all right!'

He looked away and Laurie closed her eyes, hating herself.

'I'm sorry,' she whispered, 'I don't mean to be so touchy . . . I can't seem to help it . . .'

He put an arm around her shoulder and kissed her hair. She nuzzled her nose into his neck.

'Make love to me,' she said.

'What now?'

'Yes, of course, now! It's not catching you know.'

He followed her dutifully into the bedroom, sitting on the end of the bed, as he always did, watching while she undressed, saying nothing.

She shed her clothes in record time and stood before the mirror, surveying what, until this moment, she had regarded as a pretty serviceable body. Even now it looked in great shape, with no visible evidence of the horror lurking beneath its smooth pink flesh . . . She turned abruptly from the mirror and dived beneath bedclothes, pulling the top-sheet over her face and contracting into a foetal ball, shivering at the chilly touch of the linen, waiting for him to join her.

He seemed to take for ever, fumbling with his shirt buttons and laying out his loose change on the bedside table, and when he finally slid between the sheets, a quick act of resignation – or so it seemed – she knew at once that it wasn't going to work.

'What's wrong?'

'Nothing's wrong!' His voice was muffled by the pillow, choked and strange. 'Just give me a few minutes, will you?'

She gave him a few minutes, receiving the familiar overtures impatiently, alert for any move, any slight deviation, which might reveal his reticence. And when she reached out for him, he moved swiftly away.

'Maybe a few minutes more,' he mumbled.

'It's okay,' she said, sitting up. 'It doesn't matter.'

'It obviously does.'

'No it doesn't.'

'Look Laurie, I want to ... But it's just not happening.'

She got out of bed and reached for her clothes, the first unexpected hint of her forthcoming detachment soothing her spirit and hardening her heart.

I have crossed an invisible divide ...

'Maybe you should go,' she said tightly. 'If you don't mind, I'd like to be alone.'

There was a long silence, and Laurie sat down at the mirror, combing her thick black hair. So he couldn't make it ... Or didn't want to make it ... It seemed suddenly irrelevant. There were more important things to consider.

'You think I've let you down,' Sean muttered at last, his voice still indistinct. 'But I haven't ... That is, I don't mean to ... But I'm not a bloody machine ...'

Laurie turned to face him. 'As a matter of fact, I wasn't thinking of you at all,' she said calmly. 'I was wondering who the heck's going to tell my mother I've got cancer ...'

A week in Hell. A week of hospital corridors, all of them painted a homogenous shade of grey-green, a week of much-laundered robes with missing ties so that Laurie's backside seemed permanently threatened with exposure, a week of lukewarm tea swilling in pitted pottery cups, of prescriptions and prognoses, of interminable questions and never-ending queues. A week of impenetrable medical jargon. *Lobular carcinoma. Oestrogen receptors. ER-positive. Node Status. TNM classification.*

A week of submission to strange machines which whirred and revolved and perused Laurie's body, suddenly frightening and unfamiliar, in reel upon reel of photographic images. Liver okay. Lungs okay. Bones ... sort of okay.

'A small patch of activity on the ribs,' said a cheerful and rather dashing houseman, seemingly sprung intact, Laurie thought somewhat ungraciously, from a Richard Gordon novel. 'But we don't think it's anything serious. Probably an old childhood injury. Did your big brother duff you up?'

Laurie shook her head weakly. Once, with the passing desperation known to all lone children, she had invented an older brother and called him Oliver. He had been her friend and protector. But slowly she'd realized that a real Oliver would go his own way, just as her father had done. And so he'd been disinvented.

'No big brother,' she said to the houseman.

'Ah well, then. Guess you fell off your roller skates . . .'

A week of shocks.

'Aggressive chemotherapy is the best weapon against breast cancer . . . So we in this hospital believe . . . Shrink the tumour, then operate. Back it up with radiotherapy.'

This doctor was young, female, and at least as nervous as Laurie herself.

'My hair?' Laurie asked faintly. She ran her hands through the blue-black curtain which swept her shoulders, feeling its smooth strength. *My best feature. My crowning glory.*

The young doctor nodded miserably.

'I'm afraid so. But it does come back. Quite quickly too. And sometimes it comes back curly . . .'

'If I wanted it curly,' Laurie cried, 'I'd have a bloody perm. I want it the way it is!'

'Sorry,' said the doctor, looking away.

'What else?' asked Laurie fearfully. 'What else will it do?' The young doctor looked back, forcing herself to meet Laurie's agonized gaze.

'Chemotherapy immobilizes the ovaries,' she said bravely. 'This treatment will very probably make you infertile . . .'

Laurie walked out through the grey-green corridors, into the waiting room where Gloria sat eyeing a tea-trolley laden with KitKats and crisps.

'Did you ask them about diet?' she demanded pointedly of Laurie, grimacing at the ancient volunteer behind the trolley.

Laurie shook her head, dazed.

'They can hardly know more about diet than I do,' she muttered.

'But what about anti-oxidants? Beta carotene, vitamin C?

And what about selenium and zinc? Did they mention zinc? Zinc is terribly important.'

'Nobody mentioned zinc,' said Laurie miserably, 'but I'll take it if you think I should . . .'

Gloria's response to the news had not been quite what Laurie anticipated. She'd made the announcement with precision and economy, knowing that anything else was simply postponing the moment, and she had expected outrage. A daughter of mine with cancer? *Impossible!*

There had been concern, of course, and there had been mild reproof. Had Laurie been taking her multi-vitamin? Was she still on the Pill? And why hadn't she gone back to the doctor earlier? *Answers: Yes, No, Pass.*

But mostly there had been pragmatism, the brisk assumption of control, the nonchalant confidence of cure, calmly conveyed to Laurie with a spurious authority that couldn't be countered because she longed to believe it. And underlying all this, the unspoken conviction that cancer is a failure, not of cells, but of spirit. Nasty, yes. Traumatic, naturally. But terminal? *Not unless the victim so decides.*

'You think it's all my own fault,' Laurie had wept that night. 'You think I've done something wrong . . .'

'Of course I don't!' Gloria put her arms around her daughter and hugged her close, but with unerring precision, exploded her denial in the very next moment. 'However, I do think you've lost control . . .'

'Lost control?'

'Your body is rebelling . . . Giving you messages . . .'

'What messages?'

'It's asking you to try a different way of living.'

'How am I supposed to do that?'

Gloria had smiled, a kindly, indulgent smile, meant to quell all resistance.

'I'm glad you asked me that, darling,' she replied with undisguised satisfaction. 'Tell me, have you ever heard of Doctor Dale Mitchell and the Movement for Regenerative Studies?'

* * *

Looking back, Laurie hardly knew when her feelings for Sean began to change.

Perhaps it was that very first day, when he'd scuttled from her distress like a frightened rabbit scenting a fox. Or perhaps it was during the week in Hell, when he'd received each hospital report with a stoicism that seemed to border on resignation.

Or perhaps it was that final night, when he'd exploded in unprecedented fury at Gloria's Norfolk plan, shaking and shouting and ordering Laurie to defy her mother.

Whenever it was, at the end of that night she'd felt a curious sense of release as she watched him walk towards the door.

So long had been spent in expectation and hope, so many dreams founded upon the promise of Sean's freedom, so much longing and love invested in the vision of their eventual union, that the sudden absence of desire seemed like a burden lifting.

'I'll call you in Norfolk,' he muttered, subdued again now.

'If you like,' she said cautiously, trying out the new mood.

'Do you want me to?'

She shrugged, the first time she'd been conscious of using this odd, unfamiliar gesture.

'I don't know.'

'Well, do you or don't you?'

He was looking at her with evident challenge, his face set in a grim reproach that seemed altogether inappropriate considering their respective situations, one healthy and whole, one diseased and damned.

'I don't think so. There doesn't seem much point.'

He moved towards her, making to take her hand.

'How can you say that?' he whispered.

'Because it's true,' she said brutally, turning away. 'It's better if you go. Go back to Tina . . . Or go find some- one else.'

He shook his head in disbelief, stunned.

'I know I haven't been a tower of strength,' he mumbled,

staring down at his feet. 'It's hard for me, Laurie . . . I want to help, but I don't know what to say or do . . . I only know I don't want you to go to Norfolk . . .'

She turned back to him, her heart strangely light, her mind clear.

'I also know what I don't want,' she said calmly, her icy tone finally forcing him to meet her eye. 'Believe it or not, Sean, after all this time, I've suddenly realized I don't want you.'

The first treatment was scheduled for two weeks hence, allowing Gloria to rail simultaneously against the NHS for failing to deliver its services immediately, and for employing chemotherapy in the first place.

'It's so crude, Laurie,' she said. 'All those terrible drugs blasting through your system. But of course, darling, I do understand that you want to try everything.'

On this point at least, Laurie was clear. She had no intention of defying the hospital's advice. She would go so far along Gloria's road, and no further. Complementary medicine, yes. Alternative, no.

And it was this, of course, that led to Norfolk. A simple trade-off. Chemo for Regeneration. *Don't bug me about one, and I promise I'll try the other.*

'I just know everything will be fine!' Gloria burst out suddenly. 'And it's not as though we're short of money, is it? We can pay for the very best! I'm going to ring your father at once . . . Do you want to speak to him?'

Laurie turned away.

'I've got nothing to say right now.'

'But you will go to Norfolk? I can tell him that?'

'I'll go,' Laurie retorted. 'But I won't promise to take it seriously.'

Later, alone in her room at the Centre for Regenerative Therapy, awaiting the call to supper and contemplating the first blank page of the silk-bound notebook in which all daily thoughts, bad and good, were meant to be recorded, this remark returned to embolden her.

She reached for a pen and began to write, quickly and carelessly.

Name: Laurie Davison.

Age: Thirty-three. A significant sort of age if you are into numerology or religion, or so my dear mother would have you believe. The mystical three to its own power, three times, plus three and three. For a woman, a prime-of-life sort of age. No longer the nubile naive. Not yet the exhausted old bat.

Occupation: Information technology consultant and sometime helper to the aforementioned mother at a modest health-food outlet. Our speciality: Frozen Fricassee of Tofu in Shiitake Sauce topped with Toasted Sesame Seeds (organic).

Children: None, nor ever will have.

Parents: Two. Divorced and both in rude health, thank God.

Significant Other (former): Sean Youngman, aged thirty, father of Mollie and Megan, picture-book twins, and errant husband of the avenging Tina.

Presenting Problem: I have breast cancer. I am dying.

Recommended Therapies: Surgery, chemotherapy, radiotherapy, Tamoxifen. Hypnotherapy, visualization, relaxation, meditation, playing the glockenspiel. Prayer. Touching wood. Writing this ridiculous journal at the insistence of Dr Dale Mitchell into whose hands I have been summarily delivered.

State of Mind: Superstitious. Suicidal. Scared shitless.

Chapter Three

Crompton Hall was a house of stories, many of them related by Laurie's fellow sufferers with gusto and pride during her first evening at the supper table.

There was the story of how Dr Dale Mitchell, preeminent researcher at Berkeley into the chemistry of the brain, had suddenly switched from neurology to psychology, declaring in a notorious paper, which led, so the story went, to popular deification and professional suicide, that an indefinable agent lay at the root of mental, and less plausibly, physical health. This agent, chemical in origin but subject to measurable change during thought processes, he termed the 'regenerative soul force'.

'Hardly a new idea,' Laurie said carefully.

'The old ideas are the best,' replied an elderly man with a crumbling face.

Then there was the story of how the West Coast community he founded grew so rich so rapidly, and amid such controversy – miracle cures, accusations of brainwashing – that Dale Mitchell felt constrained to quit his native land and take his message to England, where a mystery benefactor with an abiding interest in unorthodox medicine, so the story went, enabled him to acquire Crompton Hall.

'How fortuitous,' Laurie murmured politely.

'It was divinely ordained,' retorted a small, intense woman with a disconcertingly beatific smile

There was the story of how the Hall had risen from picturesque ruin to restored palace; of how dark rumblings among villagers who suspected a cult had been splashed in the *Norfolk Observer*; of how Dale Mitchell and Ruth Christianos, outraged, had threatened legal action and received both a front-page apology and a shame-faced deputation from the local parish council.

Then there was the story of each and every patient whom

Laurie met that first night: the small, intense woman, with her myriad allergies; a middle-aged man with a mystery blood disorder; a young manic depressive, a Cockney who'd had a heart transplant; two pale-faced women who were HIV-positive; then the cancer crew, one ovarian, two breast and a bowel; and the man with the crumbling face, fighting a tumour to the lung.

Val and Edie, the breasts, sat one on either side of Laurie, a show of unnerving solidarity that she neither wanted nor admired.

They all had one question: *What's your story?*

It seemed to Laurie that she had no story, and she said so.

'Of course you have a story,' Edie chided gently. 'The story of your illness . . . Which becomes the story of your life.'

So that was it, Laurie thought grimly, the Mitchell formula neatly condensed and ready for foisting upon each new arrival. She smiled at Edie, reluctant to mock but unwilling to concur, and said nothing.

'Are you married?' asked Edie, an inquiry at once both disarmingly innocent and deeply presumptious, taking Laurie by surprise.

'No . . . No, I'm not. Never have been, never wanted to be . . . Until recently, that is . . . And now I've even gone off him . . . I think I saw too much of my parents' marriage. It made me exceedingly careful.'

She stumbled over the words, furious with herself for giving so much away and with Edie for seemingly having no idea what was permissible and what was politically incorrect.

'That sounds like a story!' Val said.

Laurie stood up from the supper table, nodding politely.

'Well, that's all there is to it,' she said lightly. 'There's no happy ending, I'm afraid.'

Back in her room she lay down once more on the plush tapestry quilt, gazing out through her window on to the woods and distant meadows beyond the lake, inky black

34

now in the deepening gloom although its surface swayed with a curious green light, vegetation of some sort, she guessed.

She decided then that when the chance arose she would go walking in the woods after all, despite her stated intent to do nothing that would take her into the company of Dale Mitchell.

She'd seen no more of him since marching out of the counselling room, and now the prospect of another encounter the following morning settled heavily upon her. She certainly wasn't in awe of him, nor did she feel he might woo her into confession, for in any case, there was nothing to confess. But increasingly, she felt herself alone and adrift, irreparably severed from the life she had known, uncertain of the future, terrified of the present. In such a state, she was surely ripe for picking, or if not that, she considered wretchedly, then for regeneration, whatever the hell that was.

At breakfast, she said nothing to anyone, passing sugar and salt in mute condemnation of the prevailing jollity, picking at a slice of melon on her plate, wondering what Gloria would have to say on the subject of sugar and salt, knowing only too well, and then, as she feigned a courteous interest in the arrival of the muesli, plotting just how she'd drop these scandalous details into her next conversation with her mother. The allergy sufferer had been awake all night with a terrible itching underneath her ribs, and the conversation centred on possible causes, remedies, and psychological implications. By the time the coffee arrived, Laurie was close to cracking. But at least it was coffee and not bloody Dandelion or Miso.

Afterwards, boycotting the art class and the massage with fragrant oils, she marched out into the grounds, fighting a rising anguish that threatened to overwhelm her.

What am I doing here? In God's name, what?

The kitchen garden was secluded and sheltered, a warm patch of ground hidden from all windows, fragrant with

35

the scent of mint and thyme, its well-trodden pathways meandering between towering rods of runner beans and burgeoning raspberry canes.

Laurie sprinted purposefully between the lines of green until she came to a sprightly fig tree overhanging a gnarled wooden bench, and gasping with the effort of her exertion and the anxiety that gripped her ribcage as surely as some instrument of torture, she sank down upon it, closing her eyes against the white morning light.

Anxiety. She knew it well. Indeed, it seemed at that moment an old friend, a trusted companion whose moody ways and guiles were deeply familiar. The sweating palms, the churning stomach, the tightness in the chest . . . How many times had she felt like this?

Every time she returned for a new term at boarding school. And every time she came home again . . . Every time she glimpsed the gathering incompatibility of her mother and father . . . Every time he went away, and every time he came home again . . . The time he finally left for America, and the time he came back to introduce his new wife . . . Then her first day at college, and every end-of-term exam . . . And after that her first day in her first job . . . Then the day she finally broke off the engagement she'd been harried into . . . And, curiously, though she couldn't quite think why, the day she'd first met Sean . . .

But now, the big one. *I have cancer. I am dying.*

How foolish, how indulgent seemed all other concerns. Why had she never seen how beautiful, how blissful, life really was? How come she'd spent weeks, months, even years, worrying about trivialities? Why hadn't she come to her senses until the moment she faced losing them?

She lowered her head to her hands. And it was as she sat, a thousand thoughts clamouring to be considered, that she heard a faint rustle in the fig tree above her. Looking up, she saw the branches quiver, yet there was no breeze, and no bird to cause a flutter. The branches parted, the air moved, and she felt something pass her by, as though a shadow had briefly taken form and then melted back into the sun. She felt oddly calmed, and closed her eyes again.

But the calm was brutally brief.

'Laurie . . . There you are! Is something wrong? Are you feeling ill?'

She opened her eyes into the white glare, glimpsing only dimly the benign, concerned face of Ruth Christianos leaning down toward her. She shook her head.

'It's nothing . . . I'm okay . . .'

'You're breathing very heavily . . . Do you feel faint?'

'I've been running.'

'Running! From what?'

'From the knowledge of death,' Laurie snapped.

As soon as she said it she felt better, and part of her relief, she recognized at once, lay in transferring her own distress on to Ruth.

The woman sat down beside her, hesitant, unsure, resting her hand on Laurie's arm. In the fig tree above them, a pair of sparrows tussled over a fragment of bread, and in the dense vegetation before them, a lone bee hovered, seeking splashes of scarlet amid the green.

'I understand how you feel,' Ruth murmured at last, but Laurie, embarrassed now, waved her arm away.

'I expect you'll tell me we all have to face the knowledge of death . . . Isn't that what Doctor Mitchell would say? Death gives life its meaning, its edge? I can just hear him proclaiming it.'

To Laurie's surprise, Ruth laughed.

'Well, of course, it's true,' she said slowly, 'but that doesn't make it any easier.'

Laurie waited, expecting more, and when nothing more came, she found herself oddly comforted. Ruth Christianos, it seemed, did not deal in platitudes, nor seek to offer false consolation. For the first time since her arrival, Laurie felt herself begin to unbend.

They sat in silence for some moments, watching the progress of the bumblebee through the swaying tents of beans, lifting their faces toward the strengthening sun.

'It's very peaceful here,' Laurie said at last, feeling the

need to make amends for her brusqueness, 'I can see how helpful ... How *regenerating* ... it must be for some people.'

Ruth smiled, ignoring the jibe.

'I never come to the kitchen garden,' she said quietly, 'without thinking of all the generations of servants who must have laboured here ... All those lives, each one an individual triumph.'

Laurie considered this carefully.

'A triumph?' she asked at last.

'Yes, of course,' Ruth said easily. 'Every human life is a triumph against the darkness.' She threw a swift glance at Laurie, 'Against the knowledge of death ...'

Now Laurie smiled, a weak, polite grimace.

'I hardly imagine it seemed like a triumph at the time ... A servant's life in a house like this must have been very hard.'

'They were beneficent employers,' Ruth replied. 'Well, in later times anyway ...'

'Who were? The Cromptons?'

Among the stories Laurie had heard so far, there had been nothing about the original owners of Crompton Hall, who they were, how they'd come by such a grand dwelling, nor how they'd lost it and let it fall to ruin. She was suddenly curious.

Ruth glanced at her quickly.

'The family name was Crompton-Leigh ... An alliance of two very old Norfolk families. The Cromptons claimed descent from a kinsman of Boudicca, and the Leighs were burghers of medieval Lynn ... Very important. Very rich.'

'And what happened to them?'

Ruth stood up, shading her eyes against the light, gazing toward the house.

'Their descendants are still around,' she said vaguely. 'You must get Dale to tell you all about it ... Ah, look! Here he is. He's come to find you.'

And indeed he had. Striding through the beans like Gordon Macrae on the prairie, and dressed in pretty

38

much the same fashion, he greeted Laurie with all the boyish charm of a silver screen hero, inviting her inside to the counselling room as though it were a hoe-down and hers the first dance.

Laurie's wrath returned in a moment, and with it, the darkness.

'You're very hostile, Laurie. Why is that?'

'You tell me,' she said rudely, 'you're the shrink.'

He was amused, and the pewter eyes lightened.

'With respect,' he said gently, 'I'm not a shrink. My discipline is neurology. I'm a scientist.'

'So,' inquired Laurie, even more rudely, 'you can't tell me anything about myself?'

'I can make a few guesses,' Dale Mitchell replied.

And for the next fifty minutes, he did just that, attempting to engineer Laurie into the smallest act of revelation.

He tried to probe her feelings about illness and death.

'You know that fifty per cent of all cancers are now curable?' he asked her gently.

'Curable?' she snapped back. 'What does that mean?'

He seemed to think it over.

'I guess it means that fifty per cent of all patients go into remission . . . A remission that lasts until they die, perhaps years later, of an unconnected accident or illness, or perhaps of a different cancer . . . Cancer, after all, is primarily a disease of old age. We all have to die of something.'

He was watching her closely, and she felt herself falter beneath his gaze.

'Remission,' she muttered, looking away, 'I hate that word . . . Who wants to be in remission? What I want is *restoration*!'

'Restoration?' he queried mildly. 'A simple return to the status quo? That's a very modest ambition, Laurie . . . And a very limiting one . . .'

When this impenetrable suggestion failed to elicit any response, he moved on swiftly, taking Laurie up on her earlier remarks about Gloria. Did she truly perceive her mother as exerting total control? Did she feel she had no mind, no will, of her own? And what of her father? Did Laurie feel he'd abandoned her?

'On the contrary,' Laurie retorted, 'he's paying your exorbitant fees.'

Dale Mitchell surveyed her shrewdly.

'But if you don't wish to be here,' he said carefully, 'then your father's generosity is misplaced?'

Laurie shrugged and let her gaze stray to the picture above the mantelpiece, thinking in that moment not of Gloria, nor her father, but of the Crompton-Leighs, taking afternoon tea or playing rummy in this very room, their servants loitering like shadows behind the shutters, waiting to offer buttered bread and tiny china platters of home-made raspberry jam to their beneficent masters.

'Is there anything you'd like to ask me?' Dale Mitchell said at last.

Laurie pointed to the painting.

'That woman, the one in the foreground . . . Who is she?'

He glanced toward the mantelpiece.

'The daughter of the house,' he replied with a little smile, 'Miss India Crompton-Leigh . . . Painted in 1912 when England – and India – were at the height of their glory . . .'

'India? That's an unusual name.'

Laurie stood up and walked toward the mantelpiece. Now that she'd focused on the picture, she noticed that the composition was unusual, two women, one a jet-haired beauty, the other pale and fair, the one staring rather haughtily into the eye of the beholder, the other gazing into the middle distance. The two were so very different, both in appearance and demeanour, that it seemed almost as though the artist had been pressed to accommodate them in the same portrait, choosing to place one some distance behind the other so that each might be contained in a separate identity.

'India Crompton-Leigh was born in Delhi . . . Her father served the Raj . . . She lived there for the first ten years of her life, then returned with her family to Crompton Hall ... Her brother, Christian, was the last of the Crompton-Leighs to own the house ...'

Dale Mitchell had opened the door of the counselling suite, clearly inviting Laurie to leave, and outside she saw the allergy victim, still with her beatific smile, next in line for the regenerative ministrations.

'Who's the other woman?' Laurie asked as she walked out of the door.

'One of the servants,' he replied. 'Dutifully sitting for a portrait with her mistress ... And speaking of duty, Laurie, you will remember the commitment you made, won't you? It's the only thing we ask. You will write up your journal?'

Laurie lifted her chin.

'And what shall I write? The story of my life?'

He grinned.

'That'll do for a start,' he said, 'unless you can think of something more interesting?'

From the music room came a surprisingly melodic noise, not a tune exactly, more an orderly merging of notes and instruments, steel drums, tambourines, maracas and, underpinning all these, the melancholy strain of a piano accordion. Laurie wondered who was playing what, but as she had no intention of peeping in to find out, she hurried past up the staircase and into her room again.

The room had begun to seem a refuge, a place where she might pretend none of it were happening, and as she locked the door behind her, she had the strange sensation of pulling all that was positive and hopeful into the room with her, excluding everything that was dark and threatening.

Lying on her bed, staring out of the window toward the woods and the glinting lake, she considered that if she were home now, there would be a dozen solicitous interruptions. Gloria would arrive with parcels of vitamins, Shelley would turn up with bottles of wine and tirades against her latest boyfriend, her father would phone and

Elspeth, his wife, would dispatch one of her outrageous bouquets, hundreds of dollars' worth of exquisite blooms and berries, requiring every vase, jug and milk bottle in the place to display them.

Her neighbour, a kindly widow, would drop by as she always did whenever she saw the living room curtains closed at odd hours, and her colleagues, people she'd worked, laughed and argued with for five years, would all be checking in to see what they could do. It was even possible, she thought vaguely and without so much as a pang, that Sean might show up . . .

She wanted none of these. Other people, faced with crisis, might cling to family and friends, but to Laurie at that moment, aloneness seemed the only acceptable state. After all, what could anyone do? Nothing altered the brute fact, and alone she had to endure the consequences. At Crompton Hall she could wage her solitary battle unhindered, able to deflect all sympathizers with a curt dismissal. It would be much harder at home.

She closed her eyes, lay back on the tapestry quilt, and thought of India Crompton-Leigh.

Once she, too, had roamed these elegant corridors, strolled out through the woods by the shore of the shining lake, loitered in the kitchen garden, eaten the beans and blackcurrants that grew there.

Once, India Crompton-Leigh had been young and beautiful, full of expectation, no doubt, for a blessed future. And then what? The Great War, the decline of the Crompton dynasty, the fall of the big house . . . Death, decay and the end of consciousness, the common fate of all, rich or poor . . .

Life is a black joke. The best you can hope for is a laugh along the way.

And Laurie, finding nothing remotely funny, suddenly buried her face in the quilt and wept.

She took lunch in her room, and sitting by the window, picked up her journal with its one sardonic entry.

Okay, Laurie. What's your story?

She turned the blank pages idly, fingering the pristine parchment-coloured leaves, imagining them filled with the minutiae of her humdrum existence.

Born in Letchworth, moved to London, aged four. Father a teacher of mathematics, mother a health-food evangelist. A childhood of butterbeans and sprouted alfalfa seeds ... Of surreptitious Mars Bars and cans of Diet Coke ... An adolescence scarred by parental discord ... A first love affair, at the ancient age of nineteen, conducted with initial enthusiasm, quickly replaced by bewilderment and doubt.

'You can't want to marry me!' she'd laughed.

'Oh, but I do,' he'd replied.

And because he'd seemed so perplexed, so *wounded* by the suggestion that she mightn't wish to be his wife, she'd said yes. Or rather, she hadn't said no, and this, it transpired, was equally encouraging.

But it was Gloria who'd made the running.

'You couldn't get a better man,' she'd declared, a remark which at the time had seemed innocent enough, but which later, long after the engagement had been broken off, returned to haunt Laurie. No, she couldn't get a better man. And dammit, she'd sure as hell tried.

'Why didn't I marry Eric Russell?' she wondered aloud to the empty room. 'How would life be different if I had?'

Well, she would have had children, of course. Chestnut-haired outdoor lads like Eric himself, fond of football and boyish larks, or pink-skinned girls with freckles and pony tails, sturdy, honest, upright kids.

Kids who would now face losing their mother.

A good job she hadn't married Eric, nor anyone else for that matter. A good job she hadn't married Sean, though the chance would have been a fine thing ...

'I didn't marry Eric Russell,' she announced to the curtains, 'because he was called Eric! There, I've finally admitted it. I saw myself at endless cocktail parties saying "Have you met my husband, Eric?" And I couldn't stand the thought of that ...'

She began to laugh, a thin, high giggle which might have descended into hysterics if a sudden sharp rap on the bedroom door hadn't brought her up short.

'Everything okay, Laurie?'

Ruth Christianos seemed to have appointed herself guardian or comforter, and now she peered into the room curiously.

'I was talking to the curtains,' Laurie said, laughing self-consciously, 'telling them the story of my life.'

Ruth said nothing, though her face registered mild concern.

'Or perhaps it was something else,' Laurie smiled, the idea just occurring. 'Perhaps it was the spirit of India Crompton-Leigh . . .'

'Perhaps it was,' Ruth replied carefully. 'These were her rooms after all.'

'India's room? She slept here?'

'Very little has been changed since the day she left. The furniture, the carpet, the quilt, even the curtains . . . They're all the same.'

Laurie caught her breath, unsure why this should seem significant, yet feeling that it was.

'We seldom use these rooms . . . India's private apartments . . . It was the wish of the previous owner that they be left undisturbed . . .'

'Who was the previous owner?' Laurie inquired tentatively. 'I thought that India's brother inherited the house?'

Ruth shook her head.

'There was another owner after Christian. The name was Malone . . .'

She hesitated, then moved suddenly to a tall oak bureau which stood next to the window, half hidden by the heavy curtains, extracting from it a battered leather-bound book fastened with gilt clasps.

'India's journal,' she said, offering it to Laurie. 'Seems there was a tradition of keeping a diary long before we came to Crompton Hall . . . Here, take it! Let's have a look at the entry for today's date . . .'

Laurie opened the yellowing leaves cautiously, as though

some momentous news or secret might lie within. But what she read of that summer of 1912 was as ordinary as anything she herself might have written.

We took tea on the terrace (the first day warm enough this month) and heard Adam proclaim that he has engaged a doctor to serve the village. Mama was most impressed (as she always is by anything the Goodchilds propose) and I do declare I am much interested in Dr Luke Harte myself. Later, at Alice's insistence, we drove through the village to admire the lavender fields. They are, as she said, truly magnificent this year. I wonder what Christian has bought for my birthday?

Laurie looked up at Ruth.

'The lavender fields?'

'A local crop. It was once grown all over Norfolk. Not much of it left now. The fields at the edge of the village have long been given over to more lucrative produce . . .'

Ruth turned to the door.

'And now, Laurie,' she said firmly, 'if you really want to meet the spirit of India, you should come walking in the woods. That was one of her special places, the summerhouse over by the lake . . . You can only reach it through the woods. Won't you come? It's such a lovely day. Dale is waiting with the others right now . . .'

The woods were, in truth, no more than a spinney running from the orchard behind the kitchen garden to the lake, an area of some four or five acres.

'In the Cromptons' day,' Ruth informed Laurie, 'the woods stretched for miles. It was a huge estate and there were great shooting parties. All very English . . .'

'A golden age,' Laurie said absently, her eyes fixed upon the rangy figure of Dale Mitchell ahead, Californian man in the old country. 'If you belonged to the elite, that is . . . Like India.'

'Perhaps,' Ruth agreed. 'However, I find myself wondering what those people might have thought if they'd glimpsed the future . . . Would they see all the bad things? Or would they reckon we'd arrived at our own golden age?'

Laurie shrugged.

'I doubt it,' she said. 'Things were simpler then.'

'Simpler isn't always better,' Ruth replied.

They were joined then by Val and Edie, hanging back from the main party, Edie clutching a posy of celandines and urging them to view a clump of cowslip she'd found at the edge of the brook.

'It's very rare!' she exclaimed breathlessly. 'Do come and look!'

Obligingly Ruth veered from the main path and followed along an overhung dip toward the stream, and Laurie, finding herself alone and faced with the choice of joining Dale's gang, a couple of whom now looked back expectantly, plunged purposefully into the undergrowth.

And it was then that it happened. As she strode toward the increasingly audible tinkle of the brook, she was enveloped by a curious sense of recognition.

What happened here? Why do I feel I know this place?

She reached to brush a branch from her face, and pushing forward, suddenly saw the lake laid out before her, an opaque sheet of glass studded with swaying clumps of sedge into which the mellifluous brook fell . . .

It was all utterly familiar, as if she'd stepped into a piece of her own history, and yet she knew she'd never set foot in Norfolk before.

As though in a dream, where every movement seems magnified and each sound orchestrated, she walked down to the water's edge, knowing that in the lea of the wooden jetty she would find a rowing boat moored . . . a green-painted rowing boat, with golden lettering on its stern.

The Lady of the Lake . . .

She stared at the faded gilt words, entranced, her mind clear and still. In the trees behind her, a skylark warbled, just the way it always had, and a vague thought settled upon her.

Mama will be waiting on afternoon tea . . .

And then, just as suddenly, the sensation vanished, leaving Laurie shaken and confused, staring stupidly at the shabby boat and its faded nameplate.

'See! I told you it was cowslip!'

Edie, her face flushed with effort, was pointing toward an indistinguishable mass of leaves on the bank of the brook. Laurie could just discern a feeble flash of gold within the green.

'Cowslip,' she repeated dully.

'I'm certain of it!' Edie cried . . . 'But Laurie! Whatever's the matter? You look as though you've seen a ghost . . .'

Laurie shivered in the cooling afternoon air, then turned away.

'Well, maybe I have,' she offered curtly over her shoulder. 'Those of us who've glimpsed mortality are prone to all kinds of strange fancies, after all. Ghosts . . .'

A strange, harsh laugh escaped her.

'Hardly surprising that imagination gets the better of us,' she muttered savagely, 'given the state we're in. What else would you expect?'

Val stood up from the bank where she'd crouched to admire the flowers.

'Don't be afraid of your imagination,' she said softly, 'just make sure that you use it for the best. We can all imagine terrible things, but we can also dream wonderful dreams. Let it happen, Laurie. Just let it happen.'

Chapter Four

You might expect the summer of 1912 to have passed in a blissful haze, hot and untroubled, a carefree calm before Europe's terrible, unglimpsed apocalypse.

You might imagine the clipped emerald lawns of Crompton Hall thronged by elegant ladies in tight-waisted bustles playing croquet – the croquet pitch is still plainly visible beneath today's wayward grass – or flirting with young men in white flannels.

You might, if you closed your eyes and summoned every remembered image of Edwardian England, picture the serving girls with their silver platters of Cromer crab sandwiches, black skirts clinging to bare legs in the sultry afternoon, hair sticky beneath white lace caps; the long trestle tables on the terrace, their floating covers weighted with glass bowls of fruit punch; the discrete figure of the butler, erect and imperious, watching from the wings, masterminding the show.

You might even see someone you recognized, a slight, vivacious girl with a long dark plait swinging down her back, striding across the lawn toward some lanky, languid male, a poet, perhaps, or a painter of portraits.

In that case, you might know that you've encountered Miss India Crompton-Leigh, and, equally, that all usual expectations had better be suspended.

As it happens, the summer of 1912 began poorly with a damp, depressing May and indifferent June.

But the middle of the month saw a sudden change, and Lady Crompton dared to hope that the garden party planned for her daughter's twenty-first birthday might pass without an umbrella opened.

The party! How eagerly it was anticipated, by all from India herself to the humblest member of the kitchen staff. Pastries had been baked, tartlets had been glazed, hams had been hung and jellies left to set. A huge frosted cake in the shape of a Buddhist temple had been decorated with tiny golden bells and paper prayer wheels, this extraordinary confection being Lady Crompton's one concession to India's esoteric tastes.

Sir Robin, it was rumoured, had gone to London to see his solicitors, planning to settle a considerable fortune on his daughter, and Christian had gone with him, intending, so the whisper went, to buy a very special birthday present for his sister.

But not as special, perhaps, as that proposed by the Crompton family's neighbour and much valued friend, one Adam Goodchild, landowner and gentleman, traveller and philanthropist, whose hopes for the evening were known to him alone.

A sacred seal would surely be set upon the friendship of Cromptons and Goodchilds this birthday night, a bond that had been hopefully anticipated over long years, yet never explicitly articulated – a uniting of the two families.

They were, after all, the principal dynasties in this part of the county. And since the Cromptons had returned to Norfolk on the death of Sir Robin's father, the children of both houses had taken much delight in each other's company. What more natural than that Adam, older than India by some ten years and Christian by a significant two, should have become both mentor and protector? And what more fortunate than that Adam's little sister Marianne, younger than India by two years and much in awe of the new arrivals with their exotic history, should find in them a cure for her loneliness . . . Marianne, who, since her mother's death in childbirth and her father's subsequent disinterest, had become Adam's pride and his special responsibility . . . Marianne, who, although she had matured in his most recent absence, was nevertheless still too young to know her own mind . . .

Adam Goodchild brushed aside all thoughts of his sister. Recently returned from the subcontinent himself, he had a rare gift to bestow upon India, not only all his worldly goods, but the offer of his love and unstinting admiration, summed up in a betrothal ring set with rubies and seed pearls. The ring sat in the top drawer of his dressing cabinet, and each morning as he dressed, in an unlikely show of sentiment, he took the ring from its enamelled casket and held it to the window, watching the rubies wink in the morning sun, imagining their scarlet fire set against the pale ivory of India's slender fingers.

There was no doubt she would accept. Indeed, so certain was Adam of India's esteem that he had taken the trouble to order a redecoration of his London house, imagining a brief sojourn there before setting out on a honeymoon tour of Europe. The ruby ring was to be a birthday surprise, the crown upon India's coming of age and on her future as mistress of the Goodchild estate. He would speak to Sir Robin at the start of the evening and make his intentions known.

Adam Goodchild hummed as he drove his carriage through the village to Crompton Hall just one week short of India's party. The wide Norfolk sky stretched above him, a great dome of silvery blue. The woods of Crompton Hall rustled in the summer air as he passed. A skylark sang. He was a happy man.

For India, that day began as a perfectly ordinary English summer's day, with kedgeree for breakfast, served in the much-loved spicy style of her old home in Delhi, followed by an hour's letter-writing in the morning room, then a stroll through the woods to the lake.

It ended in much the same fashion, with tea on the terrace and a drive in Adam's carriage and pair.

'I must see the lavender fields,' India declared when an outing was proposed. 'Just this week, so Alice says, it has all come into bloom.'

An ordinary summer's day, ending in a ordinary summer's eve. But in between, such news that it later seemed to India the most significant of days, a moment when destiny alighted in the drawing room and brushed against her cheek, and, had she only glimpsed it, might still have been shooed, like an errant butterfly, from its determined path.

'I've finally engaged a doctor to serve the estate,' Adam Goodchild informed the interested company as they idled on the terrace that afternoon. 'A most unusual man, who, I believe, deserves our patronage. He has impeccable qualifications from a very distinguished university, and he has some very challenging ideas . . . He believes that we shall very shortly overcome all the major illnesses by the development of strong chemical potions which will nullify the agents of disease . . .'

'That would be exceedingly useful,' Lady Crompton observed. 'It seems to me that there are rather more diseases than there used to be, and certainly a great many more than there ought to be. Why, a girl in the kitchen has some new ailment that none of us has ever heard of . . . What is it, India? My daughter, Mr Goodchild, always takes such an interest in the servants . . .'

'Cystitis,' said India.

'There you are!' Her Ladyship exclaimed. 'What did I tell you?'

'It's a very common complaint,' India elaborated mischievously, 'but I hardly think it's new, Mama. It affects the female bladder . . .'

'Thank you, India. Mr Goodchild does not wish for all the details . . . Now tell us, please, Mr Goodchild, about your doctor . . . Is he a married man?'

'Doctor Harte has a wife and three young daughters,' Adam Goodchild replied. 'And indeed, I was wondering if they might rent the manor house at Blue Farm? It would be the perfect size . . .'

The occupancy of the manor house was not in Her Ladyship's gift, or at least, not officially so, as she most carefully explained. But Sir Robin being away on business in London, and Christian being away on some other business in London, then the matter might be provisionally settled in their absence . . . Upon the understanding, of course, that should the arrangement not prove agreeable, then no obligation would incur on the Crompton side.

'When does he arrive, Mr Goodchild?'

'They're all coming tomorrow, Ma'am. Doctor Harte will be visiting the cottage hospital, then travelling on to Norwich to meet with other medical minds in his field . . . It would be most helpful if I might show Mrs Harte the manor house at the same time.'

Her Ladyship hesitated, as though, for a moment, she too heard the beat of destiny's tiny wings, but then the intimation was gone and she smiled graciously at Adam Goodchild.

'I'm sure India will be happy to accompany you,' she murmured, glancing purposefully at her daughter. 'You could walk there tomorrow afternoon, through the woods, and pick up your carriage at Blue Farm boundary . . . Fresh air and exercise, Mr Goodchild! Those are the vital elements in good health. It has long been my view that the serving classes, particularly, get far too little of either, and I look forward to discussing the matter with Doctor Harte . . . All my servants, Mr Goodchild, are required to take a brisk walk each Sunday afternoon before tea, no matter what the weather . . .'

Adam Goodchild stood up, his expression polite and inscrutable.

'If we're to see the lavender fields before the light fades, we'd better set off at once,' he said to India. 'Shall we go?'

And at the edge of the waving lavender, India, alighting from the carriage, slipped her arm in his, inhaling the heavy scent that hung on the air, as palpable as mist.

'What's he like, your Doctor Harte?' she inquired lazily, gazing out on the rippling lake of mauve and fixing her eye on the point where it met the lilac wash of the darkening sky. 'Will all the young ladies fall in love with him?'

Adam laughed and squeezed her arm.

'Not all of them, I hope,' he said.

Lady Crompton knew nothing of the ruby ring.

Had she been aware of its existence, she might have

relaxed her unceasing connivance to steer India into Adam's company and ~~allowed herself a little~~ peace, content in the belief that a difficult, yet much-loved, daughter had met her match.

As it was, the following day she ordered Alice to lay out India's best walking clothes and send her boots to the gun room for polishing, picturing her daughter welcoming the new doctor's wife as though she were already Lady Goodchild, gracious, God-fearing and perfectly groomed.

A few moments' reflection might have reminded her that India was frequently none of these things, and had a worrying tendency to present herself as a 'free spirit', a phrase often heard upon her lips, albeit offered with a mischievous smile. But Lady Crompton, having been raised in the gracious and God-fearing school herself, was not much given to reflection, and like India in turn, clung to a belief that all would eventually turn out for the best if only one kept one's head and made the most of opportunities presented. In this respect, mother and daughter truly thought as one, but alas, their ideas of what constituted *the best* were not only various, they were often utterly opposed.

Perhaps it was well that no such gloomy meditations arrived to trouble Lady Crompton that balmy June morning, for it was hardly likely she might have imposed any restrictions upon India's heart, nor even warned against the unhappy consequences of wayward emotion, and as it was, she spent a delightful few hours while India dressed and prepared herself for the outing, fussing over buttons and the precise arrangement of the corsage.

'Why am I wearing flowers?' India objected as Alice fiddled with the pin. 'I'm not going to a wedding!'

Not yet! The hint of a smile hovered upon her Ladyship's cheeks, puckering the fine skin she'd been at such pains to protect in Delhi's fearsome heat, and she allowed herself a moment's glory as prospective mother of the bride. *Not yet!*

'You must add lavender to encourage clear vision,' said Alice quietly, fixing the spray of rosebuds on to India's lapel and adding a sprig of the purple foliage she always seemed to have about her whenever the lavender fields were in bloom. 'The scent is useful for clearing the nasal passages, which in turn allows the brain to . . .'

India laughed good-naturedly.

'Oh really, Alice! If we followed all your remedies and recipes, we'd have no time for anything else.'

She bent her head to her lapel and inhaled the fragrance of the lavender.

'But the perfume is certainly wonderful . . . And I do believe I can feel it clearing my brain! I shall have no trouble conversing with Mrs Harte on any subject she cares to raise. The water closet at Blue Farm, perhaps? Or the nutritional needs of the village children? A bowl of oatmeal each morning, and a little sweetened tea and bread for luncheon! Isn't that right, Mama?'

India laughed aloud, and Alice smiled discreetly, but Her Ladyship, overlooking this mild jest at her own prescription for the daily diet of Crompton tenants' children, seized on the more important matter at once.

'There is nothing wrong with the water closet at Blue Farm,' she declared. 'And I'll thank you, India, not to mention it to Mrs Harte. Quite apart from the fact that Sir Robin went to much trouble and expense hiring a plumber, it is hardly a subject for polite discussion.'

She frowned at her daughter, wondering whether she could really be trusted to make the right impression on Mrs Harte. Fortunately, the opinion of a doctor's wife counted for very little, but Adam Goodchild's opinion mattered a great deal. And despite all evidence of his good humour and forbearance, Lady Crompton couldn't believe he'd welcome talk of water closets.

India, sensing she'd gone too far and wondering for one awful moment whether her mother might insist on accompanying her to Blue Farm, was immediately contrite.

'I'm sorry, Mama. It was just a silly joke. I promise I'll be perfectly polite to Mrs Harte, and indeed, who knows? If she's as distinguished and intelligent as her husband, which she must surely be as he's married her, then she'll become a good friend. I should like that.'

Her Ladyship's frown deepened. She doubted that any doctor's wife might prove distinguished, and as for intelligence in women, she had seen quite enough of it already. It was to be discouraged for the simple reason that gentlemen did not like it, a self-evident fact that her daughter chose to ignore.

'We shall see,' she remarked coolly, leaving no doubt that on the matter of Mrs Harte, she had, if not seen, then already decided and determined accordingly.

Adam Goodchild did not arrive at Crompton Hall to walk through the woods as arranged.

Instead he sent his carriage and a note for India explaining that Mrs Harte would not, after all, be viewing Blue Farm that morning. But Dr Harte himself, who'd arrived alone and was even now inspecting the arrangements at the cottage hospital, would very much like to see the house.

The note threw Lady Crompton into confusion. Adam Goodchild, despite his status as prospective suitor, was nevertheless a proper companion for India on account of his long friendship with the family. And the proposed presence of the doctor's wife, whatever her personal qualities proved to be, had given the outing to Blue Farm its necessary respectability.

But Dr Harte was unknown, and his suitability therefore uncertain. It could hardly be right for India to accompany two gentlemen into a deserted house.

Indeed, now that she came to consider it, Her Ladyship couldn't imagine why she hadn't done the sensible thing and instructed Hardy, the estate foreman, to open up the house. It was, of course, her eagerness to see Adam and India together, to allow every opportunity for declaration, that had overcome her usual scrupulousness. With rueful hindsight, Lady Crompton summoned Hardy to the Hall and instructed India to change out of her walking clothes.

'So I'm not to meet this eminent doctor!'

'I imagine there'll be plenty of other opportunities to meet him, and his eminent wife too. But Hardy will deal with Blue Farm.'

India, well-practised in changing her approach to achieve her ends, and by this time determined to encounter the intriguing Dr Harte that very day, nodded meekly.

'But what will Adam think, Mama? He has sent the carriage! He surely intends me to go to Blue Farm.'

Her Ladyship hesitated. What did Adam Goodchild intend? If only she could be absolutely sure.

'Alice would come with me, Mama. It's her afternoon off, but I'm sure she wouldn't mind.'

Alice looked up and set aside her sewing.

'Another afternoon off?' Her Ladyship inquired peevishly.

'My sister's son is sick, Ma'am. If it's acceptable to you, I'm taking in some of Cook's chicken soup.'

'And some of your peculiar ideas, no doubt!' Lady Crompton was now quite out of sorts, and not at all certain what she wanted. 'Perhaps lavender will clear his nasal passages?'

India laughed a little nervously.

'Do say we can go, Mama!'

Alice stood up, folding away the square of tapestry she was working into a quilt for India's bedroom.

'I'm sorry you find my remedies peculiar, Ma'am,' she said, gazing directly into the petulant eyes of her employer, 'but I'm sure you'll agree my common sense can be relied upon. I shall, of course, accompany Miss India and ensure that everything is as you'd wish . . .'

'Of course,' replied Her Ladyship, momentarily appeased, 'I know you mean well, Alice. But no chicken soup! It's far too rich and thick for a child's stomach. Ask Cook for some thin vegetable broth instead.'

They drove into a blazing noon, India out of her walking clothes and now attired in a cream silk morning gown, a

57

somewhat lavish choice for so functional a journey, but one Lady Crompton was not to be denied.

In the rush to change, however, the corsage had been forgotten.

'So much for clear vision! Now I shall probably appear the silliest of girls, and Doctor Harte will want nothing to do with me!'

Alice smiled and shook her head.

'Is it true about lavender?' India pursued. 'I mean, that village people *really* believe it can somehow affect the thinking process?'

This question of belief, whether the simple act of whole-heartedly believing a proposition might, in some mysterious way, make it true, was among India's favourite topics. Her years in Delhi, although ending at the tender age of ten, had fostered a passionate interest in the varieties of religious experience and the nature of enlightenment, and in Alice she'd found a wise and willing ear.

Today, however, Alice seemed preoccupied.

'I can't say what village people believe,' she replied shortly. 'I can only say that all means to health, both mental and physical, should be actively pursued by everyone. Lavender does no harm, smells delightful, and may do some greater good. That is surely reason enough to test its efficacy.'

India glanced quickly at her companion, reminding her-self just how fortunate she was to have so interesting, so enlightened, a person as her maid. Alice could surely have been a teacher at the village school, or even a governess, and yet she chose to stay at Crompton Hall. She was indeed a true companion, of the spirit and the heart, and India much preferred to call her so instead of maid, a matter upon which she and Lady Crompton differed vigorously.

'I'm sorry, Alice,' she said quickly. 'You're worried about your sister's son! Why don't we take the village road and call to see him on the way? Doctor Harte will hardly mind if we're a little late.'

They drove past the purple fields of lavender, beyond which the brooding hump of Blue Farm beckoned, and stopped at a squat pink-painted cottage, its doors thrown open to the sultry day.

Alice, carrying her jug of vegetable broth, hurried inside and India followed at a discreet distance, knowing that an unscheduled visit from Miss Crompton-Leigh might throw the household into confusion.

As indeed, it did.

Alice's sister, her hair escaping its pins, rushed forward as India entered and curtseyed low, offering a glass of water, the best chair in the house and a piece of her new-baked shortbread all in one breath, unsettling a large black mongrel which lay by the window and which, fearing some unhappy intrusion, at once began to bark. A small girl darted from behind her mother's skirts, gazing up at India in undisguised awe, tripping upon a cloth rug as she ran and sliding, legs splayed, across the room. Alice's brother-in-law, meantime, rushing in from the back garden to investigate the commotion, snatched his cap from his head on seeing India and shuffled deferentially back toward the fireplace, dislodging the fire irons from their perch upon the fender with an appalling clatter.

India ignored it all.

'How is the boy, Ivy?' she inquired gently of Alice's sister. 'Is he improving?'

'He's worse, Ma'am,' Ivy said fretfully. 'We've wrapped him warmly and given him oil of camphor, but he's very feverish. I'm sure he won't take the soup, though please tell Her Ladyship that we're most grateful for it . . .'

At that moment Alice emerged from the bedroom beyond, her face anxious.

'He's sleeping,' she said, 'but not peacefully, I fear. He threshes about among the blankets and seems to imagine that myself, or someone else, is come to take him away . . .'

She looked nervously at her sister.

'He's too hot, Ivy. We should remove the blankets and sponge him with cool water. Then, perhaps, a little crushed aconite . . .'

'Don't go giving him any of your devilish stuff!'

Ivy's husband turned to confront Alice, his face angry and flushed.

'Don't go taking his blankets, neither! You let his mother decide what's best. Don't you go telling us what to do!'

India glanced swiftly from one to the other, sensing a long-running family disagreement that only marginally touched upon the sick boy.

'I'm sure Alice means well,' she said carefully, 'and cool water sounds very sensible.'

'Pardon me, Ma'am,' responded Ivy's husband, deferential once more, 'but she ain't no doctor!'

And it was then that India saw the solution, a proposition so obvious and pleasing in its simplicity, that she smiled broadly at the thought.

'Then we shall get a doctor!' she declared. 'I know exactly where to find one. We can have him here within the half hour.'

Ivy blanched and clutched at her sister's arm.

'We can't afford a doctor,' she whispered.

India waved her hand impatiently.

'I shall pay!'

She turned and swept from the cottage, the cream silk morning gown rustling as she went, intent upon nothing but the waiting carriage and Adam Goodchild's languid groom who sat dozing in the warm air.

Alice caught her before she reached the garden gate.

'India! You can't do that! Excuse me, but it would hardly be acceptable to Lady Crompton . . . You must know it!'

They stared at each other for a brief moment, two young women separated in position by a thousand years of history, yet, by virtue of temperament and individual insight, seeming at that moment to be true sisters of the imagination, pursuing their unconscious assault on the barriers of culture and class.

'Then Adam will pay,' India answered. 'After all, didn't he say he was engaging a doctor for the village? That means the whole village, including Ivy and her family. And here we have Doctor Harte not ten minutes' drive away! What could be more fortuitous?'

Alice, unconvinced, nevertheless climbed into the carriage beside India, and the Goodchild mare set off at a steady trot for the distant manor house, pulling its cargo through a landscape of purple splendour, the lavender fields that gave Blue Farm its name.

They argued for much of the journey, Alice declaring that aconite and cool water were all her nephew required, India insisting, with increasing confidence and a growing sense of crisis fuelled by the heated discussion, that professional help be sought.

They drew up outside the house to see the front door ajar.

'Ah, look, there's Adam at the bottom of the orchard, and Hardy with him,' India cried. 'Go at once and tell them what's happening! I shall find Doctor Harte.'

She descended from the carriage with as much speed as the morning dress allowed and hurried into the house, leaving Alice to gaze after her in uncharacteristic indecision before reluctantly setting out for the orchard.

Inside the hallway, India hesitated. The house was still, its furnishings draped in white sheeting above which shafts of sunlit dust hovered, and there was no sign of a visitor. Then, from a room beyond, she heard a faint yet precise tapping, as though someone were meticulously measuring the floorboards. She ran to the door and threw it open.

He was down on his knees before the window, and at the sudden intrusion he rose to his feet, startled.

'Doctor Harte? I am Miss Crompton-Leigh, and I need your help!'

He stared at the extraordinary vision in the doorway, a slender girl dressed in an extravagant ivory gown, strands of coal-black hair drifting across delicately flushed cheeks, wide blue eyes imploring, hands clasped earnestly across her bosom.

'How can I help?' he asked at length.

India stared back at a tall, tousle-headed man, fair and handsome and engagingly untidy, his necktie awry, his waistcoat undone and his shirt sleeves rolled. She held his gaze.

61

'Excuse me,' he muttered, pulling at his sleeves and reaching for a jacket which lay draped across a covered chair, 'I was inspecting the skirting board. But tell me, please. How can I help?'

He was still looking directly into her eyes, and India found herself at a loss, the impetus of the child's illness inexplicably vanished.

'My maidservant's nephew,' she managed at last. 'One of the village children. He's sick, and there seems to be a family dispute about how he should be treated . . .'

'Then let us go at once and settle this dispute!'

He smiled, and India seemed to hear a rushing in her ears, a strange pounding beneath the breast panel of her morning gown.

'That would be very kind,' she faltered. 'Thank you so much, Doctor Harte . . .'

A clatter in the hallway announced Adam Goodchild, his comfortable stockiness and bluff visage providing an unexpected shock for India, who'd never before given much consideration to the appearance of her old friend, nor found him wanting in any way.

'I hear you're being put to the test!' he said jovially to Dr Harte. 'Though Alice declares it's a fine fuss about nothing!'

This latter remark was addressed to India whom he greeted with a smile that even the most disinterested observer might have perceived as ardent. To India, however, Adam Goodchild's tone and expression were suddenly irritating.

'Why don't we let the expert decide?' she said coolly, sweeping past him into the hall where he quickly followed. 'I'm sure none of us can say just how serious the case might be . . .'

Back in the carriage, India barely spoke to Alice or Adam, seating herself to allow a view of Dr Harte's modest conveyance which brought up the rear, aware that her reaction was inappropriate and excessive, yet unsure how to temper it, and unwilling to try, mystified by her own intransigence.

She refused to be drawn on all frivolous matters, not the

beauty of the lavender fields, the elegance of her morning gown, nor the state of the orchard gate at Blue Farm, and Adam, seeing he'd caused some offence, eventually fell silent.

At last, after what seemed to them all an interminable journey, the carriage drew up at Ivy's pink-painted cottage once more.

In a moment, Ivy appeared at the garden gate urgently beckoning to Alice, and India, her senses restored and her concern alive, hurried toward them.

'Alice, I took your advice when I had the house to myself . . .'

Ivy threw a swift glance around the cottage garden as though she feared her husband might spring out from behind the hollyhocks, 'I sponged the poor mite down and gave him the aconite . . . He's right as rain now!'

India began to laugh, her earlier vexation overcome, and when joined by Dr Harte, succeeded in appearing positively merry.

'I fear I've made a drama out of a minor catastrophe,' she cried gaily as he approached. 'The boy is quite well it seems.'

'I'm delighted to hear it,' he said, plainly amused, 'but as I'm here, perhaps I should see for myself?'

He disappeared into the cottage with Alice and Ivy close behind, while India walked purposefully back to the carriage and climbed in to make her peace with Adam.

He was gazing glumly upon the lavender fields, lost in some contemplation of his own.

'I'm sorry I was cross,' India murmured, 'I don't know what came over me! I suppose I didn't like to have my judgement questioned in front of Doctor Harte . . .'

'I suppose not,' he muttered.

'But now it seems right and proper that my judgement should be questioned . . .'

He turned to face her, taking her gloved hand in his, and seemed about to make some portentous announcement when the cottage door opened and Dr Harte came into view.

'The boy's much better,' he called, smiling up at India, seeming never to have doubted her judgement for a moment, not even in the light of such conclusive new evidence. 'He's made an extraordinary recovery in the past half hour. Certainly, there has been a fever, but no trace of it now. The body has that facility, of course . . . It's a curious fact that the great majority of conditions improve without any medical treatment at all . . . Which isn't to suggest,' he added wryly, 'that we have no need of doctors!'

'I should think not!' India laughed, turning to Adam for confirmation. 'We are most happy to have you among us, Doctor Harte. We shall all be the healthier for it, no doubt!'

'No doubt,' Adam Goodchild agreed, his customary enthusiasm unusually dimmed but his good manner winning above any private reservation. 'And it's splendid news that the child has recovered. Is there nothing we can do for him? Nothing he requires?'

'He's a cheeky young chap!' the doctor replied with a grin, looking back at India. 'And he's not afraid to make his feelings known. He's asking for some of your Cook's chicken soup!'

India, entering up her journal that evening, was moved to lofty thoughts.

What is health if not a blessed wholeness of body and spirit, governing not only the physical workings of organs and cells, but also the moral impulses of personality? What wonderful things are yet to be told about the chemistry of the soul, its rising and its waning, its biological predisposition to joy and sorrow, to love and hate, to sickness and to recovery?

'Do you think,' she asked Alice tentatively, 'that you cured Ivy's little boy? Do you think he believed you'd make him well, and so it happened? Or does your aconite truly have miraculous powers?'

Alice was disinclined to discourse on the nature of sickness or health, for much about the day's events had unsettled her. She had been shaken by the censure of

Ivy's husband, and startled by India's curious behaviour as they left Blue Farm. Yet she summoned her customary compliance.

'As the good doctor indicated,' she replied quietly, 'many illnesses disappear of their own accord. It's my belief that the body has great healing power within itself. The body, or the mind . . .'

India gazed out of the window to the lake beyond the woods, now gleaming crimson beneath the evening sky.

'By the end of this century,' she mused, 'we shall surely know the answer to all these questions . . . And all diseases will be under our control . . . No more suffering, Alice! Just think of it!'

Alice bent over her sewing, flicking the needle in and out of the cloth with meticulous concern.

'No more illness perhaps, but no more suffering?' she inquired. 'I fear that can never be. We devise our own suffering . . . Or else endure the cruelty of others and live with the frustration of our true desires . . . No medicine on earth is going to change that.'

India turned to her journal again. Our true desires! What better subject to inspire a writer?

The wellspring of desire, like the fount of health, is both deep and unknown. What hidden forces feed those mighty waters, swelling that first trickle of longing into a torrent, until all impediments are swept away?

She put down her pen. Desire, she cautioned herself, was not a matter on which she had much experience.

'Have you ever known desire, Alice?' she asked dreamily. 'Have you ever been in love?'

Alice looked up from her needlework.

'I may have imagined so,' she replied cautiously.

India's eyes widened.

'Who is he, Alice? Tell me, please! How dare you keep such a wonderful secret from me?'

But Alice, for once, refused to say a word.

Chapter Five

Sometimes, if you stand on tiptoe, you can peek into the future.

In the kitchen garden the other day, picking peas, I reached to the top of the tallest stem, and suddenly I saw it. A hint of foreign colour, cobalt like a peacock's breast, and then a flash of unfamiliar clothing, pale, faded, like a working man's trousers, and with it a wafting scent of something strange and spicy, vanilla maybe, or cinnamon, then a low sighing, pinched and breathy, like the moment before tears. Not so much a vision, I suppose, as a feeling. An intuition of for ever.

There have been other times, too. Beneath the magnolia tree, peering through the creamy blooms, I've sometimes glimpsed an unknown shape flitting between the terrace and the lawn.

Spirits and phantoms. Angels and ghosts.

The county of Norfolk is much given to such things, and Crompton Hall, sprawled as it is on the site of a Bronze Age settlement, trembles with the weight of history, the collective memories of all its fallen, washing across the pale skies like a morning mist.

This is the land of the forest dwellers, Iceni warriors, rough men in blue woad and women archers who, like the famed Amazons, carved off one breast the better to fire their arrows from their bows. Out of the woods they streamed, a torrent of human fury, raging toward the Roman invaders like a river in full flood.

Or so it seems to me, and sometimes, from the corner of my eye, I think I see an arrow fly across the sun, and in the shadows by the ornamental pool, I catch the fleeting outline of a fighting woman . . .

Spirits and phantoms, future and past. Yesterday and tomorrow, interwoven with the moment like the different coloured squares on India's birthday quilt.

Angels and ghosts, divine and diabolic. Who can say he has not been touched by their ethereal embrace? And who, being aware of such things, would not wish to tell stories of the marvellous deeds he has witnessed?

I first became aware of the spirits during a severe illness, shortly before I was engaged at Crompton Hall.

I'd had several situations, from kitchen 'tweeny to housekeeper, in many diverse places, from Norwich to King's Lynn, and I wished very much to come home. I heard of the vacancy as India's maid, and travelled to Crompton at once, but before I might apply, I was seized by a mysterious malady for which there seemed no cure.

My mother, believing me to be dying, summoned the parson, and it was as they both knelt at the foot of my bed, praying for my deliverance, that I saw a third figure standing behind them. His skin was bronze, his hair the colour of new-brewed cider, his eyes a remarkable grey, sparkling deep like the heart of The Wash on a summer's day.

'You must wait a little longer,' he said to me.

'How long?' I asked, though I suppose the question must have formed inside my mind for neither my mother nor the parson raised their heads at my voice.

'About a hundred years,' he replied.

I was annoyed at this answer, for it was neither informative nor reassuring, and he must have perceived my irritation, for he quickly began to offer me practical advice.

'If you dab your temples with oil of lavender,' he said to me, 'it will cool your fever and reduce your pain.'

Now, my mother had worked in the lavender fields, and I knew of this use for lavender oil, yet gave it little credence. But finding an audible voice, I asked for lavender, and my mother, no doubt imagining herself to be fulfilling my final request, dabbed at my temples with the oil. And so it was that the parson went his way without securing a funeral fee.

Of course, it wasn't the lavender that cured me. There could be no rational basis for such a supposition. But, as predicted, the lavender cooled my fever, and perhaps that allowed my body to begin healing itself. Or more likely, perhaps the cooling of my fever allowed for the working of the medicine prescribed by a doctor from Lynn, summoned at the expense of Adam Goodchild, whose family had once employed my father as under-gamekeeper.

Whatever the truth, when I woke from my fever, the world seemed a lovelier and more precious place.

After that, and most especially after I came to Crompton Hall, the spirits were seldom far away.

But it proved beyond my powers to summon any particular one of them. I looked often for the man with the bronze face and the sparkling grey eyes, imagining I might meet him among the lavender fields, for such seemed to be the sphere of his interest. Yet though I walked many times to the fields in the months after my recovery, I never saw him again, nor came to understand his strange words to me. Perhaps he spoke of a time when the causes of mysterious illness like my own would be apparent to all medical men, and as easily treated as he directed me to be treated with the lavender oil.

The achievement of health, however, lies not simply with the care of the body, its food and drink, attention to its pains and accidents, although these are important.

Health, it is clear, is also a matter of *heart*. I felt in my heart that I would be healed once I took the lavender oil, and thus it was so.

The parson took a different view.

'You were healed through prayer,' he said.

Prayer is the power of *heart*.

I discussed it often with the parson during long and lively conversations on the holy scriptures.

'God gave us minds and hearts,' he told me. 'With our minds we must question the universe, and with our hearts we must honour humanity . . .'

It seems to me now that prayer, on the face of it the least rational of responses, is in truth the spontaneous working of *heart*, its natural response to crisis or to joy.

Some might dismiss this as illusion, mere wishful thinking, talking to oneself in the slender hope that someone else might be listening.

But if the Kingdom of Heaven lies within, as the Gospel surely teaches, then what is talking to oneself, if not a dialogue with God?

How else might we come to know our true selves or find the strength to face the pain that life presents?

As to whether prayer affects the lives of others, whether those prayed for might find themselves healed in body or restored in spirit, I can only say that each must reach his own conclusion.

I have pondered deeply on this matter, and have come to believe that the power of prayer may be tangible. A sick person, sick even unto death, may be restored by the prayers of his fellow believers. A sailor, faced with certain death on a stormy sea, may find himself miraculously delivered by the prayers of those who urgently petition for his safety. But how it works, we cannot say.

I raised this matter with the parson after my own deliverance from death, for it was he who prayed with my mother at my bedside, and watched her anoint me with lavender oil.

'Prayer was the conduit,' he told me. 'The God in each of us speaking to the God in you. And the God in you responded to the pleas of the God in us. How else did Jesus of Nazareth heal the sick?'

Yet there were those whom Jesus did not heal, and for every sailor plucked from the waves, another score perish. Is God capricious then, saving only those who have the wit to pray for themselves or the fortune to have others pray for them? Perhaps. The Bible speaks of a wrathful, jealous God, and I have seen such a God at work in the hearts of others. Vengeance is theirs, and so is moral righteousness. Some they would condemn, and some they would preserve, according to their laws.

I put this to the parson, and he shook his head.

'The God of Jesus was no avenging tyrant,' he said, 'but a loving father. And how did he raise his beloved son from the dead? Why, through prayer, of course. The prayer of Jesus was so pure, so selfless, so perfectly the prayer of God himself, that its power was unlimited. We see only a spark of that power now, and yet that spark may still work miracles . . .'

And so I concluded that prayer was in essence the energy of souls linked by the God within, communicating their heightened sensations and desires to each other by unseen waves. Perhaps one day these waves might be examined and assessed, as we are now beginning to comprehend the mysterious power of electricity? Perhaps, one day, prayer might be seen as equally rational and scientific?

Perhaps. But I fancy there will always be an element of unknowing, an intriguing possibility lingering just beyond the edge of our understanding . . .

The parson told me a story, a true story, concerning his grandfather who'd been parson in charge of a parish near Lynn in the year 1849.

At dusk one evening this good parson opened his door to a child who begged him come visit her dying mother in a village some three miles hence. The house lay along country lanes on a stretch of coast notorious for smugglers and robbers. It was scarcely safe after dark even for mounted travellers, and the parson's horse was lame. He would have to make the dangerous journey on foot.

His wife implored him to wait until daybreak, but Christian duty and the heart-rending pleas of the child took him out into the starless night with none but Faith and Hope for his companions.

Fearing she might never see him alive again, his wife immediately summoned her family and neighbours, all devout folk of the parish, and together they prayed for his safe return. Throughout the night they offered their petition, for the dying mother, sick of the blackleg after childbirth, and for the parson and young child, prey to murderers and thieves. *Oh God, who in your infinite mercy sees the fall of every sparrow, preserve unto us this man whom we love and the woman who lies sick, and her young child . . . Defend and protect them Lord, and restore them to us . . .*

At daybreak the parson returned unharmed with the news that the woman's crisis was past. She was weak, she would require much care, but she would live to raise her children. And no bandit had crossed his path as he walked with the young girl . . .

There was relief in the parish, but then the matter was quickly forgotten, with nothing much proved, nor disproved, about the power of prayer.

However, a few weeks later, this same parson was called to the gaolhouse in Lynn to absolve a murderer due to be hanged the following morning.

When the two men met, the murderer fell to his knees with wails and laments, declaring that God himself had sent this particular parson to be his confessor.

'Father, I repent!' cried the murderer. 'May God forgive all my sins, which I now confess before you . . .'

He confessed not only to the murder for which he was to pay the price, nor yet the smuggling which had been his trade for many a year, but also his thwarted intent to rob the very man who stood before him.

He told the parson he had lain in wait one dark night on the country road that links Lynn to the shores of The Wash, hoping to encounter a lone traveller. Soon he saw a man approach on foot, and knew him to be a man of God by the collar he wore. A small child walked by his side.

'I felt no pity. I would have killed you there and then for the sovereign in your pocket . . . But as I stood to strike the fatal blow, two men appeared at your side. They looked like soldiers, though their uniforms were none I'd ever seen.'

They were burly and strong, and knowing himself no match for three men, the murderer let them pass. But he followed to the next village, thinking the soldiers might go their own way and leave his quarry unprotected.

'But I saw you all go into a humble cottage, and when I peered through the window, still thinking there might be profit for me, I saw your face quite clearly, and the two soldiers standing by the bed of a sick woman . . .'

The murderer clutched at the parson's cloak.

'Your soldier friends saved your life, and I too, through

them, was spared yet another grievous stain upon my soul . . .'

The parson, astonished, delivered his absolution and forgave the man his sins.

There had been no soldiers, no companions on that journey! Who, or what, had the murderer seen?

The parson accepted this story, for nothing was to be gained by inventing it, and at no time did the murderer believe he had seen anything unusual. And after this, the tale was recounted many times, the parson always concluding with the same injunction: *Believe in the power of prayer, for it summons the angels to your side . . .*

I, myself, have never seen an angel, unless the man who once stood by my bedside was one such. But the story convinced me, and I have prayed ever since. I have prayed most earnestly for my mother and my sister at times of crisis, and I have asked all my fellow believers at Crompton church to pray for them too. *Thou hast promised that when two or three are gathered together in your name, thou wilt hear their requests and grant them . . .*

Who knows what prayer may do? Perhaps God can intervene in no other way, and must sit in Heaven, weeping and wringing his hands over all who fail to call upon him? Perhaps prayer is the only means by which we can save ourselves, and by which, alone, we come at last to peace and plenty.

As a child I went each Sunday to the round-towered church in the woods beyond Crompton Hall, neat and earnest in my velvet-collared coat, walking between my Ma and Papa, my sister's hand clutched tightly in my own, eyes wide, ears open.

I watched for angels and believed I might see one, for our church was dedicated to St Michael and All Angels. And indeed, sometimes I seemed to sense that rare and glorious being, St Michael himself, hovering on wings of fire above the altar, shaking his glittering locks and beckoning me on to Paradise. I even fancied, when the church was silver cold and still, that I could hear the fluttering of the heavenly host as they jostled their wings in the aisle and bent to kiss my bowed head, all of us one in the communion of saints.

But to sense is not to see, and never glimpsing an angel, I concluded that I must conduct my researches elsewhere.

This I proceeded to do, devouring every book that came my way, poring over faded print by the light of a single candle. Yet for all that, I learned little of angels, and even less about prayer, that mysterious process over which they seemed to hold sway. Angels, I came to see, were a matter of perception, and prayer, a matter of experience. I could read all I might, but never come to understand unless an angel tapped me on the shoulder, or a prayer fell into my lap. Or unless some wonderful story, like the one about the murderer, should seize my imagination and enlarge my understanding . . .

I had been taught to read by the parson at my mother's request, and finding me a willing and enthusiastic pupil, he went on to tutor me in Latin and Greek.

My mother was delighted, declaring that if I had a brain in my head, and most importantly, knew how to use it, I need never be dependent on a man for my ideas. I doubt I would have been in any case, for my mother herself was not, and had learned rudimentary reading and writing by her own unaided efforts, procuring a two-penny alphabet primer from a second-hand bookshop in Norwich.

My father, who could not read a word, and who duly bowed to my mother's superior understanding in most things, found her views upon menfolk and marriage endlessly amusing.

'My dear Nell,' he'd say to her, 'if those girls wed as well as you did, they'll be lucky little mawthers . . .'

My mother, who loved my father dearly, concurred with this sentiment but retained the belief that she had been peculiarly blessed, and that such good fortune in matrimony was not easily come by. Alas, this proved to be so, for Ivy married a dullard, and I have neither married, nor considered, any man at all.

Now I envisage no end to my spinster state, nor would

I wish it. I saw how my mother struggled after my father's death with a baby son to raise and two growing daughters not yet old enough to marry nor earn their keep. Marriage makes life an uncertain and generally disappointing business, and motherhood only increases its pains. So my mother had me believe, and although until my father died I had every reason to think her the happiest of women, I found no cause to dispute her wider view.

My father was killed by a single rifle bullet on the first day of the shooting season, in the first year of the new century.

There seemed a terrible logic to his death for he'd hated guns and hunting, always hoping he might one day find some other employment. He despaired of a world where three hundred birds might be killed in a day, many so full of shot they might never be eaten, and half the village close to starving.

We looked to the Goodchilds for recompense, but we found no friend there. Adam Goodchild was abroad at that time, observing the South African wars, and it was his father who forced my mother out of the estate house and into a tumbledown cottage on the edge of the lavender fields.

It was carefully explained that my father was to blame for his own death, that he had disobeyed a fundamental rule and walked into the line of fire. It was not so much an accident as a culpable act of self destruction. At the inquiry before the examining magistrate, it was even suggested that my father, fearful for his job – a box of missing cartridges, a brace of pheasants discovered at Lavender House, the home of a nearby farmer – had deliberately endangered himself. Was this, asked the magistrate, a criminal attempt by my father to gain compensation for his wife and family?

It was nonsense, of course. The cartridges were later discovered behind a dog's basket in the Goodchilds' gun room, and the lavender farmer, in one of his sober moments, entered a deposition to state that the birds seen on his table by a gossiping parlour maid were in fact bantam chickens cooked in ale – a substance which rendered the flesh dark.

But all this counted for nothing, and if the farmer hadn't offered my mother work in his fields, and allowed us to rent Lavender Cottage for a shilling a week, then we should all have entered the workhouse.

I never saw my mother weep but once.

It wasn't at the news of my father's death, nor even at his meagre funeral. It wasn't at Ivy's wedding either, although I knew she felt like crying.

It was one evening, shortly after I'd recovered from my illness, as we sat on the back step of our cottage. We were taking a glass of elderberry wine which Charlie, the lavender farmer, had sent over from his cellar, he being solicitous for my mother's comfort we now understood, on account of his poaching from the Goodchild estate while my father was employed there.

The lavender was coming into bloom, waving before us like an inland lake of deepest blue, its perfume drifting on the twilight air.

My mother raised her hand and bade me listen.

Did I hear it? That melody so sweet, so mournful, that angels cease the beating of their wings and fall from heaven in ecstasy . . .

I hardly know, but as I raised my eyes from the darkening blue of the lavender and turned to my mother, I saw tears like the shards of stars upon her cheeks.

'What is it?' I asked her gently. 'Please don't fret. I'm quite well now . . .'

She turned to me, wiping her face.

'You know, don't you, Alice? You hear it . . . You understand . . .'

'Understand what?' I whispered, although I think in that moment, for the very first time, I did begin to understand.

My mother leaned forward and touched my face, her eyes still glittering with tears.

'The language of nightingales,' she said.

How often have I heard that glorious song in moments since? How often have I pondered its sorrowful message and

76

imagined myself rising beyond the limits of consciousness, free as a bird?

How often have I dreamed, with the poet, *that I might leave the world unseen and with thee fade away into the forest dim?* Too often.

The world is a tragic place, but to dwell upon tragedy is to deny the song of the nightingale.

Certainly, my mother would have no doing with idle melancholy, and I heard no such talk again.

Instead, I heard much about the practicalities of living, the means by which contentment – if not happiness – might be secured.

You may not control what happens to you, Alice.

And I would respond dutifully: 'No, but I can control how I react to what happens . . .'

You may not be able to control your feelings, Alice.

No, but I can control the way I act upon my feelings . . .

You may not always be treated as you deserve to be, Alice.

No, but I can retain my belief about what I deserve . . .

You may meet with misfortune, Alice.

Ah, yes. But I will never despair. I know that from the purging fire of misfortune comes the trusty steel of courage.

You may suffer, Alice.

Yes, indeed. And through suffering see into the heart of things.

There are those who claim that suffering, like health, is a matter of degree.

I have heard this argument put by Sir Robin Crompton, agreed upon most vociferously by Lady Crompton and seldom contradicted by India, who seems to believe that suffering is brought about by one's own iniquities, if not in this life, then in some other imagined existence, as the Hindu people hold.

Even Adam Goodchild, whose tenants are the best served in the county, would not argue with the view that working families feel hardship less than genteel folk because they are used to it.

Only Christian dares to dissent, and then I suspect, simply because he loves to court controversy.

'Well, I should not live in a hovel,' he declared during a lively discussion about wet rot and fungus, evils which continue to blight a row of cottages on the Crompton estate. 'And why should I require others to do what I would not do myself?'

Nobody answered this question, and to my intense embarrassment, Christian went on to relate a tale I had told him of an old woman who froze to death one winter's night after slates above her bed worked loose, causing the water which streamed down her walls – a permanent feature of life in Crompton village – to become solid ice.

'She should have moved her bed into the sitting room,' India said.

'She should have replaced the slates,' said Lady Crompton.

'She wasn't a Crompton tenant,' said Sir Robin, as though this settled the matter once and for all.

Christian laughed uproariously.

'Then I hope I'm never so old that I can't mend the slates on my own roof nor pull my bed close to the fire,' he said with mock gravity.

Lady Crompton was not amused.

'The servants will do all that,' she said archly.

Underlying every such debate – and I have been a silent witness to many – is the belief that all are not equally deserving of shelter, good food, employment, nor indeed, of medical attention.

I've heard much derision of working men who fritter their wages in the village inn – as though it were only the poor who know how to waste their money – and of women who bring children into the world without the means to feed them, as though rich mothers never find themselves bearing a child they neither anticipated nor desired.

I've heard it said that poor boys go without shoes because their mothers drink too much gin – as though only the rich are entitled to liquor – and that the lower classes suffer disease because of slovenly habits, as though all might be as fragrant as the ladies of high society if only they tried a little harder.

Yet for all this heartless talk, I pity those so divorced from suffering that they cannot feel the pulse of life, cannot grasp the slender thread of conscience that unites us all. They know nothing of angels, and would not think to pray.

They will never see into the heart of things.

Chapter Six

'Do you have any belief system, Laurie?'

She blinked and said nothing.

'A set of concepts by which you live?' he pursued. 'A vision of Paradise?'

Laurie stared mutinously at the portrait of India and the woman she now imagined to be Alice, the maid. A trick of the light through the French window to the counselling suite seemed to enliven India's features, touching the wide painted eyes with fiery blue. Her tilted face was lit with glowing olive, while in the space behind her, Alice, pale gold wisps of hair curling against ivory skin, gazed into eternity with liquid hazel eyes.

We see you, Laurie. We see you.

'A belief system?' Laurie snapped, looking away. 'If you mean religion, I should point out that my father is a mathematician, and I am a rationalist. I believe in what can be seen and measured, Doctor Mitchell, by the naked eye of man himself and the instruments he has devised . . .'

'Computers?' Dale Mitchell smiled his Californian smile, startling white teeth dissecting the smooth bronze face. 'Yes, of course . . . Your chosen career, Laurie. Your point of reference.'

Laurie battled against her irritation.

'It's not a point of reference. It's what I do. The way I earn my living.'

She knew she was being churlish, and knew too that her temper had risen in response to a perceived threat. He was goading her, leading into unknown admissions. She took a deep breath and sat back in her chair. She wouldn't be led.

'I'm just trying to discover how you feel about your life,' he protested, reading her every move. 'I want to know what you want from your future.'

'I want to be well,' she said, hearing her voice quiver.

'And what will you do with your health when you have it back? Will you return to the career you've left, or will you do something new?'

She was battling against her tears.

'Take up watercolours or loom-weaving, you mean?'

He grinned, accepting the jibe, and leaned toward her.

'No, I don't mean that. I'm asking what would make you content . . . What you believe might be the secret of a good life?'

A tear escaped her and she wiped it away furiously. The paucity of her one-time beliefs rose to taunt her. *A good marriage. A happy home. Children.*

'Talking computers,' she said fatuously. 'Ones that think for themselves and give you all the right answers . . .'

'Ah,' he said, smiling, 'computers in love?'

'Why not? It would solve a lot of problems. Plug in your dream lover. Programme your desired response.'

He seemed to think it over, still smiling.

'In our lifetime, do you reckon?'

Laurie stared at him coldly.

'You talk blithely of a lifetime, Doctor Mitchell, and know what to expect. I have no such luxury.'

He was momentarily embarrassed, and she felt an unexpected surge of sympathy. He was trying to help her. He was seeking to lighten her darkness. It wasn't his fault she refused to play.

'I wanted to get married,' she heard herself offer, a change of heart that surprised her as much as him. 'I thought it would make me happy . . . Only now I'm not so sure. I mean, I have to ask why I've never married before . . . It's not that I haven't had the chance . . .'

He raised one eyebrow, awaiting more, but Laurie had said enough. For a long moment they stared at each other across the room.

'So,' he said, 'once you believed in the healing power of love, and now you no longer do?'

She shrugged.

'Does it really matter what I believe?'

'I suspect it does.'

Laurie shifted restlessly, and raised her eyes once more to India's.

'I fail to see what all this has to do with my cancer,' she said at last.

'Maybe nothing,' he replied slowly. 'And yet it has been my observation, and that of other scientists far more notable than myself, that a belief system can have a measurable effect on the progress and experience of disease . . .'

'So you can believe what you like?'

He eyed her carefully, assessing her mood.

'I wouldn't say that. To gain from belief, you'd have to believe in something good . . .'

'Ah!' Laurie's lip set in a thin, hard line. 'Positive thinking! The last resort of the quack who can't come up with a cure . . .'

He leaned forward, pressing his fingertips together, as though he'd taken the decision to plough on despite her intransigence.

'Do you believe in justice? The pursuit of freedom and equality for all?'

'Doesn't everyone?'

He pressed on.

'Or is there something else, something which underpins all our hopes of Paradise? The resurrection of the dead, perhaps?'

She shook her head, surprised.

'Reincarnation, then? The eternal cycle of death and rebirth, ending only with the overcoming of all worldly desire? Have you ever considered it?'

Laurie laughed despite herself.

'I've read Shirley Maclaine's autobiography. Does that count?'

When he laughed too, she stood up, turning from him to gaze once more at India's portrait.

'I have a physical illness,' she said tightly, pressing her hand to her diseased breast. 'The cells of my body are mutating and destroying their host. No belief system on Earth is going to change that.'

83

* * *

Gloria called, with news.

'You've got a date for your first chemotherapy.'

'Is that the good news or the bad?'

'Depends which way you look at it, darling. You have to check in the day after tomorrow.'

With unexpected dismay Laurie realized she'd be leaving Crompton Hall in the morning, and, deeply perplexed, she knew that she didn't want to go.

There was a long pause, at the end of which Gloria's voice quavered, heavy with uncharacteristic emotion.

'I'll understand, Laurie, if you don't go back to Norfolk ... It was wrong of me to insist. Your father says you should be home with your family and friends ... He's flying over this weekend ... I think he's bringing *that woman* with him!'

Laurie's fingers tightened on the telephone receiver.

Great! A parental drama at the bedside with me going bald and throwing up.

'It'll be good to see him,' she said carefully, 'but I doubt Elspeth will come. She's always so tied up with the business ...'

'Bathroom fittings!' Gloria exploded, unable to conceal her disdain for her successor even at this inappropriate moment. 'Bogs for the Bourgeoisie! Yes, maybe you're right, darling,' she added contritely, 'she won't come.'

Laurie closed her eyes, calling on all her strength.

'It will be good to get started,' she said decisively. 'No sense hanging about ... I mean, it can't be *that* bad, can it?'

Gloria's doubt was palpable, poised on the distance between them.

'What does Doctor Mitchell think about chemotherapy?' she inquired at last.

'I've really no idea, and in any case, his opinion carries no weight with me!'

Gloria, showing unusual forbearance, allowed this to pass.

'Now, one last thing, darling . . . Sean's coming to pick you up . . . Please don't be churlish, Laurie! The poor boy is positively grief-stricken. He's called me every day you've been away, and he *insisted* he should be the one to bring you home.'

Another shrug, instinctive, almost mandatory, even though Gloria couldn't see.

'It's all the same to me,' she answered.

What unknown forces feed the wellspring of desire, swelling that first trickle of longing into a torrent?

Laurie lay back on the bed – India's bed – and pulled the tapestry quilt – India's quilt – tight around her shoulders, wrapping her griefs away and, with a certain clinical curiosity, allowed herself to summon the past, as though by examining her former passion in all its intensity she might uncover the root of her present disaffection.

What was it about Sean that had marked him out from the beginning?

'Look at that gorgeous bum,' Shelley had whispered in her ear. 'Did you ever see such a neat pair of cheeks? Wouldn't you just love to grab a handful?'

Laurie had looked, vowing that never again would she invite Shelley to an office party, despite her unusual talent with things on cocktail sticks.

But Shelley was right. It *was* a gorgeous bum, fetchingly encased in tight blue denim.

'That's Sean Youngman,' said the girl from accounts, who'd overheard and obviously agreed. 'We should be chatting him up, not admiring his bum. He's looking for a new system.'

'Aren't we all?' sighed Shelley. 'But you can bet your arse – or even that little arse – we won't find it this side of paradise.'

'Ah, Laurie,' said the office manager, catching her eye and making her blush for fear he'd overheard. 'I'd like you to meet Sean . . .'

Then, of course, it wasn't his gorgeous bum, it was his

smoky blue eyes and his silky blond hair, and his engaging way of appearing to concentrate intently on everything Laurie had to say, his gaze never faltering, his attention held.

'Never mind the derrière,' Shelley hissed when at last Laurie dragged herself away, 'he's a definite AOB. I wasn't sure at first, but now I am.'

'What's an AOB?' the girl from accounts wanted to know. 'I thought he was Irish.'

'All-Out Bastard,' Laurie said thoughtfully. 'But I really don't see how you can tell at this stage.'

'You can always tell,' Shelley muttered darkly. 'If you know how to read the signs. Anyway, how come a guy that pretty is here on his own? He's probably gay – or married.'

'Which is worse?' Laurie pondered.

Later that night, flushed with pride and Chardonnay, the deal for the new system clinched and Sean having been revealed as definitely not gay, possibly not AOB, and not Irish either, Laurie found herself rewriting her usual script.

'I don't sleep with men I've just met,' was what she meant to say as they emerged from their shared taxi.

'Are you coming in?' was what she actually said.

He stood in her hallway admiring her framed theatre posters, then moved into the study where he turned on her computer and tapped out a message. *Sean Youngman woz here.*

'Electronic graffiti,' he said. 'Quickly deleted. You can wipe me out as soon as I've gone.'

'You could be saved,' she said.

He smiled, a faint, melancholy half-smile.

'I should warn you I'm not worth saving,' he said.

'Why's that?' she asked.

'I'm married,' he replied.

She had guessed as much, had noted, indeed, the faint white band on his finger shadowing a wedding ring. But still she was hoping. A recent divorce, an adulterous wife who'd vanished with a best friend, a fatal car accident or a terminal disease . . . No such luck, it seemed, judging by the hang-dog look he gave her.

'What are you doing here then?' she said sharply, snapping off the computer, angry with herself and disappointed in him, wondering why she hadn't exercised her usual scrupulous care. 'Shouldn't you be at home?'

'I suppose so,' he said, turning away.

She watched him go with heavy heart, knowing she would certainly have to see him again, imagining how they might both pretend this embarrassing little exchange had never happened. But at the front door he turned back.

'I live apart from my wife,' he muttered. 'I don't want you thinking I'm that big a bastard . . .'

So, not the all-out variety after all?

She took off her clothes and watched him undress with an eagerness that belied all customary restraints. She could scarcely believe she wanted him this much, and couldn't imagine where such incaution would lead her, except that it would surely be to deep and murky waters. And when his naked flesh first brushed hers, it seemed a shock of recognition swept across her, like a wave from a warm, sunlit sea, and she'd felt herself tugged out of the shallows and into the blue beyond.

What crap!

Laurie sat up on India's bed and reached for the phone.

A warm, sunlit sea? It was lust, pure and simple, that had driven her first encounter with Sean.

How foolish, how self-deceiving, are the ways of a thirty-something woman who fears time might be running out . . . But not any more, she thought grimly, not now that time really *is* running out.

It was all horribly clear-cut. *Where's the sense in love? What's the point of having sex when you're going to die?*

She dialled Shelley's number, barely concealing her impatience at the necessary exchange of greetings.

'I want you to collect me from Norfolk,' she said tersely. 'I want you to ring Sean right now and tell him not to come. Just do it, Shelley, please. Tell him to stay away from me.'

*   *   *

At supper, she announced her impending departure.

'Chemo isn't so bad,' Val said, squeezing her hand across the granary rolls. 'You'll see.'

'I refused it,' Edie said, 'I felt I'd rather take my chances. But of course, it's your decision . . .'

Laurie looked down at her soup. *Broccoli and coconut!* Could it really be? Gloria could hardly surpass this herself.

She raised a spoon of the green sludge to her lips, and felt her throat gag.

'This soup's a bit rum,' said a man whose name Laurie couldn't remember. Was he a bowel or a lung?

Laurie smiled uncertainly, grateful to have her opinion on the soup confirmed, and he leaned over the table toward her.

'You'll be fine,' he whispered. 'Just believe it.'

She felt the tears prick hard behind her eyelids.

'If I believe,' she muttered fiercely, 'will that make it true?'

Val and Edie exchanged knowing glances.

'Well, it's a start,' Edie murmured.

'It's the only possible start,' Val said gently. 'Not believing isn't a start. It's the end.'

Back in her room, she took out India's journal once more, fingering the gilt clasps and the ancient leather, closing her mind against the misery of the moment, summoning the past in all its imagined glory.

I am still wondering if I dare mention the matter of Christian's amour to Alice? I do so long to have her reassurance, but I am very concerned not to appear indiscreet. It's my perception that Alice carries some influence with Christian, though quite why that should be so, I can't say. Perhaps he too sees her special qualities. Certainly, I find myself ever more convinced that without her, the whole of Crompton Hall would fall prey to sickness and depression. I do so long for Christian to return. I long to hear his laugh and watch him dive into his deep, clear pool. And of course, I can scarcely wait to know what he has bought for my birthday! Dr Harte called to pay his respects to Mama this afternoon, and with him his wife Eugenie and their little daughters.

Laurie snapped the book shut. She didn't want to know what Christian Crompton-Leigh had bought for his sister's birthday. She didn't want to hear about Alice's influence on the young master, nor India's concerns about his love-life. And she certainly didn't wish to know about Dr Luke Harte and his wife Eugenie. She wanted snapshots to fire her fantasies, not facts to spoil her perception of a perfect moment, locked in time, preserved upon the very air she breathed in India's room.

Laurie reached for her own journal.

Now I know why we tell stories. Why cavemen drew on walls and wandering minstrels sang ballads. Why little girls imagined fairies at the bottom of their gardens and Enid Blyton got rid of all the grown-ups. We are filling up time and space. We are closing our eyes against the coming of the night. We are basking in the sunshine of created worlds, where skies are always endless blue and laughter carries on the breeze . . .

A knock at the door interrupted these lofty musings, and Laurie, faced by the solicitous Edie, bundled her journal into the bedside drawer. She didn't want anyone thinking she was blindly obeying the rules of the house.

'Val and I are going for a walk,' Edie said. 'It's such a beautiful night. Won't you come? No lectures, we promise . . .'

Laurie smiled awkwardly, stirred by mild shame. They were trying to be nice. They wanted to help. *If only they weren't so relentlessly positive. If only they would howl or swear or rail at the horror, the injustice, of it all. If only they'd stop pretending that everything was going to be all right . . .*

'Thanks,' she said meekly, 'a walk would be great.'

There were no lectures. Instead, a stilted inconsequentiality walked with them, along the pathways of the kitchen garden, out of the Crompton Hall woods, and on to the meandering gravel lane that led into the village.

'There's talk of draining the lake,' Edie said as they skirted the silent water with its undulating cover of green.

'Really? Why's that?' Laurie asked politely.

'Something to do with the sedge. It's got some kind of blight.'

'The sedge is withered from the lake,' said Val, as though deliberately seeking to enlarge the small talk, 'and no birds sing.'

'Not true! I heard a nightingale just last night,' Edie protested.

Val laughed easily.

'Then perhaps we'll be lucky this evening,' she said. 'Come, thou light-winged dryad of the trees!'

Laurie needed no other cue.

'Now more than ever seems it rich to die,' she quoted, her tone harsh and sardonic. 'To cease upon the midnight with no pain . . .'

'Pardon?' Edie looked up, startled.

'Keats,' replied Val, glancing quickly at Laurie.

'Yes, poor old Keats! Dead of consumption, and only twenty-six. How lucky we are that times have changed!'

Now her voice broke, and, deeply embarrassed, she marched ahead of them, veering off the village road when a footpath appeared which, she calculated, would lead her back to Crompton Hall. She climbed over the stile and set off across the darkening fields.

It was useless, this attempt to pretend solidarity with her fellow sufferers. Each must endure, or capitulate, as individual temperament dictated, and in the end, as the poets knew only too well, everyone must die alone . . .

Ahead she could see the woods, a black thickening line on the landscape.

She ran toward the trees, her breath rasping on the still evening air. Ridiculous to be this unfit. Why had she stopped going to the gym? It was Sean, of course. After she'd taken up with Sean, there simply hadn't been time . . . Now she would put that right. She would get back into shape, get fit again . . .

The incongruity of this resolve hit her with all the force of a blow in the chest, and once in the shelter of the wood, she sank to her knees with a little sob. She clasped her hands over her breasts, feeling the blessed softness of the one; the hard, moveable lump, tight as a dried pea, at the centre of the other.

Shit, oh shit. A thousand times shit. *Shit, shit, shit!* Oh, shit.

'I love it,' Shelley said dreamily. 'I've never been anywhere so beautiful. I thought Gloria told me Norfolk was wet and flat.'

'She was thinking of someone else,' Laurie said.

Shelley was sitting on the bench in the kitchen garden, spiked head thrown back against the apple tree behind her, chalky face turned to the mellowing sun, the tip of her nose glinting brazenly.

'You've had your nostril pierced,' Laurie said.

'Yes, do you fancy one too?' They both laughed. It never ceased to amuse them, the splendid contrast they presented, Laurie the smart city girl, Shelley the wild child. They should each have disapproved of the other, yet from the moment they met, aged fifteen and nothing in common from background to aspiration, they'd moved purposefully toward an exchange of sensibility so that Laurie was able to delight in showing off her vulgar friend, and seriously annoying Gloria, while Shelley could make unlimited fun of the Davison ménage.

'A bald head and a stud up my nose?' Laurie mused.

'Why not? What's to lose?'

'There's nothing to lose,' Laurie said, sober again. 'Not any more.'

'In that case,' said Shelley, lurching upright and fixing Laurie with her sooty stare, 'you should get the pants off Doctor Dale Mitchell. I would if I were you.'

'No you wouldn't,' Laurie said, laughing again.

But then she thought that Shelley probably would.

'He's an AOB,' she cautioned.

'I don't think so. I see something unusual there. I think it's called sincerity.'

'Oh, come on!' Laurie was irritated. 'He's got a line he's selling just like everyone else.'

'Maybe.' Shelley lay back against the tree again. 'But it would be fun, finding out . . .'

The meeting between Shelley and Dale Mitchell had not been what Laurie expected.

He'd seemed less than his usual beguiling self that morning, tense and preoccupied, gazing thoughtfully at Laurie as, after much agonizing and a certain trepidation, she outlined her reasons for returning to Norfolk once her first chemotherapy was done.

'Despite what everyone here appears to think,' she'd said belligerently, 'I'm not a quitter. I just don't like being fed a sop, that's all. And I like to make my feelings plain. I'm sure you approve of that?'

'Sure,' he affirmed vaguely.

'And frankly,' Laurie continued, intent now on delivering the speech she'd spent half the night rehearsing, 'I may as well be here as anywhere else. My father's flying in from Washington, and he'll probably have my stepmother in tow. That makes for a difficult family situation with my mother . . . I think life will be more peaceful here. You're providing me with an excellent excuse to be alone.'

'Do you need an excuse?' he'd inquired, a trifle testily she fancied, and for the first time, she found herself wondering about his private life. Was there no wife or lover? Was he five times divorced, like every other sun-bronzed Californian of her imagination?

'No,' she snapped. 'I can do anything I like. And if you must know, it's a matter of some amazement to me that I intend coming back here at all.'

There was an uncomfortable pause.

'Me too,' he agreed heavily.

Into this frosty atmosphere, Shelley burst like the first ray of morning sun, pale and fiery, extraordinary in the contrast provided.

'The cavalry!' she announced, winking at Laurie, and then turning her attention to Dale, surveyed him critically. 'Hiya, cowboy,' she said at last, smiling broadly.

He eyed the apparition before him in open wonder, the vertical hair, the owlish eyes, the little ebony coffin swinging round her neck, the mock silver handcuffs that dangled from her ear-lobes.

'You're a work of art!' he declared, appearing genuinely impressed. 'What wonderful jewellery . . .'

Shelley twirled her coffin.

'I make it myself,' she grinned.

'And how do you get your hair to stand up like that?'

'I give myself a fright once a day,' Shelley said, and they both laughed, long and just a little too heartily. Laurie was dismayed. *They liked each other.* This wasn't the way she'd envisaged their meeting, planning to present Shelley, as she so often did, with a brazen flourish designed to say something about herself. *Don't think you've got me weighed up. This is my best friend!*

Now she dismissed all talk of Dr Mitchell with a brisk admonition.

'I don't give a damn about men any more!'

Which brought them swiftly and inevitably to Sean.

'He's very upset, you know.'

'Is he? About what?'

'You've cut him dead, Laurie. He doesn't know what's going on.'

'There's nothing going on. Nothing that wasn't always going on anyway. The inexorable processes of life and death . . . Entropy and decay . . .'

She hadn't meant to embark on this morbid theme with Shelley, indeed, had been so cheered at the prospect of her old friend's arrival that she'd even apologized to Edie and Val, announcing her intended return to Crompton Hall with an implicit promise of new and hitherto unimagined sociability. But somehow, Shelley's banter with Dale Mitchell and her unlikely championing of Sean had pitched Laurie back into her former gloom.

Even so, she struggled against it.

'I know it's hard for everyone else . . . That's the thing about cancer . . . It isn't just the victim who suffers . . . All the same, I'm the one who's got it. I have to do what's right for me . . .'

'Of course you do,' Shelley said soberly. Then she

grinned. 'That's why you ought to get the pants off Dale Mitchell.'

Before they left, Laurie took Shelley into the woods.

'I have this curious feeling,' she tried to explain. 'A bit like *déjà-vu*, only not quite that . . . More a kind of intuition, like living out a fantasy, but knowing that it's true . . . That it really happened . . .'

Shelley shook the handcuff earrings and twiddled with her coffin.

'I'm not surprised. This place is heaven on earth. Made for fantasies . . .'

They'd reached the orchard beyond the kitchen garden, and opening the dilapidated gate into the wilderness beyond, stepped out among the beeches, taking overgrown paths away from the main well-trodden thoroughfare in case, Laurie said wryly, they should encounter the other clients.

'Clients?'

'Seekers of regeneration.'

'What is all this regeneration stuff anyway?'

'I haven't really found out. Nobody seems willing to pin it down.'

'Maybe it's dark sexual practices,' Shelley said. 'Sacrificing virgins or having it off in the blackcurrant bushes. That would be pretty regenerating, wouldn't it? Especially if you got the lovely Dale Mitchell . . .'

Laurie stopped abruptly.

'Listen! Do you hear the brook? It seems to be running deep just here . . . Maybe there's a pool . . . A pool deep enough to swim in . . .'

She closed her eyes.

I do so long for Christian to return . . . I long to hear his laugh and watch him dive into his deep, clear pool . . . And of course, I can scarcely wait to know what he has bought for my birthday!

Laurie sprang from the path and began to battle her way through the dense saplings toward the noise, beating back branches that slapped at her face and the briars that tugged at her ankles.

'What the heck's going on?' grumbled Shelley behind her, and then emerging into a brilliant green cavern, a natural clearing overhung with mallow bushes and waving willows, they stood in silence before a glittering pit of water, dark and clear as stained glass.

Laurie sank to her knees on the bank.

'Christian's pool! This is it . . .'

'You could drink this stuff!' Shelley dangled her fingers in the fronds at the water's edge. 'It's straight from the fridge . . . Don't know about swimming, though. Bit parky for that. Whose pool?'

Laurie stood up.

'Did you notice the portrait in the counselling room this morning? Two young women, one very dark, the other fair . . . An Edwardian lady and her personal maid . . . That was India Crompton–Leigh, and Christian was her brother . . .'

Shelley shook her head.

'Too busy ogling Dale, I'm afraid.'

Laurie made no reply, simply stared into the depths of the pool as though a sleek wet head might break the surface at any moment and look up through the intervening years.

'So is this your *déjà-vu*?' Shelley asked gently.

'It's nothing much. Just spirit of place, I guess.'

Now she felt embarrassed, unwilling to reveal the extent of her interest.

Maybe this is how life-threatening illness works. Maybe it robs you of all reason and loosens your hold on reality. Maybe it leads to denial and a retreat into make-believe.

'Let's get back,' she said brusquely to her bemused friend. 'There's no sense lingering. Nothing will make any difference. All this is just postponing the pain.'

They found Ruth Christianos in her office, a gloomy room off the hallway hung with mangy heads of deer and dusty rifles in glass cases.

'The old gun room,' she explained to Shelley seeing her interest. 'We keep saying we'll throw out the livestock, but somehow we never do . . .'

She came to see them off, standing on the steps of Crompton Hall in her neat business suit, calm, efficient, kindly, just as she'd appeared on the day of Laurie's arrival.

Laurie took her hand, fighting unexpected emotion.

'I'm glad to hear you're coming back,' Ruth murmured. 'I'm sure you'll feel it's worthwhile in the end.'

'I've taken my journal,' Laurie said awkwardly. 'I'll be filling it in while I'm away . . .'

They climbed into Shelley's violet Mini, Laurie balking, for the first time she could remember, at the skull motif boldly emblazoned on the roof.

'Can anyone come to be regenerated?' Shelley inquired, leaning out of the window. 'Or do you have to be ill?'

'Everyone's welcome,' Ruth replied. 'But if you're sound in body and mind, then it's not so much a question of what you'll get from Crompton Hall . . . It's a question of what you'll give . . .'

Shelley nodded sagely, waggling the silver handcuffs, and they drove away from the house in silence, out through the avenue of limes, down the hill and into the village, cruising past the pink-painted wattle cottages with their English country gardens, and out on to the motorway.

I'm leaving part of myself behind . . . A part I never knew existed . . .

Laurie smiled nervously, willing herself to look ahead to the meeting with her father, to the consolation Gloria would require, to her determination to avoid Sean.

But nothing seemed important, not even the prospect of her hospital ordeal.

She could think of nothing but India, and of the story waiting to be told.

Chapter Seven

A domestic disaster overshadowed the morning of the birthday party. Daisy, the kitchen 'tweeny, fainted in the pantry, and along with her fall from consciousness went seventeen raspberry jellies, six apple and cinnamon turnovers, a plate of mincemeat tartlets and two dozen cow-heel pies.

The resulting clamour was heard in the drawing room, prompting Lady Crompton to make an unprecedented appearance below stairs, an event of such magnitude that Cook, anticipating the apportioning of blame and wisely calculating that a more portentous disaster would eclipse the loss of the pastries, immediately gave notice, swiftly followed by two of the scullery maids.

Her Ladyship bristled with the effort at control.

'No such action is necessary,' she said crisply, eyeing the trembling scullery maids and smiling icily at Cook. 'Though I wonder about the girl. She's obviously not strong enough for kitchen work. Tell Addison or Mrs Long to give her a three-penny piece, and escort her to the gates.'

The unfortunate Daisy, recovering from her swoon just in time to hear this judgement pronounced, let out a feeble wail and attempted to rise from the trestle by the window where she'd been lain.

'It were only the heat, Ma'am,' she pleaded, but Lady Crompton, similarly oppressed by the soaring temperature in the kitchen, was already on the first stair and thus beyond concern for those beneath.

Daisy burst into tears, and Flora, the younger of the scullery maids, quickly added her own, while Cook surveyed the devastation in the pantry, plucking the odd recognizable pie or tartlet from the carnage, dusting the pottery shards from their crusts, and declaring, with more jollity than she surely felt, that the kitchen maids would be tasting some party fare after all.

'You take these pies home to your Ma,' she said kindly to Daisy, wrapping a couple of the least crumbled specimens into a cheesecloth, 'but tell her to watch out for bits of china!' This noble offer failed to dry Daisy's tears, nor indeed, to improve her prospects, and she might well have found herself at the gates forthwith in company of Mr Addison, or the feared Mrs Long, had not the champion of all downstairs maids suddenly appeared on the kitchen stairs.

'Oh, Miss Alice!' cried Flora in relief. 'There's been such a to-do! And now poor Daisy has to go . . . Without a mention of a reference! Whatever will happen to her?'

Alice said nothing, simply grimaced and took charge, leading the whimpering Daisy out into the courtyard beyond the basement, pulling a bench into the shade of the railings so the child might take the air without feeling the sun, reaching into the pocket of her gown to produce a tiny phial of powder which she then proceeded to pile on to a clean white handkerchief.

'Just put it on your tongue, Daisy,' she said gently. 'It's called the Great Reviver . . . It'll have you feeling fine in no time!'

And so it did. Within moments, Daisy's pallor vanished, her breathing calmed, her spirits lifted, and she dared to hope that Alice might prevail upon Mr Addison to intervene with Lady Crompton. Perhaps news of the disaster might even be kept from Mrs Long?

The entire kitchen staff was now gathered in the court-yard, wanting only the lofty presence of the butler and the housekeeper themselves, looking to Alice for guidance.

Alice wrinkled her nose in the sunshine, thinking it over.

'It's easy,' interjected Rose, bravest and liveliest of the scullery maids. 'Her Ladyship would never know if Daisy simply stayed and resumed her duties! After all, she never set eyes on Daisy before this morning, and probably won't again. And even if she did, she wouldn't remember the face. Daisy could cut off her hair and call herself Violet.'

Cook was horrified, and said so in the plain language of a plain cook, declaring that Mr Addison would never agree to such a ploy, and that even if he did, Mrs Long would find them all out.

'And then we'll have more to worry about than a few tarts!'

Alice shook her head and stood up.

'There will be no deception,' she said slowly. 'I shall speak to Miss India, and the matter will be resolved.'

Upstairs, however, India had other things on her mind.

She sat in the window of her chamber, a hairbrush in hand, gazing dreamily into the woods beyond which the water of the lake glinted silver through the floating bands of brilliant green sedge.

'Ah, there you are!' India motioned Alice to the window and handed her the hairbrush. 'I'm sitting here thinking very strange thoughts, Alice. On my twenty-first birthday, I am contemplating falling in love . . . I've been talking about this very thing to my Aunt Bonham . . .'

She was wearing a nightgown of turquoise Indian silk, heavily embroidered with gold, and her long black hair fell loose to her waist, a vision so striking and so innocent in its careless voluptuousness, that Alice paused at the threshold of the room, momentarily dazzled. She found herself wondering what the effect might be on Adam Goodchild, or indeed, upon Dr Luke Harte.

'I don't think a person contemplates falling in love,' she ventured at last. 'I rather think it just happens . . . And sometimes, unfortunately, the attraction is completely unsuitable . . .'

India said nothing, still staring out to the lake as if in a trance.

'My Aunt Bonham said much the same thing,' she offered at length. 'Although she did say that someone who appears unsuitable at first may turn out to be just the one you're looking for . . .'

Alice considered this in silence. Elizabeth Bonham, with

no children of her own, had taken her sister's daughter to heart, offering the kind of thoughtful counsel that Lady Crompton herself could never manage despite being minded to give a great deal of advice on a great many subjects to anyone who would listen. Aunt Bonham would never allow her niece to fall prey to caprice, or at least, not without a careful examination of all possible pitfalls.

'Did you have anyone in mind?' Alice pursued gently, pulling the tortoiseshell brush through India's thick black hair. 'Don't forget that your Mama will have to approve any final choice . . .'

India laughed gaily, awoken from the dream.

'No, of course I don't have anyone in mind! Although I do rather wonder whom I shall meet at the party tonight . . . You know that Christian is bringing a friend from London? The Honourable Timothy Harrington . . . I like that name, don't you?'

Alice was not inclined to pass judgement on a name, nor to place too much hope in any friend of Christian's.

'Don't forget that the Goodchilds will be here too,' she said carefully. 'I must say that if I myself were to contemplate falling in love, it would be with a man like Adam Goodchild . . .'

This was a well-worn theme between them, but one which, for all Alice's discreet hints, hints that had of late given way to open suggestions, India refused to take seriously. Adam was a friend, a dear and much loved friend, but nothing more, and any idea that he entertained romantic thoughts toward herself was just plain silly.

Now she frowned at Alice.

'Well, you may fall in love with whom you please,' she said crossly. 'And I hope you will allow me to do the same.'

Alice knew when to hold her tongue, and for a few moments she brushed the long hair with silent vigour, waiting for India's good humour to return, and with it the chance to raise the matter of Daisy.

India had resumed her gazing out of the window.

'I'm sitting here so I shall be sure to see Christian the

moment he comes into view! He wrote that he would approach the house through the woods. He was most specific that I should watch for him coming that way. Now why has he said that, do you think?'

Alice could not think, and in any case, didn't wish to exercise her mind upon Christian's fancies and foibles. There was quite enough of that when he was home, though to be sure, she wouldn't be sorry to see him back. The house lacked sparkle without him, even the furnishings drooped, and the curtains hung limply. Or so it seemed to Alice.

'There's been a small upset in the kitchen,' she began when at last she judged the mood to have lifted. 'A poor young girl called Daisy fainted in the pantry and some sweetmeats were spoiled. Of course, it wasn't her fault. It's very hot in there, the work is heavy, and she's only thirteen . . . I suspect it may have been monthly troubles, or perhaps exhaustion . . . There's been so much preparation for the party. Anyway . . .'

Alas, the case for Daisy was never presented, for at that moment Christian came into view through the window, striding out of the woods, a white fedora on his head and a hefty stick in his right hand, driving before him, with all the aplomb of a great white hunter, India's birthday present.

'Don't you just love her? She's called Polly!'

'A baby elephant!'

India's disbelief was matched only by that of Lady Crompton, who had been obliged to retire to her room when the news was announced, declaring that she might never forgive her son, and that Sir Robin – exactly where *were* the men when you needed them? – would surely have something to say.

In the event, Sir Robin, as was his habit, had virtually nothing to say. He had arrived very late the evening before with Lady Crompton's sister, remarking only that Christian was following on behind with the secret present. Now he merely raised one eyebrow at the revelation, soothing his wife with the private view that an Indian elephant would hardly survive a Norfolk winter.

Christian had already thought of this.

'We shall stable her come November,' he assured India, who stood, hands clasped to her cheeks, watching as the estate foreman gingerly manoeuvred Polly into the small paddock. 'I'm sure the horses won't kick up. After all, horses and elephants work alongside each other all the time . . .'

'Indian horses and elephants, yes . . . But here? Won't they frighten each other?'

'Animals are animals, the same the whole world over! And anyway, Polly *is* Indian. Shipped all the way from Bombay, just for you. She must be a tough little creature to survive that.'

'Poor thing,' India whispered.

Christian frowned.

'Give her a whack, Hardy,' he instructed the foreman, who was eyeing the shivering elephant with some alarm. 'Show her who's boss. She'll soon settle.'

Behind them, a plump, thin-haired young man emitted a shrill giggle.

'I say,' he tittered, 'you won't go short of manure, that's for sure!'

The Honourable Timothy Harrington, despite his charming name, had proved a considerable disappointment, and now India turned away in mild disgust, wanting to show gratitude for her extraordinary present, yet unable to quell her rising disquiet.

'Where's Alice?' demanded Christian suddenly. 'Why isn't she here? I can't wait to know what she makes of it all! Why, in a year or so, we'll have you riding around like a veritable memsahib . . . Won't that be fun?'

'I expect so,' India said glumly.

The Hon. Tim let out another irritating chortle.

'I say, you'd better keep old Polly downwind from the party guests tonight! They might think there's something wrong with their sandwiches.'

* * *

Alice was back in the kitchen.

She had viewed the arrival of the elephant with shock that soon gave way to resignation. It was just like Christian, of course. The extravagant gesture, the unthinking excess, always with an eye to his own reputation for unrivalled gaiety. Why couldn't he see that imprudence and frivolity would never serve him well? That no sensible woman would consider becoming his wife? Even Marianne Goodchild, widely reputed to have doted upon Christian since her childhood, would surely think twice about a man who brought elephants home as though they were puppy dogs?

In one respect, however, Polly had already served a useful purpose.

So great was her impact upon the household that all previous events that morning had been quite forgotten. Neither Addison nor Mrs Long had been informed of the incident with the pies, and Alice was now inclined to hope it might be entirely overlooked. If Daisy were able to start work again at once, the redoubtable housekeeper might be none the wiser.

'Oh, I can do it, Miss Alice,' Daisy said eagerly. 'I'm right as rain since you gave me that powder.'

Alice nodded, well pleased, and went back upstairs to find India in the library consulting her father's books, attempting to determine the proper feeding patterns of elephants domiciled in temperate climes.

The party began in splendid style with champagne, an orchestra dressed as Indian maharajahs who played as the magnificent birthday cake was carried to the edge of the ballroom, and a bank of scented candles which Addison lit at the entrance to the terrace.

Lady Crompton presented her own birthday gift, a necklet of pearls which she fastened around her daughter's throat while the guests looked on. Then Christian led his sister on to the ballroom floor for the first dance.

India was attired in scarlet satin, her long hair braided

with silver ribbon and her arms heavy with beaded bangles, her feet encased in ornate silver slippers, and a spray of white camellias at her bosom. She looked a truly exotic creature, the kind of woman who might not only have a baby elephant as a pet, but also inspire dragons or serpents to her devotion. And among those who looked on in open admiration were Adam Goodchild, reflective and unusually quiet, the Hon. Timothy Harrington, smiling broadly and clearly unaware of the poor impression he'd made on the daughter of the house, and, at the corner of the hall, his pale and silent wife standing just behind him, Dr Luke Harte.

Alice was dressed in fine style herself, an aquamarine evening silk which India had discarded after one wearing, and aware that her presence at the ball was an oddity, insisted upon by India to Lady Crompton's irritation, kept well away from the throng. Her function was to direct guests to the food, ensure that all the ladies knew where they might find rest and refreshment, and provide India with company or service should she require it.

For the moment, however, Alice allowed herself to relax, luxuriating in her preferred role of observer. She watched while Christian danced with Marianne Goodchild, folding her comfortable, broad figure into his arms, and saw Adam take India's hand for a waltz, detecting a sober note behind his customary easy manner, and then, the waltz over and Luke Harte having taken to the floor with Marianne, watched Adam invite the doctor's wife to the polka, leaving India briefly alone with Timothy Harrington. Across the ballroom, the two women exchanged a covert glance, amused and mildly despairing. Alice motioned to the terrace.

Outside in the gardens, Indian windchimes had been strung from the trees so that the very air tinkled and sang, and the guests walked upon lush turf scattered with gold powder, a festive Hindu concoction that Lady Crompton had brought home to England with this very occasion in mind. The grass sparkled and crackled beneath their feet like frost.

A long table covered in starched white linen supported

the great glass bowls of fruit punch that Addison himself had mixed, and now the scullery maids, promoted for the evening as the parlour maids were all required indoors, spooned the fragrant liquid into carefully polished glasses.

As Alice approached, she saw Flora at the near end of the table.

'How's Daisy?' she whispered to the girl. 'Fully recovered, I trust?'

Flora looked up, startled.

'I thought you'd know, Miss Alice! Daisy has gone. Master Christian came down to the kitchen, wanting a pie. Well, there weren't any pies, so the whole story came out. Mrs Long was listening, and she sent Daisy home at once . . .'

Alice shook her head in disbelief, her good spirits quenched. Christian, *of course*. The rogue element on which all plans and predictions foundered . . .

As though the thought had been spoken aloud, she turned to find him standing behind her, a pink rosebud in his hand which he now waved toward her, flicking the flower under her nose.

'Alice, you've been avoiding me!' he scolded, glancing swiftly over his shoulder to ensure there were no eavesdroppers. 'I've been looking for you all afternoon . . . But now here you are, and I've brought you this rose . . .'

'No thank you, Sir,' said Alice curtly, turning away. 'It clashes with my dress.'

'Oh, *bravo* Alice!'

Christian laughed in open delight, leaned forward, and tucked his rosebud into the neckline of her ballgown. Alice tore it out and threw it on the ground.

'Do not humiliate me!' she muttered, and to the astonishment of the awestruck Flora, she marched off across the glittering grass, the hem of her dress catching at the gold dust as she went.

He stared after her for a moment, and grabbing a glass of punch which he swilled in one gulp, set off in pursuit.

*   *   *

India, cooling herself with a black silk fan, one of her most prized possessions from Delhi, stood on the terrace with Adam at her side, scanning the milling guests for Alice. She wanted perfume from her room, a fresh handkerchief, and counsel for some vague disquiet, the root of which she could not trace. But Alice was nowhere to be seen.

'It's a lovely party,' Adam said with manifest lack of enthusiasm. 'Everyone is having a wonderful time.'

India, with no regard for any but her own unease, nodded absently and sliced the balmy air around them with her fan.

'Yes ... It's been a wonderful day. You heard about Christian's present, I suppose?'

She spoke lightly, betraying no trace of the anxiety which gripped her stomach every time she thought about Polly. How feckless, how irresponsible, it now seemed to her, bringing such a creature across the ocean to a strange, cold land. And what was she meant to do with Polly? Ride around like a memsahib as Christian had suggested? The idea might be amusing, but the reality would prove less so. India told herself that she was not inclined to grand behaviour, nor did she approve of extravagant gestures which only served to flaunt her family's wealth and prestige. She believed, instead, with the rather mischievous secondary benefit of annoying her mother, in the integrity of all living things, and the right of each to as noble a life as Providence might decree.

If pressed, she would have said that such notions were an inevitable result of her years in Delhi and her exposure to the Buddhist religion, of the literature she had read, and of the freedom of spirit which Sir Robin, for all his muted effect on his household, nevertheless encouraged in his children. But others, Lady Crompton among them, might have detected a more immediate influence, the subtle, subversive effect of an over-educated personal maid.

'I think everyone has heard you have an elephant in your stable,' Adam said gravely. 'I only hope that Christian has foreseen the difficulties.'

India laughed nervously.

'What if he'd bought an elephant for Marianne?' she teased. 'As he might well have done! It's her birthday next month, is it not?'

'Indeed it is,' Adam answered, glancing into the ballroom where his sister stood conversing with Luke and Eugenie Harte. 'And if your brother brings an elephant anywhere near my house, he will soon find himself and his gifts rejected!'

He had not meant to speak so sharply, had intended merely to indicate his reservations at Christian's whims. But instead he had conveyed a deep distaste, a sentiment which India could hardly fail to catch, and now they gazed at each other in discomfort.

'I shall have to warn him,' India said at last.

'I don't think he needs any warning,' Adam replied swiftly. 'I think Christian sees the situation quite clearly. It is Marianne who does not see.'

This was much more than he meant to say, but having begun in such frank terms, a certain recklessness overcame him, the feeling that nothing more was to be lost. He stood before his beloved as a man who sensed his hopes dwindling, though he would not have attributed the feeling to any particular event, and certainly not to any particular person. And yet hope had all but gone. He had not brought the ruby ring with him to the party. He had not spoken to Sir Robin as he'd intended. He no longer knew what the future held for himself, but upon the matter of his adored sister, he was quite certain of one thing. She would not marry Christian Crompton-Leigh, and in his new mood of sombre reflection, it occurred to Adam Goodchild that the sooner this knowledge were conveyed by whatever discreet means possible to anyone who might have influence, the better.

'I'm sure I don't understand you!' India cried, startled. 'Whatever can you mean?'

He surveyed her soberly, keen now that all should be made clear.

'I do not consider your brother a worthy suitor for my sister's hand in marriage,' he said calmly. 'Christian knows this quite well. But Marianne continues to hope, and my fear is that others may thereby be encouraged to hope . . .'

He hesitated, wishing to deny to himself the uncomfortable suggestion that Lady Crompton, anxious to unite her own and the Goodchild estates and having failed to make a match between himself and her daughter, would now direct her efforts toward Christian and Marianne. But nevertheless he determined to voice the worst.

'Your mother may wish to see Marianne happy,' he said carefully. 'I merely wish to point out the truth of the matter so that further unhappiness might be spared.'

India was dumbfounded. She had never heard Adam speak in such a forthright manner, and now she considered that he had seemed thoroughly out of sorts all evening, not at all himself.

'Are you ill, Adam?' she inquired solicitously, feeling that no other explanation would suffice.

'I'm quite well, thank you,' he snapped, and then, as Marianne emerged on to the terrace in company with Luke and Eugenie Harte, his expression softened and he smiled at India. He wanted no embarrassment between the two women, nor did he wish his sister to learn his views in any brutal manner. There was plenty of time to make plain his feelings about Christian, and indeed, he was optimistic enough to believe that Marianne would eventually come to her own realization. In this respect, India's baby elephant could only help.

'Forgive me,' he murmured to India, 'I'm spoiling your birthday. Forget I ever mentioned the matter!'

He knew, of course, that she wouldn't, but having declared himself, he now felt able to relax, waving energetically at Marianne and the Hartes, ushering them all to a table at the edge of the lawn and busying himself with glasses of punch.

Luke Harte sat down and smiled at India.

'A truly splendid party!' he pronounced. 'I was just saying to Miss Goodchild that my wife and I are fortunate, indeed, to be invited. Most kind of Lady Crompton, and yourself . . .'

India heard the words and acknowledged them graciously, but something very peculiar seemed to happen whenever she found herself in the presence of Dr Harte. It seemed as though each trite exchange were in fact a detailed masquerade, an elaborate concealment of an undeclared truth which hovered on the edge of the conversation, noticeable to no one except herself and, she fancied, to him.

Now, as their eyes met across the table, it seemed he might be saying something altogether different, something far beyond the pleasantries that came out of his mouth, and yet India had no idea what it might be.

'I was wondering about the village boy,' he said, his eyes still fixed on hers. 'Your maid's nephew? Is he fully recovered?'

India had quite forgotten that she was missing Alice, and now, tearing herself away from Luke Harte's intense gaze, she stood up and stared across the crowded lawn, searching for the aquamarine dress among the multicoloured satins and silks. Her temple seemed to pound and her head felt about to float free from her neck, like a child's balloon. India considered that she might have drunk a little too much punch and resolved to set her glass aside.

'There she is!' cried Marianne suddenly, as intent, it seemed, on locating Alice as India was herself. 'And isn't that Christian with her?'

'It certainly is,' said Adam, shading his eye against the evening sun which sat in crimson profusion upon the rim of the lake. 'Whatever are they doing?'

They were hurrying across the lawn, Alice in front, Christian at her heels, engaged in some intense debate and apparently oblivious to all onlookers.

But now, as though both sensed the eyes upon them, they drew a little apart and Christian waved at the watching party.

'What a lark!' he called as they approached. 'We've been feeding the elephant! And a hungry little lady she's proved to be too!'

He looked flustered, his dark hair glistening and his face

pink, but Alice, for all her energetic march across the lawn, appeared cool and composed.

She smiled at India, and dropped a deferential nod to the Goodchilds and the Hartes.

'There were some spoiled pastries in the kitchen,' she explained quietly. 'It seemed sensible to feed them to Polly.'

Such was Alice's calm authority that everyone immediately agreed it to be very sensible, and for a few moments the talk was all of zoo animals, which, it was generally held, were well used to a diet of buns, cakes and so forth provided by enthusiastic members of the public, and as far as anyone could tell, none the worse for it.

Christian, having refilled his glass, now drank heavily from it and regarded his sister gloomily.

'The reason old Polly got the pastries is because some wretched maid fainted in the pantry and ruined the lot,' he announced. 'And now it seems I'm responsible for her losing her position. Isn't that right, Alice?'

Alice ignored this direct appeal, and turned to India.

'I did mention Daisy, if you remember,' she murmured. 'I was rather hoping you might speak to Her Ladyship on the matter . . .'

If it seemed extraordinary, either to Dr or Mrs Harte, to Marianne and Adam, or even to India herself, that the fate of a kitchen maid should concern so many notable people on such an important occasion, then nobody voiced the thought.

Instead, Luke Harte looked wryly at Alice.

'Has this young maid received treatment for her fainting fit?' he inquired.

Alice inclined her head.

'I administered a herbal remedy, Sir. There was nothing much wrong with her. A young girl forced to rise at five o'clock every day and work until midnight may well faint from exhaustion . . . As any of us might, were we required to scrub floors and polish pans all day long . . .'

'Bravely spoken!' declared Luke in open admiration. 'I can see you are a champion of the sick and needy, Alice!'

He smiled warmly, and India, whose philosophy inclined her to a concern for the sick and needy, but whose experience of such had been necessarily limited, suddenly saw a new and noble passion opening up before her like a flower in the morning sun.

'We must help this poor girl!' she declared, turning to Alice and throwing wide her arms. 'But perhaps she will not wish to return to Crompton Hall if the work is so hard? Might it not be better to find her some new position? In a more modest household, perhaps?'

There was an awkward pause in which everyone considered this prospect and drew the same conclusion.

Then Eugenie Harte, silent until this moment, leaned forward on her chair.

'You are so kind,' she said coolly, addressing India directly so that there might be no mistake. 'But of course, we shall be choosing our own maids. And *health* is of much concern, Miss Crompton. My husband might feel himself drawn to take in all manner of weak creature, but I am of a more *practical* nature . . . We need strong girls, able to cope with the demands of a modest but *industrious* household! I am sure that your Mama would understand . . .'

India, who'd seemed barely aware of Mrs Harte in all that had preceded, now gazed at her in mute shock, unable to discount the overt note of censure that had been sounded. She glanced quickly at Luke, and caught a flash of embarrassment upon his smooth features, to be quickly replaced by a rueful smile.

'Quite right,' he agreed sheepishly. 'The women must hire the maids and decide what's needed . . .'

Christian emitted a raucous chuckle.

'Ah yes, the women shall decide what's needed!' he laughed. 'And the world will be much the better for it. We shall all be honest, upright citizens when the women are in charge. Isn't that right, Alice?'

Alice, loosening India's hair in her bedchamber that night and unpinning the white camellias from the scarlet dress, was inclined to believe it a successful night. Christian had been reprimanded for his unruly ways, Lady Crompton, through the kindly offices of Aunt Bonham, had been prevailed upon to allow Daisy back into the kitchen, while Sir Robin had bestowed a large sum of money on his daughter, a gift which assuredly marked her out as the most eligible young woman in the county. And to mark the occasion, India was to have her portrait painted, an artist from London having been commissioned and instructed to start work at the end of the month.

Only one small matter troubled Alice. Adam Goodchild had made no declaration, and she had been quite sure that he would. Whether India would have accepted was another question, but at least Adam's intentions would have been revealed, and that would have allowed for serious discussion. Alice had already rehearsed her speech.

It may seem desirable to marry out of passion, but love requires much more fertile soil if it is to flourish . . .

'Be careful, Alice! You're hurting me!'

India shook her hair and smiled reproachfully in the mirror. Alice set the brush aside.

'You've had a wonderful evening, haven't you?' she murmured. India's blue eyes clouded briefly and then she smiled pensively.

'Yes, I have,' she whispered. 'But despite my premonition, I didn't fall in love . . . And now, for some odd reason, I find myself wondering if I ever will . . . Love is so uncertain, wouldn't you say, Alice? No one can predict where the arrow will fall.'

Chapter Eight

'I'm thinking of India,' Laurie murmured groggily, and realized with dismay that she had spoken aloud.

'India? That's interesting. Would you like to go?'

Her father had opened a bottle of St Emilion, and then another. Was it sensible to flood your veins with alcohol just before they were about to be flooded with the most toxic drugs known to modern medicine? Laurie had no idea, and now it was too late.

'What would you do in India? Visit the Taj Mahal?'

She nodded vaguely. If she ever went to India, she would head straight for the diplomatic compound in Delhi, seeking the white-shuttered colonial mansion of her dreams where Sir Robin Crompton-Leigh had raised his young family.

'Fascinating country. Big on tourism these days, too. Maybe we could all go there when you're better? Maybe we'd even persuade your mother to come?'

Laurie smiled weakly, trying to appear positive. *This is the worst of it. Looking on the bright side because others don't dare to peer into the dark.*

'Maybe,' she agreed, imagining all of them, herself, her father, Elspeth and Gloria imprisoned on one of those luxury trains so beloved of TV documentaries, sipping breakfast tea and nibbling English muffins while the arid plains of India slipped by. That was surely how it would be. Gloria was no intrepid traveller, and Elspeth would never go anywhere unless the toilets met her own inimitable standards.

Laurie drained her glass. They had discussed her cancer, they had discussed Dr Mitchell, she had asked about Elspeth and he had inquired after Sean. It had all been as it should be, no excess emotion, which neither could have countenanced, no awkward questions about Gloria or Norfolk that might have led them into dangerous

territory. Now it seemed they were reduced to pleasantries.

'More wine?' her father asked, and Laurie felt her
stomach heave.

'I don't think so,' she whispered, 'I've got a big day
tomorrow.'

They grimaced at each other across their empty glasses,
both valiantly searching for the reassuring phrase that might
make everything all right.

'Hang on in there,' he muttered at last, giving up. 'We
Davisons are a tough bunch. You can do it.'

She'd wanted Shelley to drive her to the hospital, but just
in time recognized that this was hardly fair to Gloria.

The night before had been magnanimously sacrificed so
that Laurie might spend time with her father, but now Gloria
wanted her due. She was already congratulating herself on
Laurie's unexpected decision to return to Norfolk, and her old
confidence had returned with vigour. She arrived at Laurie's
flat bearing a variety of remedies, crystallized ginger to prevent
sickness, *pulsatilla* to strengthen Laurie's constitution, *ignatia*
for unwonted emotions.

'Unwonted emotions?'

Robert Davison was suffering a considerable hangover,
and his efforts at civility toward his ex-wife were strained.

'Fear, anger, resentment,' Gloria said smoothly. 'One
pill will help you put it all in perspective.' She took the
cap from the bottle and stuck it under his nose. 'You look
like you could use some!'

He laughed, despite himself.

'Are you really telling me you think a pill can deal with
all that?'

Gloria raised one eyebrow.

'What does Valium claim to do?' she inquired. 'Or
Prozac? At least you won't get hooked on my pills, and
they can't do you any harm . . .'

He held up his hand and backed away, grinning at
Laurie. He would not argue with Gloria. He never had,

preferring to retreat into books and papers whenever their differences had spilled over into outright opposition, until one day, just after Laurie's tenth birthday, he had simply packed up the books and papers and departed. Laurie had watched him do it, silent and unquestioning because she knew his reasons already. And then when he'd bent to kiss her goodbye, she'd felt his tears, cold and slippery against her cheek.

She had cried for months after he'd gone, weeping dumbly into her pillow night after night so that Gloria wouldn't hear, pretending, always pretending, that it didn't matter, that she understood, that yes, of course, she realized they both still loved her. *But why didn't they stay together, then? Why inflict such pain on the daughter they professed to love?*

It was all very long ago, yet like many an old wound, it still ached from time to time.

But today, in these new and harrowing circumstances, their studied togetherness, contrived for Laurie's peace of mind yet having just the opposite effect, was not so much hurtful as pointless. The assumption of joint responsibility, the decision taken in Laurie's absence that both should accompany her to the hospital, seemed merely to mock all that had gone before. *Does it take a whiff of death before we can all be civil to each other? What hope, then, for the human race?*

It was impossible, furthermore, to disassociate these feelings from the fact of her affair with Sean. The mystery was how she'd managed to do it for so long.

Sean was married, just as her father had been, with a father's role, a father's responsibilities, a father's love, none of which, it seemed, was enough to keep him with his daughters. Too late she saw how she'd striven to justify what could not be excused, taking his own refusal to justify himself as proof of his fundamental innocence.

'It's all my fault,' he'd said. 'I never loved her, and I couldn't stay faithful to her. I'm a shit.'

No, no, she demurred.

'The sexual revolution,' he'd said, 'is a bad joke. You get

somebody pregnant, and it's back to the dark ages. Suddenly you find yourself married, and your whole life is mapped out for you . . .'

How terrible, she'd cooed.

'One baby, and it might just have been okay. I could have supported them, visited them . . . But twins? What kind of a jerk would refuse to marry his girlfriend when she was having twins?'

That might have been better, she offered.

He shook his head.

'I'm a shit,' he repeated, and now, at last, in his absence, Laurie could agree.

But it gave her no comfort, not to think of Sean forced back to Tina, nor to witness the strained cordiality of her anxious parents, trying to atone for what could never be undone.

She felt like a little girl, gently handed into the back of Robert's hired car, carefully chauffeured in case any violent movement upset her precarious equilibrium, pampered with gifts, a special water cooler from America so that her bedside drink wouldn't get warm, a bunch of the best quality rose grapes from Marks & Spencer, a new silk dressing gown from Gloria, black and gold, embroidered with strange concentric circles which were certain to have some tantric significance for healing or inner harmony.

And all she wanted was to be left alone.

She thought of her room at Crompton Hall, the haven that had been India's bedchamber, with its fine tapestry quilt and rich wall-hangings. She thought of the lake, silver and green through the square of her window, and of Edie and Val, walking in the woods, alert for cowslips or celandines. She even thought of Dale Mitchell, lounging in his counselling suite beneath the portrait of India and Alice, meticulously unravelling the secrets of his suffering clients' souls.

'Here we are then,' said Gloria bravely, laying a hand upon her ex-husband's arm. 'Looks a bit grim, doesn't it? Still, you can't tell by the buildings, can you?'

'Don't buildings have karma?' asked Laurie jerkily, making a weak attempt at a joke. 'This place used to be an old workhouse, didn't it?'

The remark fell awkwardly between them, and she regretted it at once.

'You could have gone private,' Gloria said tightly. 'Robert would have paid ...' She glared at him, demanding confirmation.

'I didn't want that,' Laurie said quickly. 'It's enough that you're paying for Doctor Mitchell ...' Then with a little stab of guilt, she remembered how ungracious she'd been on this very point. She forced herself to consider that since her traumatic ride to Norfolk with Gloria, only a few short days before, some curious, indefinable kind of progress had been made.

'Thank you,' she said suddenly, leaning forward toward the driving seat and nuzzling her head into her father's shoulder, 'I'm very grateful. Without Norfolk ... I'd be totally ... Unregenerate!'

To her relief, they both laughed.

They left her in the care of a fiercely jolly staff nurse who chattered loudly about taking bloods, giving a specimen, filling in your menu cards and keeping your pecker up.

Laurie had insisted they go, and requested them not to visit, because once on the cancer ward a dread intimation of reality had taken over. This wasn't a bad dream, it wasn't a horror story. The long corridor of curtained bays, the prostrate forms in the beds, the drips and feeds and electronic bleeps, this was now her world. She wasn't a visitor, she hadn't come to advise on their new computer system. She was an inmate.

And like all inmates, she wanted no visible reminders of her restricted freedom. She didn't want her parents sitting in their outdoor clothes while she got into bed. She didn't even want to see the world outside the hospital window. A patch of blue might move her to tears. A tree might reduce her to sobs. Fighting the fear, she shook off her shoes and lay down on the high metal cot she'd been assigned, grateful for the drapes that concealed her from her fellow prisoners. She couldn't bear them to see her, and dreaded the time when she would have to see them.

But there were plenty of callers to her secluded little booth. The young woman doctor she'd seen on her earlier visit, perkier now, as though she'd received a ticking off for being over-sensitive . . . Then the consultant, a tall, thin, sad-eyed man who spoke in apologetic tones . . . Yes, Laurie had every chance of recovery . . . No, he couldn't say how many chances that might be . . . Yes, she was getting the best possible treatment . . . No, he couldn't predict whether it would stop her cancer spreading . . . And after him, a succession of nurses offering anti-nausea pills and sedatives, an army of domestics with cups of tea and biscuits, a trickle of timid volunteers offering newspapers, tissues and sweets . . . Then, finally, a woman with a box of wigs.

'Do I have to choose one now?' She was breathless with the shock of it all.

'It's better to get it over with. Then it's there when you need it.'

Laurie fingered the wigs nervously. They looked like acrylic rats, creatures who'd jumped into vats of dye and come out chestnut brown or strawberry blonde. She couldn't possibly wear one of these tattered rodents on her head.

'This one's very like your own hair!'

The woman held up a jet black bob with a heavy fringe, smoothing the fronds into shape. Laurie tried it on, twisting her own voluminous hair into a knot and pushing it under the wig's cap. It looked ridiculous.

'It'll look better when you've lost your own hair,' the woman said.

Laurie silenced a rising hysteria, and in her effort to appear grateful, made an unexpected and mystifying decision.

'I'll go for that one,' she said, pointing to a ragged blonde mop straight out of *Baywatch*. 'Might as well have some fun.'

The woman gathered up the wigs.

'Perhaps, after all, you should decide later,' she smiled.

'No, no! My mind's made up. I like this one. I think I'll call it Roland . . .'

The woman shook her head, and Laurie's hysteria burst forth. She let out a high-pitched giggle, halfway between a wail and a shriek.

'I'll get Sister,' the wig woman said, backing out of the cubicle. 'Just lie there and relax!'

It was then that Laurie remembered Gloria's pills for unwonted emotions. Delving into her handbag she took out the little phials, and quickly checking she'd got the right one, tipped the bottle toward her mouth. The tablets tasted of nothing, and in a moment they were gone. But not before Sister had caught her in the act.

'Homeopathic medicine,' Laurie said distractedly. 'My mother gave it to me. It's for unwonted emotions . . . To calm you down, I guess . . .'

She had expected hostility, or, at best, sceptical indulgence. This, after all, had been Gloria's experience of the medical profession over many years. But the Sister seemed genuinely interested, taking the phial from Laurie and reading its label, asking what other remedies she took, and finally noting down the name, *ignatia*.

'I might try it myself,' she said.

'Really?'

'Believe me, there's plenty of unwonted emotions round here.'

'Yes . . . All this sickness and death . . .'

'I was thinking of the senior registrar, actually.'

Laurie laughed nervously.

'Is he an All-Out Bastard?'

'It's worse than that. He's gorgeous.'

She plumped Laurie's pillows, adjusted the height of the bed, delved in the bedside cabinet to produce a stack of magazines, and promised to return with a cup of decent coffee from the nurses' room.

A second later her head reappeared through the enveloping curtains.

'Do you feel any calmer?' she asked with a grin.

The funny thing was, Laurie did.

The needle sank into the soft underbelly of her elbow, deep and clean, like a skewer plunging into a baked cake to test its readiness.

I'm a lump of meat, diseased meat. An E-coli chop or a salmonella chicken.

The butcher, a pretty staff nurse who cheerfully announced that she'd only just finished her chemotherapy training, was clad in protective apron, gloves and goggles.

'What is that?' Laurie asked, pointing to the bright red liquid pumping through the shoot into her arm. 'Drugs or nuclear waste?'

'It's strong stuff,' the nurse agreed. 'We're all warned not to spill a drop on ourselves . . .'

So, what mustn't be spilled on the skin is even now coursing through my veins. Great.

'If you feel ill,' the kindly nurse advised, 'remember that this means the drugs are working. Same thing when your hair falls out. If it didn't, we'd be worried.'

Laurie had taken all Gloria's remedies, and as the bright red liquid began to freeze her body, was bemused to find that she didn't feel even slightly ill. Was this a dubious blessing? Did it mean she was resistant to treatment? She put her free hand to her hair, testing its roots, tugging firmly and feeling the tension.

She closed her eyes and tried to visualize the drugs working in her body like detergent on a tanker spill, astringent, disinfecting, cleansing the ocean within, reaching into every last oily cell.

'Precious poisons,' said the staff nurse helpfully. 'Try to think of them that way . . .'

Then suddenly, Laurie was back on her feet, the bag of poison suspended from a rod at her side, walking toward her bed and pushing the rod on its little wheeled cart in front of her like a supermarket trolley.

When she'd dared to think about her hospital treatment,

she'd imagined herself lying motionless amid a mass of tubes and drips, sick and in pain. It was a curious kind of let-down to find herself walking around feeling normal. She got back to her bed, and for the first time that day, drew the curtains and cautiously surveyed her fellow patients.

It was as though they'd been waiting for the moment. There were smiles and waves, inquiries about the new wig, commiserations on the supermarket trolley which, Laurie would almost certainly discover during the course of the night, was the worst on the ward and had a seriously wonky wheel. There were offers of newspapers, advice about what not to order from the menu cards, opinions on anti-nausea pills and suggestions about which way to sleep so the drip wouldn't obstruct and set off the alarm.

And in the little jokes, the wry asides, the quibbles and the quips, there was, above all, an overwhelming, enveloping sympathy, that true sympathy born of shared experience.

Laurie smiled back.

In the middle of the night, she woke to a high-pitched, staccato beep above her head. The alarm.

She lay for some moments until the shadowy figure of a nurse appeared at the bedside and turned it off.

'Does that mean I've stopped getting the drug?'

'No, it just means the machine's gone on the blink and woken everybody up.'

Laurie closed her eyes, but now sleep eluded her. Her arm throbbed, and she wondered vaguely how heroin users found the courage, or the stomach, to plunge needles repeatedly into themselves. Perhaps a course of chemotherapy would cure them. She turned over restlessly and set the alarm off again.

The nurse took longer to come this time.

'You'll have to lie still,' she said snappily.

'Yes . . . Sorry . . .'

She lay like a carved saint on a tomb, arms folded across her breasts, resisting the impulse to check her lump and see if the chemo was working. Of course, it couldn't work *that* fast.

How fast, then? How soon would the lump begin to reduce? Tomorrow? Next week? Nobody had told her, and this, she recognized, was because nobody knew.

Carefully, painfully, she unfolded her arms and shifted on to her side once more. The alarm sounded out like a demented seagull.

It seemed nobody was going to come at all this time. She waited anxiously while all around her, people began to stir, muttering through their dreams.

'Get out and disconnect the bloody thing,' said a voice from the next bed, and Laurie jumped on to the floor in fright. She grappled with the wires at the base of the alarm, and gasped aloud in relief when the noise suddenly stopped.

'Don't worry,' said the next bed comfortingly. 'It doesn't make any difference. We never used to have alarms, and when the drip clogged, we just twisted it back the other way. Now we have alarms which go off when the drip's not clogged, so we get out and switch them off . . .'

She chuckled.

'Then when the drip *does* get clogged, we twist it back the other way again . . .'

'That's progress,' Laurie said.

An uncomfortable thought occurred to her.

'How long have you been coming to this hospital?' she asked.

'Six years, on and off,' came the reply. 'They can't cure me, but they're having a damn good shot at keeping me alive. I'll settle for that.'

Laurie got back into bed, but there was no sleeping now.

In her bedside cabinet she had the silk-covered journal from Crompton Hall, and having written nothing about her own experience since leaving Norfolk, she took it out and attempted to order her thoughts.

Is there really such a thing as a cancer mentality? Am I

supposed to believe that both myself and the woman in the next bed have somehow brought about our own disease? That we weren't calm enough, or strong enough, or positive enough, to stop our cells running riot? Isn't this the most crude and cruel of assertions?

She stopped and nibbled at her pen. This was just what they'd once said about consumption. *An emotional disorder. The highly strung and sensitive particularly prone to it. The creative spirit expressing itself in bacteria-laden lungs.*

It was nonsense, of course. Tuberculosis had proved to be a physical disease, triggered by virus and encouraged by malnutrition. Cancer, when its complexities were finally unravelled, would surely show the same ruthless mix of the environmental and the pathological. The will to survive, to sustain life by sheer mental effort, would then be revealed as simple whistling in the dark. *A comforting notion to keep up the spirits.*

Except that it wasn't comforting. To believe that you'd somehow generated your own cancer cells by a personality disorder, that you could postpone death simply by wanting to live, was a double insult to the sick and dying.

She snapped off the overhead light and lay down.

And yet . . . And yet . . . *I'm not dead, I'm alive! I still have choices I can make. Nothing is predetermined, nothing except death itself is irrevocable. This is me, alive here and now with a lump in my breast. Maybe it will reduce, and maybe it won't. But for the moment, here I am, breathing. Living.*

She smiled to herself in the darkness, a tight, grim little smile.

'I'll settle for that,' she whispered aloud.

She fell asleep at last and dozed through most of the following day, surfacing to receive a phone call from Gloria and a bouquet of roses from her father. The blooms smelt sweet and sickly; funereal, Laurie couldn't help thinking. And Gloria, staunchly cheerful, managed only to annoy.

'I expect it was terrible?' she chirruped.

'Dreadful,' agreed Laurie.

'But not too dreadful, darling . . . I hope?'

'No, not too dreadful . . .'

A pointless, unbearably stilted conversation, and Laurie despised herself for the ill-concealed animosity that lurked behind her politeness.

'But at least I'm alive,' she ventured at last, the ultimate pointless remark.

'Of course you're alive!' Gloria said tremulously. 'What else would you be?'

'Nothing, nothing,' muttered Laurie, realizing as she spoke that nothing was precisely the alternative on offer. 'Please . . . I have to go now . . . I'm very tired.'

It was the first time she'd used her cancer as an excuse, and she lay back guiltily, submitting to the liquid pumping through her sinews, feeling the curious movement that was somehow less than digestive juices, yet more than the passage of blood or lymph, an odd sensation of ebb and flow that made her body pulsate with new, unknown rhythms. Was she tired? No more than usual, she thought, and in any case, she'd been awake half the night. But apart from the heaviness in her limbs, she felt surprisingly normal. At least she felt no nausea, no headache, a response markedly different from all she'd been led to expect.

She took it up with the young woman doctor, whom she now knew well enough to call Kate.

'We don't know why some people just sail through chemo and others get very ill . . . But it does seem to have something to do with attitude . . .'

'Positive thinking?' asked Laurie disbelievingly.

'Perhaps the level of fear . . . The more afraid you are, the more you expect a bad experience, the more likely it is that you'll have it . . .'

Laurie shook her head.

'It has to be physiological, a matter of the individual constitution, surely?'

Kate smiled sadly. 'I'm afraid we really don't know . . .'

Laurie couldn't help but contrast this approach with Gloria's all-encompassing confidence. Gloria, who'd never had a day's serious sickness in her life, who always knew what was wrong with everybody, and why. There was always a pill or a potion to put matters right, always some other guru to offer a new diagnosis in the unlikely event that her own should fail.

Laurie, as a child, had never been inoculated against whooping cough or measles, not because Gloria feared a catastrophic reaction, but simply because she believed in building up immunity. Thus Laurie whooped, and spent three months away from school, and when she got measles, the headmistress sent a prickly note. *Vaccination against childhood diseases ought to be a matter of community conscience, not individual preference.* Gloria had written back, an impassioned epistle detailing the terrible effects of denying children a dose of the common complaints. Laurie, her eyes red and weak, her face thick with spots, had begun to wonder.

The more afraid you are, the worse it will be? I can't accept that . . .

Now she closed her eyes against Kate's kindly gaze and drifted back to the safety of her dreams.

India . . . Alice . . . Christian and Luke . . . Laurie seemed to feel the brush of branches on her face, to hear the deep, cool rustle of the brook, to smell the heavy, earthy scent of the sedge upon the lake . . .

How compelling, how immediate it all seemed, how real. How seductive was the Crompton Hall world of elegance and etiquette, the lazy harmony of summer days in which parties and outings were the only interruptions to the long, contemplative hours . . .

She longed to be back in the kitchen garden, lounging on the bench beneath the fig tree, or wandering the woods with Edie and Val, even sitting stiff-backed in the counselling suite beneath the penetrating eye of Dale Mitchell and the fiery gaze of India . . .

She recalled the odd sensation, borne in on the breeze between the beeches, that somehow she knew the layout of the estate, had been there before in some unknown guise, had felt the passions and the pains of the people who'd lived there, long ago. Almost as though, she thought fancifully, she truly were possessed by the spirit of India, woken from a deep sleep of unknowingness by tumultuous emotions she'd never experienced before. It was a trick of the mind, of course, the response of a heightened awareness to all that was beautiful, transient and tragic.

What a strange and terrible thing is consciousness, the most ferociously mixed of all blessings. The nightingale sings and might as well be deaf to its own melody. But equally, it neither fears nor anticipates the coming of winter.

Then she opened her eyes to find Sean sitting beside her bed.

'Sorry,' he said nervously, 'I didn't mean to wake you . . . I hope you don't mind me coming? Everyone said it was a bad idea . . . Everyone, except your mother.'

He looked so pale and scared that she almost relented, and yet immersed as she was in the Cromptons' long-ago world of idyll, she felt herself disembodied from contemporary niceties. She was driven by a strong desire to speak the truth. There no longer seemed time to pick a way through the misunderstandings, and she had no inclination for the task.

'I didn't want any visitors,' she said tersely, 'I thought I'd made that clear . . .'

Now she understood the purpose of Gloria's phone call and wished she'd been more openly hostile. It might have forced a cancellation.

'I needed to see you,' he said, 'I needed to know you were all right . . .'

Well now, what's the definition of 'all right'?

It was a stupid remark, but in her determination to state her case, she let it pass, struggling upright against the pull of the drip so she might face him from a position of strength.

She ran a hand through her hair. It was still firmly fixed to her scalp.

'How was Norfolk?' he asked her quickly, as though he saw what was coming and strove to deflect it. 'I gather you found it helpful . . . And that you're going back?'

Gloria had clearly been boasting. Just the slightest hint that Laurie didn't hate Norfolk, and her whole plan was vindicated.

'It's very beautiful,' Laurie said grudgingly.

We've got nothing left. Only this vacuous politeness ...

He nodded.

'I went once as a kid ... Huge empty skies and white beaches ... And fields of barley where there used to be lavender ...'

Laurie tried to look interested.

'My father's family were farmers. We went to visit my grandfather just before he died ... I must have been four or five, I guess. It was the only time I remember seeing him ... It was a long way from where we lived ...'

Laurie was surprised. She knew little of Sean's background, had never visited his home town, yet always imagined him rooted there until his twenties when he'd run away to the grubby streets of London with a wife and twin babies close behind him.

'I don't know what they did with the stuff,' he was saying. 'The lavender, I mean. It's not exactly useful, is it? They must have had an awful lot of those little sachets that you put in drawers ...'

He was babbling, and she felt almost sorry for him. But it didn't change anything.

'My father's over from America,' she told him, homing in on her purpose, 'staying at the flat. We're playing happy families. Takes me back to the time they split up ... remembering how awful it was.'

He looked away.

'A pity I didn't remember all that before,' she pressed on ruthlessly. 'If I had, you wouldn't be sitting here now. I'd have shown you the door after that first night.'

She could scarcely countenance her own brutality, but couldn't control it either. She wanted the matter settled.

'I'll tell you the truth, Sean. A month ago I wanted nothing more than to be your wife and have your children. But all that has gone now. Even if I survive, I'll never have a child. This stuff' – she gestured at the diminishing liquid in the bag above the drip – 'will shrivel up my ovaries like a couple of dried prunes. It's a curious thing. You cut off one of your options, and it changes the way you view the rest.'

He grimaced and sat back in his chair.

'So,' he said at last, 'you didn't really want me at all. You just wanted my child.'

He spoke quietly, but the words fell harshly between them, and Laurie felt her heart dive.

'No, I wanted you,' she said steadily. 'But I've moved on, Sean. Moved on to a place where something new is happening . . . Where everything seems familiar, yet I know I've never been before . . .'

She laughed self-consciously, fighting the nonsense of it, unable to rationalize, even to herself.

'I can no longer tell you I love you,' she muttered, closing her eyes against the pain on his face, 'because the person who loved you no longer exists. Somebody else is living here.'

She clasped a hand to her heart, and as she did so, made contact with the lump in her left breast.

She turned her face away.

'I no longer know who I am,' she said.

Chapter Nine

'I am Alice Harper, Ma'am. My mother works in the lavender fields, beyond Blue Farm.'

'And your father? He works in the lavender fields too?'

'My father is dead, Ma'am. There's only my mother, myself, and a young brother at home. My sister Ivy is married and lives in the village . . .'

Lady Crompton frowned and reached for her fan.

'And why are *you* not married, Alice Harper?'

'I have found no man suitable, Ma'am. And unless one finds a suitable man, one had better have no man at all.'

Lady Crompton almost dropped her fan, but behind her shoulder, India struggled to contain her mirth, and so contorted were her features in the effort not to laugh, that I found it hard not to smile myself.

'Then I don't know *what* your future will be!' Lady Crompton said sourly.

And yet I saw my future on that first day. I saw that India would prevail over her mother's reservations, that I would be hired as personal maid, and that my position in the house would become unassailable.

I say this not out of pride nor self-aggrandizement, merely to show that the future, like the past, is something which is part fixed, part flexible. We bring our visions and our determinations to the future, just as we bring our dreams and our interpretations to the past.

Spirits and phantoms. Angels and ghosts. Sometimes you sight the farther shores of heaven, sometimes you peer into the pit of hell. Sometimes you feel the past settle upon you, airy yet tangible, like dust. And sometimes, you glimpse the world that will be, the people who come after, rare and strange, yet just as tragically human as we ourselves.

The other day, I climbed into the lower branches of the fig tree to gather the more awkward fruits, and looking down to the bench beneath, I saw quite plainly, a young woman. Her clothes were strange, her face unknown. And she was crying.

I was seized by the desire to offer comfort, but by the time I'd descended from the tree, she'd vanished.

So sharp was the impression upon me, so deep the distress I had witnessed, that as we sat in the drawing room later that afternoon, I ventured to tell India about it.

'What did you say, Alice?' Lady Crompton barked.

'Nothing, Ma'am. I was merely remarking that it's quite difficult to gather all the figs unless one climbs into the lower branches of the tree . . .'

'That girl,' grumbled Her Ladyship to no one in particular, 'talks to herself.'

'Really, Mama,' India reproached, glancing round from the drawing room sofa where she and I sat gazing into the rhododendrons beyond the terrace, 'Alice was talking to me!'

'Talking to oneself,' said Christian, catching my eye across the expanse of polished wood and velvet plush between us, 'is the sign of a sensitive soul. Of a poet, no less! I do it all the time . . .'

'The figs are poor this year,' interjected Sir Robin, 'I must have a word with Hardy about pruning the tree . . .'

'It's not the figs that are poor,' said Lady Crompton testily, 'it's what's *done* with the figs . . . They should be pickled in brandy and sugar, not dried. I don't know why we can't get kitchen staff who understand these things . . .'

This was a familiar and wearisome subject, and Lady Crompton, by no means a stupid woman and swiftly perceiving the lack of enthusiasm for her views upon pickled figs and cooks, rose from her chair and pulled on the bell.

'We'll take tea on the terrace,' she announced. 'Leave us, Alice, please. I'm sure you have chores to attend to.'

I have no need to imagine the conversation after my departure, for I am well aware how it goes at such times. *A servant must know her place. Conferring privileges and friendship upon the lower classes will only lead to trouble.*

A servant so honoured will not repay kindness with deference and gratitude. No, indeed. The fruits of flouting convention are envy, rebellion and blame. Who knows where it all will end?

But Her Ladyship will not prevail. Her children have their own ideas, and since it is a changing world (the world is always changing, whether we notice or not) I am barely touched by her opinions.

She's right about one thing, though. I do talk to myself. Or rather, to the phantoms of the past and the spirits of the future that seem to haunt this place.

They are as real to me as India, sitting next to me on the sofa. And if asked how this might be, I can only reply that the world is measured by what its inhabitants observe. There is nothing outside – or above – the observer that can be considered apart from him. There is nothing that can be monitored without his mediating consciousness. The observations of one, therefore, have equal weight with the observations of another. Who can say otherwise? The eye of imagination sees beyond, above, and through, the eye of vision.

Or to put it another way, as Christian says, a sensitive soul talks to itself. To itself, or to such things as are imagined and which, in being wooed and consulted, take genuine shape and form.

So then, the spirits of the future beckon and the phantoms of the past instruct. But the present, meantime, is all.

'Alice,' calls Her Ladyship when it seems I have scarcely been absent five minutes, 'please help Hannah clear the tea things away!'

She is discontented now, for Rose has not buttered the scones as thinly as desired, Hannah has not served them with the cake tongs but has lifted them on to the plates with a knife, and, most insulting of all, the silver teapot has a faint rim of tarnish round the spout.

'When you've finished,' says Her Ladyship peevishly, 'we shall all go walking in the woods. Alice, you may accompany Miss India.'

'Or me!' mouths Christian grinning broadly behind his

mother's back. 'Come walking in the woods with me, Alice! You'll never get a better chance.'

In the event, it was only India and myself walking in the woods that day, for just as the party was about to set forth, a visitor was announced.

'Miss Marianne Goodchild, Ma'am,' said Hannah, curtseying low, hoping to atone both for her failure with the scones and the absence of the head parlour maid, who had inconveniently chosen to exercise her right to one free afternoon a month. 'Shall I show her into the morning room?'

It being the middle of the afternoon, this suggestion did not meet with Her Ladyship's approval, but her displeasure was nothing beside that of her son.

'Then we shall all go walking,' said Christian grumpily, staring hard at me. 'India, I'm sure will wish to walk with Marianne. Alice shall go ahead with me so we might examine the fig tree . . .'

'Nonsense!' cried Her Ladyship, glaring at her son. 'Marianne has come to see you, and you shan't go walking until she's taken refreshment!'

'Yes, of course,' said India swiftly, glancing at Christian. 'But I trust Marianne will excuse me, Mama? It's really time I was attending to Polly . . .'

Lady Crompton, glaring this time at her husband whom she had charged to dispatch the elephant as soon as possible and in whatever manner he deemed expedient, now found herself both annoyed and gratified in the same moment, pleased that Christian might be left alone with Marianne, peeved that India would be free to roam the woods with me when she'd reasonably hoped that some useful discussion on the matter of Adam's absence from Crompton Hall might ensue.

'I suppose the animal must be fed,' she said grudgingly, then turned her face in fixed delight to the opening door. 'Ah, Marianne, my dear! How lovely to see you. Christian has been hoping you'd come . . . And here he is, waiting for you! We had hoped to see your dear brother, too . . .'

'He's in London!' Marianne replied, hardly knowing what consternation this news might provoke. 'He's seeing to the redecoration of the house, and may not return for some time.'

With the prowess born of long experience, Lady Crompton received this unsettling information without displaying so much as a flicker of alarm. And in any case, there were always crumbs of comfort to be gleaned. A redecoration of the London house? What might that signify?

The greetings exchanged and the compliments on the party accepted, India was allowed to depart, and at once I made to enter the kitchen for cakes and buns to feed Polly.

'There's no need, Alice!' India whispered fiercely, grabbing my arm and steering me away from the servants' door. 'Hardy has already done it . . . Let's go at once to the woods!'

I could think only that she wished to escape in case Christian and Marianne should follow, and this must surely mean that she needed my counsel, but for the moment she said nothing and we marched out into the pink summer air toward the lake.

The woods around Crompton Hall are mostly beech with a scattering of oak, shading to silver birch at the rim of the estate. A brook runs through the eastern corner, and this widens into a sedge-filled lake, affording along its route a rustic bridge, a waterfall and a pool deep enough for swimming. Christian often bathes there, so he wishes me to know, pulling off his breeches and diving naked into the cloudy green. I might accompany him any time I wish, he adds and if I were to meet him there one afternoon when Sir Robin and Her Ladyship were out visiting, we should both swim until our bodies shone with health and exertion, then lie together on the grassy bank . . .

'And India? Will she come swimming too?'

'Oh, Alice, how you tease me! No, of course not.'

'Then I will have to ask her permission for this swimming party.'

'What a pathetic excuse! I can't believe that with all

your ingenuity, you couldn't contrive something a little more convincing. Rather say you don't care for me at all, Alice, and wouldn't mind one jot if I drowned beneath the waterfall . . .'

In what exquisite detail do I recall these conversations!

'On the contrary, I should mind very much if you drowned beneath the waterfall. Her Ladyship would be distraught, poor Flora would be set to cook the funeral meats, and as she says herself, she's no good at meats . . . The house would be thrown into mourning, and I should not be at all suited . . . I look dreadfully pallid in black . . .'

'Kiss me, Alice.'

'Go and jump in your pool, Christian.'

This day, however, there was no Christian to set my pulse racing and my defences rising. Instead, India wanted me all to herself, that much was evident.

She waited until we were past the pool and come at last to the shore of the lake and the summerhouse verandah where, if you keep very still, you may glimpse one of my phantoms.

India was incapable of keeping still.

'Alice, what do you make of Marianne Goodchild?' she cried, throwing off her straw hat and flinging it on to the verandah, pacing the boards and staring out upon the sedge as though it might yield up the answers to her questions. 'Do you think she's a woman who knows her own mind?'

'I would say so,' I replied steadily, guessing at what was coming. 'She has been raised by her brother, after all, and he is the most sensible of men.'

'Oh, Alice!' exclaimed India. 'Why must we always speak of Adam? I'm talking about Christian, as you very well know! Do you think Marianne hopes to marry him?'

The merest sigh escaped my lips, no more than the shadow of a breath.

'I imagine your Mama hopes they will marry,' I said.

It was common knowledge that the Goodchild estate had been equally divided upon old Sir Martin's death, and a subsequent observation that a match between Goodchild and Crompton, if not India and Adam, then Christian and Marianne, would produce an estate unrivalled in the county. Better still would be a double match.

'That wasn't my question, Alice. Is Marianne in love, do you think?'

We gazed at each other across the length of the verandah, each clasping our secrets close to our hearts and, for a moment, said nothing. India stooped and trailed her hand in the weedy water of the lake, awaiting my answer.

'Yes, I believe Marianne loves your brother,' I said at last. 'But not all women are blinded by their desires. It is possible to love and yet to see the total unsuitability of a union . . . To dream and to wish, yet still to turn away in the name of reason, or of dignity . . .'

Was there a catch in my voice as I spoke? If so, India either did not hear, or failed to understand.

She stood up and faced me gravely.

'It is very important that Christian marries the right woman,' she said slowly. 'And I could think of no better wife than Marianne. I am sure it's what Marianne wants . . . But, Alice, it can never be! Adam has told me as much, and there is something else . . . Something only I know about Christian. Alice, he's in love with another woman!'

The watery world at my feet seemed to tilt, then righted itself again. I drew a deep breath.

'Is that so?' I inquired.

India began to pace the verandah once more, her face flushed, her wild black hair escaping its pleat to drift across her cheek.

'It's terrible, Alice. She's someone much beneath him, in both breeding and education. Someone who can never be his wife!'

It seemed the clamour of my heart would be heard above the rustling of the sedge, and I reached out to the verandah rail to steady myself.

'And do you know who she is?' I forced myself to ask.

India moved to my side and slid her arm around my waist.

'An actress from the London music hall!' she announced

in my ear, pausing so that the calamity might register in full.
'Her name is Kitty Malone, and I saw them together while
we were in the city staying with my Aunt Bonham . . . That
is to say, I saw her face on a poster, and then when we were
all dining at the Gallery Coffee Rooms, in she came! You
should have seen the look that passed between them.'

'I wish I had,' I said.

India picked up the straw hat and began to swivel it in
her hands, struggling with her words.

'That isn't the worst of it. I hardly know how to tell you
this, nor indeed, know not whether I should . . . The truth
is I found a receipt upon his dressing table . . . For the
hire of rooms in Hampstead . . . Alice, I believe they may
have spent some time together . . .' She looked away from
me, her eyes downcast, 'As man and wife,' she finished
miserably.

I cleared my throat, unsure what I might say, or what
might be expected of me, an uncertainty which India
dispelled at once.

'I want you to speak to him, Alice,' she implored. 'I
have thought very deeply about this, and only now have I
decided to act. I want you to ask him about Kitty Malone
and discover whether he truly cares for her, or whether he
has merely been . . . led astray!'

I gave her to think I was considering this carefully.

'Perhaps it's Kitty Malone who's been led astray?' I
suggested at last.

She laughed, a forced, mirthless little gasp which revealed
the extent of her concern.

'Oh, really, Alice! What a thing to say . . . You can
imagine the kind of woman she is! But you do see, don't
you, that I can hardly ask him myself? It wouldn't be
proper . . .'

No, indeed. And what more proper than that I, Alice
Harper, should question Mr Christian upon his morals?

'He's so very fond of you, Alice . . . Almost as fond as I
am myself . . . And he respects your judgement. He told
me once he believed you to be very wise and mature . . .
Please advise him that if he were to mend his behaviour,

Adam might change his mind . . . Then Marianne could become Mrs Crompton, and we should all be happy . . .'

I could not hide a wistful smile at this, but still I sought to do the right thing.

'I'll speak to him,' I told her bravely, 'when the moment seems appropriate.'

'I trust you, Alice,' India said seriously. 'I know you see into the heart of things.'

I said nothing, for my heart was in my mouth.

The heart is a mere organ, but *heart* is surely the very essence of our being, the quality which most influences our lives.

I found myself pursuing this matter of *heart* with the new doctor when he came to call upon Lady Crompton three days after India's birthday, his first visit since the party, and possibly the only time, I imagine, when we shall meet him socially in future without his wife.

He had come to apologize for their summary departure that night, an incident about which he seemed much embarrassed. His wife, he said, had been concerned for one of their young daughters whom they'd left at home with a feverish headache.

'You may subdue a headache with lavender oil,' I said politely, and thought for a moment he had not heard me speak so intent did he seem upon India's progress across the room from writing desk to sofa.

'Headache is very difficult to treat,' he said vaguely. 'So many possible causes . . .'

'It may have a spiritual cause,' I suggested, there being an awkward pause in the conversation which seemed to call for some remark. 'If the stresses and strains of a particular situation become too much, then a headache may ensue . . .'

Lady Crompton reached for her fan.

'Oh, Alice will set you right about medical matters,' she said acidly. 'I do believe there's nothing she doesn't know, Doctor Harte, although she has never read a medical book in her life!'

This was not true. I have read a great many medical books, among them *The Garden of Health* which lists, along with much other interesting material, the myriad medicinal uses of lavender: *Smell often to it to comfort and cleare the sight. Shred the herbe with the flowers and distill it and drinke two ounces of the water to helpe giddinesse of the head. Seathe lavender in water and temper thy wine therewith and also make a syrope with the said water and use it against swooning and to comfort the heart.*

Thus wrote William Langham in 1579, but I have found other authors less illuminating precisely because they ignore this question of *heart*. They look upon bodily parts as little wonders in themselves, complete and unaffected by each other. The lungs to take in oxygen, the kidneys to drain waste matter, the intestine to process food. And the heart they regard merely as a vessel for pumping the blood. There is no advocacy of the heart as repository for hopes, dreams and beliefs, the very essence of a man! Yet it is plain to any thinking person that to ignore this aspect of the heart is to address only the mechanical among human complaints. To be sure, these are important, but if no attention is paid to the essence that lubricates the bodily machine, why then, good health will never be achieved.

Dr Harte smiled at me.

'I do not dismiss folk remedies,' he said. 'Indeed, I believe they can be most efficacious, particularly in illnesses which are hysterical in origin . . .'

India met his eye across the room, and I wondered if I was the only other witness to the challenge she posed, or whether Dr Harte himself understood the momentous nature of the temptation before him. Lady Crompton, the principal witness, had already noted his admiration with a keenness that belied her apparent air of self-absorption.

'Would you say that Ivy's son – Alice's nephew – was suffering an hysterical illness the day you saw him, Doctor Harte?'

India's question seemed innocent enough, and in posing it she demonstrated no guile or flirtatiousness, yet the effect upon Dr Harte was like honey applied to an open wound, purging and sweet.

'No!' he beamed. 'That was something quite different! How perceptive of you, Miss Crompton, to cite that instance. Nothing is as simple as it first appears!'

'The lower classes are much given to hysteria,' Lady Crompton declared. 'So perhaps it is fitting that these folk remedies remain confined to them ... And now Doctor Harte, do tell us when we might meet your charming wife again? India, I believe, was hoping to make a new friend ... There are so few sensitive women in the country, I'm sure you will agree ...'

I looked up in astonishment, catching Her Ladyship's eye. She stared back unabashed, and at once I understood. A rapid change of opinion on the subject of doctors' wives was deemed prudent. There was, of course, no threat, no potential danger contained in the lively exchange just witnessed, and yet it was surely right and proper that any burgeoning friendship between India and the new arrival be firmly quashed. And what better way than by means of his wife?

The doctor coughed, he fumbled with his teacup, he prevaricated and finally, beneath his hostess's steady gaze, he agreed to bring Mrs Harte to supper and cards on Sunday. Lady Crompton smiled, content.

My attempt to reprimand Christian proved ill-conceived and futile.

'Alice, I love you. She means nothing to me, I swear it.'

He'd surprised me that morning by the elephant's compound, a bag of lavender clippings in my hand, the rough stalks that my mother discarded when making lavender water. I'd thought Polly might fancy a little variety to her diet, but she plucked the bag from my hand with her trunk and tossed it to the ground, regarding me with a wounded expression, rather like Christian's when I mentioned the name of Kitty Malone.

'I'm seeking no declarations of love,' I told him calmly. 'I'm merely doing as India asked me, and trying to discover your intentions.'

He turned away, kicking a stone against the compound fence.

'India should mind her own business,' he said.

He bent to pick up my lavender bag, sulky and out of sorts with himself, yet all the while contriving, I divined, to offer an explanation that might satisfy.

'If you continue to deny me, Alice,' he said at last, 'then what am I to do? A man must find an outlet for his passion, you know!'

A tremor of disgust ran through me and I considered the curious mix of emotion that informed my feeling for Christian, part desire, part repulsion, part daring and part restraint, all of it bound together with a powerful need for self-preservation.

'So, poor Kitty serves no function beyond a means of relief from your base urges?' I said gravely, taking the lavender bag and hoisting it to my shoulder. 'You do not care for her at all?'

He smiled and shook his head.

'Kitty is not so poor,' he said lightly, 'and I am not so unfeeling. I thought you might see this, Alice. You understand the ways of the world, and you're surely too wise to judge a man at face value. You see into the heart of things!'

'And Marianne Goodchild? Does she see into the heart of things?'

His expression changed.

'What has this to do with Marianne?' he inquired coldly.

'She loves you,' I said. 'She hopes to be your wife.'

There was a long pause in which he looked at me thoughtfully, his brilliant blue eyes, so very like India's and yet without their burning intensity, fixed upon mine. He was a fine and handsome man, and if I had not determined to keep my wits about me, I should surely have been lost.

'And what of my own hopes, Alice?' he inquired at

last. 'Are they ever to be realized? Or am I simply to do whatever's expected of me . . . Good or bad?'

I was deeply irritated by this reply.

'Don't talk to me of hopes,' I said sharply. 'You who have never known privation nor suffering . . . Your hopes have already been realized! They were confirmed the day you were born . . .'

He burst out laughing, throwing back his head.

'You know, I should have bought this elephant for you, Alice! How high and mighty you would have been, seated upon it! You could surpass India, any day . . .'

I turned away, discomfited by his mockery and annoyed with my heart for its unruly hammering.

'I should like to see the best of you, that's all,' I muttered.

He reached for my hand, caressing the fingers and squeezing them between his own.

'Well, so you could . . . Any time you like . . . Now, if you wish! We could go to the pool, and . . .'

I snatched my hand away and made to march off into the beech woods, but he grabbed my shoulders and swung me round to face him.

'It was a joke, Alice,' he said.

'Then please stop joking and answer my questions that I might reassure India . . .'

'Ah yes, India! We must all seek to reassure her . . . Very well, then. You may tell India that much as I admire and respect Marianne, it seems unlikely we shall marry . . .'

I could not still the clamouring of my heart, and now I hardly dared to look at him.

'Why not?' I managed at last.

'Because her fine, upstanding brother, the righteous Adam Goodchild, will not have it! He sought me out on the night of India's party . . . Right at the start of the evening so there'd be no mistake while I was clasping Marianne's breast to mine in the foxtrot . . . Told me not to encourage her, nor to think any suit would be gladly received . . . Such presumption is astonishing! I have never declared an interest at all.'

I could not deny my relief at this revelation, but I struggled against ignoble sentiment.

'So you don't want Marianne?'

'It's you I want, Alice,' Christian said, laughing again. 'But if you won't have me, then I might decide to give Adam Goodchild a run for his money . . . After all, Marianne is the kind of woman a Crompton takes to wife . . . And it's true that she loves me . . . Not to mention the fact that a marriage between us would create an unrivalled estate . . .'

I drew a deep breath.

'So land is more important than love?'

'I'm teasing you again, Alice.'

'Then don't!'

I found myself betrayed by a high, unsteady trill to my voice, and it was then that he moved toward me, clasping me to his chest and, when I struggled to be free, pressing his lips upon mine in a passionate, hungry kiss.

I had dealt with such behaviour many times, sometimes threatening to speak to his Papa if he should continue to harass me, though never truly meaning it, and most times, I freely confess, responding with my own passion. But this time a certain recklessness, or perhaps simple pride, overcame me, and I smacked the back of my hand across his face, a hard, loud slap which sent him lurching against the compound fence. Polly snorted in alarm and backed into her drinking trough, causing such a commotion of trumpeting and bleating, that I guessed Hardy would be with us at any moment.

Christian pulled himself upright from the fence, and I hardly knew whether he would strike me back or march off to Her Ladyship and have me dismissed. Instead he merely offered me a rueful smile.

'Now I know the truth of it,' he said solemnly, rubbing his face. 'You are not as indifferent as you seem . . . And I know now I shall have you one day! Not this day, nor tomorrow, but one day soon. Be sure of it, Alice Harper! One day soon.'

*　　*　　*

I have sometime walked to the pool in the woods and concealed myself among the mallow bushes, waiting to see him swim.

I am unashamed of such impropriety, partly because it harms no one, and partly because I know that if I were to be discovered, the resulting humiliation would be all mine.

I have watched him strip off his clothes and plunge beneath the waterfall, and I have held my breath, waiting for his dark head to break the surface. I have seen him float like an otter on his stomach, and laze like a basking seal on his back.

I have seen him rise like a salmon from the shallows, and I have laughed at my own curiosity, daring myself to imagine that I too might throw off the polite impediments of society and feel the warm waves lap against my own bare skin.

Such thoughts are dangerous I know, yet none of us may be held to account for what we think.

Think what you like, Alice. But only act on prudent thoughts.

My mother would hardly be pleased to learn of my spying, and might well accuse me of tempting my fate.

As she knows, however, Fate is merely the random work of an unprincipled universe, dressed up to look like destiny by those who cannot bear the awful truth.

We may tempt it, we may defy it, we may succumb or we may refuse. But we cannot blame Fate for the state of the innermost soul, for our readiness to embrace evil or folly, for our failure of *heart*.

That burden rests squarely with ourselves.

Chapter Ten

Sir Robin returned to London and the portrait painter arrived, a slight, diffident young man who took light readings in various rooms of the house by means of an eccentric cylindrical object with dials and pointers upon it, then announced that he would paint outside, on the library terrace. India was pleased and excited, and would willingly have struck up a discourse with the artist had he wished it. But he didn't, responding to all her comments in abstracted grunts, and finally requesting that she remain silent so he might concentrate on her profile.

This left India nothing much to do but daydream during the long mornings on the terrace, a habit which quickly expanded to fill the rest of her waking hours.

Dreams and fantasies. How would we live without them? Is it conceivable that suffering humanity, impotent individuals locked into centuries of poverty, oppression, disease and doubt, would have made it this far, let alone prospered, if not for their visions, their hopes, and the fabulous tales they told themselves and each other?

India began to immerse herself in memories of her old home, the colours and sounds of Delhi, the crimson sun perching upon the minaret of the red mosque, the cool avenues of cypresses around the compound, the chattering of mynah birds beneath the railway arches, allowing herself to imagine a triumphant return.

She might become the wife of a diplomat, a dedicated man like her father, virtuously concerned (as Lady Crompton had never been) with the native children who scurried about the compound, or even with those beggarly half-shadows who swarmed in the streets beyond, their bodies thin as sparrows' legs, their eyes dark and needy.

Or she might return as a missionary, a free and independent spirit, living in a shady house beside a white-painted church. But, no. The mission women she remembered were neither free nor independent, plump wives in large-brimmed hats who hated the heat and longed for England but never dared say so.

A doctor's wife, then? Standing fearlessly beside her dedicated husband, strong in the midst of suffering and sickness, a rock to which he might cling in the rough waters of professional competition, a safe harbour from the envy or malice of less gifted men, a trusted friend, a revered companion, a beloved partner, a willing partaker in the sweet mysteries of marriage, a devoted—

'India, excuse me. Mrs Harte is come to call.'

Alice's voice broke into her thoughts, forcing an unwelcome return to the moment.

India stood up from the writing desk where she'd been pretending to enter up her journal, frowning down at the blank spaces which revealed the extent of her daydreaming. She had done nothing since the morning portrait session had finished, and now, with Eugenie's arrival, might do nothing all afternoon. She turned toward the drawing room door, preparing to set her face in a pleasant smile. It wasn't easy.

In the weeks since the party, Eugenie Harte had become a regular visitor at Crompton Hall, forging an intimate and reverential relationship, not with the daughter of the house as might once have been envisaged, but with Lady Crompton herself, finding in her a superior spirit to be emulated and flattered.

For her part, Lady Crompton had found Mrs Harte to be surprisingly well bred and fastidious, a woman, if not of her own standing, then at least after her own heart. All previous reservations about doctors' wives were shelved, if not completely cast aside. They liked each other, and took delight in many conversations about the problem with servants, the best way to encourage regular church attendance among the lower classes, and the decline of standards in the country at large.

Now, however, Eugenie had come to see India.

They stood together in the drawing room, an erect,

slender girl with a long dark pigtail swinging behind her shoulder, and an elegant, older woman, severe in dark grey morning dress, the kind of woman disparagingly called handsome, not because the adjective *pretty* failed to apply, but rather because such a light and frivolous description seemed laughingly inadequate. Eugenie Harte was tall and imposing, her abundant chestnut hair meticulously wound into a coil on top of her head, her long neck bare of pearls or gold. She clasped her hands before her in a gesture of resolution, and her eyes were flat, like pummelled steel. She smiled, but the eyes did not lighten.

'I have come to invite you to supper tomorrow evening, Miss India. With Doctor Harte and myself, to meet my young sister Frederica . . . Since my father's untimely death some six months previous, she has been residing with her aunt in town . . .'

Eugenie neglected to say which town, but India knew she was meant to believe Frederica had come down from London, and she nodded politely, affording due respect to the prospect of a visitor from the capital.

'Now, of course, she is to make her home with us. I am sure you will enjoy meeting her . . .'

'I should be delighted,' India murmured graciously, glancing quickly at Alice.

'You may bring your maid if you wish!'

Eugenie had caught the glance and interpreted it correctly, though she had no intention of emulating Lady Crompton on this particular foible, the indulging of a wayward daughter's demand for extraordinary privileges on behalf of the woman she chose to call companion but whom – as Lady Crompton had made clear – was, in truth, a servant.

'She may eat in the kitchen with my staff.'

'Thank you,' said India coolly. 'That is most kind.'

The rebuke was evident, and Eugenie Harte was startled into qualification.

'I realize that Miss Harper often dines with the family here at Crompton Hall . . . But the dining room at Blue Farm is so very cramped . . . However, I see you might like to have company on the journey home . . . Although my husband would be happy to drive you back to Crompton Hall if Miss Harper were to find herself otherwise employed tomorrow evening . . .'

Alice inclined her head.

'I have no previous engagements,' she said quietly, and something in her voice caused Eugenie Harte to look up quickly, as though she detected – but *surely not* – a hint of amusement.

'So then, that is settled,' she said crisply, fixing India with her cold smile. 'I'm sure you will like Frederica. She's just about your own age, and a most spirited girl. We must all be on our toes when Frederica is around . . .'

She nodded again, she refused refreshment, she waved aside the offer to accompany her to the front door, and she pointed at the writing desk and indicated that India should return to her journal.

India smiled politely and waited for the door to close. Then she sat down at the writing desk again and picked up her pen, rubbing it pensively against her cheek.

'Should you like to be a doctor's wife?' she asked Alice dreamily as Eugenie Harte's modest carriage clattered away on the driveway beyond the window. 'Standing by his side while he healed and comforted the sick . . .'

'I think not,' said Alice shortly. 'If I were to imagine a glorious future, it would be as a doctor myself.'

What kind of man was Dr Luke Harte? Why had he married a creature so vexatious, so stern, so thoroughly *unsuitable*, as Eugenie? In what manner had he professed love to her, proposed marriage to her, exchanged vows with her and fathered children upon her? How could he have done it?

Such questions consumed India and made her quite exhausted with speculation. It was, she told herself, a perfectly proper line of inquiry from one so interested in human nature as she, so concerned with the motivation and mystery of personality, and how else might one practise the arts of observation and deduction, if not upon one's neighbours?

Sadly, she was forced to conclude that the choice of Eugenie as bride constituted a serious flaw in Dr Harte's character. How else might his sacrifice be understood? Was she to imagine him devoted to Eugenie, delighting in her strict household management, her dexterity with an embroidery needle – for such had already been demonstrated in a new altar hanging at the parish church – her powers of concentration at bridge, or her extraordinary ability to dance a foxtrot without once inclining her head nor allowing a smile to enliven her features?

No, devotion did not seem a possibility. And that, unfortunately, pointed to expedience. Luke Harte had married for money, for prestige, or for influence. No other explanation would suffice.

India tried out her theories on Alice.

'I should say that people marry for many reasons, and they may not always understand the attraction, or the compulsion, themselves . . .'

'Be more specific!' India implored, determined to examine the matter from all angles. 'What might lead a man and woman into marriage, if not from love, the wishes of parents, or the intimation of advantage arising from the match?'

Alice hesitated. She'd decided that the attraction so clearly existing between India and Luke Harte constituted no possible threat, and gave no cause for concern beyond a vague fear that Eugenie might notice and use India's infatuation for some ignoble purpose of her own.

Still, Alice had no desire to encourage India's interest, nor to suggest that the marriage between Luke and Eugenie was anything other than blissful and contented.

'Most people marry because they reach a point in their lives when a husband or wife becomes necessary,' she said carefully. 'Perhaps a woman is running out of time to have children. Or perhaps a man sees that his career will never advance while he remains single . . . If two people were to meet at a time when their individual needs coincided, then they might very well find themselves married without having considered the matter of love . . . And be tolerably happy, I should say.'

India was not convinced. In her mind's eye she saw the wedding ceremony, heard the promises given and accepted, even smelt the orange blossom. What kind of man went through such an event and did not think of love?

Alice tried again.

'Passion is a very poor foundation for lifelong partnership,' she began. 'And indeed, passion may turn upon itself, feeding jealousies and quarrels . . . Far wiser, I would say, to base a marriage upon mutual respect and common purpose. Such a couple will surely discover that they do indeed love each other . . .'

A sound of carriage wheels from the driveway beyond alerted them both to a visitor, and India rose swiftly to her feet.

'It's Adam!' she cried in genuine delight. 'Returned from London to see us! Now isn't that a splendid thing?'

Alice, peering through the drawing room window, equally delighted and, indeed, somewhat relieved to see the Goodchild carriage pull up at Crompton Hall again, agreed at once that, yes, truly, it was a splendid thing. And to be sure, she considered privately, a timely thing as well.

Adam Goodchild had found himself in some turmoil since the night of India's birthday party. He had left for London the morning after, insisting that his redecoration must be supervised, but in truth needing time alone to reflect on the events of the previous days and of the birthday night itself. Thinking it over, he'd been unable to explain precisely why he'd left the ruby ring in its casket that evening, how he'd come to perceive his suit to be doomed before he'd so much as hinted at his hopes, and what, if anything, had happened to alter his view of India's likely feelings.

Yet he had known India for many years, notwithstanding his long absences on travels abroad.

He had known her as a gauche child newly returned

from Delhi, as an inquisitive girl growing to maturity, and as a confident poised young woman. Consequently, he had believed himself uniquely aware of her qualities and gifts. If anyone might have predicted her response to a particular subject, then it was surely he. A younger man might have been overwhelmed by her beauty and daunted by her spirit of independence, yet he, Adam, could appreciate both and allow neither to blind him to the real nature of the creature he so admired. India was clever and well informed, but she was quickly impressed by what she perceived to be noble and true, and a girlish delight in romance and adventure sometimes compromised her judgement. He'd once had to dissuade her from attending an occult seance at the home of a questionable lady in Norwich, and on more than a single occasion had found himself mildly alarmed by her professions on such matters as enfranchisement for women, views which, he guessed, came not so much from India's own musings upon politics, as from Alice Harper. It was not so much that he disagreed with these views as that he saw in India's forthright manner of expressing them a certain danger. He also knew she could change her mind very quickly, and that while in the quiet air of Norfolk her passions might pass as mere eccentricities, in the drawing rooms of London, they could prove much more troublesome.

Fortunately, perhaps, India had not been much exposed to London society, Lady Crompton having a deep dislike of the disruption involved in relocating from country to town. India went sometimes to stay with Lady Crompton's sister, her Aunt Bonham, but she had never been presented at court, nor introduced to the delights of the season.

When he considered it, this seemed an oversight on Lady Crompton's part, and now Adam found himself forced to contemplate Her Ladyship's expectations for her unpredictable daughter. Had she simply been biding her time before embarking on the business of launching India? Had she gambled it would be worth holding back, knowing that she would hardly be pressed to find a husband should he fail to declare himself? Had he been the tame suitor, the one who knew India's foibles, would not balk at them, and thereby justified the risk of waiting? If so, then he could hardly afford to delay a moment longer.

Such thoughts had devoured much of his time in London, and he'd spared little to consider Marianne's infatuation and how he might deflect it while inflicting the minimum of pain, for he had scant hope that the rebuke he'd delivered to Christian at the birthday party would influence him in any way.

But now it occurred to him that as India's suitor, he might wield some influence with Sir Robin. He could certainly make clear his concern about Marianne's extreme youth and the unpredictability of immature emotions, and plead for the intervention of someone who might temper Christian's response.

Yes, all in all, everything pointed toward him making his feelings known! He looked back upon delightful moments with India, their conversations, their walks in the beech woods, their shared suppers and card parties and dances and Christmases over many years. She had always welcomed him, confided in him, encouraged him to talk of his travels and vouchsafed her own ambition to return to Delhi . . .

And now, as his carriage drew into the driveway of Crompton Hall, Adam recalled their happy drive into the lavender fields just a week before the birthday party, how India had climbed from this very carriage and leaned upon his arm, drinking in the perfume of the purple blooms, and they had talked . . .

Of what?

Adam's face creased into a frown as he descended from the carriage and walked toward the hall.

They'd talked, he now remembered, of nothing much that day; the lavender, the weather, the beauty of the beech woods, and the imminent arrival of Dr Luke Harte.

India rose to greet him, her blue eyes bright with pleasure.

'We've missed you!' she cried, holding out her hands. 'We've been dreary and dull since the day you departed!'

Adam smiled, his heart lifting at this eager response. He took her hand.

'You'll forgive my saying that I'm delighted to hear it,' he told her solemnly. 'But I sincerely doubt you could ever be dreary and dull. It's not in your nature.'

'Oh, you'd be surprised,' India responded gaily. 'I am the dullest of creatures when deprived of good conversation. As I have been most mornings of late! My portrait is being painted by an extremely taciturn young gentleman who believes a sigh to be more expressive than a discussion . . .'

They all laughed, a trifle too heartily, revealing a collective disquiet that could not easily have been explained.

'No walking in the woods?' Adam inquired.

'I haven't walked to the lake for days . . . Not since I went with Alice on the day that Marianne last called . . .'

Adam grimaced at mention of Marianne, then quickly recovered his purpose.

'We shall remedy that at once,' he said. 'It's a splendid day for a walk. Not too sunny, yet not too cool . . .'

His eyes met Alice's composed gaze across the room and a spark of recognition leapt between them.

Alice stood up. And if in that moment she paused to wonder how India would deal with what must undoubtedly follow, then no shadow of concern troubled her deferential smile.

'Lady Crompton is resting,' she said quietly. 'I shall tell her you're here and that you're walking with Miss India in the woods . . .'

It was understood, and as the drawing room door closed behind Alice, and India reached for her straw hat, Adam dared to believe that the future lay within his grasp.

The afternoon was cloudy and still, a sticky, airless pall hanging over the beech woods that belied all earlier assertions about the weather. It was not a perfect day for walking, and by the time they reached the trees, Adam was hot and uncomfortable beneath his jacket. Yet he felt unable to discard it, not so much for reasons of propriety as for the inexplicable intuition that while he kept it on, some dignity, some restraint, might be maintained.

India took off her hat the moment they entered the woods and fanned herself with it.

'I do believe a storm is brewing,' she said.

Adam, knowing nothing was to be gained by prevarication, embarked upon his prepared speech at once.

'I have been in London overseeing the redecoration of my house,' he began, 'and I dare to hope that you might approve of the colours and the new furnishings . . .'

'I'm sure I shall,' India murmured vaguely, 'though I've no idea when I'll be in London again . . . Oh, Adam, do look! The cowslip on the bank of the brook . . . Isn't it beautiful?'

A few moments were spent admiring the cowslip before he tried again.

'I would like it if you were to come to London at the earliest opportunity,' he said gravely. 'And not merely as a visitor, India . . .'

This time she could mistake neither his tone nor his intent, and indeed, as she'd entered the beech woods and noted him perspiring uncomfortably beneath his jacket, anxiety overcame her, the warning signal of a difficult moment that, for all her disclaimers to Alice, she had nevertheless wondered if she might one day have to negotiate.

She glanced up at him unhappily, and said nothing.

He caught her reticence, but allowed himself to think it a show of girlish modesty, and reached for her hand.

'You know I have long admired you,' he whispered urgently, 'and I do believe we have been the most compatible of spirits ever since you returned to Crompton Hall . . .'

Still she said nothing, and now she would not look at him, twisting her straw hat in one hand while he held the other, staring resolutely into the cowslip.

'I have cherished this ambition for many years, India . . . You know what I'm saying, my dearest girl . . . I hold you in the highest regard and wish only for your happiness . . . India . . . Will you consent to be my wife?'

A faint gasp escaped her lips, as though the distress of what must follow was too much for her to bear, and she withdrew her hand from his, turning away to compose herself before she spoke.

'Adam, you are my truest friend, and I can think of no other person from whom a proposal would be so appreciated . . . I thank you indeed for this honour . . .'

He knew at once, and with the nobility of a true gentleman, sought to spare her the agony of refusing him outright.

'I realize that this must come as a surprise,' he said quickly, 'and perhaps an unwelcome one . . . There's no need to give me an answer right away . . . Indeed, if you wish to think it over and communicate your reply through Alice . . .'

She was close to tears, and as he watched her struggle for the words, a great surge of tenderness swept over him, the desire to deal with her gently, to allow her every possible retreat.

'May I say, India, that whatever you decide, nothing will change between us . . . I shall still be your truest friend, and I shall still ask you to come walking in the beech woods . . . Say nothing, my dear . . . There's really no need . . .'

Alas, India was too passionate and forthright to take refuge in polite dishonesty, and her own need to speak her mind obliterated all competing considerations for Adam's feelings.

'I'd like nothing more than to accept your offer,' she cried. 'I can see that it would be both sensible and suitable . . . You are a fine man, Adam, and any woman would be proud to be your wife . . .'

She drew apart from him, walking into the cowslip toward the banks of the brook, twisting the straw hat with ever increasing agitation.

He gazed after her miserably, knowing that there was now no escape. His hopes were to be dashed in the plainest, the most brutal manner. He waited, hot in his heavy jacket, the sky above him silent and brooding.

'I cannot be that woman,' India whispered sorrowfully,

155

her cheeks flushed with her distress. 'I respect you deeply, I admire your integrity, and I value your opinions . . . But Adam . . .'

The tears flowed freely now and she fumbled for a handkerchief to wipe them away.

'I'm afraid I don't love you,' she said.

The storm broke less than an hour later, a torrent of warm rain lashing the terraces of Crompton Hall, flattening the lavender fields around Blue Farm and flooding the lane into the village.

But the elemental unleashing was nothing beside Lady Crompton's own storm, a tide of anger which swept over her daughter and threatened to swamp the entire household.

Receiving Alice into her chamber, Her Ladyship had been initially curt at the interruption to her retreat, then visibly excited at the news she was given.

Adam returned! Walking in the beech woods! The London redecorations complete!

None of this would have counted for much, however, had it not been for Alice's own excitement. Lady Crompton knew enough to judge her daughter's moods by Alice's demeanour, and though she would never have confessed to taking Alice's word for anything, nonetheless, when there were no observers, she deigned to seek her opinion.

'You really believe Adam is come to speak to India?' she asked breathlessly, struggling upright from her couch and motioning for a decanter of lemonade. 'Do you think he has the ring with him? Oh, that Sir Robin were here! The men are so careless, always neglecting the important matters . . . Still, I suppose Christian may receive Adam's suit. He can give his father's permission!'

Alice declined to comment on this possibility, privately surmising that neither Adam nor Christian would readily assent to any such thing.

'An autumn wedding!' cried Lady Crompton. 'The church can be so lovely then. The last of the roses, the early chrysanthemums and the first of the winter greenery . . . We shall have to go to London to order the gown. I suppose India will say that it can all be done in Norwich, but we'll need French lace, and there's no French lace to be had outside of London . . . Long sleeves, I think, as the weather may be cool, wouldn't you say, Alice?'

Alice, who'd intended to sound a note of caution, found herself swept along by this vision, oddly moved by Her Ladyship's open delight. Lady Crompton, she suddenly divined, wanted more than the simple satisfaction of a good match for her daughter. She truly wished for India's happiness, the assurance of her lifelong security, the knowledge that her husband was the kind of man who might be relied upon, as in common with Alice's own mother, Lady Crompton clearly considered reliability a rare blessing in a man. And who could argue with her understanding of Adam Goodchild as one such? Certainly not Alice herself, and for a brief moment the two of them were united in their pleasure at so sweet, so natural, so efficacious a prospect as the coupling of India and Adam.

Yet Alice could not entirely conceal her misgivings.

'I sometimes wonder if India is a little unrealistic in her opinions upon romance,' she ventured cautiously. 'It seems to me she doesn't always value a man for his worthwhile qualities, and looks instead to superficial attractions . . .'

Her Ladyship, who might have rapped Alice's knuckles with her fan on a less auspicious occasion, allowed this impertinence to pass.

'All women have their silly notions,' she declared, signalling for her wrap, 'I dare say you've had them yourself, Alice! We've all imagined the kind of man who'd make our hearts beat fast and tell us silly things in the moonlight. But who would wish to marry such a man?'

Alice smiled and nodded, hoping India might be sufficiently sensible to reach such a conclusion herself, but wondering nevertheless.

'I do hope she will accept him,' she said warily.

The news, when it was announced, was clearly deemed all the more terrible by Lady Crompton for the unlikely intimacy between mistress and servant that had preceded it.

India, her face still pink and blotched, hurried into the house and made straight for her mother's chamber, barely pausing to meet Alice's startled glance as she passed her on the stairs.

Alice had no time to consider what might have happened, for just a few moments later Lady Crompton emitted an audible cry, and to her shock, Alice heard the smashing of glass. She ran quickly back to Her Ladyship's room and threw open the door to disclose India cowering against the tallboy, the remains of the lemonade decanter on the floor before her.

'You foolish girl!' Her Ladyship raged. 'You foolish, foolish girl!'

Then she turned on Alice.

'Get out of this room,' she commanded. 'I don't know who you think you are, nor what you imagine you're doing here.'

Alice scuttled, closing the door behind her, and ran back down the stairs, an impetuous flight which took her, unheeding, straight into the arms of Christian.

'What's going on?' he grinned. 'I've never seen you run, Alice, except when I'm chasing you . . .'

Her expression cooled his gaiety, and he gripped her shoulders tightly.

'What is it? What's happened?'

Alice was trembling.

'Adam Goodchild has proposed marriage to India,' she managed at last, 'and I do believe she has refused him . . .'

Christian threw back his head and laughed.

'Has she indeed? Well, good for her! I hadn't imagined she'd show such exquisite taste . . .'

'Her Ladyship is very upset . . . And so am I . . .'

'Well, don't be upset dearest Alice. I'm sure India will do much better for herself . . .'

He lifted her chin with his finger and moved his face toward hers, as though he meant to kiss her, which he might well have done had Lady Crompton not chosen that moment to appear at the head of the staircase. She stood transfixed, staring down upon them, her face momentarily contorted into a peculiar expression that was part outrage, part grief.

Then she pointed accusingly at Alice.

'That girl is a bad influence,' she declared tightly. 'She will leave this house today. See to it, Christian, at once!'

His mouth fell open.

'Mama! I hardly think . . .'

'At once, Christian!' Lady Crompton shook with visible fury. 'A week's wages will suffice. Escort her from the Hall, and send for Sir Robin this very night! He will have something to say on these matters, or he will answer to me!'

'Heavens above, Alice!' Christian muttered as the bedchamber door closed behind his mother once more and the sound of India's bitter weeping drifted toward them down the stairs. 'However shall we get over this?'

Alice, appalled and close to tears herself, began packing her modest valise, and it was then that the rains began, battering the window of her attic bedroom like gunshot, leaking on to the landing through a faulty skylight she had long pleaded to have repaired. Well, she would not need it repairing now.

She could go nowhere in the downpour, however, and Christian declined to summon the carriage to take her home, declaring that the lane would prove impassable.

He was unable to decide what to do. The rain seemed to offer an excuse against sending a carriage to London for Sir Robin or ordering a telegram. And yet Lady Crompton would not be denied, and he dare not simply do nothing.

'Maybe we can get India to change her mind,' he joked, seeking to cheer Alice. 'I can't see that anything else would remedy the situation. We'll have to persuade her that marrying Adam wouldn't be so bad . . . After all, it would surely be preferable to living with Mama in her current temper!'

Alice, sitting in the gun room with her valise beside her, was not amused.

'My dismissal has nothing to do with India or Adam,' she said tightly. 'It's your fault.'

He grimaced.

'I'm sorry,' he said quietly. 'But you know, Alice, I'd been thinking it would suit us both for you to leave Crompton Hall ... Then I might visit you at Lavender Cottage ...'

Alice jumped up from her seat.

'Oh, that would be very fine, wouldn't it?' she hissed. 'One mistress in London, and another in Crompton? And Marianne Goodchild as your lawful wedded wife, no doubt!'

He turned away from her.

'I'm sorry you see it that way,' he said, his voice oddly muffled.

'How else should I see it? You Cromptons think only of yourselves and your pleasures ...'

She gestured at the trophies hung around the gun room, contemptuous of all they seemed to say about her employers. A certain disillusionment had overtaken Alice, and not simply with Christian. Why hadn't India sought her counsel before dismissing Adam? She might then have advised on how to handle Lady Crompton. It would not have been beyond India, surely, to plead that she felt unready for marriage, that she hadn't refused Adam for trivial reasons, but had simply postponed the final decision. It was all so unnecessary and regrettable.

The rain continued to beat upon the terrace, and still Christian could not settle upon action.

'I'm sure Mama will see things differently once she recovers from the shock,' he offered tentatively, convincing neither himself nor Alice. 'And then we shall all return to the way things were ...'

'I think not,' Alice said primly.

'Or maybe,' Christian added desperately, 'someone, or something else, will intervene ...'

Alice couldn't imagine who, in what circumstances, might serve to change Lady Crompton's mind, and she had become quite resigned to leaving the Hall when the rains suddenly ceased and the sound of a carriage could plainly be heard making its watery way up the drive outside. The lane to the village was clearly not impassable to a determined traveller.

Christian jumped to his feet.

'Maybe it's Adam come to say that he'll never marry another, and will wait for ever for India's acceptance,' he said dryly. 'That should do it, don't you think? More than enough to make Mama forget any imagined indiscretion on our part . . .'

It was not Adam Goodchild, it was Sir Robin Crompton-Leigh, returned from London of his own volition, not upon some uncanny intuition of trouble at home, but as the bearer of bad tidings from the capital.

Lady Crompton's sister, Elizabeth Bonham, had taken a seizure and died, and as so often happens when the ultimate fact of life arbitrarily manifests itself, all lesser tribulations were immediately thrown into sharp relief.

Chapter Eleven

Laurie went home and waited for her hair to fall out.

It didn't take long. A few days, in which nervous well-meaning friends arrived with plants and grapes, Gloria dispensed co-enzymes reputed to inhibit the growth of tumours, Robert's wife flew in from Washington, and Shelley announced she had a new man, details to follow when, or if, she promised, 'things firm up'.

Then the first strands began to appear on Laurie's pillow.

Another day, and the strands became tufts. Then the tufts became clumps, and finally she summoned Shelley with a razor to take off the rest.

It was curiously purging, watching the last resistant locks fall to the floor, like a novice preparing for first vows, or an alien graduating from Star Fleet Academy.

'Pity you don't have the ears,' said Shelley as they gazed into the mirror together, 'Mr Spock would love you.'

But Mr Spock, of course, never loved anyone, which was always the great challenge.

Laurie felt herself surrounded and smothered by love, at one time both gratified and intimidated. She wanted support, but she didn't want sympathy, she wanted encouragement, but she didn't want false hope. She wanted, no less, the warm disinterest of Dr Dale Mitchell and his doctrine of regeneration.

But here she was disappointed.

She rang Crompton Hall, only to be greeted by an unknown woman who'd never heard of her.

'Sorry . . . Dale isn't here. Are you a patient?'

'I'm a client,' Laurie said testily. 'Can I speak to Ruth Christianos?'

'Ruth isn't here either . . . Did you want to make a booking?' Laurie closed her eyes and ran a hand across the smooth, shiny skin of her head. Crompton Hall with its spirits and phantoms seemed tantalizingly close, so much a part of her thinking that she hardly knew where her own psyche ended and India's began. But she didn't want Crompton Hall without Dale Mitchell.

'When will he be back?'

'That depends,' said the woman annoyingly. 'But you can make a booking anyway. All the classes are still going on.'

Laurie decided she would wait a week. That would leave another week until her next chemo. A week in Norfolk would restore and refresh her, even if she did no more than sit in the kitchen garden beneath the fig tree.

Meantime she had her family to appease, Gloria who always became alarmingly forthright whenever Elspeth rode into town, Robert, who always seemed to shrink in the combined presence of his wives, and Elspeth herself, who invariably succeeded, with unerring American directness, to home in on the unmentionable.

'Honey, you look just wonderful,' she said, greeting Laurie with an extravagant kiss and a customary bunch of preposterous blooms. 'I do believe you're losing weight!'

'No, she isn't!' said Robert, panic-stricken.

'Silly me,' said Elspeth smoothly. 'I simply meant you were looking a little more svelte than when I saw you last time . . . Maybe it's love! Where's that gorgeous young blond you had snapping at your heels? What was his name?'

'I told you,' Robert whispered desperately, 'Sean is no longer around!'

Laurie laughed. She was fond of Elspeth, for all the curious resemblance her manner bore to Gloria's. Robert Davison had replaced his first wife with another woman remarkably like her, and the fact that Laurie found Elspeth disarmingly outrageous made her realize how she might admire Gloria, if only she weren't her mother.

'I'm a single girl again,' she told Elspeth. 'I rather like it that way.'

'Honey, I know what you mean,' said Elspeth, worryingly. Nobody mentioned the hair.

So far, Laurie hadn't produced her *Baywatch* wig, hiding her bald head with a selection of silk scarves and wide-brimmed hats. But so far, she hadn't been out. The moment would come, she knew, but she preferred to choose it herself and make her first hairless foray into the world alone.

Two days later, she decided she was ready.

The morning was bright and unbearably sweet, like Eden after the fall. How terrible it must have been, to stand in view of Paradise and know you'd lost it for ever. Why had she never understood that before?

She took the wig from its cardboard box and approached the mirror uncertainly. Already she was used to being bald, finding in her stark appearance a peculiar kind of comfort, as though all pretence had been stripped away and she saw herself clearly now, for the very first time.

She had also, to her initial shock, lost her eyelashes and brows, and so alarmed had she been by this unexpected defoliation that she'd called the ward sister at the hospital to inquire if this was usual.

'Most of your body hair will go, including your pubes,' said the sister dryly. 'But wait for it, not the hairs on your legs! Those little buggers are too strong. You'll still need the Immac if you want to wear your bikini . . .'

Laurie's face, as she stared into the mirror, was perfectly smooth and clear, like a baby's, except that her cheeks were not plump, they were gaunt. Elspeth was right, she was looking skinny. She rang the ward sister again, fear constricting her chest like a vice.

'You're bound to lose weight,' said the sister, kindly and reassuringly this time. 'You're going through a big trauma. It's like losing a lover or having your parents split up, only worse.'

Laurie grimaced into the phone.

'I've been there,' she muttered. 'When do I get back?'

'One day,' said the sister gently. 'Meantime, just keep on keeping on.'

There was, indeed, nothing else she could do. Gingerly,

she extracted the wavy blonde wig from its box and put it on. The effect was astonishing, so much so that she laughed aloud.

She had tried on fashion wigs before, but they were always spoiled by the abundance of hair crammed beneath, and Laurie's own colouring was so dark, so definite, that other shades simply looked odd.

But hairless, she was like a blank page, able to design herself in a new and hitherto unimagined way. She looked astonishing, unrecognizable from all that had gone before, a creature without history or future, sprung intact from her own drawing board.

She needed new clothes. Her old wardrobe with its safe labels and staid messages wouldn't do. Quickly, before she lost her nerve, she let herself out of the flat, half fearing her neighbours might mistake her for a burglar, half wanting to be challenged so she might reveal the full extent of the transformation.

But nobody called after her, nobody even looked at her, and she walked on in growing confidence.

She bought a shiny sweater and a slit skirt, a fake leopard-skin waistcoat and a pair of daft stilettos. She bought a black leather jacket and tight black jeans, and wished for a pair of Shelley's coffin earrings to complete the look. She bought outrageous make-up, scarlet, purple and shocking pink, and before a ladies' room mirror, she painted her naked face in its vulgar new colours.

I am Laurie Davison and I have cancer. There are no rules. I can do what I like. I can be who I want to be . . .

She stuffed her old clothes into a bag and pulled on the sweater and skirt, amazed at the image she cut with her crazy shoes and lurid face, determined to test her new identity, to use it for some secret purpose of her own.

It was Saturday afternoon, a busy time at Gloria's cafe. Should she stroll in and order a bowl of lentil soup, the plucky, resourceful daughter? Or should she call at her father's hotel and pretend to be a client of Elspeth's, the zany, eccentric stepdaughter?

It came to her as she walked out of the ladies' room and

into a queue of mothers and daughters, harassed women with toddlers and pre-schoolers.

Saturday afternoon! Sean's regular date with Tina and the twins.

Her new coolness toward Sean should have argued against any such idea, but she'd wondered about Tina for so long, imagining her in exquisite detail, her height, her hair, her clothes, her style. She'd never even seen a photograph, and all mild suggestions that the quicker they met the sooner prejudice might be set aside, foundered, every time, upon Sean's stony refusal.

'It wouldn't work. Anyway, she'd never agree. It would only upset us all . . .'

Laurie boarded the bus that would take her to Tina's home ground, heart hammering beneath her shiny new sweater, eyes alert for any sign that she'd been rumbled. Suppose someone saw her? One of her colleagues? Or a colleague of Sean's? That fellow, Jim, who'd wanted her to look at their new system? Or Sean himself, heaven forbid?

Then she shook off all misgivings. She was doing nothing unprincipled or vindictive, and the worst she faced was simple embarrassment. She mightn't even be able to find the house, or, having found it, catch anyone going in or out, and whatever happened, she was unrecognizable. There was no risk. She peered at her reflection in the window of the bus, pulling at a stray frond of the blonde wig, chivvying it back into line as though it really belonged to her. Yes, it was true. A stranger, bearing Laurie Davison's name and using her credit cards with impunity, had taken her place.

She got off the bus and looked around at the suburban high street, calculating the direction she should take. Although she'd never met Tina, she knew where she lived, and in truth, had often seen herself making this journey, knocking on Tina's front door and introducing herself, suggesting they sit down and try to work it out together, no blame, no shame, no recrimination . . .

How idiotic that now seemed, how futile, and how crass. Well, Tina could have her husband back, for that was surely what she deserved. Laurie just wanted to see her making the attempt.

She walked slowly, swinging a new shoulder bag that matched her new clothes, a dinky, swanky plastic bag, quite unlike the smart leather satchel she usually carried.

There was no hurry. Tina was a woman with precise requirements, this much Laurie knew. She liked Sean to arrive on time, ticked him off if he were late, and when he'd once arrived ten minutes early had refused, so he'd told Laurie, to open the door. There was still half an hour until the appointed meeting, unless things had changed in the meantime. Was that likely? She didn't think so. Sean wouldn't be going back to Tina, whatever he felt about the end of his affair with Laurie. Indeed, it was possible he'd already found someone else. Laurie had been with him long enough to document, in painful detail, his effect on women. They quivered, they simpered, or, as she herself had done, they openly lusted. It was the heart of his problem, and Tina's too, no doubt.

She wandered into a chemist's store and began to browse through a display of sunglasses. She usually favoured tortoiseshell frames, the kind sensible businesswomen wore when they travelled abroad, and this time she chose a dark, dramatic pair, shiny black with specks of diamanté on the wings. No sense in half measures now.

Back on the street, shades in place, she suddenly spotted Sean. He was coming out of the Co-op, a carrier bag in his hand. He was on his way, and feeling faintly ridiculous, Laurie followed.

So what? I'm a sick woman. I can do what I like.

They dawdled along the high street, only a dozen yards between them, and then, improbably, he turned into a florist's, emerging a few moments later with a feeble-looking bunch of carnations. *Flowers for Tina! Oh, infamy . . .*

Laurie had to fight the urge to run up to him and wrap the carnations round his face.

So who's an All-Out Bastard after all?

He stopped and looked in an estate agent's window, killing time. She pressed her nose against the glass of a menswear store, weighing up the relative merits of striped socks, plain socks, spotted socks, sports socks . . . Sean walked on.

It was extraordinarily easy, shadowing someone who didn't have a clue they were under surveillance, who wouldn't imagine anyone would wish to follow them, and who'd never recognize the stalker if they did. Laurie soon realized she ran no risk of discovery, and she dared to close the distance between them.

Together they looked into a bookshop window. The new Jeffrey Archer, a pile of tomes about New Age prophecies, a low-fat cookbook . . .

Then he glanced across at her. Laurie's hand flew to her sun specs, cramming them tight against her nose. She swung the dinky bag onto her other shoulder and shook her blonde curls. Sean looked away.

She temporarily lost her nerve and scuttled into the bookshop, grabbing the first book that presented itself and rushing to pay, fearful that she'd lose him if she lingered too long. But when she got outside again, there he was, still only a few paces ahead of her, still dawdling.

What the hell am I doing? Maybe I've finally cracked. But maybe I'll be dead in six months. Wouldn't every girl with a married lover do this if only she had the gall? If there weren't so much to lose? And here am I with tons of gall and bugger all to lose . . .

Laurie drew breath.

She could go home now with no harm done, no deception perpetrated. That was the sensible thing to do. She no longer cared for Sean, so why was she here?

She walked on.

When he turned off the main road, she hesitated. While she might easily pass for a nonchalant shopper on the high street, among the smart semis, she'd look like a refugee from the Rover's Return. *Bet Lynch on a bad day*.

Yet still she followed, a novice mountaineer roped to an unseeing guide, drawn on by a compulsion that both startled and intrigued. Why was she behaving this way? Had the chemo really driven her crazy?

Sean had arrived at his destination, a gentrified Edwardian villa with mortgage payments, Laurie knew, that were all but crippling. She also knew he'd been trying to persuade Tina to move, a step which might have hastened their own marriage. Now she could think only that if she were Tina, she wouldn't move either. She'd hang on to this swish house in this elegant street just as long as she could.

Make the bastard pay. Don't let him get away with it.

He was ringing the doorbell. Laurie walked past, risking a glance. He had his back to her, and the door remained shut. Perhaps he was early again.

She couldn't loiter, and she couldn't stare. She would have to walk on, but where to? What would they do?

The door opened and Laurie took to her heels, careering down the street like a hooker who'd sighted a potential catch, which was how she suddenly perceived herself in her tight slit skirt and tarty blonde wig.

Shit. It's true. I'm a crazy bitch . . .

She fled away from the house not knowing where she was going, stumbling on her unfamiliar shoes, feeling the blonde wig slip against her smooth scalp, fearing for one frightful moment that it would blow away and leave her standing, as good as naked.

When the park appeared at the bottom of the street, she gasped in relief, sprinting through the gates and sinking on to the nearest bench, trembling with emotion and effort.

She felt foolish and fed up. She'd blown it after all. She hadn't so much as caught sight of Tina. Laurie dumped her shopping on the seat beside her and extracted the book she had bought.

Face Your Demons and Live to Fight Another Day.

She tossed it back into her bag, and in the next moment saw Sean at the park gate, a slight auburn-haired woman walking beside him, two fair-headed seven-year-olds gambolling in front.

So here, at last, was Tina, at once both prettier and more ordinary than Laurie had imagined, dressed in T-shirt and jeans, her face open and smiling as though she hadn't a care in the world. Maybe Sean had been spinning a line all these months, claiming Tina still loved him when in truth she was happy to let him go. Or maybe the flowers had been a peace offering now that he were free again . . .

Laurie swallowed hard.

So what? None of it matters any more.

They walked on toward the benches, and Laurie fumbled for her book again, burying her face between the pages.

'*Are you hung up and stressed out by the strains of modern life? Do you have secret fears you can share with no one?*'

They sat down on the bench behind her.

'Can we go on the big slide?' asked one twin.

'Yes,' said Tina, 'if Daddy catches you at the bottom.'

'Okay,' Sean said easily.

'Let's go on the swings first,' said the other twin. 'Watch us, Daddy! We don't need a push.'

They ran in front of Laurie and careered across the grass toward the swings. Sean and Tina turned on their bench, and Laurie began to sweat beneath her wig. His eyes were less than a yard from the back of her head. Surely he must see?

She waited in agony, scarcely daring to breathe, wondering what they might say next. Suppose she overheard something intimate, something which revealed the true nature of their dealings with each other? How could she bear it?

There was a long pause in which the twins swung ever harder and higher, and their parents watched and waved. Laurie could hear her heart beating, and she'd begun to feel sick. Perhaps it really was the chemo, or perhaps it was the intuition of the eavesdropper that something momentous was about to follow.

'So,' said Sean at last when the silence had begun to seem interminable, 'how's it going with the baked beans?'

'Well, she just won't eat them,' Tina replied.

'I thought all kids liked baked beans?'

'Not this one,' Tina said.

The normality was unbearable. Laurie rammed *Face Your Demons* back into her shopping bag and stood up. She felt light-headed, as though she were drunk and might do something regrettable at any moment, like throw up or fall down, or burst into a chorus of 'God Save the Queen' . . . Better to go before the temptation became too much.

'When did you say you were going to Norfolk?' said Tina to Sean as Laurie gathered up her shopping. 'I need to know where you'll be . . .'

'The week after next,' he answered.

Laurie froze.

'And you're just going to see if you can find your grandad's old place?' Tina said sharply. 'There's no other reason?'

'There's no other reason.'

'And you're going on your own?'

'I'm going on my own,' he said steadily. 'You can call me there if you like. It's a place called Blue Farm.'

Laurie, stunned, let a parcel fall to the ground.

'Sean, swear to me there's no one else,' Tina muttered.

'Look, I've told you before . . . There's no one else . . . Just let it go, will you?'

Laurie, trembling, picked up her parcel and crept away.

She rode home in a rage, unable to believe what she'd over-heard, yet seeing only too well how she'd been deceived. Suddenly, Sean's refusal to introduce his daughters became intelligible. *Tina knew nothing about her!* What fools they'd both been.

And yet how commonplace, how brutally banal, it all was. Every agony page in every woman's magazine could tell the same story . . . *Dear Auntie, My husband has left me because we weren't getting on. He's moved into a flat, but he swears there's no one else involved . . . How can I get him to come home?*

It was questionable, who'd been the most stupid.

Dear Auntie, My boyfriend is married, but will soon be getting divorced. He has two children, but he won't let me meet them. How can I persuade him it would be better if we all learned to get along?

And what might be the advice to such misused wives and

lovers? *Get rid of this charmer at once! You both deserve better than him* . . .

Laurie could barely control her fury. She would write to Tina the moment she got home and tell her the whole tale . . . And she would kill whoever had revealed her own Norfolk plans to Sean! It could only be Gloria or Shelley, and one of them was about to experience her wrath.

Back in the flat, she phoned her mother at once.

'Did you tell anyone I was going to back to Norfolk?'

Gloria was puzzled, and registering her daughter's mood, plainly upset, her delight at Laurie's decision to return to Crompton Hall replaced by uncertainty. She might have mentioned it to a few friends, *as one would*, and of course, to Robert and Elspeth.

'But not to Sean?' Laurie could hardly bear to speak his name.

Gloria hesitated.

'Darling, I haven't spoken to him in days . . . Not since Shelley told him you didn't want picking up from Norfolk, and he rang to ask me why . . .'

'That's a lie,' Laurie shouted. 'He came to see me in hospital. He said you told him it would be a good idea.'

Gloria faltered.

'Well, I thought it would be . . . And he seemed so unhappy . . . But that was all I said . . . Darling . . . What's going on?'

Laurie slammed down the phone and called Shelley.

A long pause greeted her terse inquiry.

'I might have let it drop,' Shelley confessed at last.

'How could you do that?' Laurie shrieked into the phone. 'And why are you seeing Sean anyway? Good Grief! He's not your new man, is he?'

'Don't be ridiculous,' said Shelley coldly. 'No married men for me, thank you very much! I'm coming over . . .'

By the time she arrived, Laurie had begun to take stock. She was behaving like a lunatic, disguising herself, following people around, shouting down the phone at her family and friends, planning to contact Tina. She would have to calm down.

She opened the door, a hairless creature again with a silk turban wound around her bare scalp, her new clothes ditched for a familiar shirt and jeans.

'Sorry,' she mumbled tearfully, 'I've had a bad day . . .'

'I'm sorry too,' said Shelley gruffly. 'That was a bitchy crack about married men . . . But really! Me and Sean?'

Laurie bit her lip.

'I didn't honestly think that . . . But I've begun to think Sean's capable of anything. I've just realized he's never told Tina a thing about me . . . She doesn't know I exist. She probably thinks he'll go back to her if she gives him long enough! And for all I know, she's probably right . . .'

Shelley looked at her carefully.

'How do you know all this?'

Her face changed from concern to incredulity as the tale unfolded, and by the end, when they'd examined the new clothes, Shelley had tried on the *Baywatch* wig, and the whole lot had been dumped at the back of the wardrobe, they were both laughing.

'You sat right next to him, and he didn't know?'

'It was like something out of Phillip Marlowe! I could have a whole new career in CID . . .'

'And he's off to Norfolk? He did ask me if you were going back, but I didn't know he was planning anything himself . . . Far be it from me to defend him, but he's very upset, Laurie . . . His friends are quite worried about him.'

Laurie raised one eyebrow.

'Okay, here it comes . . . My new man is Jim. You remember him? He works with Sean. That's how I met him.'

'Your new man?'

'He's not all *that* new. I mean, he can cook spaghetti bolognese, but I can't see him doing the hoovering . . . It was while you were away. I bumped into Sean at the pub, weeping into his whisky. Jim was with him.'

Laurie said nothing, and Shelley took her hand.

'He's in shock,' she said quietly. 'He knows he's handled it badly, but he doesn't know how to put it right. I'd guess that's why he's going to Norfolk . . . Maybe he thinks he'll meet you in the woods, and then you'll make mad passionate love and it will all be okay . . .'

Laurie closed her eyes.

'If he can't handle things at the moment,' she said curtly, 'then he's better off out of it. Pretty soon I'm going to have one breast hacked off. How do you think he'd cope with that?'

Shelley looked away.

'I don't know,' she muttered, 'but I feel he deserves the chance to find out. I feel sorry for him, that's the truth of it . . .'

'And sorry for Tina?'

'Look, Jim has told me things about Tina I didn't know before,' Shelley said cautiously. 'Maybe it's not the way it appears . . .'

Laurie fought the urge to ask what things. She wasn't in the mood for mitigation, nor did she believe there could be any.

'So Jim's not an AOB, then?' she said coolly. 'More of a Creep, by the sound of it.'

Shelley knew when she was beaten.

'Jim's got a few AOB tendencies,' she grinned, 'but he has other talents to compensate . . .'

'So things firmed up, did they?'

'Oh yes,' said Shelley smiling. 'Things firmed up very nicely, thanks.'

'Good. I'm glad. But please don't tell him anything more about me. And if you see Sean, tell him to keep out of my way.'

'So you won't be seeing him in Norfolk?'

'I don't know. I might. If I do I'll tell him to get the hell out and stop spying on me . . .'

Their eyes met, although the thought remained unspoken.

You've been spying on him, haven't you?

Laurie pulled off her turban and flung it on to the sofa beside her.

I'm the one looking over the edge of the abyss. I'm the one with cancer. I'll do what the hell I like . . .

'I'm very tired,' she mumbled apologetically. 'It's been a long day. All that stalking takes it out of a girl . . .'

Laurie bought a new wig, coal black like her own hair, but fashioned in a short, springy style, the kind of cut she'd often fancied but never got round to trying. It suited her, imparting a fragile, almost haunted look, framing the lashless eyes and curling its lifelike tendrils around her narrowing cheekbones. It was true she was losing weight, an unlooked-for bonus that reflected nothing so much as her total disinclination to eat.

Gloria, unnerved by Elspeth's comments on the matter, had taken drastic steps. A succession of unlikely delicacies began to arrive at Laurie's door, banoffi pie and chocolate brownies, almond croissants and blueberry muffins.

'I thought I was on a low-fat diet?'

'Well, darling you are . . . There's a lot of evidence to link cancer with fatty Western foods . . . But a little won't hurt, and you need to treat yourself . . .'

This was so far removed from Gloria's usual philosophy that it caused Laurie to pause. Things had to be bad to get Gloria baking banoffi pie. Maybe Laurie hadn't fully registered her mother's distress. Maybe she would drop in at Gloria's and eat something wholesome, an act of contrition.

Her arrival, however, caused surprise and, Laurie detected, a certain consternation, as though she'd been under discussion and, in her absence, agreement reached. And now, before they were quite ready, the verdict had to be announced.

Gloria was sitting at the supper table with Robert and Elspeth, a vat of cauliflower goulash between them, a bottle of best Bordeaux all but drunk. An improbable aroma drifted on the air above the table, freshly brewed coffee. The discussion had clearly turned serious.

Gloria jumped to her feet at once.

'Darling, we've been ringing you all afternoon . . . Where on earth have you been?'

Laurie pointed to the new wig, and they chorused approval. *How natural it looks! The style really suits you!*

Her father motioned her to the table and Gloria began to ladle out the goulash. Elspeth, horror of horrors, took out a cigarette, and catching her husband's eye, put it away again.

They all looked at Laurie, willing her to eat.

She took a mouthful and forced it down, wondering how long it would take them to state their case.

Robert began at once.

'We've been talking about you, Laurie,' he said gently. 'Trying to work out what might be best . . . We don't want to make your decisions for you, but we want you to know you have our total support . . .'

He hesitated, and Laurie felt her throat tighten.

'We all feel, your mother included, that you should give up this Norfolk idea, and come back home with us . . . You'll get the very best treatment there. And we can look after you . . . Who knows, you might even feel you wanted to stay in Washington. Meet new people . . . Begin a new life. Just say you'll think about it.'

Laurie looked up at Gloria, knowing what this capitulation must have cost, and felt her heart lurch in pity. She smiled at her father and reached out to squeeze Elspeth's hand.

'Thank you both . . . But I belong here. And I have to go back to Norfolk. Somehow, I feel that Crompton Hall holds the key to my recovery . . .'

She hadn't meant to sound so melodramatic, and her face flushed in mild embarrassment. Yet nobody seemed surprised, except perhaps Gloria, who reached for the coffee pot and poured herself a second cup, darting a disbelieving glance at her daughter.

'You really think this Dale Mitchell guy is on the level?' Elspeth, doubtful, was treading warily.

'I don't know,' Laurie said frankly. 'But it's got nothing to do with him. He's not the reason I want to go back . . .'

They gazed at her, waiting. 'It's not Sean is it?' Gloria asked nervously, and Laurie swallowed an instinctive reproach.

'It's nothing to do with Sean or anyone else. It's all to do with me and my imagination . . .'

She laughed self-consciously, hearing her own uncertainty.

'I feel I have another life there,' she faltered. 'Someone else's life . . . A life that's long since over . . .'

They exchanged glances.

'This Mitchell guy does hypnotic regression?' Elspeth was fighting incredulity.

'Nothing so vulgar,' Laurie said, laughing again. 'And anyway, it's more complex than that . . . As though something is unfolding before me, a story which will one day have an ending . . .'

As all stories do! What's your story, Laurie? Everyone has a story . . .

She closed her eyes against their anxious expressions, and a vista of the beech woods rose to greet her, cool green in the evening air, shivering beneath a spangled Norfolk sky.

She longed to be there, and knew she had to return at the earliest moment, no matter that Sean might be there too, or that he might try to see her.

She opened her eyes again.

'This is my story,' she said quietly, 'and I'm in the middle of it.'

Chapter Twelve

The Hall was thrown into mourning, blinds drawn, windows shuttered, engagements cancelled. The family departed to London for Elizabeth Bonham's funeral and swiftly returned, subdued and sorry. The unexpected demise of one so vibrant, so hearty, and at forty-nine Lady Crompton's elder by a mere two years, was tragedy indeed.

Her Ladyship took to her chamber, ordering camomile tea upon the hour. Sir Robin, sensing that his family needed him but having had little practice in answering any such need, retired to the library, bracing himself for calls upon his sympathy. Christian, who'd found himself overlooked in his aunt's will when he'd been counting upon a mention, retreated into gloomy introspection, confiding to Alice that he urgently needed a change in his luck. And India, grieving for a beloved aunt whose wise counsel and careful intervention on delicate family matters had so often averted discord, sank into melancholy.

She'd trusted that Aunt Bonham would take her side in the controversy concerning Adam Goodchild, certain her aunt would argue against accepting a man one did not love. Nothing else, India felt, was likely to restore Lady Crompton's good opinion of her daughter, but now this route back to domestic harmony was cruelly lost.

India absorbed herself in her journal, pouring out her troubled heart to its uncritical pages.

We turn ceaselessly on a wheel of suffering which only the conquering of desire can still . . . We are sparks of life which must one day be extinguished in the dust . . .

Alice, her usual confidante and adviser in such weighty matters, had proved preoccupied and distant, and Sir Robin, to whom India had turned in a moment of desperation, answered his daughter's philosophical inquiries with the brusque comment that 'all any of us can do is to live virtuously before we are extinguished', a well-meaning and sensible maxim which, nevertheless, didn't help at all. Alice would surely have offered something more encouraging.

But in truth a certain coolness had characterized relationships between Alice and India since the rejection of Adam Goodchild, a coolness, India knew, which was largely of her own making. Alice had made no secret of her admiration for Adam, seeing in him a rare humanity and uncommon spirit. The two women had often discussed him. No, Adam was not handsome. Yes, he was generous and kind. No, he did not like flirtation. Yes, he had an honest heart. The talks had been light-hearted, rarely aspiring to more serious intent, and India had believed that Alice understood her reservations. But now it seemed she did not. Little had been said between them on the matter of the proposal, but it had been enough.

'I pray you will find another man equally worthy of your hand,' Alice had said, her tone implying to India that such an event were all but impossible.

'Am I to marry a man I don't love?' India snapped in response, 'I should rather die an old maid like you . . .'

She wished very much that she'd never said such a thing, but she could not retract it, or rather, no opportunity for retraction presented itself. The morning after this exchange, the family had departed for London, without Alice who might normally have been expected to attend India, but whose measure with Lady Crompton was still wanting, despite the threat of dismissal having lifted.

Then when India had barely returned from the funeral, Alice asked for leave of absence to nurse her sick mother.

The request was made not to India, but directly to Lady Crompton, who then communicated the news to her daughter.

'We can manage perfectly well without her,' India was told. 'And I dare say she may never return . . . If the mother dies, then someone will have to look after the young brother . . . That will solve our problem.'

India was horrified, and ran to find Alice at once, wishing only to throw herself into the arms of her beloved companion, beg her forgiveness and implore her to return as quickly as possible. An unworthy thought came to her as she hurried to the driveway. *If Nell Harper dies, Ivy would be best placed to take the young brother* . . .

It was only when she arrived at the door to see the carriage pull away that she realized she'd given no thought to Alice's anxiety over her mother's health, nor planned so much as a word of sympathy. Heavy of heart, she watched until the carriage disappeared into the lane, resolving to wait no more than a day before visiting the Harper cottage with soup and elderflower jelly. But would Alice be glad to see her? Would she readily forget that remark about remaining an old maid? India, much affected by this new loss so soon after her bereavement, found herself close to tears.

It was in this delicate and vulnerable condition that Luke Harte came upon her, and who is to say that in other circumstances, even without a chaperone present or a mother presiding, their encounter might not have proved entirely unremarkable?

As it was, the doctor having been summoned to attend Lady Crompton, and on arrival learning that Her Ladyship was now sleeping soundly, the scene was set for an unusual exchange.

He seemed initially flustered, as he so often did in India's presence.

'I intended to give Her Ladyship a sedative,' he muttered, offering an embarrassed greeting and opening his black bag, 'but it seems she doesn't need it. I shall leave it anyway, but I suggest a little brandy might do as well as anything once she wakes . . .'

India, who had been standing by the window gazing out into the driveway as though she hoped Alice might materialize at any moment, turned to him, her face deeply troubled, her blue eyes bright with emotion.

'I thank you indeed, Doctor Harte . . . A little brandy might be the best answer for us all . . .'

She smiled, a wan, distant shadow of her normal gaiety.

'My dear Miss Crompton . . . India . . . May I offer my condolences on the death of your aunt? I know only too well that in these circumstances so little can be said . . .'

A tear escaped India's eye and rolled down her cheek. She wiped it away hurriedly.

'Please say to me whatever you would say to anyone else in such a situation, Doctor Harte! I long for words of comfort . . .'

He moved toward her, an imperceptible shortening of the physical distance between them, and yet an act of drawing close.

'I would say that the dead would wish us to go on living, and living happily . . . That although suffering may be the destiny of all mankind, we do ourselves no service by dwelling upon it . . . That we cannot allow disease, disaster or death to rob us of our hopefulness, nor dilute our purpose to better the condition of ourselves and our fellows . . .'

They were passionate words, spoken with an urgency that seemed to surprise Luke Harte himself, and India could hardly mistake them for platitudes.

'I know you're right,' she murmured meeting his earnest gaze, 'and yet I'm afraid I lack courage . . .'

She buried her face in her hands.

'It isn't only my aunt's death that distresses me,' she heard herself say, 'although that is the greatest grief. But there are other things . . . Mama is very angry with me. She has threatened to send Alice away, and now Alice has indeed gone and may not return . . .'

He seemed to recollect himself, the doctor remembering that a prospective patient stood before him, needing his professional advice, albeit upon a non-medical matter. He listened carefully, his expression calm and grave, his fleeting eagerness of a few moments before replaced by a tempered interest.

'I can't believe that Alice won't come back to you,' he said kindly. 'It's my impression that she loves you dearly, indeed that the two of you are more like companions than employer and servant . . .'

She looked up at him gratefully, feeling he had struck to the heart of the matter, seeing her true grief where others might have imagined petulance or simple self-interest on the matter of a missing maid.

'That is so,' she concurred, 'and it makes me all the more unhappy. Doctor Harte, I have been most unkind to Alice . . .' Another tear escaped India's eye, and the professional doctor vanished once more.

'I cannot believe it!' he said ardently. 'You could not be unkind to anyone!'

If she caught the admiration in his words, then she succeeded in concealing the response it called forth, but when she looked at him this time, it was with a new intimation of his regard.

She shook her head.

'I told Alice that I'd rather die an old maid like her than . . .'

She hesitated, fearing to reveal too much, yet driven on by the desire to have him know her situation.

'Than what?' he inquired gently, the slight upon Alice entirely overlooked in his need to hear the whole of it.

India took a shuddering breath and closed her eyes.

'Than marry Adam Goodchild,' she finished miserably. 'Although I do agree that he's the finest of men, and the most one might ever wish for in a husband. But Doctor Harte . . .'

He knew it then, yet still he wished to hear her say it.

'But what?' he pursued.

She gazed at him, trembling in the unwelcome realization of turbulent emotions and consequent woes.

'When I marry, I want it to be for love . . . For that blessed union of two souls who find in each other their counter-selves . . . Do you understand me?'

He swallowed hard, and when he moved to take her hand, his words were muffled.

'I do understand,' he whispered. 'We should all desire such a union, but the truth is that most of us have to settle for something far less . . .'

Her hand still lay in his and they looked down at it

together, bemused, as though they had been joined, not by the simple act of one person reaching out for another, but by some force beyond themselves. Perhaps it was this strange sensation of sacrificed control that allowed India to ask her next question.

'Why did you marry Eugenie?' she inquired faintly.

Now she saw that he too seemed overcome with turbulent emotion, and she watched while he struggled for an answer.

'Because I saw her to be a fine woman,' he said at last. 'As fine a prospect for a wife as Adam Goodchild might be for a husband . . . Honest, faithful, reliable and diligent. And I have not been disappointed . . .'

Yet he looked deeply disappointed, and despite herself, India felt a lifting of her heart.

'There is nothing more?' she pressed him, hardly knowing if she were demanding further detail of his sentiments, or whether she hoped for some new revelation concerning his marriage.

He swallowed again, as though he fought against the truth, or perhaps simply against the declaration of it, then made his decision.

'Eugenie's father was my benefactor,' he said at last. 'Without him, I would never have become a doctor. At that time both his daughters were engaged to be married. But both of them were heartlessly deceived by their suitors . . . Indeed, Frederica's reputation was scandalously imperilled, and Eugenie had to endure a bitter rejection . . . Her fiancé abandoned her for a wealthier woman . . .'

He still held India's hand in his, and now he was stroking the fingers lightly, a delicate, sensuous movement that seemed largely unconscious, an absent, innocent making of love. India felt her flesh thrill, as though she'd passed from the icy air of a winter's afternoon into the radiance of a blazing parlour fire.

'There was no pressure put upon me,' he was saying. 'No suggestion that I owed anything to the man who had paid my college bills from the very goodness of his heart . . . Yet I felt my duty keenly. I wished to relieve the family of some distress . . . And I believed I could offer myself as a suitable husband. It was then a question of whether I might choose Eugenie or Frederica . . . And it seemed to me Eugenie would make the more suitable wife . . .'

India had begun to feel a certain unreality descend upon her, the extraordinary sensation of finding herself alone with a man who, she now saw, answered all her hopes for a husband, noble, clever, kind, and yes, *desirable*. She trembled to think it, and yet, it was true. Luke Harte was desirable in a way that Adam Goodchild could never be. And he was married to another woman.

'A suitable husband,' she repeated distractedly. 'And a suitable wife! You will forgive my saying that such a thing hardly sounds exciting or loving . . .'

He bowed his head.

'Not exciting,' he agreed, 'and yet not unloving. There are many different ways to love, India . . . And my way has been to provide a home and a family for a woman who desired only that . . .'

India suddenly withdrew her hand and began to pace the length of the drawing room.

'And you, Doctor Harte,' she challenged, 'what do you desire?'

He faltered, he ran a hand through his hair.

'I have desired a quiet family life with no unnecessary distraction,' he said uncomfortably, 'such as any professional man might wish for . . .'

She moved back to the window where he stood, subdued and uncertain, as she herself now was.

'Forgive me,' she whispered, 'I have no right to question you in such a manner . . . I don't know what's come over me . . . The shock of my aunt's death . . . The loss of Alice, and of Adam too! I might not have wanted to marry him, but he was my dearest friend . . . Perhaps I, too, should have settled for a quiet family life . . .'

A sob escaped her, and he raised a hand to her face, smoothing away a tear.

'Never do that, India,' he murmured. 'Never settle for less than you deserve . . .'

She met his gaze and held it.

'But you have done that . . . And you have not regretted it . . .'

He smiled, and if such a thing had been imaginable, she
might have thought she glimpsed a tear in his own eye.

'Until this moment, no,' he said.

Despite her earlier resolve, India did not set out for the
Harper cottage the following day.

Instead she fretted in her bedroom, languishing upon the
tapestry quilt Alice had worked for her birthday gift and
gazing moodily out of the window toward the lake.

How empty and unrewarding did all future days now
seem, how bleak and joyless loomed the prospect of another
week, another month, another year and then the endless
years, of life without the man she loved.

Equally disturbing was the knowledge that she had no
one to share her sorrow, no wise aunt to dry her tears and
comfort her with tales of sacrificial love, no companion to
offer friendly advice or sisterly support. And no parent in
whom she might confide.

Regretfully, India forced herself to face an unhappy
conclusion. Her mother was a creature devoid of finer
feeling. She would never understand, much less embrace,
her daughter's distress. And her father, though he might
have understood, or even experienced the phenomenon of
thwarted love, was unable to communicate any insight. Frequently absent, invariably distant and relentlessly absorbed
by his notion of public duty, he had established no pre-
cedent for talking to his children. Little wonder, India
considered with an unexpected flash of contempt, that he'd
raised a daughter he barely knew and a libertine of a son.

And yet, she could not harden her heart toward her
family, nor could she believe that somewhere in the bosom
of those she loved, a pulse did not beat in sympathy. She
rose from her bed and went in search of Christian.

He was practising croquet shots upon the lawn, as
futile and indulgent a pastime as India could imagine

in that moment, and she paused on the terrace, dismayed.

He raised the mallet, swung it in the air, then saw her watching and waved.

'At last!' he called. 'Someone to talk to!'

He flung down the mallet and walked across the lawn toward her, his face open and smiling, a young man in the prime of life without a care to trouble him nor a vocation to ennoble him. India was shaken by an unexpected anger. Her brother was scarcely worthy to call himself a Crompton.

'I wanted to talk as well,' she began as he approached, but he interrupted her cheerily.

'I was starting to think we should be in mourning for ever!' he said. 'And I really can't believe my Aunt Bonham would have approved such a thing. She would surely wish us to be jolly.'

India shook her head and said nothing.

'There is a deep illogicality at the heart of our national faith,' he continued, taking her arm and steering her across the lawn, 'as I tried to point out to Mama this morning! Either we believe a glorious heaven awaits us – as we profess every Sunday in church – or we think that our life ends with death. Now, we all know this to be a heresy of the very worst kind . . . So what is the conclusion we must draw?'

He was walking her toward the beech woods, and all she could think was that she did not have her hat.

'What is the conclusion?' she asked him dully.

'My dear India, it's obvious!' he laughed. 'When a person dies, we should immediately begin upon a riotous celebration. Singing and dancing and drinking . . . A rare old party . . . What better way to assert our belief in the resurrection of the dead? They've gone to a happier place, so why are we sitting around with long faces? You see what I mean . . . It makes no sense!'

India was silent.

'You could extend the logic to fatal illness . . . Why weep and moan when someone contracts consumption or a fever epidemic strikes? The victims are privileged indeed! They're out of the vale of tears and off to meet their maker.'

She looked up at him dismissively, not knowing if he might be serious for once, or whether his habitual need for joking had blinded him to the fallacy of his arguments.

'Mourning isn't for the dead,' she said at last. 'It's for the living. We grieve for ourselves, not for those who've gone before . . .'

He punched the air, still laughing.

'Well, that just proves my point! If it's all about us and our feelings, then we can choose whether to be happy or sad, whichever suits us best. And I choose happiness, India. This is my way of mourning.'

She withdrew her arm from his. A wiser companion might have perceived his intention to shock, or at least to irritate, but India, consumed by gravity, saw only unthinking frivolity, and would have considered herself even more sorely misused had she imagined provocation.

'I don't want to walk,' she snapped. 'It's too hot and I don't have my hat.'

But Christian was not to be denied this slender opportunity for diversion, and he grabbed her arm again, marching her into the woods, declaring that her head needed no covering under the trees, and that once they reached the lake, they would surely find one of her hats in the summerhouse.

She allowed herself to be led because the alternative was a return to her lonely bedroom, and because she longed to share the secrets of her heart. But a new heaviness had settled upon her in the light of Christian's remarks, and for the first time she found herself staring into the chasm that divided their perception. Christian would no more understand her love for Luke Harte than she might endorse his own dalliance with Kitty Malone.

Yet on some matters, there seemed unspoken agreement between them. They had reached the path which led to the elephant's compound, but neither of them so much as looked in Polly's direction. India's birthday gift was rarely mentioned, and more rarely visited. Polly's care had fallen largely to Alice, and India hardly liked to examine her feelings on the subject. When she thought of Polly she felt only disgust.

'Has there been a message from Alice?' Christian asked her. 'I do hope her Mama isn't going to follow dear Aunt Bonham through the pearly gates. That would be rather tiresome . . .'

There had been no message from Alice, nor had India expected one, and she told him so, curtly.

He frowned.

'You are cross with poor old Alice, aren't you? And all because she felt you should consider Adam Goodchild? Well, I shall tell you this, as the subject's finally come up . . . I thought you plucky at first for refusing Adam. He really is a frightful bore, and sanctimonious with it . . . But now I wonder if you haven't been a little hasty? The Goodchild estate, though hardly comparable to our own, is nevertheless one of the richest in the county. Supposing I were to wed Marianne and you'd accepted Adam? Between us we'd own half the land worth having from Norwich to the sea . . .'

India looked up at him in disbelief.

'You will never wed Marianne,' she said steadily. 'I thought you knew that. Adam won't allow it.'

Christian let out a chuckle.

'I'll let you into a little secret,' he declared, clearly enjoying himself, 'Marianne loves me, and I consider her the very dearest of creatures . . . I might be tempted to say that I love her in return, though it is, perhaps, a rather different kind of love . . .'

He looked away for a moment and seemed to hesitate before resuming his customary banter.

'The point, my dear India, is that Adam is powerless to prevent us doing exactly as we please . . .'

They had reached the shore of the lake, but instead of walking to the summerhouse, Christian untied the boat and motioned her in.

'Do you want to row?' he asked her. 'You're rather good

at it, I always think . . . Then I could simply lie back and luxuriate.'

'You row!' India said curtly. Every word her brother spoke seemed destined to annoy her.

The *Lady of the Lake* swayed out from the bank and into the whispering sedge, its oars ploughing the dense vegetation and rising like festooned wings. India began to wish she were rowing after all. The motion might have calmed her thoughts. As it was, she felt giddy and sick. Had she truly imagined she might talk to Christian about her feelings for Luke? The very idea was now revealed as preposterous, and with this knowledge came a new and frightening sense of isolation. Her brother, like her father and her mother, could offer no bulwark against a cruel fate. Whatever she had to endure, she must endure it alone.

But the knowledge brought with it a curious kind of freedom. If Christian had no claim to know her secrets, nor she to influence his actions, then there was no need for delicacy, nor prevarication. She could say what she liked.

He had rowed the boat to the centre of the lake, and now they rested in the midst of the shimmering green, eyeing each other thoughtfully. India trailed a hand in the water and felt the sedge brush against her fingers, a living, swimming thing. She shuddered and took a deep breath.

'You are not worthy to be Marianne's husband,' she said gravely. 'She deserves a better man than you . . . I know all about it, you see, Christian. I know about you and Kitty Malone!'

His surprise was so great that he lurched toward her, grabbing her wrists and unsettling the boat.

'What do you know?' he demanded urgently. 'I've no idea what you're talking about!'

India shook her hands free and tried to stand up. The boat tilted dangerously.

'Sit down you stupid girl!' Christian roared, then seeing that he risked a serious upset, sat back. The boat steadied and he smiled uncertainly. 'What do you know?' he repeated.

'I know that you spent a night with Kitty Malone!' she

declared breathlessly. 'And that such behaviour does not become a prospective husband . . .'

A more wordly observer might have noted his evident relief, concluding that he'd escaped the exposing of some greater misdemeanour, but India did not, and so urgent was her own need for consolation that she allowed herself to accept his assurances.

'My fiery little sister,' he said laughing, leaning forward in the boat and kissing the hands he had so recently grabbed, 'how I wish we might all aspire to your high standards! But you have found me out, and I am deeply ashamed . . .'

She looked at him, believing she saw a mirror of her own confusion.

'Is that true?' she whispered. 'Are you resolved to change your ways?'

He smiled.

'I solemnly swear I shall never entertain Kitty Malone again,' he announced. 'And as for Marianne, may the best man win! If her brother can turn her heart against me, then so be it. But we shall see . . .'

'Adam intends to keep Marianne out of your way,' India said, shaking her head. 'That's why he's taken her to London. She's very young, Christian . . . Adam is only thinking of her happiness.'

He laughed again.

'Adam is only thinking of her fortune!' he retorted. 'If he cared for her happiness, he would encourage her to make up her own mind . . . But does he really believe that by removing Marianne from my company, he'll remove me from her thoughts? How foolish! Any lovestruck girl could have told him that the longer we're apart, the stronger her love will become . . .'

India said nothing, gazing at him dumbly.

'Come,' Christian said, pulling on the oars, 'I won't burden you with other confidences . . . Please, forget I ever spoke! You know nothing, and now we must go home to be with Mama and act the dutiful offspring . . . It's gone four o'clock.'

I won't burden you with other confidences . . .

India looked away, fighting her tears. There could be no sharing. There could be no meeting of minds, no shouldering of one another's woes. It was as she had thought. She, alone among all the Cromptons, must bear the burden of fine feeling. And instead of the communion of hearts, she now saw an unending charade in which trivia and pleasantry were all which might be offered.

She smiled distantly at her brother.

'Yes, we'd better get back,' she said quietly, 'Mama will be waiting on afternoon tea.'

India ordered the carriage after breakfast next morning, having first requested soup and jelly from Mrs Long.

The housekeeper did not relinquish her supplies readily, nor without evidence that Lady Crompton approved, and her insistence upon the usual sanction from above led to a delay in India's departure and a difficult exchange between mother and daughter.

'I shall be pleased to know Alice's intentions,' Lady Crompton said plainly. 'If she's unable to return within the week, then we will have to engage another maid . . .'

'I don't want another maid,' India said.

'It's not a question of what you want. A young lady in your position needs a personal maid. I've already made inquiries in the village. There's a girl called Amy who is recommended by the parsonage . . .'

'Alice will come back,' India said urgently, 'I know she will.'

'The mother is very ill,' Lady Crompton replied calmly. 'She has a swelling in the chest. Doctor Harte tells me it is serious.'

India faltered.

'Doctor Harte?' she whispered.

'He was here yesterday while you were out with Christian . . . Adam Goodchild had asked him to visit the Harper home that morning. It's very generous of Adam, I must say . . . The Harpers are no concern of his.'

India could hardly conceal her agitation. The knowledge

that Luke had returned, that she had missed him, that he had visited Alice's home, that his opinion might be instrumental in delaying Alice's return to Crompton Hall, that he might have hoped to see her and give her the news himself ... Such concerns drove out all nobler thoughts about the health of Nell Harper, about Alice's own anguish, or indeed, about the right course of action concerning Christian and Marianne. She had intended to confide in Alice and ask her advice, but now nothing seemed important except to discover what Alice planned to do.

She drove away in haste, riding through the lavender fields without so much as a glance at their purple beauty, past Blue Farm where she noted that Luke's carriage was missing from the driveway, and out to the perimeter of the fields where the Harper cottage stood. It was now nearly midday, and the blinds were closed. She feared she had come too late.

But then Alice opened the door, India almost fell from the carriage in her eagerness, and they were in each other's arms, kissing and exclaiming, all differences forgotten.

'Your mother?' India asked at last, quite overcome. 'How is she?'

'Doctor Harte has taken her to the cottage hospital ... He's going to perform an operation ...'

'But will she recover? Is there hope for her treatment? I had thought, with the blinds being drawn ...' These were hardly encouraging questions nor sentiments, but Alice, as ever, was unperturbed.

'There is always hope,' she said gently, 'but the illness can prove fatal ...'

'A swelling in the chest?'

Alice nodded. 'Doctor Harte plans to cut it out, but he can't yet say whether she will recover. Sometimes the growth infects other parts of the body. Sometimes it doesn't. Nobody knows why ...'

'How terrible,' India whispered. 'But Alice ... Aren't you treating your mother yourself? With lavender oil, and the like?'

Alice smiled.

'Of course I am! Doctor Harte knows nothing about it, however, and I'd be grateful if you would . . .'

A noise from the kitchen behind them revealed the young Harper boy peeping curiously into the parlour, and Alice motioned him in, presenting him to India, explaining that the cottage blinds had been drawn to allow him privacy to work.

'Work?'

'Johnny is studying anatomy and biology,' Alice said proudly. 'And this morning he's been dissecting a field mouse.'

India was astonished, and then impressed, not only by the boy's skill and determination, but by Alice's evident satisfaction. This was a truly remarkable family, and Alice was an extraordinary woman, a peerless companion and a rare friend. When, oh when, would she return to Crompton Hall?

They ate the soup and the elderflower jelly between them, then Johnny retreated to the kitchen once more and India was able to voice her fears.

'I realize you must stay here for Johnny at the moment . . . That your mother would wish that, although I rather hoped that Ivy might take him in eventually . . . Alice . . . I can hardly bear it without you at home! When do you think you might come back?'

India's voice quavered, and Alice reached for her hand.

'I don't think Lady Crompton wants me back . . . And perhaps it's better that I stay here . . . For all kinds of reasons . . .'

Now Alice's voice faltered, as though she too struggled with wayward emotion.

'I should tell you that a most unexpected thing has happened,' she continued. 'Something I could never have predicted . . .'

India waited, her heart thumping.

'I have received a proposal of marriage! As you know, I've not been keen to marry, and was quite content to remain . . .' Here she glanced at India and the unspoken phrase *old maid* hung awkwardly between them. India looked away and bit her lip.

'I wouldn't normally consider accepting,' Alice said quickly, 'but my mother has asked me to give it serious thought . . . And under the circumstances, I feel I must do that . . .'

'Who?' India asked faintly. 'Who wishes to marry you?'

'A farmer. You may have his acquaintance, but I don't believe you know him well . . . However, he's a good enough man . . . He owns Lavender House . . . He has been very kind to my family . . . His name is Charlie Youngman.'

India closed her eyes.

'Are you in love?' she whispered.

Alice drew a deep breath.

'As I've told you before, I consider love a doubtful proposition . . . Perhaps if you had no family cares to divide you, and there were no social constraints, nor worries about what people might say, and if you could be truly assured of your lover's faithfulness . . .'

She seemed, for a moment, close to tears and India looked up in surprise.

'Perhaps then,' Alice concluded at last, 'you might say you were in love.'

Chapter Thirteen

It wasn't too hard to locate Blue Farm.

At first Val and Edie, the only people Laurie recognized from her first visit to Crompton Hall, declared they'd never heard of it.

But then Val made inquiries, and reported back that Blue Farm was indeed nearby, although few knew it by its old name. Now it was called 'Crompton Holiday Apartments'.

'There's a new owner, so maybe she's changing the name back. Blue Farm sounds rather more evocative . . .'

Laurie was disappointed.

She had imagined Blue Farm as it was in India's day, and although she knew the lavender fields were long since gone, had pictured the wide expanse of purple blooms, dancing on the wind borne in from The Wash. She had seen Sean living in magnificent isolation, the only inhabitant of the manor house which had once been home to Luke Harte and his family. She had imagined herself calling, as India had once called upon the village doctor, being ushered into a high-ceilinged room and seated upon an Edwardian settee. And there, in period splendour, she would confront her former lover and tell him what she knew, before marching out through the portico . . .

Unfortunately, Crompton Holiday Apartments conjured no such image.

And the longer she thought about it, the less taste she had for confrontation anyway.

She despised Sean for his deception, but saw only too clearly how she'd colluded in it. She had swallowed his bland assurances, taken him at his word when any fool would have questioned his rigorous determination to keep his wife and his lover apart . . .

Worse than this, it seemed to her now that she'd made the running all along. She'd picked Sean as though he'd been a fancy item on display in a department store . . . *Oh yes, I'll have that one please . . . The one with the smoky blue eyes and the silky blond hair . . .*

She'd wrapped him up and taken him home, and though he'd never demurred, she had installed him as the centre-piece of her hopes and dreams, the trophy that justified all the waiting, the super-buy at the end of a long, fastidious spell of window shopping. *Have you met my fiancé? Lovely, isn't he?*

No wonder she'd been taken for a ride.

And yet . . . She had loved him. She had loved him, she now saw, as India had loved Luke Harte . . . Both of them glimpsing something elusive which answered their deepest desires . . . And both of them doomed to disappointment.

What might India's story reveal about her own? In the continuing absence of Ruth and Dale, whose whereabouts she'd been unable to determine, Laurie found herself aimlessly pursuing India, unable to uncover the detail she craved.

She idled away her hours in the grounds of Crompton Hall, sitting in the kitchen garden beneath the fig tree, wandering through the woods toward the lake, crouch-ing down by the decaying sedge to stare at the green-painted dinghy with its gold lettering. *The Lady of the Lake.*

Now, to her dismay, she felt no flash of recognition, no intimation of events remembered, of places known. The lake, the boat, the woods, were indeed familiar, but only because she had visited them earlier. All sense of a link with the past of Crompton Hall eluded her.

She had also been perturbed to discover that India's journal ceased abruptly in the autumn of 1912. The last entry, enigmatic and solemn, had further depressed her.

I am inclined to believe there is nothing in which one might take hope, except one's own resilience and resolve. If you cannot find within yourself the spirit and the means to overcome, why then, you might as well give up, for you will not find refuge elsewhere . . .

These thoughts were too close to Laurie's own for

comfort, and she refused to dwell upon them. India, she concluded unhappily, had come up against some intractable sorrow, rather like she herself, in the face of which only a poignant stoicism would serve. There was nothing to be learned from the journal, and no gain in uncovering India's subsequent life. Laurie's hope had been vain, her sense of identification cruel. She locked the journal away in its drawer.

On the third morning of her stay, having boycotted yet another art class, the visualization session and the practical aromatherapy, she set out for Blue Farm, wearing her new black wig, and despite the clipped style, looking uncannily like her old self.

There would be no confrontation, she decided. Just a careful weighing up.

The walk took her through the village of Crompton, past the pink and white cottages of one-time farm labourers, now gentrified into exquisite country homes or holiday lets, beside the fields of swaying barley, splashed with vermilion poppies, fields which, she guessed, had once shimmered lavender-blue, and beyond to the shady gardens, crammed with pink and cream hollyhocks, which Laurie knew at once to be the grounds of Blue Farm.

The house, though far more modest than Crompton Hall, was nevertheless a fine building, with columned portico, sash windows stretching to the ground and tall, ornate chimneys. The front door, a vast, solid oak affair, was wide open and Laurie lingered uncertainly, peering inside to a hallway cluttered with chairs, chests of drawers and assorted pieces of kitchen equipment. It looked as though the owners had just moved in.

A figure appeared at the end of the hallway and Laurie stepped back.

'You want Mr Youngman?'

The woman was flustered, pink-faced from furniture removals.

'He's staying at Lavender Cottage. Over the barley fields ... It stands all alone. You can't miss it.'

Laurie nodded politely and turned away.

'Wait a minute!' the woman called after her. 'You know the cottage is on the market? Are you interested at all?'

Laurie turned back.

'No, I suppose not,' the woman said regretfully, catching her expression. 'Oh well, we'll keep trying.'

She walked briskly, hot beneath her wig, heart thumping.

The barley fields were as beautiful in their way as the expanse of lavender must once have been, a rustling roll of golden green sweeping up to the Crompton woods. On the far boundary, a white wattle dwelling of evident charm beckoned. Lavender Cottage. Had anyone thought to rename it? What was Sean's connection with this place, and why had he come here? The questions harried her on, and she increased her pace.

At the cottage gate, she paused to catch her breath, and at once felt her senses assailed by a pungent, heady perfume. The cottage garden was crammed with lavender plants, a dozen different varieties, purple-blue, mauve and pinky white, every bush and stem combining to scent the air so that it seemed she were literally drinking it in. She could taste lavender, thick and sweet, at the back of her throat. She closed her eyes and leaned on the gatepost.

India, my dearest. I'm so glad you're here!

Laurie opened her eyes to see Sean standing in the doorway.

'You found me, then? I wondered if you would.'

He seemed unsurprised, his manner almost curt, and Laurie knew him well enough to sense anxiety. But she didn't mean to be kind.

'This isn't a social call,' she said coolly. 'I've come to ask what the hell you think you're doing here.'

'Oh ... Well, I'm just having a bit of a holiday,' he muttered foolishly. 'Although naturally, I hoped to see you ... Now that you're here, are you coming in?'

Curiosity led her to follow him inside, eyes blinking against the gloom, taking in the simple furnishings and plain distempered walls. Lavender Cottage had retained its ancient, rural air and Laurie felt herself slip back into a vanished world. *India's world.*

A tray with teapot and milk stood upon a sideboard, and she watched him fumble with crockery and spoons, trying so hard it was painful. Or would have been, had she felt any sympathy at all.

He glanced at her nervously.

'I like the hair,' he said.

'It's not hair,' she snapped, 'it's nylon. Would you like to see me bald?'

She put a hand to her head, and he took a step backward.

'Please Laurie,' he said plaintively. 'Don't . . .'

They faced each other across a pitted pine table on which stood a china pitcher filled with lavender sprigs. A little pile of flower heads lay by its side, along with a pestle and mortar. Sean, it seemed, had been experimenting with his grandfather's old trade.

He saw her eyeing the lavender, and took advantage of the diversion it offered.

'My family used to own this cottage,' he said quickly. 'That's really why I'm here . . . When I discovered Crompton Hall was near the old lavender fields, I couldn't resist coming. I even thought I might find my grandfather's old house . . . Lavender House . . .'

She said nothing, intrigued despite herself, yet still possessed by the memory of his denial to Tina and determined, now that she'd come to the moment, to make him face it.

He offered her a cup of tea, his hand visibly trembling as he poured from the pot, and she began to feel emboldened. She sat down on the sofa.

'And have you found Lavender House?' she asked politely.

He shook his head.

'It's long gone like the fields themselves. And nobody seems to remember the Youngmans. My great grandfather is buried in the village churchyard along with his wife . . . But that's the end of the story. After that, they all moved away . . .'

She smiled graciously, sipping her tea.

'And have you finally told your wife about me?' she inquired in the same casual tone.

He flushed, he looked away, he all but dropped his cup, and if she hadn't known him better, she might have thought him about to burst into tears. But tears were out of character.

'What's that supposed to mean?' he mumbled at last.

'It's a straightforward question. Have you told Tina about me?'

Now he did look at her.

'What's there to tell?' he asked defensively. 'It's over, isn't it?'

'That doesn't let you off the hook. You've been stringing me along, Sean. Letting me think it was just a matter of time . . . That it would all work out . . . And you never even told her . . .'

Now she felt her own tears start, and cursing her weakness, stood up and made for the door, bitterly aware that he hadn't even attempted to justify himself.

The All-Out Bastard finally shows his colours.

'I'm going,' she gulped, 'and I never want to see you again . . .'

He jumped up and sprinted to the door ahead of her, his arm across the frame, preventing her exit.

'Get out of my way!'

'I'm not letting you go like this . . .'

'I'll scream for help.'

'Who do you think will hear?'

She was going to have hysterics. She was going to slap his face or bite his arm or kick him in the balls. She closed her eyes and willed herself to relax. When she opened them again, his relief was palpable.

'Sit down,' he said quietly. 'Please . . . Let's talk.'

She marched back to the sofa and stretched her feet upon it so he couldn't sit beside her, forcing him to face her from the other side of the room.

'Okay,' she said coldly. 'Talk!'

He looked at her helplessly, shaking his head as though he couldn't credit the situation, measuring his words.

'Laurie, I haven't done this right at all . . . But I'm not going to make excuses . . . Nor am I going to tell you a whole lot of stuff about Tina that might explain it . . .'

'Oh, good!' she said sarcastically. 'So you're not going to claim she's a psychopath? Or that she'd kill herself if she found out?'

'Of course not!'

She saw the first flash of anger cross his face, and wondered how far she might provoke him. He had a habit of walking out on rows, but this time he was clearly motivated to stay.

'You're a shit,' she said evenly. 'A total shit. Why aren't you at home with your wife and children? What are you doing here?'

She'd given him the opening he needed, and he seized it at once.

'I'm here because I'm desperately worried about you,' he said urgently, 'and because you won't tell me anything. I had to check out Crompton Hall for myself. You can say it's none of my business, that I should leave you alone and stay away . . . But you can't stop me caring . . .'

She looked at him in dawning horror.

'Check out Crompton Hall?'

'Yes. I had to meet this Doctor Mitchell. Decide if he was genuine.'

Laurie stood up.

'You mean you've been there? And talked to him?'

'It was no big deal. I rang him up. He agreed to see me. I went.'

She was trembling, so outraged she could hardly trust herself to speak.

'Sit down,' he urged, reaching out to her. 'Just listen to me and try to understand . . . I want to help you . . .'

She smacked his hand away.

'How dare you!' she shouted. 'How dare you go there and discuss my treatment behind my back?'

He shook his head.

'We weren't discussing you . . . Obviously he's not going

to do that . . . We were discussing the esoteric theory of regeneration . . .'

She said nothing and he smiled nervously, risking an opinion.

'As a matter of fact, Dale Mitchell changed my mind about a lot of things . . . He was very interesting. And very impressive.'

Laurie looked up, astonished, her fury abating. Sean offered another cautious smile.

'I'm sorry I suggested it was half-baked . . . I think you're right to go along with it. Regeneration may be exactly what you need . . . What we all need . . .'

So now the All-Out Bastard tries a new tack.

She walked over to the window and stared out on to the waving barley fields, her mind reeling.

Regeneration, manifestly, was what she'd never discussed with Dale Mitchell herself. There had been cursory talk of beliefs, of positive thinking and the benefits of therapy. But of the mysterious doctrine of *regeneration* there'd been remarkably little and this, Laurie knew, was because she'd deliberately avoided it.

Why? Because, when all was laid bare, what could it possibly prove but half-baked as Sean had once insisted?

A curious reluctance, she now saw, had underpinned all her dealings with Dale Mitchell. She had challenged him, she had laughed at him. But she had not openly required him to state his case. And why not? Because once the full extent of his vacuousness had been revealed, she would surely feel herself compelled to leave Crompton Hall for good, and that she could not do for one reason alone.

'India!' she whispered.

Sean walked over to the window and stood beside her.

'Yes,' he said, 'India Crompton-Leigh . . . I guess she's the key to it all. That portrait, the one above the fireplace in the old library. He uses it to gauge how much input his clients require. Some of them don't even notice it. Others are drawn to it immediately. And once they start to uncover the story, the process begins . . .'

Laurie struggled between resentment and curiosity.

'What process?' she muttered tightly.

'Well, you know more about it than me. A trip into the past. The process of regeneration, I guess.'

She closed her eyes, fighting a deep weariness.

'I don't understand,' she said faintly, 'I don't know what you're talking about . . .'

He led her back to the sofa, taking her hands in his, and this time she didn't resist.

'There's nothing sinister about it after all,' he said gently. 'I was wrong to think there was. Mitchell means well, and he may even do some good . . . Positive thinking is obviously very important . . . I just wouldn't like you to rely solely on him, that's all. It's chemotherapy that will save you. Anything else is a bonus.'

She opened her eyes.

'I guess so,' she whispered.

'You look so pale,' he murmured. 'And you're losing weight too, I can see . . . But you're going to be fine! Everyone says so.'

Laurie was perilously close to tears.

'Who says? Dale Mitchell?' she jerked out.

'No, not him . . . Gloria and Shelley . . . And your Dad too.'

She laughed, a thin high sound, poignant and humourless.

'And what do they know? Wishful thinking isn't so far from positive thinking, you know. It's the next stage on . . . When hope is gone, all you're left with is wishing it wasn't.'

He squeezed her hand and pulled her close.

'Come on, now,' he said gently, his face so close he might have been about to kiss her, 'I hate to hear you talk like that. Hope isn't gone! You're responding well to the treatment. There's every chance you'll make a full recovery.'

He'd come a long way, she suddenly saw, from his panicky first response, and he seemed to have done it by a sheer effort of will. She should have been gratified, but she wasn't. And she hadn't forgotten Tina.

She struggled free of his grasp and stood up.

'I haven't forgiven you, Sean. Why don't you just do the decent thing and go back to your wife?'

'I'm never going back,' he said calmly. 'Whatever happens between us, I'm never going back. Please understand that.'

He got up from the sofa and slid his arm around her waist, drawing her close so that his chin rested on the crown of her wig.

'I love you, Laurie,' he said. 'You do believe that, don't you?'

She saw his next move as though he'd already made it, a replaying of that first ecstatic collision of bodies so long ago, the tentative taste of tongue upon tongue, the moulding of limbs into each other, the exquisite assimilation of flesh into flesh.

'No,' she whispered.

'Yes,' he said, and looped his finger into a curl at the nape of her neck, oblivious to its insecurity.

Then Laurie could think only of the touch of acrylic against skin, coarse and ugly like cancer itself, and her throat gagged. She let out a stifled gasp, which he seemed to mistake for passion, for in the next moment his lips were on hers and she felt him relax into her, a once-beloved, familiar overture which now seemed pointless and inane. She suffered his kiss only because to avoid it seemed equally pointless, but the instant it was over, she fought back.

'You still don't get it, Sean, do you?'

Her voice was muffled against his chest, and she thought at first he hadn't heard, but then he pushed her from him, searching her face with an anguish that would once have wrenched her heart.

'My world is a different place,' she said tremulously. 'The old rules no longer apply. How could they? How could it be business as usual, when all the time my time is running out?'

He swallowed hard.

'Was business as usual so bad?' he asked at last.

'It was based on lies,' she whispered, feeling her tears rise again, hot and hard. 'Your lies, and my own selfishness. On the belief that nothing mattered but our own feelings . . .'

She stifled a sob.

'There's so much more that matters, Sean. Life itself . . . For its own sake, not for what you get out of it . . . And freedom, too. Freedom from guilt and doing the wrong thing. After all, that's the only freedom we truly have, isn't it? The freedom to choose against selfish acts and personal gratification . . .'

He showed a glimmer of defeat now, directed at the lavender cuttings on the table which he suddenly swept from the surface into a waste-bin underneath.

'If that's the way you see it, I won't argue any more.'

He was visibly upset, directing all his attention to the scattered fronds and flowers on the table, pushing the lavender heads into the mortar bowl and refusing to look her in the eye.

'Thank you,' she said simply.

Then she turned and walked out of the cottage, into the waving barley without so much as a backward glance.

She turned away from Blue Farm, making for the Crompton woods. Beyond the first grove, she knew from earlier walks with Edie and Val, ran a lane which led down to the village church. She had never taken it, having scant interest in churches, but now this seemed an extraordinary omission. What was it Sean had said?

India is the key to it all . . .

As she walked, she felt her preoccupation with Sean lift and then vanish, as though a mighty burden had been shed, leaving her free to think only of India.

And now that she came to think, it seemed possible, indeed probable, that India lay buried in the churchyard, a prospect at once both beguiling and terrifying, the inevitable end of the story, yet with so much still to be revealed.

How old was India when she died? Did she marry? And if so, who had been her husband? A gravestone could tell it all.

Laurie quickened her pace, hearing her breath fall upon the afternoon air in urgent rasps. She rounded a loop in the wooded lane, and there in a tangled hollow overrun with hemlock and dog-rose, sat a curious round-towered church, its walls plastered with flint stones, a building so odd and unexpected that for a moment Laurie wondered if she had accidentally come upon an ancient fortification, a castle minimally disguised as a place of worship.

She hurried forward, then as the churchyard came into view beyond the tower, stopped short. She was not alone in her quest. Val had arrived before her.

There was no mistaking the plump, rumpled figure bent before a weathered gravestone, energetically rifling through decaying flowers and rearranging them along with fresh blooms from a basket by her side.

Laurie fought to quell a rising dismay, reminding herself that she had no proprietorial claim upon India. Sean's words returned to her once more.

That portrait, the one above the fireplace in the old library. He uses it to gauge how much input his clients require . . .

How much input, Laurie wondered, had Val required? Was everyone, perhaps, shown into India's private suite on arrival at Crompton Hall, encouraged to read her journals and speculate upon her fate, and then, the lesson learned, gently moved on to allow for the next client? But what was the lesson?

As though she felt the weight of these thoughts, Val stood up from the grave and turned, catching sight of Laurie and beckoning her into the churchyard. Reluctantly, Laurie picked her way through the briars until she stood at the rear of the grave, unwilling to read the name on the stone.

'Did you find Blue Farm?' Val wanted to know.

Laurie nodded.

'I also found a place called Lavender Cottage . . . Do you know it?'

'Alice Harper's home. Everyone knows it.'

Alice Harper's home! I've been standing in Alice's parlour . . .

Val bundled the dead flowerheads into her basket.

'There, that should do it!' She stepped back to admire her display. 'Happy birthday, Daisy,' she said.

Laurie shot round to the front of the gravestone and read the inscription.

Here lies Daisy Turner, died 1982, aged 83 years. Once She Wasn't, Then She Was, And Now She Ain't Again.

'She was a bit of a joker, our Daisy,' said Val, laughing. 'She wrote that epitaph herself as she lay dying. There was a battle with the vicar, but Daisy won the day. Cute, isn't it?'

Laurie hardly knew if she were relieved or disappointed.

'I thought it might be India,' she muttered.

Val threw her a curious glance.

'No, it's mostly maids and footmen buried here . . . Most of them used to work at Crompton Hall . . . Over there is Rose Richards, and Flora Bransome's right next to her, and then over by the wall is Joshua Addison, the Cromptons' butler . . .'

Laurie had begun to feel faint, the result of her emotional encounter with Sean and her breathless march across the barley fields. She sat down suddenly in the wiry grass beside the grave, burying her head in her hands.

Val knelt beside her, concerned.

'You should take it easy,' she said gently. 'Chemo does funny things to your system. You never know when it's going to hit. Don't push yourself so hard . . . You'll find India in due course . . .'

Laurie tried to summon her senses. If the entire company of Mitchell clients were in pursuit of India, then she had no desire to join them. She would keep her obsession to herself.

'It must be the chemo,' she agreed hastily. 'Nothing to do with India . . .'

She looked round the churchyard, seeking an alternative explanation for her visit.

'I was looking for another grave,' she said vaguely, standing up and adjusting the wig which had somehow worked its way over her eyebrows. 'The relative of a friend . . . named Youngman.'

Val pointed to the far corner of the graveyard.

'Charlie Youngman . . . Died 1945, aged 63 years . . . And his beloved wife Frederica, died 1948, aged 61 years . . . Do you mind if I give you a little piece of advice, Laurie?'

'No,' Laurie muttered, bracing herself for what might follow.

'A couple of hairgrips behind your ears would secure that wig!'

Laurie marched out of the churchyard.

She was starring in a farce. Any moment now her wig would fly off and the lead actor would appear with his pants around his ankles. Who would it be? The ghost of Charlie Youngman?

She was energetically pursued by Val with her basket of dead flowerheads, a vision that gave rise to a desperate fit of giggles.

'I'm sorry, Laurie,' Val called anxiously, and the words rang through the trees like a bizarre bird call. *Sorry Laurie, Sorry Laurie . . .*

Laurie heard her breath rise toward a great guffaw, and she forced herself to take hold. She mustn't seem to be losing her grip . . . *Or hair grip!*

She stopped short, doubled with laughter.

Val approached uncertainly.

'I didn't mean to be rude about the wig,' she began, but Laurie, unable to speak, shook her head.

'I don't give a damn how my wig looks,' she managed at last, still laughing. 'I thought you were going to say something else . . .'

Val looked doubtful.

'About India?'

Laurie, calm again, looked away.

'I don't know,' she muttered.

'You must read the journals,' Val said. 'And not just India's . . . There are dozens more. Isn't it wonderful how all the women kept journals? Daisy Turner and Alice and India, Rose and Flora and Mrs Long . . . Spilling out their secrets in little books or jotting down their thoughts on scraps of paper.'

Laurie stopped in her tracks.

'Alice Harper kept a journal?'

'Haven't you seen it yet?'

They had reached the kitchen garden when all discussion was swiftly curtailed by the appearance of Edie, announcing Dale Mitchell's return and summoning Val to the counselling suite.

'Is Ruth here too?' Laurie asked hopefully.

Her two companions exchanged a glance.

'Ruth won't be back for a while,' Edie said at last, 'so we've all got to survive without her. It's hard for Doctor Dale, but we must all do our bit . . .'

Laurie swallowed a comment that she hadn't come to Crompton to do her bit, and inquired when she might see Dale Mitchell. She had much she meant to ask.

'There's a queue,' Edie said, 'but I'll tell him you're anxious . . .'

And indeed, Laurie was. She walked up to her room perplexed and ill at ease. Sean's unexpected connection with Crompton Hall, the news that there were other journals, unknown and unseen, the intimation of something unusual about Ruth's continuing absence, all served to unnerve her. It was time, she decided, to force Dale Mitchell's hand, though no sooner had the thought formed than she realized she'd no idea what she meant by it, nor what she wanted from him.

He kept her waiting an hour, and when she finally descended to the old library to find herself facing the portrait above the mantel, her former weariness had returned with renewed spite. Her eyelids drooped, her limbs sagged into her chair, and all her senses seemed diminished, as though she saw, heard and felt through a thick covering blanket, a damper imposed on the spirit she longed to summon.

He looked tired himself, though he greeted her with warmth, asking careful questions about the hospital, the treatment, the hair. She answered hesitantly, unable to fix upon the purpose she'd so recently felt. But she still managed to rally for the crucial exchange.

'Sean Youngman came to see you,' she said directly. 'I was very surprised to learn that. It seems most unprofessional, to invite him here in my absence. Why did you do that?'

She saw then that he'd been prepared for the question, and that his defence would be Sean's own, an assertion that they hadn't discussed her. She jumped in first, fighting the fatigue.

'Sean says you didn't talk about me. Frankly, I find that unconvincing. What else would you talk about?'

He took several moments to answer, and when he did, his voice seemed distant and weak, a tremor at the edge of her consciousness.

'We talked about time,' he murmured. 'About spirits and phantoms, future and past. About how we all know we must live in the present. But how desperately hard it is to do that . . .'

She listened dully, aware only of her need to lie down.

'Then we talked about Crompton Hall,' he said. 'How beautiful it is here, how it speaks of a vanished world . . . And how, when the senses are heightened by illness or by grief, it serves as a kind of time machine . . . A means to another dimension, which is the life of the imagination . . .'

She felt drowsiness overcome her, as though she were dissolving beneath his gaze.

'A time machine,' she repeated faintly. 'Who believes in such things?'

He leaned toward her and smiled.

'Then let me put it another way . . . Sean's way. Maybe our spirits and phantoms are the software of people who once lived here . . . And maybe our minds are the hardware running their programs . . .'

She said nothing, simply stared at him dumbly as though he'd taken leave of his wits.

'But there's something more simple than software,' he said quietly, moving to his desk and extracting a book from a drawer. 'Maybe this will hold your answer . . .'

She stood up, feeling her knees fold beneath her, and for the first time, he registered her fragile state. He moved toward her quickly, lowering her back into her chair.

'You're unwell,' he said gently, 'I'll get Val . . .'

'I'm tired, that's all. Very, very tired . . . Please, I just need to lie down . . . Give me the book . . . What is it?'

He looked at her carefully, assessing her state of mind, and then nodded.

'It's Alice Harper's journal,' he replied.

Chapter Fourteen

My mother refused to die, and I refused to let her.

She lay on a high narrow bed in a busy corridor at the cottage hospital, her face white as the sheets drawn up to her chin, her chest compressed with heavy bandages. Beneath the lint lay a raw disc where her breast had been, a wound I was required to bathe and dress myself.

I painted her ravaged skin with honey, then soothed her temples with lavender oil to relieve her stress, as once, long ago, she'd done for me.

'Doctor Harte will have you burned for a witch,' she muttered.

'I don't think so. He told me he approved of folk remedies.'

'So he might when they're used for coughs and colds and kept in the kitchen cupboard. But this is his hospital, and I am his patient. He won't like it.'

I considered her words carefully, unwilling to risk any confrontation with Dr Harte and wary of the Matron who'd already reprimanded me for bringing flowers into her ward. The blooms, she said, would deplete the air and weaken the sick, a view which, to my knowledge, finds no credence in scientific opinion.

'You're going to recover,' I said to my mother, 'and I'm going to help you. If that means keeping our treatments a secret, then we must do it together.'

She smiled at me and closed her eyes. I knew she agreed.

The next day I took a dilution of mistletoe berries mixed with crushed sprigs of St John's wort into the hospital, and fed it to my mother in surreptitious sips.

'Mistletoe is a poison,' she murmured. 'You're going to kill me!'

'Many poisons are helpful as well as harmful. It depends

on how they're given, and in what circumstances. Treat like with like, the old books say. A poison to vanquish a poison.'

'Precious poisons?'

She was weak and her voice faint, yet her eyes danced. She was laughing at me.

'Mistletoe is a parasite,' I told her, 'and a parasitic growth has invaded your body. Treat like with like.'

'Why St John's wort?' she asked me.

'To lift the spirits,' I replied, 'and give the will to live.'

Her eyes sparkled with tears.

'I've got the will to live, Alice,' she whispered, 'I just need the strength to do it.'

'I'll bring you something for strength,' I said, and the next day took in a compound of comfrey and cloves. I mixed it with lettuce leaves and fed it to her on dry biscuits.

She chewed it meditatively.

'Have you considered Mr Youngman's proposal?' she asked me at last. 'There's much to be said for it, and quite as much against, and I wouldn't wish to influence your decision in any way, Alice . . . However, I would say that a certain condescension has always underlain his attitude toward us. And I am bound to say that such a quality would not be good in a husband . . .'

She was having second thoughts. It was then I knew her strength was growing, and this before the comfrey had begun to do its work.

My mother seemed more cheerful the following morning, and the scarlet wound was losing its fire. Even Dr Harte, as he met me coming out of the hospital, seemed encouraged, though his general demeanour was mournful.

'Your mother is a remarkable woman,' he said, 'and she's making good progress. But this is an unpredictable disease, Alice. I wouldn't wish to give false hope.'

He eyed me thoughtfully.

'You've anointed her with lavender oil,' he said slowly, 'I could smell it on the pillows . . . Well, it's only a scent so it hardly matters. But nothing is to be given internally,

Alice. It's very important for a doctor to control what his patient is taking.'

I nodded and held his gaze.

'You know best,' I said. 'I've given her a few biscuits spread with herbs this morning. Very nutritious. As good as your hospital fare, I've no doubt.'

My mother had done much complaining about the food the nurses served, stews of gristle and bowls of colourless gruel. Dr Harte, I was sure, would not argue with me.

He hesitated, and I saw then that hospital food was the very last thing on his mind.

'When are you returning to Crompton Hall?' he asked at length. 'I'm sure Miss India misses your company . . .'

'I miss her too,' I told him. 'But I have no plans to return. India must manage without me.'

He looked down.

'I'm told she is very melancholy. Her mother and father are quite concerned . . .'

'A melancholy state must be challenged, not indulged,' I replied, rather more sharply than I'd intended. 'Forgive me, Doctor Harte. I'm not immune to India's distress, but at the moment my mother's health is my primary concern.'

It struck me then that it was curious, his use of the word *anointed* when speaking of the lavender oil, for I wouldn't have used it myself, yet it seemed to describe most appositely the service I had performed for my mother.

'She will recover,' I told Luke Harte, and in that moment, knew it to be true.

'I pray to God,' he said fervently, and without registering my surprise, he strode off through the hospital doors.

As I said to India, Charlie Youngman was a good enough man.

He had laughing blue eyes and hair the colour of straw, and although he drank too much and lost more money than was sensible at cards, he would have made a tolerable husband, and Lavender House, for all its lack of elegance, a tolerable home. I liked him for his unconventional ways, and had seen nothing of the condescension my mother remarked, although I sensed some lingering indebtedness toward us which I could never quite fathom. He had a quick wit, and a daring dislike of authority. I remembered well his defence of my father after he died, and his service to my mother when she was forced to leave her home.

But though I gave it serious consideration, I could not accept his proposal. It was plain to me that my mother had only suggested it because she thought she was dying. She imagined me alone and unloved, and she wished to spare herself that painful vision. However, once she began to recover, all thoughts of my becoming Charlie's wife were swiftly set aside.

'You weren't meant to marry, Alice. It's not in your nature to serve any man and have him order you hither and thither.'

I agreed, although I added the rejoinder that if one married the right kind of man, he would surely consider it part of his duty, even his pleasure, to serve his wife in return.

'And where would you find such a man?' inquired my mother frostily. 'Not at Crompton Hall, I fancy!'

This, of course, was a reference to Christian, for my mother had seen enough to know where my heart lay. *My heart, but not my head!* I should never marry a man like Christian, even supposing our relative positions in society did not render such a thing impossible. I have too great an instinct for my own preservation.

'I know good men exist,' I said, a trifle testily. 'My father was one such man ... And Adam Goodchild is another. Where would we be now if not for his generosity?'

It was Adam who had ordered my mother's admission to the cottage hospital, he who paid the bills, and Adam who, on learning from Dr Harte that my mother would not eat the hospital food, had insisted a new cook be hired, one who understood the principles of nutrition and who might work toward improving the health of all patients.

Yet we had never seen Adam, nor been afforded any opportunity to thank him personally for his kindness. Since his rejection by India, he had returned to London, taking Marianne with him. No one knew when he might return.

'Ah yes, Adam Goodchild,' said my mother mistily, for this name alone served to modify her view of menfolk, 'what a husband he might make! A pity you weren't born with ten thousand a year, Alice.'

'A pity indeed,' I replied.

My return to the hardships of life at Lavender Cottage had been more difficult than I'd anticipated. I missed good food on my table and warm water in my washing bowl. Worse, I was greatly concerned about the state of the cottage, the constant damp upon the walls and a gaping hole in the roof above the scullery which we had stopped with strips of bark. Our repair would not survive the winter, and I considered how, while rejecting his advances, I might also suggest to Mr Youngman that he endeavour to maintain his own property.

He received my refusal with grace, good humour, and a certain wry perception which later caused me to wince.

'You'd have made me an excellent wife, Alice. And for you, I might have given up the whisky . . .'

'You should do that anyway,' I told him gravely, 'for yourself.'

'But we all need our pleasures, Alice. Those little compensations for the trials that life presents . . . Your father liked a glass of whisky too.'

'My father was a loving husband,' I said.

'And so might I have been.'

'I should have made you give up gambling,' I told him, joking now, yet still with some modest hope of influencing his behaviour. 'Lavender farming yields little enough, and I wouldn't have seen my daughters go without Sunday hats while you squandered your earnings at cards.'

He smiled.

'You must blame your friend Christian for my bad habits,' he said slowly. 'And you must agree that mine are scarcely so grievous as his . . .'

He looked closely at me then, and I felt my colour rise.

What had Christian said of me over cards and whisky at the village inn?

'It is only a matter of degree,' I said faintly. 'Gambling and drinking are poor traits in any man, and a lesser sin may always lead to greater . . .'

I had not meant to lecture him, nor to sound so disapproving, but I was ruffled by mention of Christian, and I found myself attacking to defend.

Charlie laughed, and reached for his hat.

'Alice, I shall embarrass you no further. I see your mind is quite made up, and I respect you for your opinions. Your father had strong opinions too, and since we have already spoken of him, I shall remind you once again that he might not have been the ideal husband you imagine . . . Your mother was hardly the perfect wife either, and yet they achieved a rare contentment together.'

This was true, and for a moment I do believe my resolve faltered, for I saw most clearly then what I had always known to be the case, that every marriage is a compromise, and that my mother's own had weathered many idiosyncrasies, on both sides.

Perhaps he saw that momentary hesitation, and perhaps, having considered himself conclusively rejected and experiencing a certain relief alongside his disappointment, he then sought to secure his freedom, for he hurried to establish acceptance of my answer.

'I need a wife to help me run the lavender farm,' he said squarely, 'which may not be the most excellent reason for contemplating marriage . . . Marriage should, of course, be a union of purpose, and this, I see, you have understood . . . In asking for your hand, Alice, I have aimed too high. I should have known better.'

'Please, there's no need to say such a thing . . .'

'Oh, but there is. You're a woman of principle. May you find the husband you deserve!'

This whole exchange left me sorely unsettled, and I could not but think I'd shown myself to be prim and unforgiving, not at all the judicious and considerate friend I had wished to appear, refusing Charlie Youngman for his sake as much as my own. We should not have been suited, and would never have made each other content. I had done him a service, and my only consolation was the thought that he had glimpsed this at the last.

But there was little else to cheer me. Charlie Youngman's offer, though I never truly considered accepting it, had the effect of making me realize how much I'd sacrificed by my refusal. A woman of my age and circumstance can hardly expect to be asked again, and it seemed to me then that I should never know a lover, nor a husband, nor ever have children of my own, matters which had concerned me little enough before, yet which, now they were irrevocably settled, became the source of unexpected disquiet. A terrible melancholy overcame me as I pulled the blind upon the parlour window, shutting out the sight of the lavender fields beyond, unable to shut out the thought that Lavender Cottage belonged to Charlie Youngman, that we lived there by his favour, and that I had no real home to call my own. Even this one was falling down around me, and I hadn't found the courage to ask him about repairs. How might I have gained in security and comfort if I had only swallowed my pride and deigned to move into Lavender House!

Yet even as I lamented, I reminded myself that there is no security, no rock on which we may build a happy home, except a peaceful heart and a firm trust in God. *If only we might always act upon what we earnestly believe!*

It was dusk when Charlie left me, and I must have dozed in my chair by the open window, inhaling the last of the lavender blooms as they began to wilt on the stem, for I dreamed that I was back at Crompton Hall, but not the Hall as I had known it. I saw the rooms filled with curious furniture, couches, stools and easels set up for painting, and I heard strange music coming from the morning room, a mournful, haunting sound. I saw men and women I did not know, and wandered among the unknown inhabitants like a ghost, for no one seemed able to see me, and then

I walked into the library. To my astonishment, I saw a portrait of India hanging above the mantel, the portrait which, I imagine, is even now being finished. But even more unsettling, when I looked closely at the picture, I seemed to see a second figure standing behind India at some distance . . . I moved toward the mantel, and suddenly stepped back with a little cry. The second figure was myself.

I woke with a start, and must have sat there in the silence for what seemed a half-hour or more, contemplating this strange vision, wishing I'd brought Johnny from Ivy's house where he'd been boarding while I prepared the cottage for my mother's return, half hoping Charlie might come back, not to renew his suit, but simply to reassure me of his continuing goodwill toward my family.

When the door knocker sounded, I was quite certain it was he, and I ran to welcome him, anxious to make amends for my previous ill humour.

Instead, I opened the door to Christian.

He stood on my step looking flushed and ill at ease, his usual boisterous demeanour entirely lacking, and I immediately feared some new disaster at Crompton Hall.

'India?' I inquired anxiously. 'Is she unwell?'

I had seen nothing of my dearest friend in the previous weeks, all my time being taken with caring for my brother and visiting my mother. She hadn't come to see me again, and although I'd heard of her low spirits from Dr Harte, I'd not imagined any serious condition that time would not mend.

Christian shook his head.

'Don't trouble yourself with India. Your mother's health should concern you much more. How is she?'

'She is recovering, thank you,' I said cautiously, sensing in him something I had not seen before, indecision, hesitation, I might almost have said anxiety.

'And you?' he pursued. 'You're quite well? You're happy to be home with your family? You're not thinking of quitting Lavender Cottage?'

So that was it. His drinking companions had told him

of Charlie Youngman's proposal and now he had come to discover my intentions.

'I'm staying here for the moment,' I said mischievously. 'But I can't say what I might do when I've considered all the offers open to me . . .'

He caught my mood and smiled.

'Alice . . . May I come in?'

He had never visited my mother's cottage before, and to my shame I found myself embarrassed by its dank squalor, an unworthy emotion which, thankfully, he mistook for simple fright.

'Oh, for goodness' sake! Do you think my mother's hiding in the lavender waiting to catch us? There's no one for miles around.'

Once in the parlour, he paced around the room, then recovering something of his customary jauntiness, sat down on my mother's threadbare settee, resting his feet on the stool.

'Is there any whisky, Alice? I could do with a shot.'

There was no whisky, but my mother kept a decanter of Charlie Youngman's elderberry wine, and I poured us both a glass, feeling that I, too, needed sustenance for whatever might follow.

He downed the liquor in a couple of gulps, then leaned across the table to the chair where I sat and grasped my hand.

'I wish I knew what you wanted,' he said.

I wanted nothing more than to tease him as he'd so often teased me, and I threw back my head and laughed.

'Well, I haven't yet decided, Master Christian, Sir!' I said gaily. 'What should an out-of-work maid want for herself, do you think?'

'Be serious, Alice. Please.'

'Why should I be? You are never serious yourself.'

He looked away.

'You really believe that, don't you, Alice?'

'I've seen nothing to persuade me otherwise,' I said smartly.

He seemed to consider for a moment, then to reach a

decision, for he suddenly released my hand, rose from the settee and strode to the window where he turned once more to face me.

'Well then, I've come to say goodbye, Alice. I'm leaving for London this very night, and I've no idea when I'll return. I couldn't go without seeing you . . .'

I looked up at him, and felt a chill settle on my heart.

'To London? To see your friend Mr Harrington?'

I could think of no other reason why he might go, for he had no business nor public duty to call him, and for one rapturous moment, I allowed myself to believe he'd finally decided upon a purpose in life, a commission in the Army, or a course of study at the university. But I knew that could never be, and I knew too that some unworthy plan was underway.

'I shan't see Tim Harrington,' he said shortly. 'And I've no idea when I'll see you again, either.'

He hesitated, groping for his words.

'Alice, I hardly know how to explain myself . . . There is nothing I can say that won't have you thinking the very worst of me . . . So it seems I had better say nothing at all . . .'

I saw then that whatever he intended doing in London, a woman was involved, and I guessed that woman to be Kitty Malone. He was right that I wished to hear nothing, but, of course, it was not in his nature to end any exchange on such a note.

'If I thought you might ever love me, or that you might believe I could be true to you . . .'

I waved my hand impatiently.

'I should find it very hard to love a man who has no goal nor ambition in life. And I should never hope you would be true to me! Faithfulness is not in your nature. You wouldn't like it.'

He looked across at me.

'Do you know what I'd really like?'

I felt my heart begin to pound beneath my bodice, and though I'd no desire to have him tell me lies, I heard my own voice whisper: 'What?'

'I'd like to marry you and live here in Lavender Cottage . . .'

I laughed aloud, relieved by the preposterous nature of this idea.

'And should you like to live with my mother and little brother also? And should you like to wash and cook and sit and sleep in four small rooms, all of them damp and unhealthy, and with not a quarter-acre garden outside? We've no space for elephants here, I'm afraid.'

His face darkened.

'Don't mock me, Alice. And don't mention that damned elephant to me again.'

I turned away, angry that such words should be spoken in my mother's house, and at once he was by my side again.

'I'm sorry, but that creature has caused me endless trouble . . . India has no interest in it, and Hardy is always pestering me to find new foodstuffs, or a bigger harness, or some means of clipping its toenails, and now the poor thing has fallen sick . . .'

He shook his head and I found myself surprised by his emotion.

'It was a joke, Alice, and a pretty poor one, I admit. I thought it would appeal to India's lofty idea of herself. But I also thought she might cherish it. I didn't think for a moment she would neglect it in such a cruel fashion.'

However sincerely he might regret the elephant, I would not listen to any slur upon India, and I held up my hand.

'If you must go,' I said to him, 'then you'd better go at once. There's nothing to be gained by criticizing your sister to me.'

He looked down for a moment, then met my eye again.

'Kiss me before I leave,' he said.

Ah, such is the power of a significant moment that later we may feel it touched by Fate, its processes inexorable, its consequences inevitable. But of course, there's no such thing as Fate, only the desires and machinations of individuals which, occurring singly, might be contained, but which, interwoven or reflected by the dreams of others, most often prove calamitous. I fell into his arms as though it were my destiny.

'I meant what I said,' he whispered, kissing my face, 'I wish I could marry you and live for ever in this place . . .'

'That's nonsense,' I murmured, shivering as his lips moved to my neck.

'Then I wish I could marry you and take you back to Crompton Hall . . .'

'That's a greater nonsense, and you do me dishonour by suggesting it. I'm no fool, Christian. I know what it is that you want.'

He held me from him, and gazed deep into my eyes.

'And what do you want, Alice?'

Could I have said what I wanted, even supposing I'd known it? I'd told myself I would never marry a man like Christian, yet in that moment I wished for nothing more than that he might truly make me his wife, and take me back to Crompton Hall . . . And this so futile, so exalted a dream, that I embarrassed myself for allowing it . . .

Perhaps, if he hadn't come upon me so soon after the encounter with my previous suitor, or, perhaps, if I hadn't glimpsed my eternal spinsterhood and unexpectedly found myself lamenting a loss I'd never recognized before, then I might have resisted.

But perhaps not. We are, each one of us, creatures of contradiction, declaring our freedom in one breath and sacrificing it the next, imagining ourselves in control, then finding to our peril that our hold upon order is tenuous and frail. We are often less ourselves than we would hope to be, and sometimes more ourselves than we would dare to be, and for this complexity, must pay the price.

He began to unbutton my dress and I watched the progress of his fingers as if in a trance, all senses suspended except the exquisite one of touch, all reason subsumed by emotion.

'I would do nothing you would not have me do,' he muttered. 'And nothing that might harm you in any way . . .'

I knew exactly what he meant, and was grateful for this small consideration, yet he need not have worried. I was not about to deliver my fate into any man's hands, not even one I wanted this much.

My dress fell to the floor and I stood before him in my petticoat. I felt him tremble against me, and felt my own flesh rise beneath his caress, and as I led him to the bedchamber, I thought of all the nights I had lain in my attic room at Crompton Hall, wondering if he would ever come to me, and whether I'd have the strength to refuse him if he did, reflecting that if it weren't for my mother's illness, then this would never have happened, and considering whether I might have cause for regret or whether, as I sought to convince myself, I were striking a brave blow against the solitary state that surely awaited me.

But such a blow could not be blind to consequences, for then it would be no brave act, merely a dangerous folly.

'Wait for me,' I said, showing him into the bedchamber, 'I'll be with you in a moment.'

I went into the kitchen and reached for a bottle of white spirit vinegar from the cupboard. This I mixed with a weak solution of juniper and rue. Then I took a piece of sea sponge, collected by my mother from the foreshore at Wells with many domestic purposes in mind, and this one too. I cut the sponge into the shape of a pine cone and soaked it in the vinegar mixture. Then I inserted it into myself.

I smiled to myself as I did it, splashing my body with lavender water to kill the smell of vinegar, recalling my mother's remark that Dr Harte would burn me for a witch if he knew the full extent of my meddling in medical matters . . . And she too, I mused, for who else had told me about sea sponge and white vinegar?

I was grateful indeed for this knowledge as I walked back to my bedchamber, and grateful, too, that my mother had shown me how to break the hymen while still a girl. She meant to spare me pain when I went to my husband, and considered it no contradiction that she never foresaw me having a husband. She believed it a mother's duty to prepare a daughter, and a daughter's right to intimate information. Such knowledge might never be needed, but should the moment come, it would greatly ease a wedding night and the subsequent path through matrimony. Even Ivy, for all her willing subordination to a rough, insensitive husband, has but three children when all the other village women have six. The choice lay within her power, though unknown to her husband, and her life was the happier for it.

Christian was lying on my bed, chewing an unlit cigar.

'What the devil have you been doing, Alice? Another moment, and I'd have smoked this thing.'

'Then I'd have shown you the door at once. A gentleman doesn't smoke in a lady's bedroom.'

'What *does* a gentleman do, Alice? Do you know?'

'Show me,' I whispered.

I lay down on the bed beside him, and his breath sounded feverish, rapid, in my ear. He began to mumble, his hands tugging urgently at the ribbon in my stocking.

'I love you, Alice. You know that, don't you? There's no woman I want half as much, nor ever will be . . .'

'Hush,' I said, removing my stockings to assist him, 'there's no need for all that.'

His hands ceased their fumbling, and he sat bolt upright on the bed.

'But it's true! Why won't you believe me?'

'Because I know you too well,' I replied. 'And because I remember what you said to me at the elephant's compound . . .'

I shall have you one day! Not this day, nor tomorrow, but one day soon. Be sure of it, Alice Harper. One day soon!'

He lay down again.

'Why is it,' he said reproachfully, 'that you give credence to every damn fool thing I say, yet refuse to take me seriously when I tell you the truth?'

He came into me with a sigh, and seemed encouraged at what he found for he showed none of his promised reserve, and when I moved my body in rhythm with his own, he gasped and bucked like a wild thing, a hare or a badger caught in a trap, so much so that I wondered if I were the cause, not of rapture but of pain, and in my ignorance, made to pull away. But this served only to increase his ecstasy, and we thundered upon the bed like two wrestlers brawling on a bar-room floor. I found myself both amused and faintly appalled at the bizarre nature of this activity, yet could not say that it wasn't pleasurable.

When the moment came to withdraw, he shuddered and moaned, and lifted from me, but I held him close and would not let him rise.

'Oh, sorry, Alice,' he whispered when it was over, and I felt a shadow touch my heart, as though in misleading him I'd lost any right to his concern. But I shook off all such thoughts by reminding myself that he was a gentleman, and I no more than his sister's servant. By taking advantage of my bed he was proving true to generations of Cromptons and others of their class.

'So that's what a gentleman does!' I teased, but now he was in no mood for jokes, and he buried his face in my hair.

But at last he raised himself and smiled down at me.

'No,' he murmured. '*This* is what a gentleman does . . .' and he began to finger my body with the most exquisite, gentle strokes until it seemed to me that the space between us dissolved, time hung suspended, and we were truly one.

Such is the power of the flesh. In one brief moment, transported upon physical sensation, all previous doubts were vanquished. I believed myself honoured and adored, and could scarcely credit my former reservations. Why had I never seen how much he cared for me? I rose to his touch like a bird beaten from the undergrowth, flying high and free before the fatal shot is fired.

Finally, he kissed me one last time, rose from the bed and climbed into his clothes.

'I'm going now,' he said.

'To the arms of Kitty Malone?' I inquired pensively, although in truth I was unconcerned now by anything he might be planning. I felt that what had passed between us had sealed our mutual devotion, and that Kitty's power was ebbing, if, indeed, not already extinguished upon the tide of the passion we had shared. I hoped she might be the kind of woman to bear her loss lightly, and I offered a quick prayer for her preservation, as well as for my own.

He said nothing for a long moment, then came to the bed where I still lay prostrate, following my mother's instructions to the last. *The sea sponge must not be disturbed for eight hours after loving, thereby allowing the vinegar to do its necessary work . . .*

Christian knelt by my side and took my hand. He pressed the fingers to his lips.

'Don't think too badly of me,' he said.

He left me then, and as I drifted toward sleep, the perfume of lavender heavy on the air around me, the song of distant nightingales sweet in my ear, I thought of all that had passed that day in my mother's cottage, my rejection of one suitor and my succumbing to another, the empowerment I enjoyed through my use of ancient remedies, the future I'd glimpsed as the *old maid* India once called me, and the steps I had taken to thwart that destiny.

I allowed myself the luxurious thought that I had misjudged Christian, that by his tenderness toward me that night he had shown his genuine regard, and that the *good enough* man, as husband or lover, might come in many guises.

And in a final flush of happiness, recalled upon many a painful moment thereafter, I considered that if by some rogue chance I ceased to be this very night, then I surely would not die in sorrow, nor in regret, but rather, should go to meet my maker a contented woman.

Two weeks later I set out to walk to Crompton Hall, carrying my lavender bag packed with a variety of remedies.

I had passed a worrying time. Ivy had come to me in tears, declaring herself to be expecting another child.

'But the vinegar and the sea sponge?' I asked, bewildered.

'I used them, Alice. They didn't work.'

I felt a chill hand clutch at my heart, but concealed my distress in deference to Ivy's own. How fervently I wished that we lived in future times, a time when women might have sovereignty over their fertility, a time when the last inequality between man and womankind will surely fall away.

Anxious and afraid, I prayed for my deliverance. I sought forgiveness for my sin, if any there had been, for a mortal sin can only be one which harms another, or which defiles the gifts of God, and I asked that I might be given insight. I did not feel myself to be defiler, nor defiled, and could only trust that the instinct proved sound.

On the morning of my walk, it truly seemed that my every prayer had been answered. I did not carry Christian's bastard child. Ivy was reconciled to her fate. And my mother was home, growing stronger by the day. Indeed, so robust did she seem that Dr Harte had cause to wonder if the new hospital cook had discovered some secret cure for the canker, or whether the improvement were simply due to her broiled beef stew!

He looked at me keenly as he spoke, and I fancied myself under scrutiny, as though I might have been the one to effect a cure. But although I continued to give my mother the tincture of mistletoe, I revealed nothing, and quickly turned the conversation to India, for this, I knew, always gained his interest.

'Her little elephant is very sick. And she is very distressed. So much so, that Lady Crompton inquired if I might help in any manner . . .'

He looked away.

'But of course,' he said briskly, 'I am a doctor, not a veterinary surgeon. There is nothing I can do.'

It was then that I resolved to visit Polly as soon as possible, to see if I might treat the creature myself, and to offer India whatever comfort she might need.

I had made no decision about returning as her companion, and whenever I considered it, found myself thrown into confusion. I wondered whether some other calling awaited me, though I had no idea what it might be, and there were yet more personal matters which seemed to preclude a return to Crompton Hall. I didn't know when I might see Christian again, nor had I any true intimation of how he might regard me when we met, but I felt sure a new understanding had been forged between us, one in which banter and teasing had been set aside to be replaced by honesty. And yes . . . by love. But such a love, I reasoned, could only be nurtured if I maintained a distance from Crompton Hall.

The morning was crisp and fair, a first intimation of autumn with the lavender fields bereft of their summer blue, and the leaves on the beech trees turning to gold. I walked quickly, avoiding the Hall and its gardens, taking instead the route to the lake and the elephant's compound, rejoicing in the pale warmth of the sun and the fresh misty air of the woods. My heart was light, my head clear.

When I arrived at the compound, I found Hardy unloading a new bale of straw.

'Well now, Alice, I'm very pleased to see you,' he said gravely. 'I think we all have need of your calming presence.'

'Is Polly worse? Not dead, I hope?'

He shook his head and motioned to the stable.

'She's pining away,' he replied. 'But I hardly think Polly's plight will rouse much interest at the Hall today. They have more important matters to concern them.'

I opened the gate to the compound and made to undo my lavender bag.

'What's happened?' I asked carelessly, imagining some household dilemma involving a leaky roof or a theft from the kitchen, matters known to incense Lady Crompton, thereby throwing the Hall into regular panic.

Hardy motioned me toward the bale of straw.

'Sit down,' he said, 'and I'll tell you.'

I sat down suddenly, my heart leaping to the back of my throat.

'It's Master Christian, wouldn't you know? We heard this morning that he'd run away to Scotland with Miss Marianne, having made the most elaborate plans to deceive Mr Goodchild who believed his sister staying with a cousin in Winchester . . . A fortnight was lost, and when they were discovered, they were already man and wife! Sir Robin is sorely vexed, Lady Crompton has taken to her bed, and Miss India sits weeping in her room . . .'

He hesitated.

'Crompton Hall needs you, Alice. You must persuade them all to toast the happy couple and get ready for their return! Only you have the good sense to make the best of things.'

Chapter Fifteen

Lady Crompton, having been raised to overcome the social rebuffs and slights of etiquette that life invariably threw up, was highly skilled at turning disaster into triumph.

But the other way round proved rather more difficult.

While Sir Robin paced the terrace, grim-faced, and India retreated to her room in distress, declaring with unfathomable conviction that it was all *her* fault, Lady Crompton was hard put to muster a sigh.

Of course, it was thoroughly reprehensible of Christian to have deceived Adam Goodchild in so concerted a manner, and since being apprehended, he'd shown not an ounce of remorse. But the ways of true love were beyond reason, and the passion of young people beyond recall. Only the most stern and unforgiving parent would view elopement as a crime.

Lady Crompton was neither stern nor unforgiving, or so she told herself. And if everyone else continued to view the wedding as if it were a funeral, then it surely fell to her, mother-in-law of the motherless bride, to show compassion. She could scarcely wait to begin, indeed had already ventured to consult Cook about baking sweetmeats – a difficult matter since she didn't wish to give too much away – and she longed to know the detail of Christian and Marianne's return.

But Sir Robin, a mild man at the best of times, and a forbearing one when times worsened, was, for all that, a formidable presence when times became genuinely tough. He was the only person to have spoken to Adam Goodchild, and the only one who knew what might happen next. Yet Lady Crompton dared not approach him, and having no patience with India's garbled assertion that she'd guessed what Christian planned, indeed might have prevented it had she spoken out, found herself in urgent need of an ally.

Alice, arriving unannounced, was therefore greeted with unprecedented joy.

'My dear girl!' Her Ladyship cried, waving her into the morning room. 'Maybe now we shall get some sense into the household, and some preparations underway for our dear son's nuptials! I wonder if you might speak to Cook about baking the sweetmeats? We shall need iced fancies, some of those little almond tartlets, and a celebration cake . . .'

She hesitated. 'You've heard the news, of course?'

Alice looked pale and serious, as though she personally were in possession of unhappy news.

'I'm told by Doctor Harte that your Mama has made an extraordinary recovery!' Lady Crompton said quickly. 'We're so very pleased, Alice. We've all been waiting on your return.'

Alice nodded absently.

'I thought I should see Miss India,' she muttered, 'I gather she's very dismayed . . .'

Lady Crompton frowned.

'There's no call for dismay. The sweetmeats must be our first concern. I'm sure India will welcome her brother and his new wife . . . As indeed we all will, once we've got over our surprise.'

India, however, showed no sign of recovering from the surprise, nor indeed, of taking any pleasure in her brother's marriage.

She remained closeted in her room, lying face down on her tapestry quilt until Alice knocked upon the bedroom door. Then at once the lament began.

'Oh Alice, he is the very worst of men! He has deceived us all. There's been no thought for anyone's feelings but his own. And do you know who is most deceived?'

'Tell me,' said Alice steadily.

'Why, it is myself! He dared to tell me he meant to pursue Marianne, and trusted me to say nothing! How wickedly have I been misused . . .'

India paused, reconsidering her words.

'And then there is poor Marianne,' she added carefully. 'Imagine it, Alice. Your life irrevocably bound to a man who can never be trusted . . . Who has married you simply for your money and your land!'

Alice sat down on the quilt. For a moment she covered her face with her hands, as though she might be praying – or crying – but when she looked up, she was utterly calm.

'You don't know that,' she said gently. 'And even if it were true, Marianne certainly doesn't know it. In any case, marriage can change a man. Where once he imagined himself acting purely from self-interest, he may later find himself genuinely bound in honour and duty.'

India sat bolt upright on the bed.

'Honour and duty! Christian? I think you know him better than that.'

Alice looked away.

'The very worst thing,' said India unsteadily, 'is that he has besmirched the name of Crompton . . . He does not deserve to be part of this family.'

Alice said nothing, unwilling to contemplate what, in India's view, might best deserve the name of Crompton.

'I have allowed my own feelings blind me!' India cried. 'I knew that Christian would not be thwarted, but I felt unable to warn Papa for fear of what he might do . . . And I didn't feel ready to approach Adam so soon after rejecting him . . .'

A sudden thought occurred to India.

'Alice, what of your own marriage proposal? Have you come to tell me that you're soon to be Mrs Youngman?'

Her lip trembled and a tear escaped her eye. Alice took her hand and stroked it gently.

'I've decided not to accept Charlie's offer,' she said at last. 'I don't know what the future holds for me now, but I'm sure I shall be given the strength to endure it . . .'

The future had never before seemed something to be endured, not to Alice at least, but since the revelation of her own feelings for Luke Harte, India felt she had gained some understanding of endurance.

'We shall endure together!' she cried passionately, throwing her arms around Alice's neck. 'We shall be old maids one and all, and never think ourselves deprived or rejected . . .'

Alice laughed, despite herself.

'We shall be ourselves,' she said.

India was already thinking ahead.

'When Christian and Marianne return,' she declared, 'I shall be gracious and polite. I shall greet them as a loving sister should, but I'll not condone their actions. By this deception they forfeit all right to indulgence. And I shall view this whole episode as a warning lesson, Alice. Unbridled passion brings its own terrible reward!'

On a less portentous occasion, Alice might have advised a more charitable response – while remarking that in this instance no terrible reward seemed to have ensued – but as it was, she merely inclined her head.

'Yes,' she agreed soberly, 'unbridled passion would make fools of us all.'

They rode up to the Hall on a fine autumn day, horses' hooves throwing out a cloud of fallen leaves so that it seemed the bridal carriage flew on a cloud of golden confetti.

But beyond this spontaneous tribute, no concession had been made to celebration. Lady Crompton had wished for garlands to deck the portico, but Sir Robin had sanctioned no garlands. Nor were there any sweetmeats.

'It would be entirely improper,' Sir Robin told his wife sternly, 'for this family to indulge in festivity. Let Adam Goodchild give a party for his sister if he wishes. That is his privilege as guardian of the bride, though on this occasion, he may decide to forgo it.'

Lady Crompton had begged to differ in her usual unimpeachable manner, but finding this accomplished nothing, had begun to wheedle, and then to plead. They could not let the moment pass without so much as a sliver of wedding cake! There must surely be a bouquet – or if not, a posy – in the hall? Hardy had remarked only that morning on the fine display of late camellias in the conservatory . . . A few camellias would hardly constitute a festival?

Sir Robin remained deaf to all petition, and so it was

that a small and subdued group of well-wishers stepped out to greet the carriage. Sir Robin himself led the way, his wife by his side, all her pleasure in the occasion meanly thwarted, and her expression plainly registering that fact. Behind them walked India, pale-faced, head held proudly aloft, and in the rear, equally pale yet with none of her mistress's defiance, hanging back as far as she might without seeming to show reluctance, came Alice.

'Mama! How splendid it is to be home!'

Christian sprang from the carriage and took his mother in his arms, briefly closing his eyes against his father's forbidding frown and his sister's impassive stare. He turned back to the carriage, oblivious of disapproval, or at least, intent on ignoring it. He seemed not to have noticed Alice.

'And I now present Mrs Christian Crompton-Leigh!'

Marianne smiled uncertainly and accepted her husband's hand, glancing anxiously at Sir Robin and dropping a deferential curtsey to her mother-in-law. She was dressed in bridal blue, and wore a corsage of rosebuds at her collar.

'I'm very happy to be back,' she said meekly.

Perhaps it was her modesty, her genuine lack of guile, or simply her youth that melted Sir Robin's frosty composure. Whatever, he suddenly moved toward her and took her gloved hand, pressing it firmly in his own.

'My dearest girl,' he said gently. 'My dear daughter . . . Come inside at once! You must be tired from your journey, and in need of refreshment . . .'

Above Marianne's head he caught the eye of his wife, who raised her gaze heavenward. *Refreshment indeed!*

'What a wonderful day this is!' Lady Crompton cried, needing no further encouragement to allow her feelings full reign. 'We're so happy for you both! Of course, there's been no time for baking sweetmeats, but I know Cook won't let us down . . .'

She kissed Marianne on both cheeks, then turned quickly to Alice.

'You'll organize it, won't you, Alice? Some cold ham, and perhaps some potatoes? And if there's any apple pie . . .'

Christian had turned to his sister, presenting her with a

silver thistle necklet from Scotland as though he'd guessed she might prove his most formidable opponent and had sought, by slender means of a trinket, to secure her goodwill. At his mother's words he spun on his heel.

'Alice!'

She moved forward, bowed politely and held his gaze.

'Welcome home, Sir,' she said.

If he seemed flustered, then none but Alice noticed, and if he took time to recover himself, then it was only a moment.

'I'm delighted to see you back!' he said quickly. 'We've all missed you, I'm sure.'

Alice bowed again, unsmiling.

'You're too kind, Sir,' she said.

'I wonder if Cook has any jellies or custards,' Lady Crompton pondered tetchily. 'Please go at once, Alice, and sort it out . . .'

Christian laughed, a little too heartily.

'Oh yes, Alice will sort it out!' he said jovially, turning to his sister's companion with a broad smile as though he suddenly perceived the wisdom of assuming his old manner. 'You'll find her a great help, my darling!'

This last was addressed to Marianne, whose arm he now tucked into his own, leading her into the Hall while Alice strode ahead of them, the sound of his laughter still echoing in her ears.

Inside the house, just beyond the green door, she paused to take breath. She found herself unexpectedly glad that she enjoyed the status of mere servant in this house, that she was not some impoverished aunt or distant cousin who would be required to sit and chat to the newly-weds, making polite conversation while her heart cried out in protest.

As it was, she could claim duties in the kitchen to keep her well away from the family, providing India, of course, did not insist upon her presence. This was the only reason Alice ever found herself taking tea on the terrace or supper in the dining hall – because India wished it and because Lady Crompton, indulging her daughter on inconsequential matters while retaining the veto for weighty ones, permitted it. And yet, Alice determined grimly, on this occasion India would be overruled, not by her mother, but by her trusty companion.

As she hurried toward the kitchen, however, a new thought occurred. Strictly speaking, she was no longer in Lady Crompton's employ. She'd received no wages since leaving to care for her mother, and had made no final decision about returning. Everyone, from Her Ladyship to India, and indeed to Christian, had simply assumed that she was back to stay. But she'd said nothing on the matter herself, and need not consider herself committed. She could put on her coat and leave the moment she chose.

She threw open the kitchen door and found the maids in a flurry, rushing to and fro with creams and curds, anticipating just such an emergency as was now announced.

Cook, however, had not stirred from her afternoon perch by the sunny window where she sat with a small tot of whisky in hand, regarding the bustle around her with wry unconcern.

'It's too late for sweetmeats!' she declared, waving her whisky glass at Alice. 'And if Her Ladyship's thinking of apple pie, then you'll have to tell her it's all gone. When folk rush off and get married without a by-your-leave, they can't expect the fatted calf . . .'

A titter from the scullery confirmed that the maids were listening, and Daisy Turner's face appeared in the crack of the door.

'Or even the fatted goose?' she inquired cheekily. 'We haven't got a calf.'

'There's the fatted piglet,' somebody said behind her.

'Or the fatted turnip,' Daisy suggested. 'There's a huge one in the kitchen garden! Just right for Master Turnip-Head Christian and his new Missus . . .'

Alice blanched. She was not used to hearing the Cromptons mocked in such a way.

She sat down at the kitchen table, nodding absently as a variety of morsels were submitted for her approval. The talk among the maids was becoming raucous, but rather than reprimanding them, Cook joined in the laughter. *A turnover for the new Mrs Crompton? Well, she'd had one of those already!* Everyone, it seemed, was laughing at the expense of the Cromptons. High-born they might be, but not so high they couldn't be brought down by a bit of a ribbing . . .

Alice clasped her trembling fingers in her lap. It seemed a subtle change had occurred since she was last at the house, a precarious movement toward the waiting future, so slight it was barely perceptible, yet in the maids' laughter, in the Cook's whisky, it was there. The unquestioned acceptance of hierarchy was faltering. Respect for the old order was dying. The servants were becoming contemptuous of their employers.

And then, in a strange, unsettling flash of intuition, Alice glimpsed the end of an era. She saw the kitchen in which she now sat, not staffed by laughing maids and garrulous cooks, but empty and silent, a redundant room which echoed to a solitary step on the stairway beyond. She saw the gardens beyond the terrace choked by briars and hemlock, moss between the paving slabs like velvet slime, and the lake – the beautiful green and silver lake – swaying beneath a rotting platform of sedge.

'Good Heavens, Miss Alice, whatever's the matter?'

She saw the turrets on the east wing crumble, and the fig tree in the kitchen garden bend beneath a burden of uncut branches. She saw a family displaced, and a house in ruin.

'Miss Alice! You look as though you've seen a ghost!'

Daisy was bending toward her anxiously, and Cook was waving the whisky bottle under her nose.

'You need one of your potions,' Daisy said.

'You need a little nip of this!' Cook said.

Alice, returned to the present, smiled and shook her head. She knew exactly what she needed.

'Call the parlour maids and have them lay the table in the dining hall,' she said quickly. 'One of them can tell Lady Crompton what's to be served . . .'

They looked at her expectantly, as though they sensed a portentous announcement.

Alice stood up.

What she might have said, had emotion not threatened to betray her, was that her duty to India had ended. That India would now have Marianne for a companion. That her own mother and young brother needed her more than the new Crompton household.

Instead she simply held out a hand to Cook and kissed Daisy on the cheek.

'I'm going home,' she said.

It had been confidently expected by Lady Crompton, and therefore by virtually everyone else, that the young couple would move into Crompton Hall, occupying Christian's old quarters.

Indeed, so certain had Her Ladyship been of these arrangements, that she had taken the trouble to consult a supplier of fabrics from Norwich. A bundle of swatches was already in the drawing room awaiting Marianne's approval, the decisions to be made, quite naturally, with considered advice from her mother-in-law.

It was not to be.

'They're moving into Goodchild Manor,' Sir Robin told his wife shortly, not a fortnight after the happy couple's return. 'It has all been discussed with Adam.'

The news surprised Christian as much as his mother, and led to a terse exchange between father and son.

'I should think, Sir, that I might be allowed to live where I choose with my wife!'

'I should think,' said Sir Robin, 'that without the means to support yourself or your family, you'd be damned grateful to live anywhere.'

Christian, finding his mother curiously unwilling to tackle her husband, not on the subject of the allowance he had reasonably expected upon marriage, nor on the vexed matter of the living quarters, appealed to India for help.

'You'd like to have Marianne here, wouldn't you? She'd be splendid company for you! And that would mean more free time for Alice to look after her mother ... Where is Alice, anyway?'

India, shocked to find her companion departed once more, and this time without so much as a goodbye, had made no move to discover Alice's intentions. Since the day of Christian's return she'd been out of sorts and in no mood to indulge anyone else, least of all her wayward brother.

'I'm sure Adam wishes Marianne under his own roof again,' she snapped. 'That seems very sensible, I must say. And please don't worry about me, dear Christian. I shall be perfectly fine – without Marianne or Alice!'

Christian frowned.

'I really don't see why you're so bad-tempered! I should have thought you'd be glad to have a new sister ...'

'And so I might,' replied India haughtily, 'if my new sister had been won by honest means.'

His face darkened.

'Don't criticize me,' he said sharply. 'And don't presume to judge what you can't understand.'

India tossed her head.

'Exactly *what* do I fail to understand?' she demanded. 'The facts seem straightforward to me. You have deceived us all. You have preyed upon Marianne's infatuation, and you have used her to create a profitable alliance for yourself!'

He turned away.

'Not so profitable at the moment,' he said with a tight little laugh.

India, who'd startled herself somewhat by her forthright attack, considered herself vindicated by this remark, as well as severely provoked.

'How cruel are the ways of a fortune-hunting husband!' she cried bitterly. 'How misused is poor Marianne! You are surely the most wicked of men, and my own brother too ...'

He swung round to face her.

'I am no fortune hunter,' he said angrily, 'and Marianne is no fool. You know perfectly well that an alliance between our families has long been wished by all parties. It was merely a question of who it was to be – you and Adam, or myself and Marianne. All I have done is to precipitate the matter.'

'This marriage was not wished,' said India hotly. 'Not by Adam . . .'

He raised one eyebrow.

'No, of course not. Kind, generous, devoted Adam! He who has spent so long wandering the world, so many months and years away from home, that he knows exactly what his sister needs . . .'

India had never considered Adam anything less than faultless in all matters of judgement, but now that she thought about it, she saw the truth of this suggestion.

'He *is* kind!' she countered, unwilling to allow Christian any small victory. 'And I know he is devoted to Marianne. He doesn't deserve to have his feelings so sorely abused . . .'

Christian smiled grimly.

'I find it touching, your deep concern for Adam's feelings. It was rather different a short while ago, was it not? No concern, I seem to remember, when you told him you didn't love him?'

India was angry beyond measure.

'How dare you speak of love!' she spat. 'You who know nothing of it!'

His own anger seemed to have vanished, and now he regarded her thoughtfully, his face grave, his eyes downcast.

'Ah India,' he said quietly, 'how wrong you are! I have been in love, and have known my love to be utterly in vain. She would not have me, and made it clear that she never would . . . Can you imagine such a fate? To love, and yet to know that you will never be united?'

India hesitated. She could imagine such a fate only too well.

Christian moved to the window, staring out beyond the terrace to the beech woods and the lake.

'So what is a man to do?' he asked over his shoulder. 'Live in sin, or in celibacy like a monk? Or is he, instead, to find a partner with whom he might establish a bond of compatibility and mutual regard, a lifelong companion whose own assets – yes, I freely admit it – would complement his own? Might it be the case that such a marriage, undertaken not in passion but in hope, could flourish and grow?'

India sat down suddenly upon the chaise longue.

Hadn't Alice expressed many such similar sentiments in their private discussions upon marriage and love? Discussions which had preceded her own refusal of Adam Goodchild, and which knew nothing of her infatuation with Luke Harte ... Sentiments which seemed inappropriate to her own situation, yet which now, so far as Christian were concerned, seemed to be borne of a wisdom she had carelessly dismissed ...

She took a deep breath and looked up at her brother.

'You have not behaved as a Crompton should,' she said, 'but you may yet redeem yourself. You may demonstrate your concern for Marianne by agreeing to live at Goodchild Manor ... At least until Papa changes his mind ...'

He nodded.

'Perhaps so,' he said heavily.

'It is always better to heal a rift where one exists!'

'As always,' he replied, 'you are right!'

'And once Papa sees you settled and Marianne content, he will relent and increase your allowance.'

He moved away from the window and sat down beside her.

'I certainly hope so. And I'd be very grateful if you'd persuade Mama to speak to him ...'

India shook her head.

'You must first show your changed ways ... Then it may all be as Alice encouraged me to hope! She said that marriage would change you. That where once you might have thought yourself acting purely from self interest, you would later find yourself genuinely bound in honour and duty.'

Christian's face contorted, and he stood up again, turning toward the door.

'Alice said that?'

'Yes. She has always believed the best of you. And where others rush to condemn, she counsels loving forgiveness . . . It is a lesson to me, Christian.'

She waited, hoping he might also acknowledge the edifying effects of Alice's measured musings.

But he did no such thing. Instead he walked swiftly from the room, in such a hurry, for some unknown reason, that he did not pause to close the door behind him.

The move to Goodchild Manor was duly settled upon, but the departure was delayed.

Since her arrival at Crompton Hall, Marianne had been unwell, an indisposition which caused her to faint at the supper table, and which kept her closeted in her room most mornings with a large china bowl by her bedside.

Lady Crompton insisted that Dr Harte be summoned, a precaution nobody else deemed necessary but which Her Ladyship calculated might be the means of further prolonging the happy couple's stay beneath her own roof.

'One can't be too careful,' she informed her husband and her son, while India, mystified, offered Marianne a tiny platter of crystallized ginger which, she recalled, Alice had always recommended to ward off sickness.

But Marianne, wretched and distressed, refused to consume anything beyond the occasional spoonful of scrambled egg or finger of dry bread. And she certainly didn't intend to take any unorthodox medicaments.

'I couldn't possibly!' she gasped as India soothed her forehead with a damp flannel and indicated the plate of ginger yet again.

'Why ever not? It can't do you any harm!'

'I have to be careful,' sobbed poor Marianne. 'Your Mama says I must be very careful . . .'

Even then India did not understand, and when she heard that Dr Harte was to call, set aside her own agitation in genuine relief that Marianne was to be helped.

Nevertheless, as the hour approached for his visit, she

found herself growing ever more restless, until the anticipation of seeing him again became an agony of doubt and imagined embarrassment. Suppose he failed to meet her eye, or hurried past her in the hall? Suppose there were no covert acknowledgement of what had happened between them, no fleeting exchange of private understanding? Indeed, now that she thought about it, how could there be? Such a thing would be deeply improper.

She had been sitting alone in the drawing room, ears alert for the first sound of an approaching carriage, but now she leapt to her feet and pulled on the bellrope for Daisy – unexpectedly promoted that week from kitchen to parlour – demanding her cloak.

'It's cold outside, Miss,' said Daisy proffering the cloak.

'A brisk walk will warm me,' said India distractedly.

'You shouldn't go near the lake, Miss. It's swollen past its banks and the paths are very slippery . . .'

Daisy was taking her new duties seriously, and had even allowed herself to imagine that with Alice gone, she might find herself elevated to personal maid. Self interest had tempered her disaffection with the Cromptons and now she gazed at India eagerly, anxious to demonstrate her suitability for any task that might be required.

'Perhaps a scarf as well as the cloak?' she suggested. 'There's a nasty throat going about the village. A young boy brought it back from his cousin in Lynn . . . They say the cousin has a bad fever with it . . .'

But India offered no encouragement, sweeping from the room without a backward glance, leaving Daisy to reflect that the Cromptons were indeed a funny, stuck-up lot. She pursed her lip. The new Mrs Crompton might prove a better prospect altogether, especially as Daisy happened to know that her personal maid was set for a hurried wedding too. Yes, Marianne, with husband-trouble in her belly, was far too weak and needy for airs and graces . . .

India walked quickly, veering away from the main thoroughfares and into the beech woods, heading toward the summerhouse beside the lake, despite Daisy's warning about slippery banks. The route took her along the path to

Polly's compound, and with a guilty start, she remembered the ailing elephant, absent from her thoughts since the fuss about Christian and Marianne – and, it had to be confessed, more especially since the fateful day she'd recognized the extent of her feeling for Luke Harte, and found herself overtaken by romantic dreams.

To be sure, she'd inquired after Polly's progress whenever she saw Hardy, and had expressed concern when told of the elephant's accelerating decline. But she had not visited. A certain squeamishness overcame her whenever the subject came up, not so much at the elephant itself as at the knowledge that it had been presented in expectation of her delight. There was something monstrous about this assumption, as though Christian saw something she did not. With an intuition she could not quite unravel, India had come to view Polly as her nemesis.

Now, however, she stopped and peered anxiously along the track toward the compound.

At once Hardy appeared around a bend as though he'd been awaiting her arrival this past month or more.

'Miss India . . . How very fortunate! I have with me this very morning an expert from the Regent's Park Zoo. Master Christian, before he . . . went away . . . contacted the zoo with a view to having Polly removed to a more suitable place . . .'

India nodded, embarrassed.

'Is the elephant much worse?' she asked tentatively.

The foreman's eyes brightened.

'Well, that's just it! Thanks to Miss Alice, Polly is completely recovered. One of those little pills, and she was up and running round right as rain . . .'

He chuckled.

'Miss Alice is a regular wonder-worker,' he beamed. 'I've told everyone how she cured that elephant! I reckon if you can cure a creature like that, you can cure anyone of anything. Miss Alice should set up in business!'

So open – and so ardent – was his admiration that India saw in that moment a myriad of possible futures for Alice. Wonder-worker, nurse, counsellor, purveyor of potions and pills, maybe even the next Mrs Hardy . . . Alice would surely never need to return as her companion. There were too many other prospects.

Was this why she had departed so summarily? Had a line been drawn beneath their friendship as she left to embark upon a new career?

Hardy coughed nervously.

'Should you like to say goodbye to Polly, Miss?'

'Thank you, no,' said India coolly, turning to resume her path toward the lake.

She took her time, meandering around the shores of the lake, taking care to keep away from the slippery banks, debating whether she might take the boat from its moorings, or simply idle in the summerhouse. The longer she stayed away from the Hall, the less likely she was to encounter Luke.

But like all desperate lovers, she found herself both wishing to avoid him and to see him. Thus it was that while she lingered over-long in the summerhouse, once her mind was made up, she set off toward the house at speed.

She'd reached the orchard behind the kitchen garden when she met him, inexplicably on foot and making considerable progress himself toward the village. For a moment they stared at each other in silence, and in that moment India knew that she need hardly have feared embarrassment or slight. His face was a mirror of his emotion.

'I thought I wouldn't see you,' he muttered.

'You nearly didn't.'

'And yet here you are!'

'Here we both are . . .'

Further irrelevancies spilled forth. No, he had not meant to walk through the beech woods, but Eugenie and Frederica had required the carriage at the last moment . . . Yes, it was true that Polly had been miraculously restored . . . No, he would not be visiting Marianne again before her departure to Goodchild Manor . . . Yes, a new home had been found for the elephant . . .

Still they stared at each other.

'So Marianne is not seriously ill?' India inquired at last.

'Good heavens, no. She's in excellent health. The first three months are always the worst.'

'Oh, yes, I know,' said India foolishly, finally seeing Marianne's situation.

'And you? Your own health is good? I hear from Lady Crompton that you have been in low spirits . . .'

India nodded, holding his gaze.

'And I too,' he whispered.

Later, when each returned to this moment, they would imagine that the other had made the crucial movement, that in surrendering to the irresistible impulse, each was guilty of compromising the other, yet in truth their coming together – no more than the brushing of lips, the entwining of limbs and the mingling of breath – was a mutual act. She drifted into his arms like a feather on the breeze and he reached to catch her as though she were an autumn leaf tumbling toward the earth.

It lasted only a second.

'India, forgive me . . .'

'There is nothing to forgive!'

He stepped back from her embrace.

'Yes there is! I am risking your good reputation and sullying my own conscience. We must never meet like this again!'

'No, never,' she agreed and the words fell between them like pebbles in a well, thudding, echoing, sunk without trace.

He brushed a hand across his face, and it seemed to India that the wheel of desire upon which all suffering life must inescapably turn had come full cycle at last, and now cranked with an audible groan toward its next torturous revolution.

She leaned against the orchard wall, seeing before her an endless future of frustrated hopes.

He waved, then marched swiftly into the gathering dusk, his shoulders hunched against the growing chill of the evening.

India swallowed a sob.

Above her in the beech trees a nightingale warbled its first few ecstatic notes, but she, immured to any sensation beyond her own thwarted longing, registered nothing of that melancholy voice, nor sought to catch the mystery of its sad and noble song.

She turned and walked slowly back to Crompton Hall.

Chapter Sixteen

'Which breast am I removing?'

Laurie, naked beneath her theatre gown, bald head covered by a gauze turban, watched the lights in the ceiling above her face begin to dim.

'The left breast,' she replied tersely.

'And why am I removing it?'

Was the man a complete fool? Didn't he know what the hell he was doing?

She took a deep breath and felt her limbs float away. Her eyelids flickered. Nothing remained but the faintest spark of consciousness. She would have to rally for one last glorious gasp.

'Because I have cancer, stupid,' she said.

The consultant's pink cheeks crinkled above his surgeon's mask.

'Just checking,' he said, amused. 'Can't have you suing because I took the wrong one off.'

Laurie dreamed she was back at Crompton Hall, but not the Hall as she had known it.

There were no treatment rooms, no refectory, no low, plush sofas nor musical instruments set out for play.

And there were no people either. It was all as it must have been a hundred years before, and yet there were no parlour maids scurrying to light the drawing room fire, no butler hovering in the shadows with a silver tray, no sound of croquet from the lawn, nor clatter of carriage wheels on the driveway. The place was utterly empty.

Laurie wandered the familiar corridors, marvelling at their transformation. Heavy furniture, tallboys, chests and dressing tables, covered every spare foot of wall, and behind their dark polished opulence, she glimpsed ornate wallpaper, green and gold with a bold peacock motif.

She walked downstairs to the room where she'd first encountered Dale Mitchell, throwing open the door to let in the light. It was no longer a counselling suite but a library, the walls lined with thick leather-backed tomes, the air musty with cigar smoke. She lingered in the doorway, trembling, afraid to enter. Then she walked swiftly to the centre of the room and turned toward the fireplace.

The portrait hung in its usual place, and India's piercing blue eyes sought out Laurie's own. *But there was no second figure in the painting!*

Laurie let out a little cry. Where was Alice?

She ran from the room, upstairs toward her bedroom, and to her great relief, found it just as she, and India before her, had left it. The tapestry bedspread was rumpled, as though someone had recently risen from it, and the casement flung open.

Laurie moved to the window and looked out upon the beech woods. She saw at once that they stretched much further than she remembered, and that the sedge on the lake had lost its rotting hue. Now it drifted vivid green, and as she watched, she made out a small vessel at its centre, riding the swaying fronds. *The Lady of the Lake.*

For a long time, she stared at the boat, wondering if it might head for the shore and if she might glimpse a figure walking back toward the house. But the boat remained still, and as she watched, the sky above the glittering lake turned from pale lilac to violet, then to black. Her eyelids began to droop.

She walked back to the bed and lay down on the tapestry quilt, feeling the sturdy stitches beneath her fingers, the softness of the folds. She floated toward sleep, then heard the bedroom door open.

She sensed, rather than saw, the shape bending toward her over the bed.

'Who is it?' she asked drowsily.

'Hush, my dearest,' said an unknown voice. 'Lie still.'

'What are you doing?' Laurie asked distantly, aware

of silky fingers caressing her forehead. 'And what's that scent?'

'Hush,' repeated the voice softly, 'I am anointing you with precious oil . . .'

The odour filled her nostrils, heavy and sweet, tantalizingly familiar. She wanted to ask about the painting, but the words would not come. There was nothing beyond the sensation of smell.

Laurie woke in a pastel room filled with flowers and fought to place herself, dimly recalling her new circumstance. No cancer ward this time, but a private suite.

For a moment she thought she was lying in a funeral parlour. A heady scent hung upon the still air, and in her drugged state, she seemed to drink in the fume of mourning blooms, lilies or carnations. But then, in a concerted re-entry to the world she had known, she placed the perfume. It was lavender.

'Ah, you're back with us! Take it easy now. Everything's just fine . . . The op went really well . . .'

A smiling nurse emerged from a shadowy corner filled with rosebuds and beamed down.

'That smell,' murmured Laurie groggily. 'Lavender . . . Where did it come from?'

'You've had bouquets arriving all afternoon! Aren't they lovely?'

Laurie raised her head, a momentous effort which sent a laser ray of pain searing through her temple.

'But the lavender?' she croaked. 'Can't you smell it? There's no lavender in these flowers, surely?'

The nurse took her hand.

'I expect someone's given you some nice soap,' she said gently. 'Lavender soap. It'll be here somewhere.'

Laurie lay back and closed her eyes. Where her left breast had been, she could feel a pulsating bandage, tight and constricting. So he *could* tell left from right!

A clear plastic tube ran from the depths of the bandage to a plastic bucket at her bedside. The tube was filled with pale pink liquid and at once the thought occurred. *Blood and gall.* She felt the bile rise in her throat and signalled urgently to the nurse.

'There, now . . . Must be the anaesthetic upsetting your tummy . . . You'll feel better in a moment . . . Then you can get some rest . . .'

More rest? I've been out like a hundred-watt bulb for the last three hours!

The room lurched, the fume of the flowers filled her head. She lay back and the world vanished again.

'I am Alice Harper,' said the unknown voice, declaring itself. 'My mother works in the lavender fields beyond Blue Farm . . .'

'Hiya, kid! How you doing?'

Laurie opened one eye and swiftly closed it again.

'Okay, for a girl with only one titty,' she said.

'Who needs two, anyway? Come to think of it, why do we need any at all? They're only there for the boys. It's a sexist plot.'

Laurie opened the other eye. A small silver coffin on a chain swung into view, topped by a white deathmask. Two bejewelled vampire bats bobbed from its ear-lobes.

'I've died and gone to Hell,' she said. 'You're the queen of the underworld.'

'You say the sweetest things.'

Laurie laughed, then wished she hadn't. A knife shifted between her ribs and she moaned.

'Hey, take it easy!' Shelley leaned toward her in alarm and the bat earrings gyrated madly. 'Don't do anything you're not supposed to do.'

'You mean like speak or move? And here's me wanting to try archery . . .'

'Archery! Look, don't say another word . . . You're still drugged up to the eyeballs. I'll just sit here and look pretty till you come round.'

Laurie tried to shake her head and settled for flicking her eyelids instead.

'Archery . . .' she repeated. 'Like the Amazons. They carved off one breast so they could fire their bows better . . .'

She'd no notion where this idea sprang from, yet once voiced, it sounded oddly familiar, like a tune dimly remembered and yet unplaced.

'Crikey! Did they really? Sounds like fun!'

Laurie closed her eyes again, drifting away from the world, back toward the dark. It was a place she didn't want to go. Nor did she wish to wander the empty corridors of Crompton Hall again like a survivor surveying the aftermath of some unknown disaster.

'Keep talking,' she said faintly. 'Tell me what's been happening. Just say anything.'

Shelley ran a hand through the spiked hair and drew breath.

'Um . . . well, there's Jim for a start. It's all over. Turned out to be an AOB . . . A bit like Sean, really. Not that I think Sean's an AOB after all, but there are a lot of similarities. I mean, I knew Jim had an ex-wife, but guess what? The "X" was silent!'

Laurie tried to concentrate.

'You know what I'm saying? Silent as in "We're still married" . . . Great, huh?'

'Yeah,' Laurie whispered. 'Great.'

'What else? Well, Gloria and Elspeth have discovered Sisterhood. Your poor old Dad doesn't know what's hit him. They go shopping, they go to the cinema, they go to the hairdressers. They've even been out looking at bathroom stuff together. Research for when Elspeth goes home!'

'I don't believe it,' Laurie said absently.

'It's true. They'll be here soon so you'll see for yourself. We were all told we couldn't see you before three o'clock, but I conned my way in . . . How did she do that I hear you ask? It was easy. I said I was representing Doctor Dale Mitchell from the Centre for Regenerative Studies, and that I was monitoring your mental condition . . . Worked a treat, particularly as the lovely Dale had been here himself . . .'

Laurie decided she was hallucinating, but still she struggled to connect.

'Doctor Mitchell was here?'

'Seems so. He was visiting someone else, but he inquired about you. Of course, they all knew who he was. I heard a couple of nurses talking about him, so I piped up with lots of stuff about Norfolk. Invited them both down to have a look for themselves . . . They let me in right away.'

'Clever girl.'

'I thought so. And let me state for the record that your mental condition seems pretty good to me. Archery's a great idea. I might even try it myself. 'Course, I wouldn't be as good as you, what with me having two boobs . . .'

The dark was sucking her in, long fingers of black pulling at her reason.

'Keep talking,' she murmured.

'Okay, let me think . . . Hey! You'll never guess who I bumped into the other day . . . Go on have a guess . . .'

Laurie could smell lavender again, heavy and pungent like a field of cut sprigs after rain.

'Alice Harper,' she whispered.

'Who? Well no, not her. It was Eric Russell! Remember Eric? You were going to marry him . . . Except that you weren't, and never would have in a million years. Do you remember getting drunk one night and telling me you couldn't marry him because his name was Eric?'

Lavender Blue, Dilly Dilly, Lavender Green . . .

'Do you remember, Laurie?'

'No, I don't . . . Please keep talking . . .'

'Here comes the hilarious bit. He's not called Eric anymore! He calls himself Rick. I thought that was kind of sad . . . I mean, if he'd thought of it fifteen years ago, he might have stood a chance . . . Not much of one, but even so . . . Rick Russell is a definite improvement . . .'

Lavender Blue, Dilly Dilly . . .

'Now he's divorced with a couple of kids like every other sodding male in the known universe . . . How do they do it? I mean, how come a whole generation of women, presumably mentally competent, actually married these guys in the first place?'

Lavender Blue . . .

'I think you need to sleep now, Laurie . . . I'll come back later.'

'Talk!' The word was a desperate croak, a final attempt to beat back oblivion.

'Whatever you say . . . Um . . . Sean gave up his job. Just walked out one day . . . Seems he came into some hefty insurance his mother set up. Kept that one quiet, didn't he? Most guys would have done a bunk to the South of France and I bet that was Jim's advice . . . Anyway, Sean paid off Tina's mortgage, or most of it, and cut loose . . . Well, when I say *cut loose*, they're still not divorced of course. But it's a step in the right direction. Now he's broke, but happy. At least, that's what he says, but he doesn't look very happy to me . . .'

Laurie was concentrating.

'Sean?' she inquired distantly.

'Come on, you must remember him! Very pretty, blond . . . Lovely bum . . . And here's some bits you don't know. As well as the splendid derrière, he's been sitting on some choice information about life chez Tina . . .'

'Tina?' repeated Laurie, trying hard.

'Seems she wasn't quite the doormat of popular imagination . . . More like one of those metal boot-scrapers that trap you by the heels . . . Would you believe she once dumped five hundred quids' worth of his CDs in the river? Or cut the crotch out of all his underpants?'

'Underpants?' said Laurie vaguely.

'He didn't have a single pair to go to work in. And he lost his entire Motown collection . . . It's either hilarious or heroic, depending on your point of view. I mean, in some circles, she'd be a feminist icon, wouldn't she? Circles not a million miles from here.'

Laurie managed one last sigh.

'Poor Sean,' she murmured.

'Good!' said Shelley. 'I was hoping you'd see it that way.'

Laurie was sitting before the dressing table mirror in India's bedroom, surveying her long luxurious hair.

'It grew back!' she said joyously, running her fingers through the unaccustomed thickness, reaching for a tortoiseshell brush which lay on the table beside her.

'I'll do it for you,' said a voice from behind, and a slender hand floated into view, smoothing the stray fronds of Laurie's fringe.

'Thank you, Alice,' she murmured gratefully.

The brush slid through her new hair like skates over virgin ice, and the sound was not dissimilar, a clean swishing that cut the silence of the room.

'It's even darker than before,' Laurie marvelled, 'I was frightened it might come back mouse brown . . .'

'Take it as a sign,' said Alice softly. 'A sign that you will be healthy and strong again. Believe it.'

Laurie felt her heart lift momentarily, then fall again.

'That's all very well for you to say,' she muttered. 'But you never know with cancer . . .'

'None of us knows,' said Alice. 'We are all in remission from the darkness . . .'

The brush pulled through Laurie's hair, clean hard strokes tugging at her forehead.

In remission from the darkness . . . If only that insight might have been seized before the deadly illness struck . . . How precious, how infinitely beautiful and fragile life would have seemed . . .

'I wish I had the strength to believe,' Laurie said to Alice, watching the hands in the mirror massage the hair at her crown.

'Pray for strength,' said Alice, 'and it will be given.'

Laurie smiled wistfully.

'Do you really think prayer can change the course of events?' she whispered. 'Can it cure a cancer?'

Alice bent down so that her face appeared in the mirror beside Laurie's, a face utterly familiar with its liquid hazel eyes framed by pale gold curls. The face from the painting above the mantel.

'I don't know. I only know that prayers can be answered in extraordinary ways . . . Do you remember the story about the parson?'

Laurie struggled to recall. No, she couldn't remember any such story . . .

'There was a man who went walking among robbers and thieves,' Alice said softly. 'It seemed he must die, and yet he escaped . . .'

She smiled.

'Believe in the power of prayer,' she murmured. 'It summons the angels to your side.'

She set the tortoiseshell brush down on the dressing table and motioned Laurie toward India's bed.

'Lie down now,' she said kindly, 'and I shall dress your wound.'

Laurie closed her eyes. The tapestry bedspread was soft and comforting, Alice's hands gentle and cool. She felt the bandages at her chest loosen and the skin beneath begin to relax.

'What's that smell?' she asked. 'It's not lavender, is it?'

'It's honey,' said Alice softly. 'Honey can mend a tear, and it prevents infection. I gave it to my mother when she too lost a breast, many years ago . . .'

'Thank you, Alice,' Laurie whispered. 'I feel it beginning, really I do . . .'

'What, dearest?' said Alice. 'What is it that you feel?'

Laurie sighed happily.

'Regeneration,' she replied.

She woke to find the jolly nurse bending over her, adjusting the vile tube with its stream of pale pink liquid.

'All right now? I've changed your dressing while you were asleep . . . That should do you for a few hours . . .'

Her chest was patched by plaster, and beneath the unaccustomed flatness, Laurie could feel her skin contracting.

'Your Mum was here . . . She was hoping you'd come round, but I told her to give it a couple of hours . . . She'll be back soon. And she's left something for your tea!'

On the bedside table stood a pack of oatmeal biscuits and a jar of heather honey.

'Would you like some now?'

The nurse loosened the lid of the jar, and the scent of honey wafted toward the bed. Laurie struggled upright, negotiating the tube so that it wouldn't detach.

'I think I would,' she said.

So it was that Gloria found her, nibbling on the biscuits and licking the honey from her lips.

'Darling, you look just fine! And you've had a marvellous sleep . . . I sat here and watched over you . . . Just like when you were a baby . . . There wasn't a flicker!'

Laurie smiled and shook her head.

'I was dreaming,' she said, reaching out for her mother's hand. 'A wonderful, peaceful dream . . .'

Gloria looked down at the hand clasping her own and swallowed hard. She seemed to be searching for words, and yet she said nothing.

'I'm going to be okay!' Laurie said. 'Suddenly, I feel it. My body has been torn apart, but my spirit has been regenerated . . .'

Gloria looked at her daughter doubtfully.

'It takes a long time for anaesthetic to wear off,' she said at last. 'You won't be feeling yourself for quite a while . . .'

Laurie laughed.

'You don't believe me, do you? Well, it's true. You'll see! It's all to do with the power of prayer . . .'

Gloria blinked rapidly.

'Whatever you say, darling. We've all been praying, of course. Although, one never knows exactly what – or who – is being prayed to . . . I imagine some sort of friendly giant living in a lovely garden full of perfect fruit and vegetables . . . A kindly old organic farmer, ploughing the Elysian fields with a couple of shire-horses!'

They both laughed.

'There's something else,' said Laurie. 'Honey! It's amazing that you should have brought me a jar . . . When I get this dressing off, I'm going to smear some on the scar!'

Gloria smiled brightly.

'You're going to do *what?*'

'Well, why not? Didn't they treat amputees in the First World War with honey? It's a natural disinfectant. I thought

262

you'd know all about it. In fact, I assumed that was why you'd brought it . . .'

Gloria looked uncomfortable, disorientated by this unexpected turn of events.

'Once we get you home,' she said carefully, 'we can do whatever we like. But while you're still in hospital, it might be better to toe the line.'

Laurie gazed at her mother in disbelief.

'I never thought I'd hear you say such a thing!'

Gloria picked up the honey jar, hands trembling as she replaced the lid. To Laurie, watching, she seemed suddenly older, less robust, no longer the battling evangelist whose nutritional theories might change the world if only the world would listen . . . Instead, she looked like a woman deeply distressed . . . *A mother who'd faced losing her child.*

'Everyone thinks I forced you into Crompton Hall,' Gloria faltered, 'and everyone thinks you shouldn't go back. We all want you home with us. Your father and Elspeth are staying on . . . We want to look after you . . . I realize now that I should have let you make your own decisions in the first place . . . I shouldn't have filled your head with my ideas. You're the one who's ill. You have to make your own way through. We want to help you do it.'

Laurie fought against a wave of irritation. *Just when we start to agree, you change your mind!*

She fought, and won.

'You have helped,' she said gently. 'By sending me to Norfolk, you've done more than you could ever know . . . Don't give up on it now, Mummy . . . Stay with it, for my sake . . .'

Gloria looked up.

'That's the first time you've called me Mummy in years!' she whispered.

There were few visitors to the little hospital room.

Robert came with Elspeth, but the people from Laurie's office, her neighbours, her old school friends and regulars at the New Leaf, sent cards and gifts instead.

The only surprise visit came from her hairdresser, full of bright ideas for the new growth which was just beginning to shadow her scalp like a faint blue haze on a summer horizon. Laurie was deeply grateful, but wished that others had braved the cancer scourge too.

Instead they sent flowers and grapes and magazines and wine. Some sent chocolates, some sent biscuits, and one, who'd suffered endless lentil suppers at the New Leaf, ordered a takeaway parcel of tandoori chicken to be delivered. The room reeked of spice, and Shelley had to dash to the hospital shop for a perfume spray.

There were no flowers or cards from Sean.

'But he did call to find out how you were,' Shelley said.

'I'm sorry he hasn't visited . . . I was going to quiz him about the underpants.'

Shelley looked shamefaced.

'Maybe I shouldn't have told you that. I don't think he's ever talked about it, except to Jim . . . Still, that's rather to his credit, don't you think? It shows restraint.'

Laurie grimaced.

'Restraint or embarrassment?'

'Shall I tell him to come so you can find out?'

'No thanks!'

'I thought you were building bridges?' Shelley had also seen a change in Gloria, and clearly hoped to utilize Laurie's new-found forbearance.

'I am. But I'm a bit short on nuts and bolts . . .'

Nevertheless, her earlier toughness was dissolving, the strident certainties she'd embraced appearing now as fragments of a self shattered by fear. She was experiencing what she secretly continued to call *regeneration*, a lightness of heart upon waking that was utterly foreign to the victim she'd so recently felt herself to be, a cleaving to the future in growing confidence, a nurturing of that rare and delicate bloom, the tiny bud of hope, visible now for the first time amid the withering foliage of terminal disease.

She had removed the dressing on her chest in the privacy of her hospital room. She'd been apprehensive, fearing an

264

ugly raw disc or a weeping gash. Instead she saw skin smoothly joined, no more than a faint puckering across the flat expanse of her ribcage, still red where the knife had cut, but already knitting together. She took the jar of honey and dribbled a thin stream across the wound. It was fragrant and soothing. She licked her fingers and laughed at herself.

Her remaining breast hung forlornly, a lone embarrassment in the memory of her former symmetry. But she would get used to it. Already she'd begun to experiment with the breast-shaped bits of silicone and foam she'd been given. Perhaps she'd use them, or perhaps she wouldn't. Perhaps she would flaunt her lop-sided profile like a battle scar, the Amazon displaying her warrior status . . .

It wasn't over yet, of course. Radiotherapy still to go . . . Yet she couldn't believe anything would prove intolerable now. She had come through! Gloria, Dr Mitchell, Edie and Val, they'd been right all along . . . Beating cancer was a matter of positive thinking, of right attitude, of *will*.

She had only to believe in order to survive.

How simple, how clear, how *obvious* regeneration had turned out to be!

The opportunity to extol this new understanding arrived precipitously, with no time for the inevitable cooling off.

'Hi there! You're looking good . . .'

Dale Mitchell, by contrast, was looking tired and pale, his eyes bloodshot and his skin sallow. Laurie was startled by his appearance, but immediately gratified by his arrival. There was no one else she'd rather see.

After a few hurried preliminaries, she began at once.

'I dreamed of Alice,' she announced. 'I was back in Crompton Hall, sitting at India's dressing table and Alice was brushing my hair . . . She spoke to me. It was so real . . .'

He nodded politely.

'Alice was quite a girl,' he said.

'She was more than that . . . She was an angel! Do you

believe in angels, Doctor Mitchell? You should. They can be summoned to your side . . .'

He looked uncomfortable, and Laurie had the wit to realize how odd, how very unlike her usual cool and rational self she sounded. It wouldn't do to have him think her barmy.

'Excuse me,' she muttered, 'it's just that everything has suddenly fallen into place . . . I understand now what it is that Crompton Hall offers. Regeneration is surely belief in a future which is itself dependent on a vision of the past . . . Nothing changes, does it? We are all required to work out our own salvation, no matter which era we find ourselves in, and no matter which challenges we are forced to face . . .'

He smiled uncertainly.

'That's one way of putting it, yes . . .'

'How would you put it?' Laurie asked sharply. Just when she would have welcomed his all-American enthusiasm, he, like Gloria, had retreated into vagueness. She might almost think him humouring her.

At the familiar note of antagonism, however, he sat up.

'I would say that serious illness brings about a state of heightened awareness. That with all senses on red alert, a sick person may tune into a mode of being that the rest of us can only imagine. Insights, visions, a telepathic connection with the past . . . An intuitive understanding of the workings of the universe . . . A religious experience, a spiritual transformation, a creative surge. I've seen them all. All are equally valid and may provoke their own kind of regeneration . . .'

He hesitated and Laurie hung upon his next words.

'Regeneration may even have a physical dimension,' he said at last. 'It is possible, though not yet proven, that chemicals released by the brain during these heightened states of awareness may have a retarding effect on the progress of disease. Such substances may boost the immune system, or even shrink a tumour . . . We just don't know.'

'But you believe it to be true?'

He looked away.

'With certain reservations, yes.'

Laurie struggled upright, feeling the tube in her chest pull against its moorings. She hauled at it impatiently.

'What reservations?' she demanded. 'Does it work for some and not for others? Tell me, please.'

He shook his head.

'I don't know,' he said. 'I wish I did.'

This uncharacteristic reserve was suddenly unnerving, and Laurie had a fleeting presentiment of disaster, of something that she wasn't being told.

'Will it will work for me?' she asked tremulously.

'I hope so,' he answered, facing her now and offering a more confident smile, 'and I hope you'll come back to Crompton Hall so that the process may continue . . .'

Laurie nodded.

'I will,' she whispered, 'though I'm rather afraid of what I might discover . . .'

The smile faded and he looked at her quizzically.

'The journals,' she said with difficulty, voicing a doubt which had floated beneath the surface of her new-found assurance yet only now came up to break the calm, 'I've been reading, although not too much . . . It's odd. I feel so close to Alice, and at times I almost feel I *am* India, but I don't know what happened to either of them . . . I'm scared to find out.'

'What do you think might have happened?' he asked.

'I wondered about the war,' Laurie said awkwardly. 'Whether they lost the men they loved. Christian and Luke, and Adam Goodchild too . . . It was so soon after that golden summer . . .'

She felt foolish, and was relieved when he stood up from his bedside chair to walk across to the window.

For a moment he said nothing, and Laurie rushed on into anxious qualifications.

'I suppose death in war is random too,' she prattled. 'Just like cancer. The bullet or the shell that has your name on it . . . The tumour that shrinks or grows according to rules that we don't understand . . .'

Still he said nothing, and she heard her voice fall away into embarrassed silence. For a long moment she stared at

267

his back, and when he turned to face her again, she guessed that he had wrestled with some inner conflict, and had prevailed. He looked serene and composed, once more the laconic cowboy she'd met on her first visit to Norfolk.

'Christian Crompton-Leigh was killed at The Somme,' he said slowly, 'though it could hardly be described as a random death. He showed great bravery under fire, dragging several wounded men to safety before he himself was hit . . . He could have saved himself, but he chose not to . . . A true officer and gentleman, you might think. He was posthumously awarded the Victoria Cross.'

Laurie was astonished by this news, and her hands flew to her ears, an instinctive unwillingness to hear more.

'Sad to say, Adam Goodchild was also lost. He volunteered for the Navy and went down at Jutland . . . But Luke Harte's services were required at home. He pioneered a treatment for shell shock. It involved using St John's wort to combat depression . . . He also investigated the use of honey as a disinfectant for wounds, and wrote a notable paper on the subject.'

Tears began to prick behind Laurie's eyelids.

'I wish I knew what it all meant,' she whispered.

He smiled, displaying for the first time the wide sunny smile she remembered so well and which, in its absence, had changed him from guru into something much more cautious, into modern medicine man.

He moved back to the bed, and in an unexpected gesture, reached for her hand.

'It means whatever you want it to mean,' he replied gently. 'Read on, and make up your own mind.'

Chapter Seventeen

The portrait was finished, but India was not pleased.

It was certainly she who stared out from the shining gilt frame, and yet she scarcely recognized herself. The hair was true, the colour of the skin exact, but the eyes were icy blue and her gaze an outright, almost offensive, challenge to the viewer. She shuddered to look upon those eyes.

Now she wished for some other interest in the painting, a little lapdog she might have cuddled, or a piece of embroidery she could have been working. Anything to detract from that stare.

Sir Robin took a different opinion, and declared that the portrait should be hung in the hallway so that all visitors might immediately register the beauty, the elegance, of the daughter of the house. Since Christian's departure for Goodchild Manor, he had spent many gloomy hours reflecting upon the duty of a parent, concluding that, in some vital respect, specifically the inculcation of honour, he had failed most miserably.

But he would not fail with India. In her he saw a fledgling nobility, a refinement of spirit which might be nurtured toward greatness. He foresaw no splendid calling, for he was a man of his time, limited by perception of what a woman might achieve, but he imagined a fine marriage. And now that he came to reconsider, his earlier hope of Adam Goodchild seemed misplaced. He had aimed too low for his precious daughter, yet she had instinctively understood her own worth. She had refused Goodchild, and in so doing surely invited a more illustrious fate.

With her father in such adulatory mood, it was easy to relocate the painting.

'I should like it hung in your library instead of the hall,' India said artfully, 'so I might always be there as your private inspiration . . .'

Sir Robin attributed this desire to modesty, imagining fondly that daughterly duty had served to concentrate all natural feelings of reserve, but still he wished to be sure.

'You do like the portrait?' he inquired earnestly.

'Oh, yes! Although I rather wish I'd had some companion pictured with me . . . I seem to be so very intense, don't you think? As though nothing matters to me except myself . . .'

Sir Robin frowned.

'A companion?' he echoed. 'You mean Alice?'

India had *not* meant Alice, and the idea would never have occurred, not least because Alice was no longer mentioned in the Crompton household. Lady Crompton had been most severely aggrieved by the presumptuous nature of her departure, a grief tempered by the satisfying knowledge that she'd been right all along about Alice. The girl had got above herself, an uprising encouraged by India's failure to keep the servants in check. Such a mistake would not be made again, and India, seeking to maintain a precarious peace in Christian's absence, duly agreed.

In that moment, however, she thought wistfully of Alice. She knew that the days of their comradeship were gone for ever, and she'd no idea how Alice might earn a living now that her career as personal maid seemed finished. The other roles she had whimsically envisaged – wonder-worker, potion-purveyor – were no more than unkind, idle imaginings. Alice would surely have to seek another situation, but she would have to do it without recommendation. Lady Crompton would never supply a notice, and for some time India had secretly entertained plans of writing her own reference and sneaking it out to Lavender Cottage.

But in truth, she too felt aggrieved. Why had Alice departed so hastily? Could she not see how much she was needed? Was it truly the case that other claims outweighed all they'd once meant to each other? India did not know, and a certain pride kept her from finding out.

The portrait, now that she considered it, seemed to speak of that pride in its cold, aloof stare, reproaching her for her intransigence.

'If I'd thought of it at the time, then I might have asked Alice to sit for the picture, too,' she said pensively, 'but I doubt that Mama would have agreed . . .'

Sir Robin put an arm around his daughter, an odd, self-conscious act that betrayed his discomfort with any show of emotion.

'I know you miss Alice,' he said with difficulty, 'but we shall find you a new companion!'

India shook her head sadly.

'I am done with companions,' she said quietly, 'though I will accept a personal maid. I know Mama thinks I must have one . . . The parlour girls are too busy for dressing hair . . .'

The subject of the new maid was vigorously pursued each morning by Lady Crompton, and India knew she could hardly refuse much longer, although she trembled to think of another assuming Alice's intimate duties. It was a great pity, she now reflected, that Daisy Turner had gone with Marianne . . . Daisy would have suited, and the break with Alice might not then have seemed so final.

Sir Robin smiled at his daughter.

'Don't rule out a new companion,' he said quietly. 'A new companion for a new life! I have been thinking, India, that we might spend more time in London. Christian is planning a honeymoon trip . . . They will stay for a time in London until Marianne is stronger, and then travel on to Brighton . . . Maybe you'd care to go with them?'

'No!'

This instinctive refusal startled them both, and India immediately sought to qualify her dismay. Of *course* she was concerned for Marianne, but equally concerned for her Mama, who would surely be *lost* without her. And Crompton Hall was where her heart truly lay. She could not *bear* to leave it, nor to be separated from her dear Papa . . .

With a shock India recognized her own deviousness. She could not bear the thought of inhabiting any landscape which did not contain Luke Harte . . . Just to be near him, to know that he lived not a half-mile away, was to be happy, even though they might never speak intimately again. Anything else was desolation.

She smiled nervously, trying out her new duplicity.

'Everything I want is right here,' she told her father truthfully, if indirectly. 'I have no need to be anywhere else.'

Sir Robin, concealing disappointment beneath a customary bluff acceptance of matters beyond his comprehension, nodded sagely. In a short time, he reasoned, India would become bored without a brother or companion. She would be ready for entertainment. She would seek diversion. Until then, he would wait.

India, meanwhile, consoled herself.

The prospect of separation from Luke had been averted. And the horrible portrait was to hang in the library, not the hall. It was a triumph, of sorts.

There was no sense of triumph at Blue Farm.

Luke Harte, no longer content with his marriage, his family life and his hitherto all-consuming vocation, had found himself distracted beyond reason.

Night after night he paced the drawing room, pounding the very floorboards on which he'd been kneeling when he first encountered India. How much had passed between them since that day! How much, and yet how little . . . And how fervently he wished it might be more!

But what was to be done? Elopement, in the style of Christian and Marianne, but without a wedding at the end? No, not that. Divorce, then? A celebrated case had just been heard in the London courts, provoking much righteous censure among those who could read newspapers, and much ribald debate among those who couldn't. The matter hinged upon the wife's immorality, and this, it seemed, was the only justification on which a decree might be granted.

But Eugenie was incapable of anything less than exemplary behaviour. Indeed, so firm was her grasp upon matters of continence that she had long since forsworn her husband's bed, wisely observing that Christian duty lay in overcoming temptation and embracing abstinence. And though she might have cause to accuse him – treachery of heart surely ranked with betrayal of the flesh – she would never do so. In any case, even if he were to divorce and pledge his entire fortune, meagre enough, he could never desert his daughters! Lucille, Charlotte and little Sophia . . . His darlings! There was no way out.

Too late he saw that in settling for domestic comfort above love he had violated the finer aspects of his nature, distancing himself from all that was noble and true in a human relationship. He had believed ambition, rooted in service, to be sufficient, indeed, to be the very cornerstone of a successful life. How wrong he had been.

A more robust man might have pushed aside all such thoughts and committed himself to ambition anew, but Luke Harte did no such thing.

Instead, he allowed himself to dwell on what might have been. He imagined himself arriving at Blue Farm a single man, feted by all as the saviour of the community. He saw himself welcomed to the dining room at Crompton Hall, a worthy guest and valued friend, openly admired for his principles and dedication. He indulged a vision of Sir Robin listening to his suit and India, adoring, pleading with her father to let love have its way.

He did not imagine Lady Crompton's response to the match, nor ponder how, once married, he might support a high-born wife. The future, with India by his side, was a flawless vision. Together they would have proved indomitable.

As with all such golden fantasies, reality soon began to seem ever more tarnished.

Luke Harte lost sympathy with his wife and patience with his daughters. He snapped, he sulked, he retreated into his study for hours at a time. Worse, he quarrelled violently with his wife's sister, declaring that gossip surrounded her friendship with a drunken lavender farmer.

Eugenie, deeply angered, reminded him of promises made to her father, and out of loyalty to his deceased

273

benefactor, Luke withdrew the charge, finding himself forced to offer a humiliating apology to Frederica.

In retaliation, he refused to attend Crompton Church picnic, an event to which the whole village had been invited. He would not accompany the sisters on a trip into Lynn. He declined to play cards on a Saturday evening. In short, he became a creature repugnant to himself and unrecognizable to those around him.

It was, most surely, a situation heralding domestic disaster, but Luke, by no means a cruel nor insensitive man, drew back from the brink. He peered into the pit and saw himself estranged from all he'd once held dear, feared by his innocent children and despised by his blameless wife. What kind of individual aimed to serve suffering humanity and yet, in his own home, inflicted discord and doubt?

He began to make amends. He bought skipping ropes for Lucille and Charlotte, a velveteen doll for Sophia, a new hat for Frederica, whom he now reluctantly accepted as a permanent feature of his household, and a box of silver cutlery for Eugenie.

He did not demur when his wife complained about the servants and discharged a girl who'd spilt a pail of milk.

He bit his tongue when she consigned Sophia to bread-and-water rations for refusing her porridge, even though the selfsame punishment – imposed for mixing with bad boys at the Crompton Church picnic – had only just been lifted.

He did not argue when Frederica demanded the carriage, requiring him to make his rounds on horseback, nor did he balk at the request for new curtains in her boudoir. And he welcomed Charlie Youngman to his dinner table, finding him an agreeable companion after all, and daring to hope that he might yet rid Blue Farm of his tiresome sister-in-law . . .

But still he thought of India. He thought of her mischievous laugh, of the way her chin tilted when she listened, the sweep of her long black plait when it fell down her back, or the coil of her chignon when her hair was piled high. He thought of that perilous, stolen kiss, of the blissful moment when she'd drifted into his arms, and of the nightingale's song that haunted his every step away through the beech woods . . .

He knew such a moment would never return, and if the knowledge pained him, then he also knew that only by renouncing the fantasy would he ever enjoy peace of mind.

He was not a man cured of love, but in fighting his despondence, he believed he had avoided disaster. He had checked his irrational behaviour. He had struggled to show goodwill. He was reconciled to his wife and family. After many a sleepless night, he could rest easy again.

Alas, true disaster is not so easily thwarted.

It may come swiftly, like a torrent or a fire, or it may come stealthily, like poison or famine. Always it comes like a thief in the night, plundering security and banishing joy.

The communication from the Office of Public Health at King's Lynn arrived as Luke Harte was taking breakfast.

He read it in growing disbelief, mortified that such a potentially calamitous event had escaped his notice.

How had this happened? He hadn't neglected his duties over the preceding days, but nor had he applied his usual rigorous attention to the bits of gossip that came his way. Instead of listening, he'd been dreaming. And now he'd been caught out.

Luke rode to Goodchild Manor at speed. Summoned to attend Marianne once more, his thoughts were far from the expectant mother. And as Adam waited on his driveway, the doctor leapt from his horse and strode toward him, quickly dismissing all questions about the new Mrs Crompton.

'Why wasn't I told that a child in the village was dying? What is the point of engaging a doctor if people are not encouraged to consult him?'

He was worried and deeply upset, but even at the height of his concern, perceived his anger to be misplaced. Adam Goodchild, sorely anxious about his sister, had barely registered the fatality in the village, and in any case, it was hardly his responsibility. Luke struggled to control his agitation, waiting for the right moment to reveal his unhappy news.

Adam ushered his guest into the drawing room, reaching for a decanter of brandy.

'A child has died? Yes, I do recall my sister's maid saying something about it . . . I'm afraid I didn't gather any details . . .'

Adam was grateful for the doctor's continuing attention to Marianne, and anxious to atone for any perceived short-coming on his part.

'I've been thinking about ways to encourage health and hygiene among our villagers, and wondered about your giving a series of talks in the village hall . . .'

Luke swallowed his brandy and stood up.

'This child's family . . . The Wainwrights . . . It seems there are cousins in Lynn. I understand they were visiting their relatives in the town . . .'

He hesitated, calculating, as doctors always will, how to communicate the facts without causing alarm.

Adam's anxious frown relaxed.

'Ah yes, the Wainwrights . . . That explains it. This family lives right on the village boundary. I imagine they thought it too far to send to Blue Farm. The child was probably buried at St Margaret's over the hill, so we wouldn't have been informed. But I understand your concern! The message must be reinforced. We do not quibble about parishes. You are here to serve everyone . . .'

Luke waved aside the returning brandy decanter.

'I'm afraid the situation is potentially serious,' he said carefully. 'I have received this morning a letter from the Officer for Public Health in Lynn . . .'

Adam blinked.

'Concerning the Wainwright child?'

'Concerning his relatives, yes. A number of children in Lynn have died, some of the Wainwrights among them . . . The Officer, in making his inquiries, discovered that our Wainwright boy had died too, but without benefit of a doctor's diagnosis. It seems he was attended by a village woman, but not, unfortunately, Miss Harper . . .'

Adam's face registered his growing fear.

'You mean some kind of infectious disease?'

Luke nodded gravely.

'Our task now must be to establish when this child fell ill, and what he did while the infection was incubating . . .'

Adam stood up.

'Good grief, man!' he cried. 'What are we talking about? Not diphtheria, for heaven's sake? I've heard something of diphtheria while travelling abroad . . . It's a terrible thing!'

Luke inclined his head, still seeking to establish calm.

'Not diphtheria,' he said, 'we have all but beaten diphtheria. Most of your village children will have been immunized against it . . . No, it seems that we're talking about the scarlet fever . . .'

Adam looked relieved.

'But that's similar to diphtheria, surely? An infection which attacks the throat and air passages? We must begin a vaccination programme at once!'

The doctor looked away.

'Your confidence is humbling,' he said quietly, 'but I'm afraid it is misplaced. There is no vaccination against scarlet fever. This particular disease continues to elude us . . .'

For a moment the two men gazed at each other, one imagining the worst, the other wishing not to voice it. Adam Goodchild broke the silence.

'Do we have an epidemic on our hands?'

Luke fingered his empty glass.

'I hope not, but all precautions must be taken. As I said, we must discover what happened during the incubation period . . . The other children in the family must be isolated, and we must endeavour to trace all other contacts.'

'Of course! We shall talk to the maid!'

Adam paced to the mantel and yanked on the bellrope. At once there came a knock at the drawing room door, and on the command to enter, Daisy Turner appeared, dropping a curtsey in the doorway.

'Excuse me, Sir,' she said to Adam, 'Mrs Crompton is asking for the doctor . . .'

Adam waved the girl inside and closed the door behind her.

'The very person I wished to see!' he said briskly, all thoughts of his sister overtaken. 'Now sit down, Daisy . . . The doctor has some questions he'd like to ask.'

Daisy looked alarmed, and Luke Harte was equally discomfited. It would not do to encourage rumour, and Adam Goodchild seemed to be reacting to the news with uncharacteristic dismay, risking an outbreak of panic among his household staff. For the first time, Luke considered that Adam had endured more than his share of grief, both in matters of the heart and in family fortunes. To be rejected by India was surely worse than his own pitiable situation. And to see a beloved sister wedded to a wastrel such as Christian was surely to know despair. It would hardly be surprising if Goodchild behaved with less than usual restraint.

Luke smiled encouragingly at Daisy, anxious to dispel any untoward fear. There was no need for a maid to be told the full facts.

'Do you know a family called Wainwright?' he enquired gently.

'Yes, Sir. Little Harry died last Tuesday. He had a fever, Sir . . .'

'Is that what you've heard?'

'Yes, Sir. It was the Scarlet . . .'

'I see. And how do you know that?'

'Everybody knows, Sir. He had a terrible red face and he couldn't breathe. Obviously the Scarlet . . . Anyway, his cousin in Lynn died of it too . . .'

Luke swallowed a bitter laugh, scarcely able to credit his own stupidity. Every serving girl from Crompton to Lynn might know of a rising epidemic, but not he . . . Not the noble, the professional, the lovesick doctor . . .

'Then perhaps you can help us with other information,' he said curtly. 'Are there more children in the Wainwright family?'

Daisy shook her head.

'No more, Sir. Harry's brother run away to sea, and his sister run away to Norwich . . . Long time ago.'

'I see. Well, thank you very much. We shall speak to his father and find out what poor little Harry was doing before he died . . .'

'Oh, I can tell you that, Sir. When he got back from Lynn he took to his bed, but then he felt a bit better, so he upped and went out . . . To the church picnic on St Michael's Day. That was the only time. He never went out again . . . Sir.'

Luke Harte felt his blood chill. *The picnic which he himself had refused to attend! The picnic at which his precious Sophia had played with the undesirable villagers . . .*

'Would that be St Margaret's Church picnic?' he asked faintly.

'Oh no, Sir! Our own Crompton Church. St Michael and All Angels! Everyone was there . . . Except me. Poor Mrs Crompton couldn't do without me, so I stayed right here.'

Adam let out an audible groan, whether in rage or in anguish, Luke could not tell. He strode across to the sofa where Daisy sat and planted himself before her, a stern, commanding presence that would not be denied.

'Does nobody understand the danger?' he bellowed. 'Does nobody know that this fever can be fatal?'

Considering that he himself had not known only a few short moments before, Adam's wrath was both excessive and unjust, yet another indication, the doctor could not help noting, of his unusual state of mind.

Daisy Turner bridled. She'd come up in the world since India's birthday and the unfortunate fainting fit in the pantry. She was no longer ruffled by the tempers and tantrums of the upper classes, nor inclined to think herself dependent upon their patronage. Mr Adam Goodchild had better watch his words, or his sister would be looking for a new maid . . . Not so easy to find these days, and her with a sickly disposition too . . .

'I expect you don't know much about the fever, Sir,' she said coldly. 'It starts with a nasty throat, but that could be any bad throat, couldn't it? Harry's cousin, he had the nasty throat, but the red face came later. Same with Harry. You don't know you've got it, Sir, till you're past all saving . . . Then it kills you!'

She drew her palm across her throat and emitted a strangulated gurgling sound, uncommonly like the noise Luke Harte had heard many times at the bedside of fever victims. The girl certainly understood disease, or this particular one, at least.

Daisy stood up and curtseyed again, an exaggerated gesture that less preoccupied onlookers might have perceived as impertinent. These two, however, seemed to register nothing untoward.

'Will you be coming to see Mrs Crompton, Sir?' Daisy enquired politely. 'She's terrible sick again . . .'

Luke reached for his bag and followed the girl out of the room, nodding at Adam as he went. Then as Daisy moved out of hearing, he turned back.

'I would advise that Mrs Crompton be kept from anyone who attended the picnic. Her condition makes her vulnerable, and the vomiting has weakened her . . .'

Adam nodded gratefully.

'They're taking a honeymoon trip,' he said. 'I've suggested some time at our London house until Marianne is stronger . . . And then they'll set off for Brighton. I am hoping India will go with them.'

'India?'

The name fell between them like a melody, haunting, elegiac, soft as fallen snow, sharp as a blade. For a moment they stared at each other, and though no word was spoken, in that moment it seemed to each that the other understood.

Luke swallowed hard.

'That might be best for everyone,' he said.

If the history of humankind is also the history of disease, and the battle between them a great heroic drama, then the triumph of medicine lies in telling the tale, and telling it true, with insight, interpretation, and, where practical, intervention.

Luke Harte went home to his wife and told this particular chapter of the tale, gently, carefully, without undue alarm, and yet with gravity. He tried to reassure her that not every child in contact with the fever necessarily fell victim, and that every child who fell victim, did not necessarily die. Then he examined his daughters and found Charlotte to be suffering from a headache. The following morning she was confined to her bed with a sore throat.

In the bitter days that followed, Luke Harte found himself telling the tale a hundred times, each version tempered to the understanding of the listener, and with scrupulous attention paid to individual circumstance and capacity for grief.

The Wainwrights needed comfort, the assurance that everything possible had been done, even though it hadn't. Supposing they'd summoned Dr Harte upon the boy's return from his cousin's house in Lynn? The doctor shook his head sadly. Their son would still have died. But supposing they'd realized it was the Scarlet, and stopped him going to the picnic? Luke Harte did not hesitate. They must not blame themselves, he said, nor think that an outbreak of virulent infection might be so easily contained.

Throughout it all, he did what he could, and consoled himself that the battle, the great heroic drama, was still playing out. The curtain showed no sign of coming down.

And yet he was sick at heart. A doctor may do much. He may relieve pain, ameliorate distress, administer potions and advise upon precautions such as the separate washing of linen, the boiling of cutlery, and the airing of a sick room. He may not reverse the process of a yet unconquered disease.

Charlotte Harte was taken to an isolation ward at the cottage hospital as soon as her fever appeared, and died within hours. Her sisters quickly followed her into the hospital, along with Charlie Youngman's small brother, Sam. Lucille died a week later, Sam within the fortnight.

But Sophia Harte, youngest and most vulnerable of the

doctor's daughters, did not die. Her breath rasped in her throat, the red skin on her face flaked and peeled, her pulse grew weak and her eyelids swelled. Yet while others perished, she lingered. There was no reason to it, and no comfort the doctor could offer his anguished wife. He still did not know if the child would survive.

In all, thirty-seven children from the village of Crompton were taken, as well as two young mothers, three serving maids, a garden boy from Crompton Hall and a trainee footman from Goodchild Manor. Scarcely a household in the village escaped . . . Except, Luke Harte calculated one dark morning from the depths of his distress, the Harper household and the children of Alice's sister, Ivy . . .

He had no idea how this might have happened, but he knew a rational explanation must exist, and he resolved to seek it in due course.

Meantime, the doctor's vocation demanded that his work never cease. No time for private grief. No time for regret nor self-reproach, although such sentiments were never far from his mind. There was always something to do, Luke Harte told himself bitterly. Visiting, advising, writing death notices. Always something, except the work that was a doctor's true vocation . . . The work that begged to be done. The work he could not do. The work of healing.

He took the short walk to the Harper cottage on a heavy, overcast evening, tramping across the dying stubs of the lavender fields, remarking now that he had not seen Alice at all during the height of the epidemic, nor heard her name mentioned among any of the families he'd visited. She'd not presumed, it seemed, to dispense any of her folk remedies and for this she was to be commended.

He rapped firmly on the door and was greeted by Alice's mother.

'Doctor Harte! What a pleasure . . . But you haven't come to see me, I hope? I assure you, I'm quite well. There are others who still need you far more than I . . .'

In truth, Luke had barely given a thought to his former

patient nor to the surgery performed upon her, and knowing he could do nothing more himself to aid her recovery, had consigned her cure to Nature.

'I'm so sorry about your daughters,' Nell Harper said quietly, ushering him into her modest parlour. 'It has been a terrible thing, this fever. So many families in mourning.'

Luke felt his eyes cloud with tears, the first time he'd allowed his grief to have sway, and he clutched at the arm of a threadbare settee for support, sinking into it with an embarrassed gasp.

'There now . . . You've come to see Alice, no doubt. She's in the garden with the children. I shall call her, and make you a cup of tea . . .'

He composed himself in her absence, taking in the detail of the room, an ageing pianoforte, a writing desk stacked with papers, an extraordinary assortment of books. *The Sanitary Condition of the Labouring Population of New York. The Water Cure in Chronic Disease. Pathological and Surgical Observations on the Diseases of the Ear. The Garden of Health*. He was immersed in the *Organon of Rational Healing* when Alice entered bearing the tea, and he felt the need to establish his goodwill at once.

'You have some surprising reading matter,' he said brightly, motioning toward the books. 'I hadn't realized you took such a detailed interest in the history of medicine . . .'

Alice looked pale and drawn, her eyes shadowed, her hair drawn back sharply from her face so that she seemed older, thinner, than before. She smiled warily and handed him a cup and saucer.

'Most of the books are my brother's. He's studying anatomy. The parson brings them from a second-hand shop in Norwich . . .'

She did not sit down herself, but moved quickly to the window, peering nervously between the curtains as though she expected some unwelcome visitor.

There was a long silence in which he sensed her growing discomfort and longed to put her at ease.

'I haven't seen you around the parish since the fever,'

he began, and saw at once from her expression that he'd
begun badly.

She turned from the window and walked toward him.

'I've taken charge of my sister's children,' she said
sharply. 'Ivy is expecting another baby, and since I've
had . . . time on my hands . . . I gladly took them over.
Naturally enough, I've kept them in isolation. I'm sure
that's what you would have advised?'

He was perplexed by her surly tone, and sought for some
innocuous remark. He failed to find one.

'So you weren't at the church picnic?' he enquired at
last, deciding to risk the question he most wanted answered.
This, it seemed to him, most readily explained the escape
from fever.

She took a long time to answer, standing above him
with her steady, hazel eyes focused upon his face, seeming to measure what she might say and what she must
keep secret.

'We were all at the picnic,' she said finally, turning away
again. 'Why wouldn't we be? The whole village was there.
Your wife and your daughters, and their Aunt Frederica . . .
The Youngmans and the Wainwrights. India and Christian.
Everyone except yourself and the Goodchilds. Adam chose
to stay at home with his sister that day . . .'

Luke sipped at his tea, trying to make sense of her attitude and of his own growing disquiet. If they'd all been at
the picnic, then what was he to conclude about the Harper
children's fortuitous survival? He decided to confront her.

'Did you see the Wainwright boy that day?'

'I saw him, yes!' she replied smartly. 'I saw that he was
ill. But I did not diagnose the scarlet fever, Doctor Harte.
I'm not qualified to do that!'

He looked down and saw his hand tremble upon the cup.
No doubt she hadn't intended to strike at the heart of his
pain, but that was what she'd done. He was the one qualified
to diagnose. If he'd been at the picnic, he might have acted
to contain the infection . . . Perhaps. But perhaps not. He
might never have seen the Wainwright boy. And if India
had also been there . . .

'Forgive me!' said Alice suddenly. 'I don't mean to sound angry. I've been placed in a most difficult position by Mr Hardy's tales about the elephant . . . It's a dreadful thing to be thought a miracle worker! But how dreadful for you too, Doctor Harte . . . And to lose your lovely daughters . . . May God console you and your poor wife!'

The teacup lurched upon its saucer.

'For a long time I believed Sophia would live,' he whispered. 'It seemed she was gaining strength . . . But the complications of scarlet fever are insidious. Now I fear her kidneys are failing.'

Alice leaned down and touched his shoulder.

'While she lives, there is still hope . . .'

He nodded. 'Perhaps.' His voice broke as he spoke. 'And yet I had hope for Lucy and Charlotte too . . .'

'There is no justice in such deaths,' Alice whispered, 'but maybe there is comfort in considering every life complete and worthwhile, however short or tragically curtailed. Your daughters were beautiful, happy girls! Their lives were of infinite value, and they will never be forgotten . . .'

They were the first words of true understanding he had received among all the well-meant sympathies from sobbing women, and all the gruff condolences from red-eyed men.

He stood up from the settee and walked quickly toward the door, no longer able to stall his tears.

Outside he set off for the beech woods, stumbling over the stubbly fields until the darkness engulfed him.

Free at last to indulge his desolation, he sank to his knees, pummelling the sodden earth beneath him and howling his protest to the starless skies above.

Chapter Eighteen

'I shall not go to the Crompton Church picnic,' I said to my mother. 'I have mending to do, and letters to write. You and Johnny may go by yourselves.'

Since my flight from Crompton Hall, I had taken in sewing and offered my services as scribe to any who needed letters or notices written, though I earned scarcely more than a halfpenny here and there for such efforts, and knew there were many who could not pay at all.

There had also been a rather curious development since my treatment of India's little elephant. Hardy seemed to fancy that I possessed miraculous powers of healing, and had told everyone in the village that they should come to me in time of sickness or indisposition.

At first I was alarmed by the trail of visitors to my door, thinking I should surely incur the censure of Dr Harte. But then I heard that he had sunk into some gloomy fit of brooding and seemed little concerned about medical matters beyond his own round, and indeed, when I met him one day out upon his horse, he passed me by as though he'd not even noted my presence.

I treated all manner of burns, cuts and bruises, attended to women's troubles and attempted to halt the progress of coughs, colds and sore throats. Some of my remedies worked and some didn't, but I found a curious relation between the people who were helped and their willingness to believe in the efficacy of a cure. Since I had read in my medical books that many conditions improve by themselves with no intervention from doctors, I concluded that the best treatments were those that worked with the body to bring about a natural recovery. And the patients most likely to recover were those who determined that they themselves would influence, if not the course of their illness, then certainly the extent to which it hampered their daily lives.

One thing I would not do. I would not treat conditions which seemed to me potentially fatal, insisting that any with a growth or a palsy consult Dr Harte at once. And I refused all money for my services, accepting instead a sprig of thyme or rosemary from the garden. It seemed wrong to take payment for a service to restore health. Such services should be free to all, and in any case, there was little money in Crompton village for much beyond the bare essentials of life. Medicine was a luxury, and one that few could afford.

None of this helped my family. I was anxious not to burden my mother nor take food from the mouth of my young brother, but in truth our meagre piece of land barely supported the two of them, and my small, uncertain earnings from mending and writing made no significant contribution. My savings had all been used during my mother's illness, and once again, we found ourselves relying on Charlie Youngman's generosity. On Sundays he sometimes sent a rabbit or a half-dozen eggs from the kitchen at Lavender House, though he did nothing to stem the damp on our walls nor mend our roof. It was a situation I found intolerable without knowing how I might end it.

I could not but reflect upon the change in our circumstances since I'd left Crompton Hall. My wage had ensured that there were always shoes for my brother and good sheets upon my mother's bed. A supply of left-over pastries, cold meats and soups from the Crompton kitchen had kept them well fed. Now we faced an uncertain future.

'You should go to the picnic,' my mother said, frowning. 'There may be folk from St Margaret's there. Maybe somebody knows of a maid's place or a governess wanted . . .'

This was a matter of some dispute between us. My mother thought that Reading and Writing qualified me to teach the children of the gentry, and that Latin and Greek made it certain I'd be snapped up at once by some likely Sire or Madam, keen to see as little of their offspring as possible.

But I'd never had any desire to instruct reluctant children, nor to find myself at the beck and call of reluctant parents. I'd been happy with my role as India's companion.

However, nor did I wish to apply for any other situation as companion or personal maid, even supposing I might get one without a notice from Lady Crompton. I'd had my fill of well-to-do ladies and gentlemen, and planned instead to apply for a post at the Ragged School in the London borough of Hackney. I had already written to the mistress in charge, and had received a reply to say that my letter was under consideration.

But I could not leave the village until I saw my mother fully well again, and I would not so much as hint at my hopes. I knew she wished me to find some situation nearby, and I couldn't let her know I meant to move so far away.

By ironic chance, a nearby situation had indeed become vacant, and it would have been mine for the taking. A letter from Adam Goodchild arrived within a week of my quitting Crompton Hall, containing information that would have made me laugh aloud, had it not been so bitter.

My dear Alice,

I do not know the circumstance of your leaving Crompton Hall, but I am certain that it will be none which reflects ill upon you. If you no longer wish a situation as India's companion, whatever your reason for that decision, then I should like to offer you a place in my own household. Mrs Crompton's maid is leaving to get married herself, and I have need of a mature, responsible person to care for my sister at this delicate time. If you would give this your closest consideration, I would be most gratified. Mr and Mrs Crompton occupy the west wing at Goodchild Manor, and there is ample room in those quarters for you to have both private sitting room and bedroom next to theirs. Furthermore, although I would not wish to tempt you with extraordinary inducements, if you have ever felt a desire to visit the South Coast, then you may be interested to know that Mr and Mrs

Crompton plan a honeymoon trip to Brighton very shortly, my sister's condition permitting. It would greatly ease my mind to know that you were with them, and that both might rely upon your common sense and good nature.

I remain Yours Most Truly . . .

I stared at the letter for a long time, attempting to compose an appropriate reply. I could think of an inappropriate one all too readily.

My dear Mr Goodchild,

I am greatly honoured to learn that you consider me a suitable companion for Mrs Crompton. However, as Mr Crompton is my lover, I fear you must revise your opinion and I must refuse your offer. I am sure Mr Crompton would find it most amusing to have me installed in a bedroom next to him and his wife, but I am not so easily entertained. Furthermore, as I intend never again to set foot under the same roof as Mr Crompton, nor to speak to him, nor indeed, to give so much as a civil glance in his direction, then it is difficult to see how I might accompany him and Mrs Crompton upon their visit to the South Coast. I am most heartily sorry that you have been deceived as to my common sense and my good nature. As far as Mr Crompton is concerned, I am afraid I can demonstrate neither.

I remain Your Humble Servant . . .

Of course, I wrote no such thing, and settled in the end for protesting my need to remain with my mother, and thanking Adam Goodchild for his consideration. I then took the liberty of recommending Daisy Turner as personal maid until some older, more suitable female might be found. Daisy, I had guessed, was growing weary of life at Crompton Hall, and a change of scene might avert her own precipitous departure from Lady Crompton's employ.

I did not tell my mother about the letter. Although she

had not enquired about the detail of my brief return to Crompton Hall, she knew of Christian's marriage, and knew too that I felt myself sorely misused. There was no need to say anything more.

But why did I feel myself so slighted and abused? What I'd done, I'd done freely and willingly. I'd never thought that he might be faithful to me, nor that his protestations of love were genuine. And when he left me, I'd believed him bound for the arms of Kitty Malone. Why was the deception he'd perpetrated so much worse than the one I had anticipated?

I supposed, though I did not welcome the thought, that it was the fact of the marriage and the coming child which so disturbed me. After all, nothing else would have kept him from me so finally.

But it was more than this. Much of my disappointment, I knew, centred upon Marianne. I hadn't imagined he would settle for so little, and I despised myself for that thought.

But she too, it seemed to me, had settled for less than her due. So wealthy, so feted, so protected, she had been born with every advantage, yet in the unthinking betrayal of her adoring brother, she had shown herself to be enslaved, guilty of acting only in the name of desire. In that respect, she was truly no different from me, but she, with so much to lose, with so much promised for her, should have thought again.

For his part, Christian might surely have drawn back, too. Even by his own standards, his action had been deeply dishonourable. Despite all my protestations to India, I felt it to be so, and was forced to accept that I had fooled myself. I'd imagined I saw into the darkest corners of his soul, but I had not believed him capable of this, and now I saw that pride in my own powers of discernment had blinded me. Perhaps the uncomfortable truth is that each of us receives in return the full measure of our self deception.

For all that, Marianne surely deserved a better husband, and her husband deserved a wiser wife, one who might have steadied his desires by matching them to her own. And who would have made him such a wife?

I could not bear to contemplate this question, and upon many a tearful night was brought to acknowledge the full depths of my longing. Although just a short time ago I'd been able to temper my passion for Christian with recognition of its unworthiness, now I could no longer do so. I wanted him, and this in all knowledge of his true nature. Such feelings made a mockery of my former assurance, of all my fine speeches to India on the subject of love, and drove me into more fervent determination to escape Crompton for good so that I might never see him again.

But I could not escape the church picnic.

'Ivy is sick,' my mother announced on the morning of St Michael's Feast. 'She is sick when she wakes, sick through the day, and sick again every night.'

'Has she taken the ginger?' I asked, looking up from my writing. I had no sewing, no letters, and so had taken to recording my thoughts in a daily journal. It was a means of keeping myself occupied.

'That fool of a husband won't let her take the ginger!'

My mother's contempt for her son-in-law was ill-concealed at the best of times, and not at all when out of his presence.

'We shall have to keep the children for a few days,' she said. 'They may sleep in the scullery – and since I'm feeling out of sorts myself, you shall take them all to the picnic!'

And so it was that I set out upon that fateful day.

The first person I met was Eugenie Harte, who pretended not to know me.

We crested the hollow above the church and stood for a moment looking down at the trestle tables set out in the meadow, watching the village children load their plates with jam tarts and madeleines. The food was provided by the Crompton Hall kitchen, and it marked one day in the year when all might eat freely.

It was a mild, sunny day, not always so for the Feast of St Michael, and I was in good humour, having set aside all thoughts of Christian and the vexed matter of my future occupation in delight at my nieces' and nephew's high spirits.

'Good day, Mrs Harte,' I called as we wandered down into the hollow and she rounded the church tower with her daughters in her wake, 'I hope you and your family are keeping well?'

She fixed me with her steely eye and said nothing, pushing past me and instructing her girls not to dally. I was astonished and not a little perturbed at this slight, and couldn't think what I'd done to deserve it. But then I considered that if Mrs Harte had had occasion to meet with Lady Crompton, and if, as was customary between these two, the subject of servants should have arisen, then the manner of my leaving Crompton Hall would surely have been discussed. And if so, Mrs Harte would certainly know what opinion to take.

In the next moment, close behind the Harte family, I encountered Charlie Youngman and his small brother Sam. To my surprise, Charlie had a young woman upon his arm, a slight and pretty creature wearing a bold and extravagant hat, cream straw trimmed with vivid satin cherries and a trail of bright red ribbons.

Charlie seemed embarrassed to see me, though we'd met many times since the night I'd refused his proposal, and I had perceived no discomfort nor censure on his part.

'Ah, Alice,' he said awkwardly, disengaging his arm from his companion's, 'may I present Miss Frederica Clayton . . .'

Frederica emitted a giggle and dropped a mock curtsey in my direction.

'So here you are at last!' she declared exuberantly. 'I'm most delighted to meet you, Miss Harper!'

Another peal of laughter, a few more curious pleasantries, and they were gone, her arm once more clasped in his, leaving me to reflect unhappily that my history and situation were surely known to her, and as a matter of some amusement, no less. She had not even required to be told my full name.

Now, of course, I perceived her to be Mrs Harte's younger sister, and remembering that Charlie had declared himself in need of a wife to help run the lavender farm, and having formed the distinct impression that while I would have been a suitable choice, he did not consider me irreplaceable, I guessed that Frederica Clayton had met her match. If so, I wished them well. I was by now not merely resigned to my spinsterhood, but positively enamoured of it.

Across the churchyard, I next spied the Wainwrights, a family my sister knew well from having minded the young boy Harry while his mother went to Norwich to search for her runaway daughter.

'There's your friend, Harry,' I said to my nephew, waving at the boy who was sitting dejectedly upon a tombstone. 'Go take him some of this rabbit pie . . .'

We'd brought our own food to the picnic, the tradition being that while the Hall provided the mainstay, the villagers should also contribute, but my nephew would not share with young Harry, and ran away instead to join his sisters in a game of hide-and-seek.

I walked on toward the trestles and set down my pie, greeting my old friend the parson, nodding to the Coopers and the Smithsons, families who'd provided me with sewing, and stopping to chat with Constable Clarke who'd asked me to copy out a deposition to be sent to the courthouse at Lynn, and whom I hoped might be a source of further work.

Children darted between the tables, laughing and ribbing each other, rolling on the ground and dancing over the tombstones. I saw the Cooper boys jostle each other, and I saw Mrs Harte's girls run to the stone where Harry Wainwright sat, and watched while the youngest pulled him from his perch with much merriment. He looked feeble and dull-eyed, and had barely the strength to scramble up from the grass again.

Then I saw India and Christian walking out of the beech woods toward the church, deep in conversation.

My heart leapt into my throat. I turned quickly and

threaded my way between the tables, almost knocking a plate of fancies to the grass as I went, hurrying to the rear of the church where tangled banks of hemlock and long-neglected sepulchres afforded some seclusion. My breath came fast and my hands were trembling. Although India had attended the Crompton Church picnic before, Christian, to my certain knowledge, had never been anywhere near it, and I'd not expected to see either of them that day. I'd thought that India would be attending her new sister-in-law, and that her brother, if not at the bedside himself, would have found more entertaining ways to pass his afternoon. Whatever, he would not pass the time of day with me.

I sank down behind a great marble edifice which announced the long-previous demise of one Elijah Hepplewhite, and resolved to wait. The children would not miss me, and in any case, they could find their own way home. I planned to remain concealed until the picnic was all but over and I could reasonably expect my enemy – for so I considered Christian – to have departed.

I believe I must have dozed in the warm afternoon air because some considerable time seemed to have elapsed before I sat up with a start at a footstep on the path. I peeped out from behind my stone, and there was India, not a yard away.

'Alice! I've been searching for you everywhere! Whatever are you doing? Are you hiding from me?'

She looked injured, and not a little perplexed. I stood up, embarrassed.

'Of course not! I was merely taking a little nap . . . Why should I hide from you?'

She stared at me, half annoyed, half concerned.

'A nap behind a tombstone? Are you ill, Alice?'

I shook my head, though in truth I did not feel at all well.

My head ached and my limbs were numb. My mouth was dry and my stomach in turmoil. Such are the rewards of misplaced love!

'You *are* ill!' India said, moving toward me and taking my

hand. 'Oh, Alice, does this explain it? Is this why you've not been to see me?'

She looked so earnest, so anxious, and so in need of consolation that for a moment I seriously considered a judicious lie, a deception that would wave away all difficulty between us and restore our lost friendship. But of course, no lie can ever achieve any such thing.

I passed my hand across my eyes and sat down on the sepulchre again. She sat down beside me and I struggled to regain composure.

'I am not ill,' I began at last, 'but I am not myself. That is to say, I am not the person you have always believed me to be . . .'

She was listening intently, and I faltered, unable to voice the brute fact of my intimacy with her brother. But could it be that she remained entirely unaware of all that had played out around her? Had she never guessed at my emotion, nor thought him overly attentive to me?

'We have talked many times about affairs of the heart,' I said unhappily, 'and I have always warned against succumbing to desire . . . Against loving unwisely . . .'

She looked away, her eyes cast down.

'We have also discussed the means by which passion might lead us to make fools of ourselves . . .'

I was about to confess it all, to swear my own greater culpability so that she might not think too badly of him, to beg her forgiveness for my deception and ask her never to mention it again, when suddenly she leapt to her feet and turned away from me in distress.

'Oh, Alice,' she cried, turning back, 'you have found me out! You have seen into my heart and uncovered the dark thoughts that lurk there . . . I might have known I could never escape! You know me too well!'

I gazed at her in astonishment, but she, seeming to see comprehension where in truth there was only confusion, sank down beside me again, eyes wide and imploring.

'I hardly know how to live with myself!' she declared. 'I cannot rid myself of thoughts of him . . . I see him in my mind's eye, sitting in his parlour with his wife . . . And

I relive those precious moments we shared together, time and time again. They will not leave my head, until it seems I am being driven wild with longing for him. Oh, Alice! You cannot know how painful it all is . . . I do most fervently wish I had never set eyes upon him!'

I shook my head in wonder, and then in the next instant, I understood.

'Doctor Harte!' I muttered.

Now her tears began to fall, and as she began to relate the detail of their intimacy, I pulled her to me, cradling her head against my shoulder, marvelling at the madness which had seized us both, and fighting a strong urge to shriek aloud. How foolish we both had been! And yet she had exchanged no more than a furtive kiss with her lover, and considered herself a sinner for this, while I had mingled body and soul with mine, and had believed myself so brave and free. I saw myself as tainted and tawdry beside her, a creature without finer feeling or restraint. I stroked her hair and tried to calm us both.

'To see Eugenie with their daughters,' she wept, 'and to think that they will all be together this evening, talking and laughing and enjoying a happy family life, while I . . .'

Her voice tailed away and I trawled for words of comfort, insisting that such feelings could be overcome, that time would prove the great healer, and all the while endeavouring to swallow my own medicine. Any thoughts of confession were gone. Now I wished only to conceal my own shabby secret.

So it was that when she dried her tears and turned once more to the manner of my quitting Crompton Hall, I sought to find a different explanation, not simply my mother's illness, for it was well known that she was recovering, but something that might legitimately have kept me from the Cromptons for good.

'Lady Crompton does not like me,' I said, suddenly inspired. 'I have always known it, and I no longer care to endure it. I am very sorry, and hope you will understand . . .'

India bit her lip.

'I *do* understand,' she whispered, 'Mama is so very

severe in her judgements ... But Alice, I hope *you* will understand how sorely you are missed. Not only by me, but by Christian, too. He came here today just so he might see you, and was most disturbed when your little niece told him she thought you'd gone home ... Perhaps he meant to ask if you would reconsider becoming Marianne's companion ... They are travelling to London and wish me to go with them, but of course, a maid is needed too ... At first I felt I could not go! I could not be so far from *him* ... But then, I confess, I have been thinking that if you were to come too, it would seem a much happier prospect.'

I struggled with a rage that threatened to engulf me, and succeeded only because I determined to show no hint of my turmoil.

'I thank your brother for his kind offer,' I managed at last, 'but I am not able to travel so far from home ... However ...'

She looked at me hopefully, and I drew a deep breath.

'I think you should go,' I said. 'The change would do you good.'

Her face fell.

'Maybe you're right,' she said finally. 'I know I can hardly see Marianne set off without a friend to care for her ... And with Christian so low and out of sorts ... Alice, it seems he too has endured a hopeless love! He told me all about it. He wished to marry Kitty Malone, but – thank God for this – she would not have him ...'

I felt then the last remaining illusion fall away, the tiny, lingering hope that I had been loved for myself and not merely the opportunity I presented, felt it fall, and let it go like an injured bird scurrying away into the undergrowth. I smiled at India.

'And what of everything else at Crompton Hall?' I asked her bravely, leading her out at last from behind the sepulchre and setting us both back on the path to recovery. 'I do miss many things, you know! Our walks in the beech woods, and strolls by the lake. Sitting in the summerhouse upon a sunny afternoon ... And I often imagine all that must be happening, and what you find yourself doing. How is your portrait coming along? Is it finished?'

India was not cheered.

'I hate the portrait,' she muttered darkly. 'The eyes are devilish, and I don't care for the composition. It needs another figure in it . . .' She turned to me with a distant smile.

'If such an idea weren't preposterous,' she said sadly, 'I would have said it needed *you*, Alice.'

The picnic was over, the children had gone home without me, and Christian, mercifully, was nowhere to be seen. I kissed India goodbye and promised I should hear all the tales of her travels when she returned. Then I walked back to Lavender Cottage, planning a new life in Hackney in which I would vanquish all memories of Crompton Hall and dedicate myself to service and to education.

Ivy's boy seemed feverish that evening, so I gave him *belladonna*, knowing that it settled temperature and warded off infection. As a precaution I gave the others a dose too, and although I found them well the following morning, administered a second dose because such is the philosophy of treating like with like. *The Belladonna would increase a temperature, but if taken early in the diagnosis, a minor dosage at night, at morning, and at night again, will afford relief . . .* I gave the children a third dose, and forgot all about it, preoccupied by the detail of a trip I was undertaking the following day.

Ivy's children were to visit their father's sister at Wells, an arduous journey which we must make on foot, and at the end of it, I knew, a dour, unwelcoming woman uncommonly like her brother. But in the event our brief excursion proved pleasant, and when we got there, we walked along the shores of The Wash and felt the autumn breezes lift our spirits and rosy our faces. We flew a kite upon the sands, and to the children's excitement, heard that the King and Queen were come to Sandringham and might be visiting the seaside. Alas, they did not make the trip, but the whole town enjoyed much fun with flags and streamers in the hope of their arrival.

I learned as soon as I returned that Harry Wainwright was dead, and that scarlet fever had seized Crompton village.

My mother was waiting anxiously, and as we walked into the cottage, rushed upon the children, searching their faces and prodding the glands behind their ears.

'Ivy is desperate with worry,' she breathed when they were safely in the scullery with their bread and honey. 'There are children falling sick every hour . . . And Alice, there have been people at the door night and day! They want you to treat their little ones. They say you cured the elephant, and anyone who did that must be able to stop the fever . . . I told them you'd given ours the belladonna . . .'

I stared at my mother in alarm.

'I cannot cure the scarlet fever!' I cried. 'No one can do that! The belladonna may work if it's given at once, but when the fever has hold, there's nothing will help. Even a doctor may not help . . .'

She nodded and spread her hands toward me, a despairing gesture which I was to repeat myself many times in the dark days that followed. In the next moment, there came a knock upon the door. Word of my return had already spread.

'I cannot cure the scarlet fever,' I repeated. 'You must consult Doctor Harte . . . I'm sorry, you don't understand. Yes, of course, you may take the belladonna if you wish, but it won't make any difference now . . .'

I cannot cure the scarlet fever. I'm sorry, you don't understand. You must consult Doctor Harte.

How many times in the terrible days that followed did I find myself intoning these words like some dreadful litany? Some took the belladonna, some didn't, and those who did found, as I'd predicted, that it made no difference at all, though a few said afterward that their children had died easier for it . . . I begged them all to say nothing that might incriminate me, and for three weeks did not leave the house for fear I might be ambushed and marched to a fever cottage . . .

In the space of a week I'd become a prisoner in my home, peering out from behind my curtains and hesitating to answer my door. I'd once heard of a healer charged at the Lynn courthouse with claiming false cures, and although the case hinged upon the extraction of money, I had never forgotten the horror this story aroused. I could not risk the wrath of Dr Harte, nor the anguish of those who believed I might cure their children and then found I couldn't.

I refused many callers, but there was one I could not deny.

The hammering on my mother's door came late one night when we were all in bed. Our children had been kept away from any of their village friends, and my mother, at first anxious to admit all and to help whom we could, was now loathe to risk contact with fever families.

'Who is it?' I whispered to her as the pounding continued. 'Can you see?'

'It is Eugenie Harte!' my mother replied. 'And she looks half mad to me . . .'

Her coil was unpinned, her eyes wild, and her breath came in short, heavy gasps. I opened the door and she fell into the room, clutching at my arm. When my mother helped her to a chair by the dying fire, she began to shiver, pulling her cloak tight around her shoulders.

She looked up at me through wisps of drifting hair.

'You must save my daughter!' she pleaded. 'I have only one daughter left to me, and I beg of you, Miss Harper, to give the potion . . . I have heard that the elephant was saved! If you can save a dumb creature, you can surely save a little girl who is dying . . .'

She began to weep, and I sank to my knees beside the chair, taking her hands in mine, shocked by her distress, though what else I might have expected, I hardly knew.

'My dear Mrs Harte, I'm sure you know there's nothing I can do . . .' I spoke gently, trying to calm her yet knowing I could not offer false comfort. 'Your husband is the only one who can help . . .'

She gave a little cry and buried her face in her hands.

'He can do nothing!' she said bitterly. 'All his fine medicine and his learning will not save her!'

My mother had fetched *ignatia*, which is said to calm troubled spirits, and I administered the droplets in a sherry glass, urging her to drink. The effect was immediate and dramatic.

She stood up and fastened her hair back into its customary coil. She was Mrs Harte, the doctor's wife once more, and though still discomposed, no longer mad.

'I will supply the belladonna if you wish,' I said carefully, 'though I must insist that you tell your husband before giving it to your daughter . . .'

I handed her a small phial of the dilution which she accepted and plunged deep into the pocket of her cloak, as though she imagined I might seize it back at any moment.

'I will not tell him,' she replied with dignity. 'It is as I said. He can do nothing, so I must do what I can . . .'

Then she was gone, and I was left to consider that few things in the world are worse than a family tragedy where husband and wife may not turn to each other in grief, nor suffer together in the hope of providing some small respite . . .

I thought of Dr Harte, and the terrible burden of the medical man who might not heal his own children. I thought of India, and how she would now feel only love and compassion toward Eugenie, not any rivalry nor discord. I thought of angels, and wondered if any were listening.

But mostly I thought of the scarlet fever, and all the other terrible diseases that had faced mankind. The black death, the palsy, the consumption, the canker . . .

I thought of my own observations concerning patients who believed in a cure, and of the strange process which seemed to strengthen and regenerate those who passionately wished to live.

And I concluded that there were no answers to the mystery of suffering, nor assurances that there might ever be, nor hope that if the known diseases were conquered new ones might not arise, nor comfort that even if this were so, those other deeper ills, poverty, hunger, oppression, would not survive to rob us of all peace.

Chapter Nineteen

Laurie discharged herself from hospital.

A curious realization had seized her as she lay in her pastel suite surrounded by flowers and cards. *She wanted to be back on the cancer ward.*

With unexpected nostalgia, she thought of her time in the chemo unit, her fellow patients with their drips and their pouches of poison, the nursing sister who'd joked about Gloria's pills, the woman with the wigs.

Here, in perfumed isolation, Laurie felt herself estranged from all that had sustained her. She hadn't known it at the time, but looking back, she saw that her pain had been transformed by sharing it.

This was true of Crompton Hall, too. She had not wanted to share, indeed, had hugged her pain to herself like a dark secret. She'd fought against Edie and Val, as though they were trespassers, invading her private grief. And in refusing to share, she had become immune to their pain. She didn't even know if either of them still had cancer.

She was quite clear that she herself did not.

'I'm no longer a cancer patient,' she told her surgeon as she demanded her discharge. 'I'm just someone who once had cancer . . .'

He'd been cautions, but yes, she saw it, he'd also been impressed. He tried to dissuade her from leaving, but when she insisted, he didn't demur.

Her family, too, had been impressed. Her father had squeezed her tight, almost dislodging the plastic drain which she still wore, tucked inside her blouse. Then he'd kissed her face and stroked the burgeoning stubble on her scalp, declaring she'd never looked so beautiful.

Elspeth had bought the biggest bunch of flowers anyone could remember seeing, and finding a woeful lack of vases in Laurie's flat, had trawled the city for antique jars and ethnic bowls, displaying them like trophies.

Gloria had been deeply relieved. Her customary briskness had returned, but with it an obvious gratitude for Laurie's new-found calm.

'It was the ignatia,' Laurie told her, laughing. 'When I took it, all my unwonted emotions just melted away . . .' And Gloria laughed too.

Laurie began to feel her old life slipping back into place, its familiar shapes and colours sharpened by her absence. Her flat was blissful and serene, a haven of solitude that she'd never truly appreciated, always seeking to fill it with parties and guests. The New Leaf Cafe was warm and vibrant, alive with old compatriots and new eccentrics, buzzing with theories about dolphins and campaigns to outlaw battery farms. The office, which she'd scarcely given thought to since she'd taken leave, was suddenly as dear as her old school. It now appeared as her alma mater, a place of learning, testing and forging a way ahead. A place, she knew instinctively, from which she would soon be moving on.

All her relationships, too, had mellowed. Not just with Robert, Gloria and Elspeth, but with colleagues and neighbours, friends and casual acquaintances. She no longer cared that the woman upstairs left her rubbish bags in the hall. She endured the complaints of the girl from accounts who hated the man from advertising. She rang Shelley, not for comfort, but to offer it herself, realizing that she'd uttered not a single word of sympathy upon the loss of Jim.

'Jim who?' demanded Shelley. 'Did I tell you about the heavy metal fan who's into Edgar Allen Poe?'

'How many ex-wives does he have?'

'Don't know. Haven't asked him yet.'

'He may have a couple walled up in his basement.'

'I hope not,' Shelley said. 'Anyway, he hasn't got a basement. He's moved in with me. Temporarily, of course.'

Neither of them mentioned Sean. Shelley knew when to let things drop. Enough had been said, and any move now lay with Laurie.

But she didn't make a move. Instead, she allowed her old life to ebb and flow around her, depositing ideas, hopes, reminiscences and ambitions like so much flotsam on the virgin shore that was her future. She didn't know where she might go, or what she might do. But in the meantime, she meant to go back to Crompton Hall.

She'd intended to tell Gloria and seek her blessing, but Robert and Elspeth's proposed departure for Washington cast an unexpected cloud. Gloria didn't want them to go, even suggesting that Elspeth might start up a bathroom business in England. And while Elspeth herself seemed willing to consider it, Laurie's father was not. They left on a grey autumnal evening, extracting promises that Gloria and Laurie would visit in the spring, a development so astonishing that Laurie could have laughed aloud. She had never felt so hopeful, so happy, about her family circumstances.

There had been only one difficult moment.

'I wasn't a good father,' Robert muttered awkwardly as they kissed goodbye. 'Not when you were growing up anyway . . . I just hope it isn't too late?'

'We're still warm and walking,' Laurie joked. 'And in that case, it's never too late . . .'

Back at the New Leaf, Gloria delivered a further surprise.

'I know you want to go back to Norfolk, so you must leave any time you please . . . I'm glad you want to go, and I'll be glad when you're ready to come back.'

'You're sure you'll be all right?'

Gloria smiled ruefully.

'I'm supposed to say that to you, darling.'

'Oh, I'm all right,' Laurie grinned. 'I used to have cancer, but not anymore . . .' She tapped her padded breast. 'See? All gone!'

Gloria looked away.

'Off you go then,' she said brightly. 'Remember me to Mrs Danvers. What was her name again?'

'Ruth,' said Laurie enthusiastically. 'Ruth Christianos. I hope she's back by now. I'm sure she will be. The centre manager can't stay away for weeks on end . . .'

But when she rang Crompton Hall to make her booking, not only did Ruth fail to answer, nobody else responded either. There was only a recorded message, a voice Laurie recognized as Val's, instructing the caller to write for details.

Puzzled, and somewhat put out, Laurie determined she would go anyway. If she found India's room occupied, then she would simply request another. Maybe Alice Harper's attic retreat . . .

She packed the journals into her suitcase and set off early the following morning, taking the route she'd travelled with Gloria on that distant day, a whole lifetime ago, when Crompton Hall was no more than a name in a glossy brochure, and India Crompton-Leigh a forgotten ghost.

The Hall looked forbidding in the dull noon light, the avenue of limes dejected and wind-torn. Laurie noted a long damp stain on the west wall as she approached, and she saw at once that the windows of the counselling suite were shuttered. She felt her heart begin to pound as she stepped from her car. Had Dale Mitchell shut up shop?

The thought was no sooner faced than dismissed. There'd been no hint of any such plan when he'd visited Laurie at the hospital. Indeed, he had invited her to read on in Alice Harper's journal, with the implicit suggestion that all she found there would later be discussed. Laurie had many questions about scarlet fever, and much she wished to know about the fate of India and Alice. She could hardly wait to begin.

The front door was firmly closed, and her energetic hammering produced no response. She'd assumed the bell to be defunct, but now it seemed there was no one to receive callers. And yet the Hall was not unoccupied. There were cars parked outside, including a glossy black saloon she knew to be Dale Mitchell's.

She looked around nervously, her imagination racing with improbable scenarios. A mass murder? An accident on the lake with everyone drowned? It had to be something serious to take every single resident, client and staff, away from the house, and Laurie was now quite sure that the place was empty.

She walked past the west wing and into the kitchen garden, remarking as she went that all the other windows were shuttered too. Crompton Hall looked like a house in mourning . . .

Then Laurie began to run, through the garden and past the fig tree, across the orchard and into the beech woods, taking the path that led to the round-towered church in the hollow, Crompton Church, St Michael and All Angels, where the fever epidemic had started so many years ago and where now, she suddenly knew, another tragedy was playing out.

On the lip of the hollow she paused to take breath, and then drew back as the door of the church below opened to reveal a team of pall bearers, the polished handles on their burden gleaming in an unexpected ray of sunlight.

Immediately behind the coffin stood Dale Mitchell, and behind him Val, Edie, a number of other people Laurie recognized, and many she didn't. They were still streaming out of the church, and now she could no longer bear to look. She sank down on the grassy bank with her head bowed until the sounds below her ceased and the party processed behind the church, out of her view.

She waited in an agony of unknowing, unable to think or to act. And as she waited, a picture began to form in her mind, a picture of Dale Mitchell's ravaged face on the day he'd come to visit her, a day when he'd surely been visiting someone else too . . .

It was some time before she realized that the mourners weren't going to re-emerge. Clearly they hadn't walked through the beech woods as she herself had done. They had arrived by car at the road behind the church, and were even now driving back to Crompton Hall . . .

Slowly, nervously, Laurie made her way down into the churchyard, bypassing Daisy Turner's grave and glancing only fleetingly at Charlie Youngman's.

As she reached the tower, her pace quickened. She

rounded the corner and found herself among a row of tilting slabs and crumbling sepulchres, beyond which a patch of hedgerow had been cleared to allow for a fresh grave.

Laurie knelt down beside it. Although she'd guessed who lay there, the wording on the tombstone caused her to cry aloud.

Ruth Christianos Mitchell, beloved wife of Dale. Flights of Angels Sing Thee To Thy Rest.

She found Val in the room that had been Ruth's office.

'Why wasn't I told? She was in the same hospital as me, for God's sake! I could have visited her . . .'

Val leaned across the centre manager's desk and grasped Laurie's hand.

'That wouldn't have been a good idea,' she said gently. 'Ruth died very shortly after you were admitted, and she wasn't conscious . . . It could only have proved deeply distressing. And you needed to focus all your positive energies upon yourself . . .'

Laurie snatched back her hand.

'Positive energies! Don't tell me Ruth didn't have positive energies. A fat lot of good they did her!'

Val sat back in her chair, her face grave and strained.

'Ruth was a very positive person. She believed in life and she lived it to the last. None of us can do more.'

Laurie pressed her trembling hands into her lap.

'What killed her?' she whispered.

'Advanced breast cancer,' said Val, looking down. 'Sorry to have to say it, but there it is.'

Laurie began to weep.

'I'm going to die,' she jerked out. 'It's going to kill me, just like it killed her . . .'

For a moment Val said nothing, simply tidied the pencils on the desk, regarding Laurie with silent compassion, struggling for the right words.

'I know how you feel,' she said at last. 'I've been there. But it hasn't killed me . . . Not yet, anyway, and that's the only way to look at it. Maybe you could take me as an example, instead of seeing only Ruth?'

Laurie lowered her face to her hands and howled.

Val got up from the desk and walked to Laurie's side, putting an arm around her, stroking the black nylon wig and pulling her close.

'There's no way out of this,' she said softly. 'The only way is through . . . But you *will* come out on the other side. We all do.'

'Not Ruth!' sobbed Laurie. 'She didn't come through.'

'Well, maybe she did . . . She lived a good life. A happy, fulfilled life . . . And anyway, maybe death is not the end . . . She didn't think it was.'

Laurie stood up.

'That's crap!' she shouted. 'Complete and utter crap! Don't insult me with that stuff! Of course death is the end. Why don't we just die now and get it over with?'

Then, as quickly as the rage had seized her, it departed, and she crumpled into her chair again, shoulders still shaking, this time with uncontrollable mirth.

Val bent toward her in consternation.

'Are you laughing, Laurie?'

Laurie dared to look up.

'Yes, I'm laughing. Pass the god-damn razor blades, I'm going to slit my wrists.'

Val raised one eyebrow, and then suddenly she was laughing too, a great guffaw of relief that lifted them both.

'One packet of razor blades coming up,' she hooted. 'After you, when you've finished.'

Laurie was shown up to India's suite by a pale and subdued Edie, who insisted on carrying her bags.

'You mustn't lift straight after a mastectomy,' she said firmly when Laurie protested. 'Didn't they tell you that?'

Laurie shook her head.

'They didn't tell me lots of things,' she muttered.

But what the hell would I have wanted to know? That breast cancer kills? That you can't just pretend you never had it? That however strong and positive and hopeful you think you're being, the daemon always sits upon your shoulder, waiting his moment to pounce? Well, obviously! So who's a stupid cow, then?

Always less comfortable with Edie than Val, she didn't want to discuss Ruth's death any further, but there was something she had to ask.

'Why didn't they tell everyone they were married?'

Edie shrugged.

'Because they weren't. They'd been together for years, but they didn't marry until a week before Ruth died . . . We all went to the wedding. It was lovely.'

Laurie swallowed the lump in her throat. So far she had not encountered Dale, and she dreaded the moment when she'd have to see him. It didn't help to think that while she'd prattled about regeneration and her dreams of Alice Harper, his wife had been dying . . . Or maybe even lying dead.

And then there was the discomfiting memory of her first visit to Crompton Hall, when she'd fled into the kitchen garden and Ruth had found her sitting beneath the fig tree . . .

'I've been running,' she'd said.

'Running! From what?' Ruth had asked.

'From the knowledge of death . . .' Laurie had replied.

She could hardly bear to recall her curt, dismissive manner, her total obliviousness to any distress but her own.

I expect you'll tell me we all have to face the knowledge of death . . . Isn't that what Doctor Mitchell would say? Death gives life its meaning, its edge? I can just hear him proclaiming it!

And Ruth, so close to death herself, had revealed nothing. What was it she had said?

'Well, of course, it's true . . . But that doesn't make it any easier . . .'

Laurie could have wept, except that she'd done quite enough weeping already.

'Why didn't Ruth talk about her cancer?' she asked Edie tightly. 'I wish I'd known.'

Edie frowned.

'She talked at great length to anyone who wanted to hear. But I expect she thought you weren't ready. And you mustn't blame yourself for that. In the beginning it's important to express how you feel ... Anger, grief, resentment, fear, whatever gets you ...'

Laurie nodded miserably.

'But I was getting over it,' she muttered. 'I really thought I'd beaten cancer! I felt so good, so positive ... I felt ...' Her voice broke as she said the word: '*Regenerated!*'

Edie turned away.

'I wish it was that easy,' she said. 'You take one step forward, then someone dies, and you take two steps back ...'

She looked round and smiled at Laurie.

'But eventually,' she said slowly, 'you have to set all that stuff aside. You have to do it because if you don't, you'll find life's not worth living ... And if life's not worth living, then you might as well be dead anyway ... See?'

'Yes,' Laurie whispered uncertainly. 'I see.'

She couldn't face supper, and still felt unready to face Dale Mitchell, so she lurked in India's room, requesting soup to be brought up, hoping it wouldn't turn out to be the loathsome broccoli and coconut.

In fact, it was a very palatable mushroom, delivered by Val and accompanied by a large glass of white wine.

'You look tired,' Val murmured. 'You shouldn't have driven down here, you know ... Not so soon after major surgery.'

'I'm all right,' Laurie said defensively, but in truth her left arm ached and her ribs felt numb. Considering what had been done to her body, the discomfort had, from the beginning, seemed remarkably slight. Now, however, she found herself contemplating the damage. Muscles and tendons had been sliced, flesh had been displaced, lymph nodes had been extracted. And fluid had begun to collect on the site of her vanished breast so that it rose like a tiny nubile bud, a mocking shadow of its former fullness.

'Sit on the chair in front of the mirror . . . I'll massage your shoulders for you . . .'

Laurie closed her eyes.

Alice Harper, speak to me. Come to me now, with your strong, gentle hands and your scent of lavender . . . Talk to me of angels and miracles. Pray for my soul, and tell me what you want me to believe . . .

Val's fingers caressed her spine and her neck, prodding, stroking, pummelling, an endless, unceasing rhythm, calm and comforting.

Alice Harper, speak to me . . .

The room was so familiar, so peaceful and enfolding, and Val's ministrations so soothing, that Laurie seemed to sink into a trance. She took a draught of wine and felt it flush her face. She was fatigued, all energy drained by the emotion of the day, and as she stared into the mirror, she began to feel her senses drift away.

'Does that feel better?'

'Yes. Thank you, Alice . . .'

'Here, why don't you take some of this? It'll give you a good night's rest . . .'

'Whatever you say, Alice . . .'

'Lie down now, Laurie. Get some sleep.'

As she lay down upon India's quilt, Laurie felt the night close in upon her. She had driven too hard, she had drunk too much, she had allowed death, Ruth's death, to unnerve her.

The light from the casement was dwindling, the stars were glittering above the beech woods, and in the distance, as she drifted toward a deep and dreamless sleep, Laurie thought she heard a nightingale sing.

She woke with a start, unsure where she was, unable to fathom the time. How long had she slept?

She fumbled for the bedside light and consulted her watch, making no sense of the hour it read. She snapped off the light again and lay for a moment in the silence, feeling it wrap her like a shroud. Was she drugged, or still anaesthetized? Or drunk, maybe? It felt that way.

She was thirsty, and in her efforts to locate a tumbler without lighting up the room again, knocked over the water jug. It bounced with an ominous crash into the iron legs of the bedside table.

She got out of bed and surveyed the damage, blinking in the soft light of the lamp, scarcely able to force her eyelids apart. There was no need to clear the glass that moment, and yet she felt compelled to do so. She reached for her gown and walked toward the bedroom door, gliding across the carpet like a phantom, light as air, insubstantial as ether, a spirit in search of a dustpan and brush.

She was wearing the gown that Gloria had bought, the luxurious black and gold silk with the curious embroidered symbols, presented on the day she'd first set out for hospital. She'd grown fond of the extravagant garment, and though she would never have confessed as much to Gloria, had imagined in a fanciful moment that the symbols might really be ancient healing runes, summoning psychic forces and channelling her energies toward recovery.

Now, in the gown, and with her head naked but for its blue-black stubble, she looked extraordinary, a creature from another world, and with a curious, calming detachment, she felt like one. Perhaps she too, like India and Alice, like Ruth, was dead. Perhaps she was a ghost, invisible to all except those whose regenerated vision allowed them to see beyond the moment . . .

The Hall was still awake, dimly lit, peaceful and quiet, and Laurie floated down the stairs without making a sound nor hearing one. But at the bottom of the flight she registered people in the sitting room, a low murmuring in which nothing could be distinguished, and glancing along the corridor, saw the door to Ruth's office ajar and a lamp burning beyond. She moved slowly toward it, and peered into the crack of light.

Nothing prepared her for what she saw.

315

. Standing by the window, dressed in the same grey two-piece in which she'd first appeared, was Ruth Christianos, her face turned away from Laurie, yet her profile clearly recognizable. In front of her, sifting papers on the desk that had been hers, sat Sean.

With a little cry, Laurie flung open the door to the old gun room, certain now, in her strange, dreamlike state, that she had entered another dimension.

'Ruth!'

The figure at the window turned toward the light.

'Laurie! Goodness, you scared us!'

At once the image of Ruth melted into the solid figure of Val, moving swiftly across the room to catch Laurie as she slumped against the door.

Val's voice was reassuringly familiar.

'What on earth are you doing up and about? You should have been flat out till morning!'

Laurie closed her eyes. Unprotesting, she allowed herself to be led upstairs, grateful for the strong arms around her shoulders, head aching, limbs so unbearably heavy she could scarcely drag them along.

Yet she hadn't lost all grasp on reality.

'Mind the broken glass,' she murmured as Val lowered her down onto India's bed. And then remembering the reason for this mishap, added faintly: 'I'm so very thirsty . . .'

Val busied herself with the glass, disappeared for a moment, and then presented a mug of water, propping up Laurie as she drank.

'What was that stuff you gave me?' Laurie muttered as she sank back into her sheets. 'Never mind magic mushrooms, you could make a fortune . . . What was it?'

Val laughed.

'Nothing psychedelic,' she said firmly. 'Just calcarea carbonica to help you sleep . . . But you've got a very potent stew sloshing round your system, Laurie . . . Chemotherapy, anaesthetic, all your vitamins and remedies . . . I shouldn't have given you that wine! No wonder you think you're seeing things . . .'

'I saw Ruth,' Laurie whispered. 'I know I did. Just for a moment, and I realize it was simple illusion – it was you all the time – but even so . . . I saw her.'

Val switched off the lamp and moved to the door.

'Tell Dale I'm sorry,' Laurie said distantly. 'Bursting in on you both like that . . . He must have got an awful fright . . .'

Val turned in the doorway.

'Dale?'

'When I saw him sitting at Ruth's desk, I thought he was someone else . . . Someone I used to know . . . I don't know why the hell that happened . . . Are you sure you didn't give me magic mushrooms?'

'Sleep now,' said Val quietly, closing the door. 'We'll talk in the morning.'

In the morning, Laurie felt remarkably refreshed, if somewhat embarrassed. She dressed slowly, wanting to miss the breakfast chatter, allowing herself time to reflect on the events of the previous night.

It made sense, of course. The emotion of the day, her exhaustion after the drive, the wine, Val's insomnia remedy – as if she needed such a thing – all had combined to heighten her sensitivity.

Explaining it, however, wasn't the same as accepting it. Laurie wasn't used to seeing things, and she disliked the thought of having made a fuss. She was particularly concerned that Dale, who surely needed comfort and support after the funeral, had been confronted by an excited client claiming to see his wife's ghost. She planned to apologize the moment she could.

But the door of the counselling suite was closed, and she could hear no sound from within. The treatment rooms were empty, and so was the music room. Only the kitchen showed signs of life, and Laurie wandered in uncertainly, accepting the proffered bowl of oatbran and taking up a solitary seat in the dining room.

It wasn't long before Val found her.

'Where is everyone?' Laurie demanded. 'Where's Dale?'

Val sat down and waved for coffee.

'There's hardly anyone staying at the moment. We haven't been accepting bookings over the past couple of weeks ... Dale needed time to recover. Right now he's still in bed ...'

'You gave him magic mushrooms too?'

Val grinned.

'It's a perfectly harmless remedy. And I've never seen it have that effect before! I give it to everyone ...'

Laurie looked at Val curiously.

'I hadn't realized you were so much a part of the set-up ... That you were involved in running the place. I thought you and Edie were just clients, like me.'

'At the start we were. And so was Ruth. But Crompton Hall has a very powerful effect ... People come here, and they want to stay. They look for some way they can contribute. Even casual visitors get hooked on the place. There's just something about it ...'

'Spirits and phantoms,' Laurie said meditatively. 'Angels and ghosts ...'

'Yes, all of those.'

They sat in silence for a moment, and Laurie felt a wave of calm enfold her. It was true. There really *was* something powerful, something regenerating, about Crompton Hall. Maybe it was nothing more than the sheer beauty of the place, the promise of its future, the magnificence of its past. And yet it was something more tangible, something strange and wonderful, just as real, and as elusive, as the nightingale's song in the beech woods ...

'So, are you going to be the new centre manager?' she asked Val at last. 'Are you taking over where Ruth left off?'

Val looked up.

'No, not me ... I feel it's time to get back to my own life now ... But I'll always be part of Crompton. And I know I'll keep coming back ...'

She hesitated.

'Dale *has* found someone else,' she said slowly. 'Not a

former client this time, but someone who's been visiting us over the past few weeks . . .'

Laurie smiled. It was hard to contemplate a replacement for Ruth, but if everyone else could do it, then so could she.

'Good,' she said brightly.

'I hope you think so when you hear the full story,' Val replied carefully. 'Laurie, that wasn't Dale you saw in Ruth's office last night . . . It really was Sean . . . He's our new centre manager.'

She was initially astonished, then aggrieved, and finally, merely bemused. It seemed she hardly knew Sean at all. And perhaps the truth, right from the start, had been better than she'd imagined. But in any case, it made no difference. She'd come too far for turning back.

'I hope he hasn't been reading my case notes,' she said stiffly to Val, 'and I hope he's going to stay out of my way.'

'He's been told to,' Val responded quickly. 'Dale would have postponed the appointment until you were finished with Crompton . . . But the fact is, we need Sean. He's done some grand things already. Installed a new computer system, and got us linked up with cancer sufferers all over the world . . . Offering each other support. Swapping stories . . .'

Laurie acknowledged the merit of this idea.

'But you didn't need Sean,' she said grudgingly. 'I could have done it.'

'Well, I know. But you've had other things on your mind. And Sean is very well organized. Efficient in a way that Ruth, through no fault of her own, couldn't always be . . . Also, he's working for less than half his old salary. Not many folk can do that . . .'

Laurie said nothing. The state of Sean's finances were a mystery, and none of her business anyway.

'He'll have a hard job replacing Ruth,' she muttered. 'Although I didn't realize when I first met her, it seems to me now that her first-hand experience was crucial . . . Sean knows nothing about cancer. He has no idea how it feels.'

'Ah, Laurie, that's where you're wrong . . . Cancer claims many victims, and not just those of us who've got it . . . Believe me, Sean knows exactly how it feels . . .'

This was too much, and Laurie stood up from the breakfast table, pushing away her coffee cup.

'How long before I get to see Dale?' she asked tersely. 'There are some things I'd like to clear up . . . Once I've done that, I may find there's nothing more to keep me.'

She was back at the beginning again. From the calm of only a moment before, she had returned to her old antagonism. The realization hit her like a blow, and she felt tears rise hard in her throat. Would she ever establish a lasting peace? Or was she condemned to endure an endless alternation of elation and depression, each false dawn swiftly succeeded by the darkest of nights?

Val reached for her hand.

'Take it easy,' she said gently. 'Maybe I can help. What things would you like cleared up?'

'Things about India,' Laurie muttered defensively, 'about the scarlet fever epidemic, and why nothing was done to check it . . .'

'The epidemic? Well, very little could be done to check it . . . The causal agent of scarlet fever wasn't identified until 1924, and by the time a vaccine was developed, healthier living conditions had improved resistance anyway . . .'

Val looked up at Laurie, assessing her mood.

'It was poverty, malnutrition and inadequate housing that killed the children of Crompton village,' she said slowly. 'Politics, Laurie. That's what did it. Just like every other human disease. Just like cancer.'

Laurie blinked.

'I don't understand,' she murmured.

Val reached for Laurie's chair, motioning her to sit down again.

'Think about it,' she invited. 'We pump young women's bodies full of artificial hormones, and call it the sexual revolution. We poison the environment and call it progress.

We stuff ourselves with food while half the world is starving, and call it freedom ... No wonder a third of us get cancer ...'

Laurie sat down, taken aback.

'I've never thought of it that way,' she said.

'Very few people do ... And yet we're all in it together, Laurie. Once you see it, there's no escaping it. That's the unexpected gift ...'

'The gift?'

'The gift of suffering,' Val said.

Here I go again. Any moment now, I'll start wailing like a bloody banshee. Dear God, get me out of this! I don't want the gift of suffering ...

Val smiled, reassuring.

'Now, what else did you want to know?' she asked gently. 'The rest about India ... That, too, is easily answered. She survived and prospered. She married well, and lived to be a grand old woman.'

Laurie, back in the depths, felt her spirits rise once more. She'd hardly dared to contemplate the unravelling of the story, and though longing for its denouement, had dreaded the moment when Dale Mitchell might reveal some tragic twist.

'So she *did* marry! I've been afraid to ask ... And afraid to look in the churchyard ... Tell me, please! Did she have children?'

Val nodded.

'She certainly did. There were three sons. One of them is still alive today, along with eight grandchildren, and thirteen great grandchildren ...'

Laurie closed her eyes. *Three sons to replace three lost daughters*. The future might be uncertain, and yet the past surely offered hope.

'A happy ending,' she whispered.

Chapter Twenty

A small incident served to change India's mind about the honeymooners' trip.

The morning after the picnic, Eugenie Harte called upon Lady Crompton, bringing her sister Frederica, attired in a most monstrous hat.

'We came, Ma'am, to express the gratitude of the village for your generosity. Such magnificent food, and in such abundance ... My only concern was that the village children might make themselves sick! A great many ate far more than their share ...'

Mrs Harte was, she explained, overwhelmed by Lady Crompton's beneficence, a largesse which the villagers in no way deserved. They would hardly come themselves to give thanks, nor so much as collect a few flowers from their cottage gardens to fashion a rude bouquet, and so it fell to her, the doctor's wife, willing intermediary between the upper and lower classes, to show good manners where working folk could not.

'I am sure my husband would agree that in attending to the nutrition of the poor on this occasion, you are making a most remarkable contribution to health,' she said solemnly.

'Oh yes,' said Frederica, giggling. 'A remarkable contribution.'

Lady Crompton was initially nonplussed by this unexpected tribute, and then suspicious. What did the woman want? Crompton Hall had always given food for the picnic, yet Her Ladyship had never been thanked before. Nor did she desire any thanks. It was quite enough to feel that duty had been done.

'You are too kind,' she said cautiously. 'But naturally, one tries to help one's neighbours whenever possible ...'

This proved an unfortunate remark, confirming Lady Crompton's fears in the next moment.

'I knew as much!' Eugenie exclaimed, turning to her sister. 'Didn't I tell you, Frederica, that Lady Crompton would look kindly on our request?'

India listened in astonishment as the petition unfolded, hardly daring to catch her mother's eye.

'You may not know, Lady Crompton, that Frederica is soon to be married. A most respectable gentleman . . . Mr Charles Youngman of Lavender House . . . We are all very happy . . .'

'Oh yes!' Frederica dimpled. 'Very happy!'

'My husband would like to give a wedding ball for Frederica . . . Naturally, with her having no father, he assumes responsibility . . . But the problem, Lady Crompton, lies with Blue Farm. It simply isn't big enough for a wedding ball. We need some other, larger establishment with a proper ballroom . . .'

Lady Crompton had begun to feel faint, and she signalled urgently to India.

'The salts!' she cried. 'Send for the salts!'

India pulled upon the bellrope, and an anxious parlour maid was swiftly dispatched to Her Ladyship's boudoir, though without any expectation of speedy return.

'Quickly!' shouted Lady Crompton as the frightened girl departed. 'Oh, if only there were some trusty servant one might rely on!'

She fanned herself energetically.

'Forgive me, my dear Mrs Harte . . . I have had a great deal to contend with just lately . . . Not least the problems with our servants! You may know that Alice Harper has repaid our generosity most grievously, walking out without a care for our needs . . . And I had to let Turner go with Mrs Crompton . . . They have proved irreplaceable, and we are most vexed . . . You understand, of course, that with our retinue depleted, we would be unable to commit to any entertainments . . .'

'We should bring our own servants,' Mrs Harte ventured.

'Oh, Sir Robin would not hear of such a thing! India – what has happened to that wretched girl?'

The parlour maid had not returned and India escaped thankfully, searching out the salts and returning some moments later to find Her Ladyship restored to full fitness and Eugenie Harte vanquished.

'I'm sorry to have suggested such a thing, Lady Crompton,' the doctor's wife said gravely. 'I do see how the Harper girl has left you with a serious difficulty . . . We shall find some other venue for the wedding ball. Perhaps Mr Goodchild will oblige once his sister has departed for the capital . . .'

The prospect of Frederica's wedding ball, at Goodchild Manor or any other establishment that Mrs Harte might procure, was so fearsome to India that she almost felt in need of salts herself.

How unrefined, how vulgar, was the household in which her beloved Luke found himself! How agonizing might it be to receive an invitation to the ball, to witness Luke, the family man, doing his duty by the dreadful Frederica! How far had he fallen, and how far had she, who only hours before had confessed the depths of her feeling to Alice, committed herself to repeated humiliations in the name of love?

Perhaps Alice had been right. Perhaps a change of scene would do her good. By absenting herself from Luke's proximity, she would spare herself the contemplation of his tragedy.

For indeed, knowing nothing of genuine tragedy, it seemed to India as though the marriage of Luke and Eugenie Harte – so ill conceived, so unworthy, so *wrong* – was by its very nature tragic. How else was she to view the ignominious enslavement of a fine and noble man?

Adam Goodchild was much relieved at India's decision, conveyed by letter not an hour after his portentous interview with Dr Harte.

He went at once to tell Marianne, anxious to offer any little comfort that might cheer her.

In the difficult days after her return with Christian, he had been distant and cold toward his sister, unable to forgive

325

what he'd seen as a rejection of the love and guidance he'd faithfully offered.

But news of the coming child had softened his anger, and Marianne had been so miserable, so thoroughly transformed from the carefree young woman he had known, that he longed to restore something of her former zest.

He found her risen from her bed, taking a cup of weak tea and a shortbread biscuit, and daring to think that the worst might be over.

'Dr Harte says I shall be better when I'm past the three month . . . By that time we'll be leaving London and setting off for Brighton . . . Won't we, Christian? I'm sure I shall enjoy the sea air . . . Don't you think?'

Christian was slumped in a chair by the bed, but at this poignant appeal from his wife, he looked up and smiled.

'Oh, everyone enjoys the sea air!' he declared. 'It's a well known fact of life . . .'

Adam bit back the observation that Christian seemed peculiarly well placed to enjoy himself anywhere, and contented himself with announcing his news. He said nothing of the scarlet fever, and did not mention Dr Harte's anxiety, urging Marianne to contemplate a restful and recuperative excursion in the company of her sister-in-law.

'India?' said Marianne in surprise. 'But I thought she didn't want to come . . . And I was hoping for Alice Harper . . .'

'I was hoping for Alice too,' Adam said, 'but she's quite clear that she can't leave her mother.'

Marianne frowned.

'I'm sure Christian could persuade her,' she said tentatively. 'Alice always listens to Christian . . .'

Her husband stirred uneasily in his chair.

'I'm afraid that isn't true,' he said awkwardly. 'Alice never listens to me . . . But India will make a tolerable companion. We shall all have to do without Alice.'

Adam looked up.

Something in his brother-in-law's expression puzzled him, a certain undertone to the casual timbre of the voice, a faint wistfulness that no one would ever associate with

Christian, yet which, undeniably, had surfaced when he spoke of Alice . . .

Adam stared at Christian. His puzzlement had suddenly connected with one that persisted concerning Alice's refusal. He could not understand why his offer had been so summarily dismissed. Nor did he see why Alice, so devoted to India, had left Crompton Hall so hastily . . . Unless . . .

But, no. It couldn't be! Such an idea was preposterous, or worse. It was obscene.

And then suddenly, a host of trivial incidents rose to confound Adam Goodchild, snatches of conversation, the memory of exchanged glances, a vision of Alice striding across the grass at India's birthday party, Christian close on her heels . . .

Without a word, he turned and walked from his sister's room, his spirit in turmoil, his heart angry and cold.

Of course. Now Alice's speedy departure from Crompton Hall became intelligible, as did her curious refusal of his own offer, when everyone knew that old Mrs Harper had made a miraculous recovery . . .

He pressed his trembling fingers into his palms.

How could he safeguard his beloved sister's happiness? How could he protect her from wanton infidelities or shameless betrayal? How best might he keep Christian true to his marriage vows?

He paced the drawing room, his brow furrowed, his face dark.

There was only one way. He would confide his suspicions to India and ask for her help.

India set out for the summerhouse by the lake, strolling slowly through the beech woods in the mild autumn air, idly registering the splendour of the burnished trees, picturing herself in London, upon the pier at Brighton, and savouring the prospect.

Her course of action now seemed clear. She would go, and she would return, and she would pin her hope upon some change of circumstance in the meantime. She was vague about this hope, and couldn't imagine what the change might be. But a fatalistic streak, born of her studies into Eastern philosophy, encouraged her to embrace the idea of inevitable consequence. Something *would* happen. It might be good, it might be bad, but it would initiate change. Only change was constant. There could be no going back, and no standing still. The inexorable process of change would have its way.

The lake was swollen with seasonal rain, the sedge drifting toward the banks until it formed a solid platform, firm and deceptive until a stone was thrown upon it or a branch disturbed its surface. India kept well away from the banks and settled herself in the summerhouse with a book, a most absorbing account of a Victorian adventuress whose travels had taken her to the subcontinent . . .

It was there that Adam found her, and in disturbing her solitude, causing her to gasp and jump up from her chair, black hair floating loose and face delicately flushed, discovered that his longing had not abated. Indeed, in the intuition of Dr Harte's own admiration for India, it had only increased.

'India, I'm sorry I startled you. I had to hurry here at once to tell you how delighted, how deeply gratified, I am at your decision to go away with Marianne . . .'

They had met only fleetingly, and always in company, since their last agonizing encounter in the beech woods, and now each regarded the other with judicious interest. Adam adjusted his collar. India fumbled nervously with her hat. For a long moment, neither of them spoke.

'I'm very pleased to be going to London,' India said at last, sitting down again on her deck chair. 'I hope Marianne is feeling stronger, and that the trip will not upset her . . .'

Adam hesitated. He was reluctant to discuss Marianne's condition, finding it a matter of some embarrassment, and he had already determined to say nothing to anyone about the scarlet fever scare. He still had hopes that it might come to nothing, and wanted simply to see his loved ones safely away.

But the matter of Christian had to be addressed.

'Marianne is feeling a little better . . . And I'm encouraged to believe that all will be well . . . As long as she is assured of her husband's devotion . . . And indeed, his best behaviour, then I'm sure there will be no problem . . .'

It was not well put, and as he heard his own clumsy words, he had no expectation of being understood. But India sat up at once.

'Best behaviour?' she repeated.

Adam's hand flew to his collar again. He gazed at India unhappily, knowing he had set himself a most delicate and difficult task.

'It's not my intention to criticize your brother in your hearing . . . Nor to suggest that his love for my sister is anything less than sincere . . . But it has come to my attention . . . That is to say, I have guessed at a liaison between Christian and another woman . . . And I'm most anxious to ensure that he remains true to Marianne . . .'

India jumped to her feet.

'You know about Kitty Malone?' she asked incredulously. 'How can you possibly know that?'

'Kitty Malone?' he echoed foolishly. 'Why, no! Who is she?'

India, seeing she had unwittingly revealed more than was necessary, began to pace the summerhouse floor, twisting her hat between her hands in restless agitation. For all her earlier censure of Christian, she did not want his misdeeds discussed among outsiders, and could not bear the thought that Adam might consider a Crompton to be anything less than position demanded.

'Kitty is no one!' she declared ardently. 'She is an actress from the London Music Hall . . . So you see, she is no one at all! I do believe Christian had her acquaintance some months ago when he was in the city . . . And I regret that he may have been led astray . . . But it's all done with now. I have his word upon that.'

This was far more than she need have said, and much worse than Adam Goodchild might have expected. The seduction of Alice Harper was one thing, an affair with a

London actress quite another. He stared at India in growing anger, all his thoughts upon Marianne and the burden her protection imposed.

'I know nothing of Kitty Malone,' he said tersely, 'and I'm most discomfited to be told of her now ... I was referring to another matter entirely. I was referring to your brother's liaison with Alice Harper ...'

India stopped dead and turned to face him.

'I beg your pardon!'

'Alice and Christian,' he said quietly, feeling now that he had nothing to lose, and possibly a considerable amount to gain. 'It may seem incredible, but I believe it to be true. Certainly, I believe Christian to be capable of so low an act ... The compromising of poor Alice ... I'm sorry to say it, but I think that if you search your memory, you will find evidence of an intimate relationship ... And that is why Alice left Crompton Hall when Christian returned. Why she refused my offer of a post as Marianne's maid ... This much, at least, we may feel is to her credit ...'

India had become deathly pale, the white mask of her face punctured by two livid spots upon her cheeks. Her breath was rapid, her eyes like pools of blue ice. She pressed a hand to her heart.

'It's not possible,' she jerked out.

'If you need evidence, then I suggest you ask Alice herself. I've no hope that Christian would tell the truth ... But poor Alice would surely feel the need to confess when confronted ...'

And then, as with Adam himself, a host of small incidents and half-remembered conversations rose to taunt India ... *The pitfalls of love, its social constraints ...*

She drew in her breath. How wickedly had she been deceived! How false had her beloved companion proved to be! Using her position, the extraordinary privileges she had gained, to wheedle her way into India's trust ... And all her fine speeches no more than subterfuge so that she might ensnare the heir to Crompton Hall.

'*Poor Alice!*'

She spat the words as though poison had suddenly

infected her tongue, and Adam stepped back in surprise, alarmed by her vehemence.

'My dear India, we must surely conclude that he bears the greater blame . . . After all, he is the future master of the house, while she is merely . . .'

'A *servant!*'

Adam shifted uncomfortably beneath his constricting collar, perplexed by this unexpected response.

'Well, no matter,' he said uneasily. 'I'm not suggesting that anything of an improper nature continues now . . . I think we both know Alice too well to imagine that . . . But I am, nevertheless, concerned for my sister. I need your help, India. I need to know that you will be his conscience. That you will be vigilant for any sign of waywardness . . . That you will challenge him if you have cause for concern, and that you will tell me everything that happens while you are all away together . . .'

India said nothing. She offered no hint that she would comply, she gave no sign of sympathy, she uttered no word of consolation.

She merely fastened her hat over her unruly hair and walked out of the summerhouse, striding away through the trees as though she'd heard not a word of his petition, let alone considered it. She did not even take her leave, as simple courtesy demanded.

He called after her.

'India! Please wait! I'm sorry if I've upset you . . .'

She turned, her face impassive.

'I must hurry,' she said. 'Mama will be waiting on afternoon tea . . .'

Adam watched her go with foreboding, sensing that in the space of this short encounter they had moved from mutual affection and pleasure in the recovery of their former friendship, to estrangement and discord beyond anything they'd previously known. Too late he saw he'd been wrong to share his fears. She didn't seem to care about Marianne's future. She didn't even seem to care that her brother had behaved with despicable callousness. She seemed only to care about some perceived infringement of a mistress's right to her servant's loyalty . . . Adam Goodchild shivered suddenly in the cooling autumn air.

Although India did not know it, the crucial change she so eagerly anticipated was about to take place.

There was a moment, fleeting though it seemed, a resolution, insignificant enough in itself, upon which her future hung suspended, waiting for the wind to blow. It might have taken her either way, toward a defiance of convention, a relaxing of the barriers that falsely serve to separate one section of society from another . . . Or toward a fatal hardening of heart.

As she walked back to Crompton Hall, the decision was made.

She would not mention Adam Goodchild's insulting accusation to her brother, nor would she attempt to question Alice. Whatever the truth, it was a matter for Alice's conscience, not hers.

She would not spy upon Christian either, as Adam had dared to request, as though his brother-in-law were some low-life reprobate. Instead, she would place her confidence in good breeding, and yes, in family character. The Cromptons were no come-lately crew of adventurers, as the Goodchilds might be considered by those *less charitable* than herself. No, the Cromptons claimed a fine and noble lineage, stretching back to the earliest settlers of Norfolk, proud people who'd learned to manage their land and their business affairs in their own way, without heed for the carps and jibes of those beneath them . . .

Now she saw that despite her earlier misgivings, she could indeed trust her brother's instincts. He had done the right thing, quite contrary to all she'd previously believed. He had not eloped with Kitty Malone. He had not allowed any other dalliance to deflect him from his course. He had married the woman for whom he'd always been intended, and he would make her an eminently suitable husband. He would do it, because such was the nature of all he had been raised to enjoy and expect . . . He would do it because he was Christian Crompton-Leigh, and because commonplace restraints did not apply ... It simply fell to the family to deal with his wilder instincts, as families throughout the centuries had dealt with their wayward heirs ...

And did India, in that moment, stop to contemplate her own romantic dreams and longing? Did she, as Luke Harte had done, imagine the situation in which he might have arrived at Crompton without wife or family to blight his prospects? Did she see herself as the doctor's consort, ministering to the low and humble of the parish? Or think of life at Blue Farm, with its uncertain water closet, its cramped parlour and its lack of a suitable room for ballroom dancing?

At the edge of the beech woods, where the orchard met the kitchen garden, she paused to take breath.

From this point, a splendid vista of the Hall rose to meet the onlooker, mellow stone glowing in the dying afternoon light, lawns and terraces stretching into the sculptured distance, everything perfectly in its place. She closed her eyes against the flickering sun, feeling its faint warmth touch her face like a caress. She was strangely calm, and this despite the emotion raised by her encounter with Adam, as though a shutter had closed upon her senses, immuring her to further unnecessary pain. She opened her eyes once more, and Crompton Hall beckoned, a haven of ideals, a repository of hopes, a fortress against encroaching uncertainties ...

India smiled to herself, and walked on.

They departed within the week, setting out for London from Crompton railway station, their train delayed for several minutes while India's hat boxes and Marianne's furs were loaded into the guard's van.

Adam's carriage had taken them into the village, but neither the Goodchild conveyance, nor the Crompton coach, could be spared for the full journey.

'This is the last time we shall travel by train!' Christian declared, lowering the leather strap on the window and leaning out to grasp his brother-in-law's hand. 'We shall return by automobile!'

Marianne, her delicacy beginning to swell into fecundity and her face flushed with excitement, clapped her hands like a child on a Sunday school outing.

'Will we buy it as soon as we reach London?' she asked her husband breathlessly. 'Oh, I do hope we will!'

'The very moment we get there!' he cried, laughing and pulling her close. Marianne put her arm around his waist and nuzzled her cheek into his shoulder.

To Adam, watching, they were in that moment the ideal honeymoon couple, perfectly matched and deeply in love, poised upon a golden future. And it was true that for all his lingering reservations and dark suspicions, he'd seen nothing in the time they'd been living in his house to suggest anything otherwise.

'Please take care,' he said nervously. 'These automobiles are wretchedly difficult things to drive . . .'

'Nonsense!' said Christian, whose reconciliation with his father and the consequent change in his fortune had greatly improved his spirits. 'I've driven Tim Harrington's a dozen times . . .'

Adam nodded.

'Well, then . . . Have a lovely time!'

India, seated in the far corner of the carriage, had barely spoken a word since leaving the Hall, and only now stood up to bid farewell.

She extended a gloved hand through the window, and smiled distantly at Adam.

'We shall send you a postcard,' she said.

'Thank you,' he replied awkwardly, looking up. He had never noticed, until this moment, how cold, how unfeeling, her brilliant blue eyes could sometimes appear.

Marianne leaned forward and kissed her brother on the cheek.

'I shall think of you tonight, all alone at Goodchild Manor while we are dining with Lord Harrington . . . We'll be having such fun, and you will have no one to talk to . . .'

Adam, who'd considered himself resigned to the departure, and who, indeed, was much relieved at the prospect of his sister escaping a fever epidemic, now surprised himself by his depth of feeling. He was truly alone, with no family to relieve his isolation, and no prospect of ending that unhappy state. He smiled bravely at Marianne.

'I shall be happy as long as I know you are safe . . .'

'Safe!' remarked India sharply from the back of the carriage. 'Why should she not be safe?'

Adam frowned and took his sister's hand, ignoring India and addressing himself only to Marianne.

'I mean merely that as long as you are well,' he said gently, 'and that you do nothing which might endanger your health . . .'

Marianne laughed gaily.

'Oh, I shall do nothing dangerous!' she declared. 'I shan't lift a valise, nor even stretch up to pull a curtain! I shall let my husband do all that . . .'

'Or your new maid,' said India pointedly. 'I hope we shall be hiring maids as soon as we get to London, not buying automobiles . . .'

Marianne raised her fingers to her lips as the train began to pull away.

'Dearest Adam,' she whispered to him, 'you need have no more worries about me! I've never felt better . . .'

And indeed, as the train disappeared in a cloud of steam, and as Marianne leaned from the window to wave a last goodbye, he considered that, truly, she looked healthier, and happier, than ever before.

Perhaps marriage and motherhood would prove blessings, and Christian Crompton-Leigh as good a husband as might have been wished. Perhaps the happy ending he had so earnestly desired for his orphaned sister might come about after all . . .

As he drove home to his lonely supper that night, Adam Goodchild dared to hope.

The epidemic bit hard into Adam's conscience.

Why were so many dying? Was it true, as Luke Harte had suggested, that only the betterment of living standards, the improvement of sanitation, family hygiene and nutrition among the lower classes, would bring about an end to scarlet fever? He had tried, in the years since his father's death, to improve the lot of the Goodchild tenants. And certainly, the cottages on the Goodchild estate were in better condition than those owned by the Cromptons. But there were far fewer Goodchild cottages, a point Sir Robin was quick to make when any discussion of tenants arose between them. It was all very well for Adam to install weather proof windows and provide new tiles for the roofs of some forty cottages. The Cromptons had nearer a hundred and fifty, and the expense would be enormous. In any case, Adam was forced to conclude that his new windows had made no difference to fever susceptibility. Goodchild families had not escaped the epidemic, and he had no reason to think his tenants were faring better than Sir Robin's.

Dr Harte had reassured him with a bitter observation.

'There is no easy answer. The standards of all must be raised before disease can be eradicated . . . You might consider that at Blue Farm we have more than adequate standards, and yet my daughters have not been spared . . . On the other hand, Lavender Cottage is surely one of the least hospitable homes in the village, but the Harper children have escaped . . .'

Adam had seen nothing of Alice Harper since the epidemic began. It seemed she'd shut herself off from a stream of desperate villagers demanding a cure for the fever.

This much he had gleaned from Daisy Turner, relegated to the Goodchild parlour in Marianne's absence and looking for new ways to make herself indispensable. It wasn't difficult. She found Adam Goodchild a much more enlightened and kindly employer than previously encountered, and quickly undertook to keep him informed on village matters. And he, with too much time on his hands and too few companions at his dinner table, found himself listening eagerly to a parlour maid's gossip.

'Alice Harper has a rare way with cures, Sir. Everyone knows she cured that little elephant . . .'

'She'll not cure the scarlet fever,' Adam said gloomily.

'No, Sir. But they say she gives the belladonna, and if it's given in time, or if the patient has a fighting spirit, it might work . . . She gave it to the doctor's daughter, little Sophie Harte . . . And she's not dead yet, Sir . . .'

Initially startled by this revelation, Adam dismissed it upon reflection. It was unthinkable that Luke Harte should seek a folk cure for his daughter, and highly unlikely that his wife would do so. This was one piece of maid's gossip he could safely ignore.

But as the days wore on, as the epidemic worsened and Sophia Harte still did not die, he found himself wondering about Alice and her cures. Indeed, thoughts of Alice often rose to unsettle him. He began to remember things he had barely noted at the time, Alice's constant good humour in the face of Lady Crompton's slights, her gentle correction of India's fanciful ways, her command of conversation and her considerable learning on an astonishing variety of subjects . . . It seemed, now he came to think of it, hardly surprising that Christian had pursued so rare and fine a creature under his own roof . . . The surprise was surely that Alice herself had responded.

The longer he thought, the more convinced he became that Alice had indeed responded. He had not been mistaken in his original suspicion, he had simply been wrong to convey it to India. It was done for the best reasons, of course, to protect his beloved Marianne . . . And yet somehow, instead of igniting India's concern, he had succeeded only in provoking her wrath. How different India's behaviour now seemed to that of Alice herself . . . Alice, who would always rank her own cares below the distress of anyone else, and who would never cause hurt nor despondency . . . Alice, who would never have refused a suitor as India had done, declaring to his face that he was not loved . . . Nor walked away from his legitimate concerns without so much as a goodbye . . .

He didn't care to dwell upon India's coldness that day at

the lake, preferring to hope that whatever spectre had risen to discomfit her would soon be vanquished by a change of scene.

And yet, in that one small, insignificant encounter, the light of his longing had been severely dimmed, if not completely extinguished . . . He suspected now that he had loved a fantasy, a splendid vision whose lack of substance might only be revealed in conditions of adversity . . . Where once he had seen playfulness, he now perceived mischief . . . And in the imagined depths of her sensitivity, he now believed he glimpsed selfishness . . .

If he'd needed assurances about Christian, he should have sought them from Alice, not India. And perhaps, he persuaded himself, it wouldn't be wrong to approach her now . . . Not in any spirit of censure, of course, but with the hope of securing her confidence . . . There might even be some way he could help. Perhaps by pressing Charlie Youngman to repair Lavender Cottage, or by offering some thoughts upon window frames . . . And thereby, he mused, discover Alice's feelings on the matter of Christian's marriage to Marianne . . .

Alas, no such opportunity presented itself.

Adam continued to wonder about Alice until one morning, when the fever epidemic was subsiding and the village daring to raise its head once more, a telegram was delivered to Goodchild Manor.

He tore open the envelope, knowing that it came from London, and that it surely contained urgent news.

What he read inside drove all thoughts of Alice from his mind, and rendered any discussion between them utterly, tragically, irrelevant.

Chapter Twenty-one

It was such a silly death.

India, though shocked, could not avoid this conclusion. Nor could she avoid conveying it to Adam, who appeared calm and composed on receiving his sister's coffin at Crompton railway station, unlike Christian who, in the terrible days since the accident, had seemed half mad with grief.

'It was so ridiculous,' India said earnestly to Adam, 'such a slight and unexpected thing ... We weren't travelling above five miles per hour, much slower than if you were driving in a carriage ...'

He had walked to the railway station instead of riding with the hearse, his mind unable to grasp the finality of his loss, needing to take the air on this most sterile, most suffocating of mornings.

Not a month before he had waved her off from this very platform, daring to believe her bound for a secure and happy future. He had taken her hands in his own, and had not known that he should never touch them again, nor see her precious face break into smiles at some new excitement ... Now he would not see her mature into womanhood, nor take her child, the eagerly hoped for nephew, into his arms ...

At the station, he had watched the unloading of the long polished box, had seen India and Christian alight, and could not believe that Marianne too might not step from the carriage at any moment ...

And yet even at this darkest hour, he had known that his suffering was matched, was understood, by dozens of families in the village of Crompton ... He was not alone. And in standing beside all those who'd lost loved ones in the epidemic, and most especially beside Luke Harte, had felt himself to be both humbled and uplifted in one curious surge of shared emotion. It was Luke he thought of now. The doctor's one remaining daughter, who'd fought so valiantly against her fever and seemed to be winning, had died the previous night. A gentle passing, so it was reported, and yet for all that, perhaps the Hartes' most devastating bereavement, striking just as hope had begun to flourish . . .

Adam had chosen to ride home in the Crompton carriage, sent by Sir Robin and put at his disposal for the difficult days ahead. He'd been unsure whether India and Christian might come with him, or whether they should return to Crompton Hall, and it was India who announced their destination as Goodchild Manor while Christian stared blankly into the grey noon sky, and while he, Adam, sought desperately for something comforting to say. He mumbled a few words about blaming no one, but still Christian said nothing, bowing his head as though he did not trust himself to speak.

And it was then that India began her account.

It seemed scarcely credible, she asserted, that anyone might be killed in such a way. Automobiles were generally held to be the safest form of transport yet invented . . . The open-topped ones even more so as they allowed for immediate escape in the event of an accident . . . And this one had been driven so very slowly and carefully . . . As *of course*, you would expect with an inexperienced young woman behind the wheel.

'Marianne was driving?' he asked incredulously.

'No, it was me! I was driving. Just that morning Tim had promised he'd give me my very first lesson. Christian had gone into the city on some business, and so Marianne and I were left alone . . . She was sitting in the back.'

They had rounded a bend, the car had hit a sudden dip in the road, Marianne had been kneeling on the seat, leaning out to gain a better view of Lord Harrington's Italian gardens, and she had simply toppled into a ditch . . .

'We thought she'd barely be winded, let alone wounded . . . But the ditch contained a boulder, and . . .'

Here India faltered, remembering the horror, the denial,

of the moment they had run to the ditch ... It was impossible. Marianne could not be dead. Such a thing was unthinkable. It was so very ... silly.

Adam fought to control his emotion.

'It wasn't your fault,' he said haltingly.

India had not imagined that it was her fault, nor that anyone else might think so either, and now she blinked at Adam in surprise.

'It was my fault! I am to blame! If I'd been there, it would never have happened ...'

They were the first words Christian had spoken, and they were accompanied by a desperate sob such as Adam had never expected to hear.

He put his hand on his brother-in-law's shoulder.

'I'm sure that's not true,' he murmured gently.

'But it is! I should never have left her ...'

Adam's eyes met India's above the bent head of her brother, and to his shock, he saw there a flash of impatience.

'It would still have happened,' she said impassively. 'If you'd been sitting right next to her, you wouldn't have caught her because you'd never have thought she was going to fall ...'

She looked away.

'If anything's to be learned from this disaster, it is surely that there ought to be some kind of restraint fastened to automobile seats ... Something that would prevent passengers tipping into ditches if they should be so unwise as to lean out when the vehicle is taking a corner ...'

This suggestion was both sensible and simple, but it found no favour with India's companions, producing only a terse nod from Adam and another sob from Christian.

'We should write to the Government,' India pursued. 'To Mr Asquith himself ... Perhaps there could be an investigation, and we could give our evidence ...'

Adam nodded again and forced a weak smile. She was trying to make sense of the incomprehensible, to extract from it some shred of meaning and hope. Her remarks were inappropriate, but they were well meant.

'I should never have bought that car! If Papa hadn't given me the money, I couldn't have bought it . . . And Marianne would be alive today . . .'

Adam's heart went out to the bereaved husband, and for a moment he thought he might weep aloud too. He tightened his grip upon Christian's shoulder, and India leaned over toward her brother.

'Unfortunately,' she said, 'that is true.'

To Adam's relief they had arrived at Goodchild Manor, and now he sprang from the carriage, waving urgently at Daisy Turner who stood waiting to meet them. She rushed forward to take charge of India's gloves and parasol, then stood back as Adam helped Christian into the house.

'I've set out the brandy, Sir,' she said.

But Christian did not want brandy, nor sweet tea, nor any other sustenance. Most of all, he did not want to sit in the drawing room with his sister.

'Please,' he whispered brokenly to Adam when the two of them were left briefly alone, 'please send India back to Crompton Hall as soon as possible . . .'

Adam also did not wish to sit with India, but it was impossible to dismiss her at once, and having left Christian lying upon the bed he'd so recently shared with Marianne, found himself forced to pass an agonizing hour with the woman whose company he'd once prized above all others.

They talked of Marianne's delight in Italian gardens, of Lord Harrington's splendid estate in Hampshire, of the unexpected discovery that he owned tea estates in Darjeeling, and finally, of automobiles, their defects, their possible improvements, and their imagined benefits to society.

When nothing more could be said on the subject of Marianne's death, they turned at last to the epidemic.

'Mama wrote to tell me that some Crompton children had fallen ill . . .'

'I'm afraid it's been much worse than that. Some thirty or more already dead. And poor Dr Harte lost his last surviving daughter this morning . . .'

'Dr Harte?'

Adam shook his head in sorrow.

'Most terribly tragic . . . Those lovely little girls . . .'

India suddenly rose to her feet, her face flushed.

'And Dr Harte's wife?' she whispered urgently. 'What has happened to his wife?'

Adam looked up, puzzled.

'To his wife? Why nothing, as far as I know . . . She is no doubt distraught . . .'

What India imagined, or perhaps desired, in that moment was beyond her own understanding or indeed, her wildest hopes, and she at once retreated from unworthy fantasy.

But whatever vision rose to tempt her, whatever hint of resolution had been glimpsed, whatever long-expected change now seemed about to reach its zenith, she could no longer sit talking to Adam. She had to go. She reached for her hat and called for Daisy, declaring that she would send the carriage back just as soon as she reached Crompton Hall.

'Mama will expect to see Christian,' she said as she climbed into the carriage, 'so perhaps you will return him to us in the morning . . .'

Adam risked a contradiction.

'Christian may stay here as long as he pleases . . .'

India raised one eyebrow.

'That's very kind. I'm sure Mama will be most gratified . . . But my brother's place is at home with his family . . . There is nothing to be gained by staying here . . .'

He watched the carriage drive away with a heavy heart, unable to fathom how the tender emotion he'd always felt for India had vanished so entirely. Now he experienced a chill when he gazed into those brilliant blue eyes, a sense of falling into icy waters and flailing against a wicked undertow. The loss seemed to compound his greater loss, the tragic death of Marianne, and yet it also served to concentrate his resolve.

He would set aside all previous doubts about Christian. He would allow him time and peace to grieve. He would not suggest quitting Goodchild Manor while any small remnant of comfort might be gained from remaining. And he would never abandon his sister's husband to the heartless vacuity of his own family . . . All this he would do for the sake of Marianne, who had loved them both.

'I have a confession I wish to make. I am sorry to force it upon you, yet nevertheless, it must be done . . . It must be done before we stand together at her graveside . . .'

They were sitting at breakfast in the vast emptiness of the Goodchild dining hall, consuming food, as they were required to do in order to function, but tasting nothing. A jug of cold coffee stood between them, a mound of congealing eggs by its side. Adam removed the eggs and called for more coffee. He did not wish to hear any confession, and yet he understood Christian's need. He found himself hoping the revelations wouldn't centre upon Alice Harper.

'On the morning of Marianne's death, I was in Hampstead . . . Visiting a woman I used to know . . . A woman who was once my lover . . . And who had recently given birth to my child . . .'

Christian's face was white as the tablecloth before him, yet he spoke clearly and steadily, his eyes downcast.

There was a long pause. This was worse than anything Adam might have expected, and he gripped the table, flexing his knuckles in an effort at control, reminding himself of his earlier resolution.

'It doesn't matter now,' he said at last. 'Marianne is dead. I stand by what I said. It wasn't your fault, and you mustn't blame yourself.'

Christian looked up.

'It matters that you hear it from me,' he said quietly, 'and that you understand my feelings on the subject. I have most bitterly regretted this mistake, and I will not claim it as my only one . . . But this particular mistake I have tried to make good. I've bought a house in Ireland for Kitty and her son, and I have settled an income upon them . . . I want you to know that I had no expectation of seeing them again. That I should never have been unfaithful to

Marianne, nor brought any shame or embarrassment upon her . . . I wished only to make her happy.'

Adam fought against his pain.

'You did make her happy,' he said simply.

A shadow of grief fell upon Christian's face.

'Thank you,' he whispered.

They sat in silence for several moments, each lost in his private agony, and then Adam spoke, seeing that the moment might never come again and that all future accord rested upon their mutual honesty.

'I am glad you felt able to confide this news . . . And I have my own confession to make . . . I realize now that I wasn't exactly the diligent guardian . . . That I left Marianne too much alone and imagined I knew what was best without truly understanding how she felt . . .'

He broke off, hardly able to contemplate the memory, then took a swallow of his coffee and struggled on.

'I believe you knew her better than I . . . And that you saw what she wanted . . . It's true that I never liked you, Christian, nor considered you in any way suitable to marry my sister . . . But it seems to me now that I was wrong . . .'

Christian shook his head.

'You weren't wrong. I was deeply unsuitable. But I should have become suitable . . . And I should have done it for one reason. Marianne always believed the best of me. She alone saw beyond all the fooling . . .'

He hesitated.

'There is one other matter I should like to raise . . .'

Adam held his breath, feeling they were surely approaching the matter of Alice.

'It may have been suggested that I married your sister for her fortune . . . That my main interest was to unite the Crompton and the Goodchild estates . . . I may even have said something very like it myself . . . To tease India, I suspect . . .'

Now he looked a little sheepish, and Adam nodded. He could see how India might have been provoked in such a manner, and for the first time, understood why someone would wish to do it.

'It's true I needed money . . . And now you know why
. . . But it wasn't Marianne's fortune I sought, merely an
increase in my own . . .'

'I never suspected you of that,' Adam said gently. 'It
made no sense . . .'

'Then thank you again . . .'

There followed another long silence in which Adam
sought for some way to offer Goodchild Manor as a home
without thereby seeming to criticize the Cromptons.

'Have you thought what you might do next?' he inquired
carefully.

'I mean to seek a commission in the Army. It may seem
an odd choice, but I can think of no other career . . . And
I'm bound to say that the moment has come to apply myself.
I cannot escape that conclusion. Out of tragedy, perhaps,
may come some little good . . .'

He suddenly stood up, and Adam knew that if Alice were
ever to be mentioned between them, it had to be now. Did
he want to hear his suspicions confirmed? Or did he wish to
have his admiration for Alice preserved, thereby sparing his
grieving brother-in-law, and himself, any further distress?

'I'm going to walk in the grounds,' Christian muttered.
'Will you come with me?'

Adam hesitated, and then shook his head. He would
seek no more confessions, nor subject himself to any other
turmoil.

'I shall write some letters,' he said heavily. 'And then we
shall visit the parson to discuss the funeral hymns . . .'

Christian walked the entire perimeter of the Goodchild
estate, noting as he went the condition of Adam's tenanted
cottages, their sturdy window frames and weatherproof
roofs.

At the edge of the lavender fields, where Goodchild land
met the Youngmans', he veered quickly away from Adam's
neat and sculptured acreage toward Blue Farm.

He had no wish to encounter Luke Harte, sorry though
he was at the news of his loss and keen to express his

sympathy when the moment seemed right. For now he had another purpose in mind, and he saw no reason to delay.

As Lavender Cottage came into view, he paused, suddenly uncertain. He'd rehearsed the speech he would make to Mrs Harper a dozen times, yet he had been unable to envisage her likely response. Worse, he could not imagine what Alice might say, and had concluded that his only option was to request an interview with Nell Harper alone. But would Alice countenance such a thing? Christian did not know, and he had no stomach for an argument. His best hope was that Alice might yield in the light of his recent bereavement.

But there was a better hope that he had not considered.

'Master Christian!' said Nell Harper in surprise. 'You've come to see Alice . . . But I'm afraid she isn't here . . . She's gone to visit poor Mrs Harte . . .'

He shook his head, enormously relieved.

'I've come to see you, Ma'am,' he said.

She led him into the damp and shabby parlour where he'd last sat drinking elderberry wine with Alice, motioning him down on to the same shabby settee, and as that memory returned to haunt him, he forced himself to confront another fear.

'Is Alice well?' he asked nervously.

'Tolerably well, yes . . . We have mercifully been spared the scarlet fever in this house . . .'

He nodded and tried again.

'So Alice is not indisposed in any way?'

'Indisposed? Not that I am aware . . .'

She was looking at him curiously and he felt his face start to flush. He hid his confusion by moving rapidly into his speech, finding that emotion had rendered him less prepared than he'd hoped.

'It may surprise you to hear you have a new landlord,' he began unsteadily. 'One who will undertake to repair your cottage and keep it in good order. The matter has been settled with Mr Youngman, who kindly agrees to oversee the renovations even though he himself has no further interest in Lavender Cottage . . . And you will pay only a peppercorn rent. One shilling a year . . .'

He swallowed hard.

'You will naturally wonder why I am doing this. Suffice it to say that I am settling my accounts. I shall be leaving Crompton after my wife's funeral, and I wish to see those whom I have . . . That is to say, those whom I shall . . .'

His voice tailed away.

'Should you mind if I took a cigar?' he asked faintly.

Nell Harper delved into the cupboard behind him and produced her elderberry wine.

'I think you need more than a cigar,' she said gently. 'It's a terrible ordeal you're going through . . .'

His hand shook upon the glass and Alice's mother sat down beside him.

'Well, now . . . I hardly know what to say . . . Except that I am deeply grateful . . . Alice, I fear, may be less grateful. She wants to be free of all worries about landlords. Just this morning we learned she has gained a post in London where she will earn five shillings a week . . .'

Christian closed his eyes.

'I'm not doing it for Alice,' he said with effort. 'I'm doing it for you . . . Because you deserve a better home than this one . . . And because you have raised a fine and rare daughter in impossible circumstances . . .'

Nell considered this carefully, weighing her words.

'I have often wondered about your interest in Alice,' she began tentatively. 'And of course, her interest in you . . . She has been very low ever since you married Miss Goodchild . . .'

He struggled to maintain his calm.

'I should never have done it, but for Alice. I mean no disrespect to poor Marianne in saying that . . . Yet it is true. Since the day your daughter walked into Crompton Hall, I have wanted no other woman. And if Alice had understood that, then I should have had no other . . .'

Nell Harper was astonished, and not a little doubtful.

'And how might your sister's maid have understood

the attentions of Crompton Hall's son and heir?' she inquired dryly.

Christian looked up, hearing in the mother a tone he knew all too well in the daughter.

'By considering that a man may not always be judged by his circumstances,' he said haltingly. 'By seeing into the heart of things . . .'

And it was then that he finally burst into tears, weeping with an abandon he had not previously allowed himself, burying his face in his hands and requiring Alice's mother to set aside her wine and cradle him in her arms, rocking him back and forth as though he were her own dear son, whispering to him that all grief and suffering would one day surely cease, but not, alas, upon this day, nor any day, so far as she could see, that would be soon to come . . .

India was writing a letter in the morning room when her visitor was announced.

> My dearest Tim,
>
> We are so grateful for your kind offer to poor Christian, but he insists that he will accept his commission instead. I myself should most dearly love to visit Darjeeling, and cannot imagine why Christian thinks the Army a more delightful prospect! But he is much out of sorts, as you might expect, and we barely managed to persuade him to return to Crompton Hall to spend time with his family before departing for Sandhurst . . .

'Excuse me, Miss India. Alice Harper is here. She wishes to see you.'

India stood up and walked to the window, staring out into the dank autumn day.

'Do you know the whereabouts of Master Christian?' she demanded of the maid. 'Is he in the house?'

'No, Miss. He went out walking in the woods . . .'

'Very well. Show Miss Harper in.'

Alice looked thinner, pallid and heavy-eyed, dressed in a plain black frock such as a poorly placed governess might wear. She smiled eagerly and held out her hand, withdrawing it uncertainly as her eyes met India's cold blue gaze.

'Sit down Alice and tell me why you have come.'

Alice was distracted, and for a moment said nothing at all, perching uncomfortably upon the edge of the sofa where she'd sat so many times in deep conversation with India, staring unhappily at her former mistress.

'I have come to offer my condolences on the death of Marianne,' she muttered at last. 'I am sorry it has taken me so long . . . To be truthful, I found it very difficult to return here . . .'

India made no visible response, and Alice faltered.

'I have also come to say goodbye . . . I am leaving for Hackney where I have a new post at the Ragged School . . .'

India sat down.

'That should suit you very well,' she said calmly.

There was a long pause.

'I was utterly shocked to hear of the accident,' Alice began again, but India held up her hand.

'I shall convey your sympathies to Lady Crompton, though I'm bound to say that they may not be well received . . .'

Alice's face registered open shock, but she said nothing.

'Was there anything else?' India asked, reaching for the bellrope.

Alice's hand flew to her hair, tucking the stray wisps into her neck in plain agitation.

'I had also hoped I might see Christian,' she faltered.

This was a tactical mistake, and one that Alice, with her wits about her, would never have made.

India's face darkened.

'Mr Crompton is not receiving visitors,' she said coldly.

Alice looked down. 'Then I wonder if you would be so kind as to give him this letter . . .'

She began to fumble in the pocket of her frock, and as

the letter appeared in her hand, India leaned forward and snatched it.

'I will deliver no letter!' she declared, tearing it into shreds before Alice's incredulous gaze. 'And I might inquire what business you think you have writing letters to my brother, except that I should not wish to hear your answer . . . I suggest you leave this house immediately, and never set foot on Crompton land again! If you do, I may be forced to have Hardy escort you away . . .'

Alice laughed in disbelief.

'India! What on earth is this? I don't know what you may have heard, but I can assure you, I've done nothing of which I am ashamed . . .'

India pulled on the bell.

'Then you are even less honourable than I'd thought! Rose . . . please show this woman out!'

'Of course, Miss,' replied the startled maid, glancing at Alice. 'Right away . . .'

At the door, Alice turned back, head held high.

'India, I cannot believe that after all we have been to each other, you are simply to send me away like some . . .' She struggled for the word, but did not find it, rubbing a hand across her eyes as though she could not credit the scene unfolding before her.

'Like some dismissed servant?'

Now India laughed, a cold tinkling sound, thin as the wind, icicles clinking on glass.

'But that's *exactly* what you are, Alice,' she said.

India waited a few moments, then called for her cloak.

The parlour maid might well have told Alice that Christian was walking in the beech woods, and if she meant to pursue him, then India determined she would be thwarted.

In the days since Marianne's funeral, she had taken most seriously her mission to reform her brother, calling on him every day at the Goodchild Manor, pressing him to return home where he truly belonged, and where his family might care for him.

She was, after all, the only one who knew the full extent of his iniquity. It was her duty, therefore, to protect the Crompton heritage, to ensure that its noble line should not be sullied, a matter which seemed even more urgent now that Christian was single again.

His commission had set the seal upon her efforts, restoring him to his father's favour with miraculous effect, and confirming his mother's enduring faith. There had been rejoicing and relief, albeit necessarily muted, and it seemed now as though Marianne's death might have been a true blessing, the means by which the heir to Crompton Hall would at last assume his rightful position in the world . . . So long as nothing, *or no one*, succeeded in tempting him back to his old ways.

India walked quickly toward the lake, alert for any sign of her brother, or of the woman she now regarded, with no evidence at all beyond her own intuition, as his seducer.

At the pool where he so often swam she paused, peering into the surrounding mallow bushes, but the morning was poor and the water cloudy grey. It was not a day for swimming.

She walked on. The lake was still swollen, its banks dark and slippery, the sedge riding high against the sodden planks of the jetty, green and vivid like a silk carpet. India walked cautiously along the jetty and untied the *Lady of the Lake*. She stepped inside and began to row to the lake centre, pulling easily upon the oars. Then she let the boat drift and lay back on the cushions in the stern. From this vantage point she could see all the main paths through the beech woods, as well as the track to the orchard and the compound, and the summerhouse.

Christian, she was sure, would eventually arrive at the summerhouse. He had taken to walking endless miles around the Crompton and Goodchild estates, visiting no one, returning to the Hall only for meals where he sat in polite silence, answering when spoken to, but volunteering nothing. Sometimes he would be missing for hours upon end, and once Sir Robin had sent to Goodchild Manor in alarm, fearing he might have wandered on to Adam's land and injured himself, so long had he been gone from the Hall. But finally, he might usually be discovered in the summerhouse, sitting in lonely contemplation, gazing out upon the lake.

India had become a trifle impatient with his continuing reticence, thinking that grief should surely be eased by the kind words of loved ones and the company of relatives. But he received her ministrations without comment, never offering a sign that he were grateful or comforted.

She had tried many ways to ease his unhappiness. She had sent Addison all the way to Norwich for a bottle of finest Napoleon brandy, but Christian, though courteous in his acceptance, had not touched it. She had ordered his favourite dishes from the kitchen, sending two maids into Wells to buy fresh crabs, but he ate frugally, taking no pleasure in treats. All her suggestions of diversion, a carriage drive to Hunstanton, a trip to the theatre at Lynn, a weekend invitation to his closest friend, Tim Harrington, met with firm refusal. Yet he would have to recover his spirits before leaving for Sandhurst, otherwise he would surely risk blighting his new career, a prospect India could not bear. She'd tried to make this point, most tactfully, but had received no indication that he understood or respected her concern.

This Christian was so unlike the brother she had known that it almost seemed a different man had taken his place. Now he did not play croquet, nor visit the village inn, and when she'd proposed that they might throw a ball once mourning was over and his first leave confirmed, he'd looked at her as though she might be mad.

Now, as she floated on the lake, India considered the extraordinary changes that had come upon Crompton Hall, and upon her own life, in the past few weeks. Marianne's death had been the significant event, but it was more than this, more than the transformation of Christian and the revelation of Alice Harper's wickedness.

It was also the terrible epidemic that had ravaged the village in her absence, the experiences she herself had enjoyed while away from Crompton Hall, and the curious ambivalence toward her old life that she'd felt on her return.

It was this confusion, as though she were poised between the girl she had been and the woman she would become, that had kept her away from Blue Farm. The girl might have overcome all personal consideration and rushed to console both Luke and Eugenie. The woman was content to wait and see.

Certainly, she'd sent a short note of sympathy to Dr and Mrs Harte. And she'd quizzed her mother most eagerly after Her Ladyship made an unprecedented call upon Eugenie, offering, in a fine show of solidarity, the Crompton ballroom for Frederica's wedding after all.

'I don't think there'll be any wedding ball,' Lady Crompton reported candidly on her return. 'I think that woman will die of a broken heart . . .'

Beyond the note, however, India had done nothing. Nor did she feel there was anything to be done. It would be the very worst hypocrisy to pretend concern for Eugenie when she disliked her so intensely, and in any case, Mrs Harte would not want her distress observed any further by her superiors . . . That could only prove embarrassing once she recovered from her loss . . . Assuming she were to recover . . .

India didn't really think Eugenie would die of a broken heart. But she allowed herself to imagine a wonderful resolution in that unlikely event. There would be a period of mourning, there would be a time of enforced separation, perhaps a long time, some months, or even a year, then there would be a gradual rehabilitation, taking perhaps a further three months, in which Luke, without wife or daughters, would resume his place in society again.

And that place, India told herself, would not be the one he currently occupied . . . She had, during her sojourn in London, observed the time taken up and the money spent by ladies with various ailments that required the ministrations of a specialist doctor. If Luke were to gain some extra qualification, he might then begin a practice in London ... With plenty of time still available for his humanitarian concerns. Indeed, a doctor with a suitable private income was surely better placed to pursue humanitarian concerns? For how might you help the poor if you numbered among them?

As she drifted in the *Lady of the Lake*, settling a rug around her shoulders against the greyness of the day, India opened her heart to sunny thoughts. A quiet wedding, as would befit a widower who'd lost his entire family, a modest honeymoon, perhaps in Brighton, which she'd been disappointed to miss owing to Marianne's unfortunate death ... And then a townhouse in Fitzwilliam Square, somewhere near Tim Harrington's own splendid mansion ...

She floated on, reflecting now, in the philosophical manner that was her habit, about the nature of change. Nobody knew what the future might hold, nor when death might strike as it had struck at poor Marianne ... And there was nothing that might be done to avert such change. Death was inevitable, and if one believed in the Eastern doctrine of karma, one might hold that the manner and moment of death were somehow pre-ordained ... Although it was hard to imagine what poor Marianne might have done to deserve such an end ...

India sat up and reached for the oars. She was drifting from the lake's centre, toward the sedge, and a few swift strokes sent her back to her vantage point.

It was then that she saw Eugenie Harte.

The doctor's wife seemed, impossibly, to be dressed in her nightshirt, and even at some distance, looked distressed and wild, tangled hair flying around her shoulders, hands clasped before her in the manner of prayer.

As India watched, Eugenie, seeming to see neither the boat nor its occupant, stepped on to the jetty and walked slowly to the tip.

For a moment she stood poised, a swimmer before the plunge, and then with a faint cry, like a falling bird, slipped from the jetty and into the swirling sedge.

With a little gasp, India reached for the oars, but as she made to strike out for the flailing figure in the depths –

indeed, she *surely* did mean to strike out – a curious inertia overcame her. She could not pull, would not attempt to pull . . . She raised the oars once more and lay back in the boat. She closed her eyes.

We turn ceaselessly on a wheel of suffering which only the conquering of desire can still . . . We are sparks of life which must one day be extinguished in the dust . . .

She floated on.

The wellspring of desire, like the fount of true health, is both deep and unknown. What hidden forces feed those mighty waters, swelling that first trickle of longing into a torrent, until all impediments are swept away?

She pressed her hands to her ears. A great splashing and gurgling seemed to be coming from beneath the sedge, which might be some fish or water bird feeding . . . And then, from the shore, an urgent cry, which might be some village child trespassing on Crompton land . . .

India lifted her head and peered over the side of the boat. Alice, her black frock billowing behind her, was running toward the jetty, arms waving in a desperate plea.

'India! For God's sake, help her . . .'

The cry was borne on the breeze above the lake, but India told herself she did not hear . . . She lay back again, drifting, uncaring and serene.

We turn ceaselessly upon a wheel of suffering . . .

From the shore, came a second shout, loud, insistent, strong. India sat up. On the jetty beside Alice stood Christian, kicking his boots from his feet and stripping his coat from his back. A moment more, and he was in the water, swimming with swift, sure strokes toward the sedge where Eugenie, like some monstrous leviathan, flapped and bobbed among the green, and then, as he reached her at last, slid into the blackness beneath.

Raising himself for a mighty gulp of air, Christian dived after her, while on the bank, Alice screamed.

India watched, unmoving, as if in a trance, waiting for his crown to break the sedge. A dozen times he surfaced, and a dozen times he plunged back to the depths. Alice began to pace the jetty, wringing her hands, until at last, when he could dive no more, Christian swam slowly back and hauled himself to safety. He lay panting upon the boards, while Alice, shaking, wrapped her shawl around his shoulders and stroked his dripping hair.

India pulled the *Lady of the Lake* toward the shore with firm, unhurried rhythm.

'Someone must send to Dr Harte,' she said to Christian as she alighted. 'And you must come home before you catch your death of cold!'

He rolled over and looked up at her, his face incredulous.

'You did nothing!' he gasped.

Alice was more forthright.

'You watched her drown!' she shouted. 'You watched your brother risk his life . . .'

'We must raise the alarm,' India replied. 'And we must arrange for the lake to be drained. I'll fetch Hardy at once!'

As she strode back to Crompton Hall, India was untroubled.

There was nothing to conceal, nor any reason to reproach herself. She had been frozen in shock, unable to move a muscle . . . And in any case, supposing she *had* rowed to the drowning Eugenie and offered an oar? Would the woman have grabbed it? Why should a dedicated suicide embrace her would-be rescuer? No, all that had happened was surely meant to be . . .

She breathed deeply in the bracing autumn air, permitting herself no philosophical musings, concentrating instead upon the mundane – and persistent – observation that this was the second silly death she'd witnessed inside a month.

'What do you mean he's gone?'

'Just that. He's closed up Blue Farm and left. It seems he's gone to London. Nobody knows precisely where.'

'But Adam must know . . . He engaged him . . . He surely has some right to be kept informed?'

Christian glanced at his sister oddly.

'It's not a question of anyone being kept informed. A man so bereaved has the right to do as he pleases.'

India bit her lip.

'But to leave this quickly? Without even waiting for the lake to be drained . . .'

Christian said nothing, and India, desperate for news, risked a dangerous question.

'What was he told about the accident?' she whispered.

'Alice was the first to see him,' Christian replied quietly. 'And I imagine he demanded the full facts from her as principal witness . . . If I understand anything about grief, it is the obsessive need to know exactly what happened, to examine each tiny detail of the fatal incident and discover its precise cause and effect . . .'

There followed a long silence in which India glimpsed her future, suspended upon the moment, all she had ever been, or might come to be, poised for realization, potential about to be made actual, for better or worse.

'And then you spoke to him?'

'Some hours later, yes.'

'And he said he was leaving?'

Christian fixed his eyes upon her.

'He was quite definite about it. He'll return for his wife's funeral, of course. But that apart, he declared there was nothing to keep him in Crompton a moment longer.'

Chapter Twenty-two

Laurie knocked on the door to the counselling suite.

She felt she could wait no longer. She had to see Dr Mitchell, had to register her presence and offer her condolences on Ruth's death, even though she knew the need for sympathy was hers, not his.

'He's got somebody with him,' Val warned.

'Not Sean?' Laurie asked warily. In the space of twenty-four hours, she'd become accustomed to the idea of Crompton Hall's new manager, but she didn't want to meet him just yet.

'Sean's working from home today . . .'

'Home?' Laurie threw Val a startled glance. 'You mean the centre manager doesn't live here?'

'He's bought Lavender Cottage . . . I thought you knew that . . . Didn't you visit him last time you were here?'

Laurie nodded dumbly. There seemed no end to Sean's subterfuge, and no explaining the extraordinary shift from city man to country dweller. She would ask him about it, of course. Some time.

'Go in,' said Val, indicating the counselling suite. 'You may be interested to meet Dale's visitor . . . And he may need rescuing by now.'

Laurie threw open the door at his quiet command, then gaped in astonishment. She swayed and leaned back against the doorpost. She truly *was* losing her senses, her grip on reality so weakened that she could no longer distinguish fantasy from fact . . . The guest who turned abruptly to face the intruder was . . . India Crompton-Leigh.

Laurie's gaze flew to the painting above the mantelpiece. The match was extraordinary, the same long black hair in the same extravagant pigtail, the same ivory skin, and the same piercing blue eyes . . . A casual observer might not have seen it, but to Laurie, who had dreamed of that painting, that face, the resemblance was no ordinary likeness. For a long moment, India lived again.

Dale stood up from the sofa.

'Good to see you, Laurie,' he said gently, holding out his hand. 'Here, let me introduce you . . . This is Miranda Harrington . . . Miranda, meet Laurie Davison, one of our most interesting clients . . .'

The woman stood up, her intense blue eyes holding Laurie's own.

'You see,' she said to Dale, waving at the portrait but still staring at Laurie, 'she noticed right away . . .'

'Well of course she did,' Dale said patiently. 'Anyone would . . . And Laurie has been quite captivated by the Cromptons. Particularly India. She's very taken with the portrait . . . Isn't that so, Laurie?'

Laurie sat down suddenly on the sofa, her head pounding. She glanced anxiously at Dale, registering the pallor and distracted expression of the newly bereaved. Miranda Harrington, however, seemed unaware of her host's distress, or chose not to notice.

'You look as though you've seen a ghost,' she laughed at Laurie. 'All very gratifying as India was *the* society beauty of her day . . . But I can assure you I'm plain old flesh and blood . . .'

She sat down on the sofa herself, crossing a startling pair of legs and flipping the pigtail over her shoulder.

'I am India's great granddaughter,' she confided brightly. 'My great grandfather was Lord Timothy Harrington, and Crompton Hall is my ancestral family home, so to speak . . .'

Dale shifted in his chair.

'No it's not,' he said quietly. 'This house, and everything in it, belongs to Kathryn Malone. It is *her* family home and we're all of us here, including you Miss Harrington, only because she's kind enough to allow it . . .'

Miranda threw back her head.

'I'm not interested in the old family feud,' she said curtly, 'so please don't drag it up. This has nothing to do with Kat Malone, and you know that perfectly well, Dr Mitchell.

She has delegated the decision ... She trusts you to do the honourable thing!'

Dale stood up, his face taut and strained.

'Then I, too, delegate the decision,' he announced. 'I leave it up to Laurie ... Make your case to her, Miss Harrington. Whatever she says is okay by me ...'

He walked toward the door, grimacing at Laurie as he passed.

'Take it as a compliment,' he muttered. 'You're part of the place now ...'

Laurie, bewildered, had begun to doubt her ears as well as her eyes, yet she could not mistake his urgent need to quit the room − and to be free of the persistent Miss Harrington, though what it was that she wanted, remained unclear. And now Laurie, who'd wanted only to talk of Ruth, found herself drawn back to India. She stood up from the sofa and stared at the portrait. It really was an extraordinary likeness.

Miranda opened her handbag and produced a pack of cigarettes.

'I've never heard of anything so ridiculous,' she snapped. 'Who are you to make any decision about Crompton property?'

She waved the cigarette carton under Laurie's nose.

'Do you want one of these?'

Laurie shook her head.

'You're not going to tell me they cause cancer?'

Laurie smiled coldly, appalled at this jibe.

'I wasn't,' she said steadily, 'but they do.'

Miranda stood up and strode over to the fireplace, gesturing at the portrait.

'I'll come straight to the point. I want that painting. It's right that I should have it. I am India's only direct female descendant ... And you've already seen how alike we are. It's only natural that I should wish to own it and restore it to its proper condition.'

Laurie looked up.

'It's proper condition? It looks perfect as it is to me ...'

Miranda shook her head.

'It's been defaced. You see this figure here?' She pointed at Alice Harper, standing her distance behind India. 'It was added at a later date, and by a different hand. The original painting showed only the daughter of the house . . . Not any upstart maidservant.'

Laurie was intrigued and affronted at the same time.

'You want to remove the second figure? But that would destroy the special significance of the portrait!'

Miranda Harrington glanced at her oddly.

'What special significance? There's nothing special about it, except to me as India's great granddaughter . . .'

'I meant the story,' Laurie faltered, unwilling to discuss any meaning she had personally bestowed upon the painting and suddenly unsure of her ground. 'The story revealed in the journals . . .'

Miranda frowned.

'It may be just a story to you, but it's my family history. The good bits and the bad . . . I'd like to salvage the good, I suppose. That sounds reasonable, doesn't it?'

'It sounds like changing history,' Laurie said.

They stared at each other for a moment, then Miranda smiled, a conciliatory twitch of the lips which failed to register in her icy blue eyes.

'Look, I simply want to buy the painting. I'm getting married this year, and I want to hang it in my new home . . . I'm prepared to pay a fair price – say five thousand – and I'm able to offer another painting of India in exchange. I have it here with me . . .'

She indicated a wrapped canvas which stood in the corner of the room, then walked over to it.

'Do you want to see? If you're really empowered to speak for Doctor Mitchell, then I think you should . . .'

Laurie was still uncertain about this commission, not knowing if Dale truly meant her to decide the fate of the portrait or whether she were merely required to deflect the determined Miss Harrington until some more appropriate moment.

'I'll have to talk to him,' she murmured, 'I'm sure you

realize this is a very difficult time ... His wife just died ...'

Miranda smiled, but Laurie caught a flash of impatience in the brilliant blue eyes.

'Yes, of course. Very sad. Fortunate perhaps, that they weren't married long ... And her death was hardly unexpected, was it?'

With a peculiar jolt, Laurie recognized the tone of this observation, an unthinking acceptance of the inevitable which, while true enough, was deeply unfeeling.

'Did you know India?' she asked suddenly. 'Was she still alive when you were born? What was she like?'

Miranda paused in the act of unwrapping the canvas.

'I was three years old when she died. I think I remember her, but one is never quite sure. There were so many tales, they passed into family legend. She was an irascible old lady and everyone was scared of her. She lived most of her life in Darjeeling, but all her time was spent trying to regain the title to Crompton Hall ... There are hundreds of her letters here! She hated the Malones, and couldn't bear the thought of them living at Crompton ... Understandably so. They had no legal right to the property.'

Miranda laughed and looked up at the portrait.

'She caused all kinds of trouble. She once tried to have Michael Malone certified insane ...'

'Michael was Christian's son?' Laurie asked, seeing the pieces fall into place.

Miranda wagged her finger in the air.

'And as everyone knows, an illegitimate son cannot inherit ... Unless, that is, he has powerful friends who arrange his adoption and contrive to change his name to the family's own ...'

She snapped a stray piece of string from the wrapped canvas and stood back.

'But like I said, I've no wish to fight old battles. My father still abhors the Malones and won't hear Kat's name mentioned, but none of that bothers me. I'm only interested in India and the portrait ...'

She laughed again.

'I suppose India was a little mad and bad,' she said carelessly. 'But that's true of all interesting women, don't you think?'

Laurie said nothing, staring down at the canvas which was finally emerging from its covering and which Miranda now held up for her approval.

'Of course, she was much older when this one was painted. She had three sons, a household of four hundred servants and seven tea-estates to help administer . . . But she still found time for her pleasures . . .'

The picture which met Laurie's eye was gaudy and bold, its colours strong, completely unlike the muted tones of the portrait over the mantel. It showed an imperious middle-aged woman, unmistakably India, long black hair coiled beneath a cream chiffon sun hat, glittering eyes staring resolutely ahead, lips set in a thin hard line. She was surrounded by native servants waving silk canopies, and she was seated upon a monstrous bejewelled elephant.

'The memsahib in her element!' said Miranda Harrington admiringly. 'She owned a whole string of elephants, but that one was her favourite . . . So what do you think, Miss Davison? Isn't she simply splendid?'

Laurie blinked.

Oh India, I loved you, truly I did. I loved your passion and your promise, and everything you seemed to say about belief and hope . . . Now I've lost you . . . And I can scarcely bear it . . .

She smiled weakly at Miranda.

'Splendid,' she said.

Miranda Harrington departed without the portrait, leaving behind the elephant painting, she explained carefully, as a gesture of goodwill. Laurie promised to consult Dale, and now, as she walked back into the house, she wondered how soon she might do it.

Crompton Hall was unusually quiet, and with remorse, Laurie realized just how presumptuous she'd been to arrive without a booking, or even so much as an inquiring letter.

364

She had imagined the centre existing only to answer her needs, oblivious to all other tragedies playing out within its walls.

She hadn't guessed at Ruth's illness, nor thought to inquire about the other clients she'd met. Indeed, now that she considered it, she was still expecting Dale Mitchell to grant her an audience, to receive her condolences just because she wanted to make them, to answer her questions about India and the Malones, and this in the face of his obvious grief and need for respite.

She decided she would not seek him out. More than this, she would ascertain from Val whether she ought to stay at all. Despite Dale's comforting remark about her being part of the place, she didn't mean to presume any further. If he wanted to be alone, she would depart at once. She would write a note giving her thoughts about the portrait, and leave it at that. It seemed only right.

Val was nowhere to be seen, however, and nor was anyone else. The door to the old gun room remained firmly closed, but the counselling suite was still open as she'd left it. She walked in and surveyed the new picture of India, propped against the edge of the desk where Miranda had stood it.

There *was* something splendid about it, of course, the Englishwoman presiding over the last throes of Empire, the languid air of luxury which seemed to pervade the scene, the vision of a leisured class enjoying its last moment of supremacy. But there was also melancholy, a sense of futile ritual and empty gesture, and the longer she looked, the more Laurie began to perceive the waste, not just of India's life after Crompton Hall, but of all lives dedicated to maintaining privilege and thereby perpetuating the suffering of others . . .

As though we wilfully close our eyes against the obvious . . . the only conclusion . . . That the happiness of one is inextricably linked to the well-being of all . . .

Behind her the door opened softly, and Laurie turned to face Dr Mitchell at last. For a moment they stood in silence, each assessing the other's mood, and then he smiled.

'So what's the verdict?' he asked, indicating the picture.

'I loathe it,' Laurie said quietly. 'And I can't see any way it could hang in here . . . It doesn't belong. That's the India who lived at Crompton Hall!'

She pointed to the portrait above the mantel and he followed her gaze, scrutinizing the painting as though he were seeing it for the first time.

'You're right, of course,' he said at last. 'And yet, the India who lived here was also Lady Harrington, last of the great memsahibs . . . Our portrait has something of what she would become. The artist saw it, and so did India herself . . . I guess that's why she hated it so much.'

He smiled again.

'Maybe there's something to be gained from displaying this new picture,' he said. 'And I'm kind of inclined to let Miranda have her way . . . There she is, all got up in pigtails like her grandma, and we nasty guys won't let her have the portrait that shows it off . . .'

Laurie shook her head in surprise.

'But she wants to paint out Alice! She'll ruin it if she does that . . .'

'Not so,' he said. 'She'll improve it. The original artist has become very collectable . . . But the guy who added Alice was nobody special. If Miranda paints her out, she'll have a valuable picture on her hands . . .'

'She only offered five thousand!'

'Oh well,' he shrugged, 'it's not about money. Not for us, and not even for her, though it's true the Harringtons have fallen on hard times. Death duties, and all the rest of it . . .'

He paused, fixing Laurie with the pewter eyes.

'No, it's about creating a story. India's story . . . You've got your version, and Miranda has hers. Both of you want props to back it up . . . Paintings or journals . . . Letters . . . There are hundreds of letters in this house! Letters from India, Christian's letters from the Front, letters between Alice and Adam Goodchild . . . Letters from Luke Harte . . . And dozens of letters concerning the Malones . . .'

He smiled at her.

'It's all waiting for you . . .'

'I see,' said Laurie, wondering whether she did.

'However, I meant what I said,' Dale added quickly. 'The decision on the portrait is yours. You tell me you don't want it to go, and it stays right here!'

Laurie said nothing, imagining India on her favourite elephant hanging above the mantel. It would surely be preferable to have no painting at all . . . Except that future visitors to Crompton Hall would then have no vision of India to challenge them . . .

'I don't know,' she whispered.

'Well, let's see how the replacement would look.'

He reached up and swung the old portrait from its hook, and a moment later the elephant painting was in place, its colours harsh and overstated against the pale wall.

He nodded toward the door.

'Let's leave it a while and come back . . . I was going to take a walk . . . Want to come?'

He laughed.

'I haven't managed to persuade you into those woods since the day you got here,' he said.

They walked out through the kitchen garden, Laurie remembering the first time she'd come upon it, when Ruth had found her sitting beneath the fig tree, when she'd first experienced that curious sense of presence that seemed so much a part of Crompton Hall.

She pointed to the fig tree.

'The last time I sat there,' she murmured uncertainly, 'I felt someone watching me . . .'

'Spirits and phantoms . . . Angels and ghosts . . .'

Laurie looked up at him, startled.

'Not so much a vision,' he said softly, 'as an intuition of for ever . . .'

'Do you know Alice Harper's journals off by heart?'

'Pretty much,' he grinned. 'They've always been a big part of my life. I guess now's the time to tell you a bit about my family history . . . My grandfather was John Harper, Alice's younger brother. He qualified as a doctor in the Twenties and emigrated to America where

he quickly became very rich and moderately famous . . .
Despite having some pretty unconventional ideas about
medicine . . .'

He smiled.

'Or maybe because of them,' he said.

Laurie was astonished, and a little peeved. She sat down
on the bench beneath the fig tree.

'Why didn't you tell me that before?'

'Because it would have spoiled it. The idea's that you
decide how much you want to know . . . As it is, I have
to stop my mother jetting in to give impromptu lectures
on Alice's methods to my clients . . . You just missed her.
She flew home right after the funeral.'

'Your mother?'

'Doctor Eleanor Harper Mitchell . . . The most unconventional of us all. Good thing we have my father to keep
our feet somewhere in the vicinity of solid ground . . .'

Laurie nodded uncertainly.

'I hope I'll meet her some day,' she said.

'I'm sure you will. And Kat Malone, too.'

The name was familiar, and yet Laurie, trawling her
memory, couldn't quite place it.

'Why do I think I've heard of the Malones?' she asked
Dale. 'Are they famous?'

They were walking now through the beech woods toward
the lake, their feet crunching upon dry autumn leaves, the
glittering stretch of water with its banks of brown and green
sedge beckoning them on.

'Michael Malone made his money in the theatre. Big
musical shows after the Second War. He lost his mother
when he was just a boy, but he was still very much her
son . . .'

'And Kathryn was his daughter,' Laurie mused, 'and
you and she are friends?'

'The Malones and the Harpers are like one big family,'
he said easily. 'Kat is my godmother, and although she
owns the Hall, she gives me free use of it . . .'

'Why do I think I know her name? Is she in the
theatre too?'

'Not quite. But Kat is also after her grandmother's stock ... She runs a film company. They shot a version of Jane Austen's *Mansfield Park* right here at Crompton Hall ...'

Laurie was transported back to the moment she'd first glimpsed the Hall, driving along the avenue of brilliant limes with Gloria, frightened, sick at heart and hostile ... *Looks more like Manderley than Mansfield Park*, Gloria had said, *And here comes Mrs Danvers ...*'

She had been looking at Ruth Christianos, Ruth who'd appeared on the portico steps in her smart grey suit, warm, welcoming, reassuring ... Ruth, who'd been quietly dying of cancer ...

Laurie stopped suddenly on the brink of the lake.

'I want to talk about Ruth,' she said, her voice catching, 'but I don't really know what to say ... Except that I'm desperately sorry ... And very grateful for everything she offered me ...'

There was a long silence in which he stared into the darkening water then kicked a stone on to the jetty where it bounced into the tethered boat.

'We'll talk about Ruth,' he said at last, 'but not right now if that's okay ...'

'Of course,' she whispered, 'whenever you're ready ...'

He kicked another stone and they both watched as it skimmed above the *Lady of the Lake*.

'Now we've stopped fighting and look like we're finally communicating,' he said cautiously, 'there's one other matter I'd like to raise ...'

'You mean Sean?'

'I want you to know the decision wasn't lightly made. I had to think long and hard about whether it was right. In the end, I concluded he'd got a lot to offer Crompton Hall ... But that doesn't mean I'm insensitive to your feelings. I'm very sorry you found him sitting at Ruth's desk ...'

'It's my own fault. I shouldn't have turned up unannounced.'

He raised one eyebrow.

'You can turn up any time you like,' he said wryly. 'That was one hell of a cheque your father wrote me ...'

Laurie caught his eye and they both laughed.

He took her arm and steered her away from the treacherous bank, a comfortable, unforced gesture that seemed to consolidate their new understanding.

'Better get back,' he said. 'It's getting cold and we mustn't be late for supper . . .'

'Broccoli and coconut soup?' she wondered.

'I don't think so. We have a new chef as well as a new centre manager, and to be frank, it's not working out so well . . . We may get pork pie and chips.'

They laughed again.

'I don't suppose,' he inquired solemnly, 'you have any old boyfriends who can cook?'

After supper she set out for Lavender Cottage, slipping away quietly so she mightn't be seen, keeping close to the hedge along the path that led to Blue Farm, though why she felt the need to hide, she couldn't have said. Perhaps she imagined that Dale or Val might tip off Sean . . . And yet, she reasoned, it would hardly matter if they did . . .

As she walked, she thought of Alice Harper taking this same route so many times, going home to her mother and the little brother who'd become Dr John Harper . . . How gratifying must that have been, yet how sad and unfulfilled Alice's life had come to seem, deprived, by simple fact of her lowly birth, of all that might have been hers had she been born a half-century later . . .

She knocked on the door, remembering Alice's account of the night Christian had called upon her . . . How many times, Laurie wondered, had Alice replayed that scene, wishing it might have ended differently . . . How sweetly had she treasured their lovemaking once Christian was gone, and how bitterly had she reconsidered her misjudgement . . . At least she, Laurie, in full knowledge of the brevity and uncertainty of life, would make no such mistake. She had come, instead, to make her peace.

Unlike her earlier visit to Lavender Cottage when he'd seemed to expect her, she caught Sean off guard.

'It's you,' he said uncomfortably, motioning her inside. 'I thought it must be Val . . .'

'Sorry to disappoint you,' she said lightly, cursing herself for sounding sarcastic when she meant only to be conciliatory. Maybe her bad habits were becoming ingrained.

The cottage was bright and inviting, walls painted a pale sunshine yellow, floorboards sanded and polished. Her eye was caught by a painting of the lavender fields, a slightly lurid oil which nevertheless gave atmosphere. Sean had been busy.

'Everything looks lovely,' she said, seeking to establish her goodwill and walking over to admire the painting, but he was in no mood for small talk.

'I know what you've come to say,' he began, 'and I want to tell you it's not the way it looks. You must feel I've invaded your sanctuary by taking this job . . . But it wasn't planned, Laurie. It just happened, and a lot of things in my life have fallen into place as a result. In truth, it doesn't really have anything to do with you at all . . .'

'Oh,' she said, taken aback. 'Well . . . Good.'

She gazed at him, remembering how much she had loved and wanted him, trying to see him anew, standing outside the history they shared.

'What things?' she asked uncertainly.

'I don't want to hurt you,' he said quietly. 'Particularly now when you're so vulnerable. But I don't want to lie to you either. I've done too much of that . . .'

It wasn't going the way she'd planned. Laurie sat down suddenly, remembering their last encounter in this room when he'd entreated her to stay, had even seemed as though he wanted to make love. Now he'd clearly changed his mind.

'So don't lie anymore,' she muttered. 'Just tell me how it is . . .'

He then offered what she perceived to be a prepared speech. He hadn't anticipated making it this soon, and as a result it was imperfectly delivered, yet nevertheless it appeared to contain all the required ingredients.

'For a start there's my career,' he said steadily. 'I haven't been happy with it for a long time, but I could never explain that to you. It would have sounded like copping out. Right away you would have seen it as a threat to our future . . .'

He paused.

'Then my divorce . . . I've done nothing about it. I said I had, but that was untrue. I just couldn't decide what was right . . . And there's more. The night we met, I told you I was married but no longer lived with my wife. Well, that was a bare-faced lie. It took me three months to leave, and the flat I took you to meantime was Jim's. He even gave me some of his furniture when I finally got my own place. Just so you wouldn't suspect.'

She said nothing, fighting a rising anguish that she knew might engulf her at any moment.

He looked away.

'What Shelley would call an All-Out Bastard,' he said quietly.

'You and Jim, both,' she muttered.

He reached for a bottle of wine on the table behind him and poured himself a glass, raising an eyebrow when she declined to join him, clearly needing to fortify himself for what would follow.

'You were right that I'd never told Tina about you . . . I always knew you'd work that out one day . . .'

She held up her hand, knowing now she had to make her own confession.

'I didn't work it out. I followed you one Saturday and heard you tell her there was nobody else . . .'

It took a long moment for this to sink in.

'You're kidding me?'

'I'm not. I was wearing a crazy blonde wig, a pair of stilettos and some tarty black clothes. Even so, I was amazed you didn't recognize me . . .'

He stared at her, bemused.

'Does Shelley have a name for you?' he asked at last.

'Psychotic Bitch?' she suggested. 'Or maybe just Stupid Cow . . .'

He laughed and refilled his glass, drinking it slowly

this time, regarding her quizzically, as though he'd just encountered someone he didn't know at all.

'So . . . Was she what you expected?'

Laurie hesitated.

'No, not at all . . . But I know things aren't always what they seem. Shelley repeated some stories Jim had told her . . .'

He turned away.

'I'm not going to tell tales,' he said. 'Suffice it to say that Tina has a terrible temper. I never know what she's going to do next. She can scare the hell out of me without even trying . . . I suppose that's why I backed off telling her. Too much of a coward . . .'

He took a heavy draught of the wine, and seemed for a moment to have lost his nerve, glancing at her anxiously, weighing up her mood, judging how much more he might reveal.

'There's one other thing I should tell you,' he said. 'The insurance that paid out on my thirtieth birthday . . . I kept it quiet because I thought you'd put pressure on me . . .'

'Pressure to do what?' she asked shakily.

He held her gaze.

'Pressure to pay off Tina and marry you,' he replied.

She looked down.

'But you have paid her off?'

'A big chunk from the mortgage, yes . . . And she's finally accepted that our marriage is over, so there will eventually be a divorce. But it was my decision . . . Our decision . . . And it could only be made once you were no longer around.'

So there it was, and now that he'd said it, she saw that it wasn't unreasonable. But how seriously had they misunderstood each other? And how much time had been wasted in all their moves and countermoves? She had wanted him, but not at any price . . . And not in any way which violated his conscience . . . So why had she never made him see this?

'Can't you patch things up?' she asked him haltingly. 'Wouldn't that be best all round?'

He shook his head.

'Now I've finally broken free, I'm not about to go back. It went wrong a long time ago, Laurie. Nothing to do with you at all. That much wasn't a lie . . .'

She turned away, feeling the tears start.

'I loved you, Sean,' she whispered. 'Truly I did. And I thought you loved me . . .'

'Oh Laurie,' he said helplessly, 'I did . . . I do . . . And I know you loved me. It was terrible, the night you said you didn't want me anymore . . .'

He sat down beside her on the settee and took her hand.

'But I came to see that you'd never really wanted me the way I was . . . You just wanted what you hoped I'd become . . . A free man who'd father your children . . .'

'That's what most women want,' she said, smiling through the tears. 'There's nothing peculiar about it.'

'No, of course not. But life's not that simple anymore . . . If it ever was. The fact is I have a wife and two children, and one way or another, I've mucked up their lives. Somehow . . . and I still don't really know how . . . I've got to make it good.'

He squeezed her hand

'You said it yourself,' he murmured. 'Here in this very room . . . You said that the only freedom we truly have is the freedom to do the right thing . . .'

She was crying openly now, burying her face in her hands and leaning away from him.

'I've always been full of fine talk,' she sobbed.

'No, I don't think so. You've changed. We've all changed . . . You, me, your mother and father, even Shelley . . . It's changed us all.'

'Cancer?'

'That's what I've come to see about Crompton Hall and the work they do. You can lie down and give up. That's what I wanted to do when you were first diagnosed . . . Or you can use it to regenerate whatever life you've got left . . . And none of us knows how long that might be . . .'

She looked up at him.

'I know it's been much harder for you,' he said quickly. 'I'm not claiming I've suffered the same kind of trauma . . . But it *was* hard, Laurie. I thought you were dying . . . I was drinking too much, I kept breaking down at work . . . And you just froze me out! I couldn't reach you. I couldn't even make love to you . . .'

She fumbled for a tissue and blew her nose.

'You should have taken your last chance,' she laughed jerkily. 'Now I've got no hair and only one boob . . .'

He shook his head and Laurie saw that he too was close to tears.

'I wouldn't care,' he whispered.

He walked her back to Crompton Hall through the beech woods, and she asked if he'd ever heard a nightingale sing.

'I don't think so. I'm not sure I'd know if I did . . .'

'You'd know,' she said.

The moon hung high above the lake, and they skirted the muddy bank in its full beam, taking the path that led past Christian's pool and back toward the house.

'You're thinking of Alice,' he said as they passed the cavern of mallows shielding the pool. 'I think of her too . . .'

'She made love to Christian in your cottage,' Laurie said wistfully. 'Don't you find that unbearably sad?'

He looked down at her.

'Sad? I know he was killed in the war, but they were happy together before that . . . It's more than many people achieve . . .'

She stopped on the track.

'Happy together? What do you mean?'

He stopped too, looking back toward the summerhouse and the glittering stretch of water where the *Lady of the Lake* still bobbed against the jetty.

'Ah, you don't know,' he said quietly. 'You haven't read on . . . After they'd both left Crompton, he went to find her. She was living in Hackney, and she was very lonely . . .'

Laurie held her breath, listening to the dry rustle of the beech leaves, waiting for his next words.

'They were married in the spring of 1914. He was on leave from his regiment and she'd given up her post at the Ragged School ... Sir Robin had died from a stroke the previous winter, so his son inherited the title ... They took a honeymoon in Paris, and they set up home in the London house ... And then Christian brought Alice back as mistress of Crompton Hall ...'

He smiled.

'I bet the nightingales sang that day,' he said.

Chapter Twenty-three

A party of well-wishers came to meet us at Crompton railway station, Adam Goodchild, newly returned from some adventure abroad, my mother, my little brother Johnny, my sister Ivy and her husband and family, as well as my old friend the parson and several curious villagers.

I greeted them all as I imagined I should, but found myself embarrassed when a small girl presented a posy and dropped me a curtsey. The day will come, and not too far away, when such deference will be seen for what it is, a crude means of keeping people divided from one another.

My husband, fine and handsome in his scarlet uniform, had not been in his best mood owing to a small disagreement about the railway accommodation.

The first class carriages were all taken, and I suggested we might travel in the second class, it being a short journey and the carriages seeming perfectly comfortable and clean.

He frowned at me.

'Lady Crompton does not travel in the second class!' he declared, and then disappeared to have some unfortunate person evicted from one of the superior carriages so that we might occupy it.

'A pity I'm not wearing my tiara,' I said as I clambered in. 'Then everyone should see how high and mighty Lady Crompton is . . .'

'Oh Alice, do shut up. Otherwise I shall send you to the attic the moment we arrive . . .'

He was nervous, and so of course was I. We'd received no indication of the reception we might expect, although we could well imagine. All Christian's letters to his mother had gone unanswered, and the invitation to our modest wedding had been acknowledged by no one, not India, nor Timothy Harrington, nor by Lady Crompton herself.

We had therefore delayed our return to Crompton Hall, and might not have visited at all until the following year, had it not been for India's own wedding. But she was to marry Timothy Harrington at Crompton Church, and a brief letter arrived requesting that Christian give her away.

I did not anticipate the occasion with any joy or confidence, and had done much private fretting about which pew I should occupy during the ceremony, a matter I didn't dare raise with my husband for fear he would have me yoked to his side throughout the day. Already he had altered the seating plan for the wedding breakfast, posted to him by India without so much as an accompanying comment, and returned in the same manner. He was determined I should sit at the table head with him, an arrangement that would surely outrage both his sister and his mother.

'I want you where I can see you,' he'd said, half-laughing, half-serious, 'so I can stop you rushing off to supervise the sweetmeats . . .'

There was also the question of what I should wear. He had bought me many fine clothes, some of them a trifle too fancy for my taste, and he would have me in the most fancy of all for the wedding.

'The blue silk, Alice,' he'd said, 'and the cream chiffon for the wedding ball . . . With the tiara, of course.'

I would have preferred the neat brown suit in which I travelled back to Crompton Hall, and my high-necked black lace gown for the ball. And by choice, I wouldn't have worn the tiara, nor carried any such item in my luggage at all. But it was his wedding gift to me, and I would not hurt him by refusing to wear it.

'I don't really want a tiara,' I'd said when he proposed it. 'But I'll tell you what I *would* like as a wedding gift . . .'

'Name it!' he'd said with all the reckless generosity of a besotted bridegroom, 'Whatever you want is yours . . .'

It was a week after our wedding, and I had waited until an intimate moment, one which was not totally consumed by our long-thwarted passion and in which, I judged, I might prevail against his natural instinct.

I took a deep breath.

'I should like to qualify as a doctor,' I said, crossing my fingers beneath the bedsheets. 'Luke believes I can pass the entry examinations ... He says my Latin and Greek are better than many medical students' ... And indeed, he has already taken me to meet with the principal tutor at St Bartholomew's. I think they would accept me. But of course, the training is very expensive ...'

He looked at me as though I were quite mad.

'A doctor! You've spent half your life as a scivvy, and now you want to spend the rest as nursemaid?'

'Not a nursemaid,' I said steadily. 'As a doctor ... Shouldn't you like a wife who had a professional calling? Who would bring a living wage into your household?'

He laughed uproariously.

'Indeed, I should not! The very idea ... I should like, Alice, a wife who would devote herself entirely to me and my comforts ...'

'Well then,' I teased, kissing his back and moving my hand so I might attend to his comforts, 'maybe you shouldn't have married me ...'

In the end, it was Luke Harte who persuaded him, Luke who, since I'd first arrived in Hackney, had sought me out on the information of his sister-in-law Frederica, and had become my friend and confidant, reassuring me through all the doubts that assailed me on assuming the title of Lady Crompton, and encouraging me in my medical ambitions.

I, in my turn, had offered what comfort I could upon the loss of his family, consoling him when it was found that Eugenie's body could not be recovered, remarking to myself that in all our long conversations about life and suffering and death, India's name was never once mentioned between us.

'I fear you're a bad influence on my wife,' Christian told Luke solemnly. 'And I am no influence at all ... She will somehow contrive to have me do exactly as she pleases ...'

But he still bought me the tiara, and he would still have me wear it at India's wedding ball.

The Crompton carriage had been sent to the station to convey us home, and I found myself wondering who had ordered it. Perhaps Hardy had simply taken it upon himself, for I'd heard from my mother that the running of the Hall had become a shambles since Sir Robin's death, with India spending much of her time at Lord Harrington's estate, and Her Ladyship left alone to manage as best she might. It was a matter, I knew, which Christian would have to address, and I wondered anxiously in what way I might be called upon, if I might be required to organize the servants or report upon their suitability. I should not relish such a task.

But all my worries about the boundaries of class were eased as I stepped from the train to receive Adam Goodchild's tender congratulations, and to see him greet Christian as though he were a true brother. He must surely have remembered that unhappy time, not much more than two years before, when Marianne's coffin had been borne from the station, yet his delight in our marriage was both evident and sincere. He took my hand and pressed it in his own, smiling at me with genuine warmth, and I could not but reflect how happy we might all have been had India been marrying him the following day. Yet perhaps Adam was, in truth, a solitary man, more intent upon his adventures than any domesticity, and perhaps, at the last, he had come to accept this.

It was not only Adam's kindness which moved me. The scene at the railway station was astonishing, with Christian kissing my mother and Ivy upon both cheeks and sweeping up my little niece into his arms, declaring that she had found herself a new uncle. Even Ivy's husband earned a generous handshake, and for Johnny, Christian had, unknown to me, bought a present, a splendid atlas which he offered without show or ceremony, and which my little brother fell upon with shouts of glee.

I looked then at my new husband with overwhelming love and admiration, forgiving him all foibles concerning railway carriages and tiaras, knowing that whatever differences we might have, of experience or expectation, they could all be overcome. And in that moment I determined that nothing I might encounter at Crompton Hall should distress me, nor bring me low.

A solitary maid, whose face I did not know, stood beside Hardy as our carriage drew up outside the Hall, with no sign of any to greet us, not Her Ladyship, India, nor Timothy Harrington whom I still imagined to be Christian's friend, though I knew they had not met since Marianne's death.

'Welcome home, Sir Christian!' said Hardy, glancing uncomfortably at me. 'And Your Ladyship too . . .'

Christian turned to the maid.

'Take Lady Crompton's bags into the Hall!' he commanded. 'And send someone to tell my mother we are arrived . . .'

I followed him into the house, my heart thumping beneath my strange new clothes, every step that I took familiar to me, yet every sight that greeted my eyes, the carpets, the furnishings, the floral display upon the carved hall-stand, utterly changed by the knowledge of my relationship to them.

I am mistress of Crompton Hall, I am mistress of Crompton Hall . . .

Alas, it didn't matter how many times I repeated this incantation, I could not believe it, and when a door opened on the stairway above me, I turned and scuttled into the gun room as though I were an intruder about to be caught and punished.

He came after me at once, slamming the door behind him, his face black.

'If you will not behave as my wife,' he said furiously, 'then no one will think you deserve to be! Myself included . . .'

I flushed at this rebuke, and was about to beg his forgiveness when the gun room door suddenly opened.

'Well now,' said India, surveying us both with icy calm, 'I'm pleased you're making yourselves at home. But you no longer need to hide away in corners and cupboards. You may come out at last where we can all see you . . .'

For a terrible moment I feared he would strike her, but instead he grabbed her roughly by the arm and marched her out into the hallway.

'You're hurting me,' I heard her say, still in that odd, impassive tone. 'Let me go at once!'

'If you insult my wife,' Christian replied, his voice low and bitter, 'I shall walk out of this house. You may find someone else to stand in at your wedding . . .'

'You have brought scandal on the Cromptons yet again!' I heard her respond. 'You wouldn't have dared do this if your father had still been alive . . .'

They moved along the hall and out of my earshot, leaving me trembling in the gun room, feeling foolish and angry with myself, unsure about how I might now retrieve my dignity. Certainly I should not do it by cowering in any corner or cupboard. I opened the door and stepped out.

And there a great shock awaited me. Her Ladyship stood on the stairway above me, but not the Lady Crompton I had known. Her face was sallow and drawn, her eyes vacant and despairing, and the neck button of her dress was undone, as though she'd just risen from her bed. I stared at her in disbelief, astonished by the transformation.

'Is it you, Alice?' she inquired faintly, moving slowly toward me down the stairs. 'Have you come back to us?'

I dropped a curtsey, not caring who might catch me.

'Yes, Your Ladyship,' I said steadily. 'It's Alice. I have come back.'

She reached the bottom of the stairway, and so frail and uncertain did she seem that I rushed forward and took her arm, leading her into the morning room and seating her upon her favourite chair by the window. She waved a hand in the air and absently pulled upon her chignon which was matted and unkempt.

'Some tea, I think, Alice . . .'

'Of course, Ma'am. I'll see to it.'

'And some buttered scones, perhaps? We've not had buttered scones for weeks . . .'

'I shall speak to Cook right away . . .'

I sped from the room, heading for the green baize door with all the haste my heavy clothing allowed, unable to banish the thought that in my maid's frock I should have travelled much more efficiently. My fingers were on the handle when he caught me.

'And where the devil do you think you're going, Alice? I swear I shall send you straight back to London if you so much as . . .'

He saw my expression at once.

'Your mother!' I muttered. 'You must go to her. Something's terribly wrong . . .'

I pointed to the morning room and watched him run to the door. I heard him exclaim, and then, because I did not know what he might expect of me, because I could not think what else to do, and because so much of my time in that house had been spent overseeing culinary detail and averting domestic discord, I hurried away down the kitchen stairs, intent on nothing but the buttered scones and tea.

Later that night I washed her poor hair and filled a tub with hot water as I'd done so many times before, thinking it a sad and curious turn of events that had spared me her wrath. She'd no idea I was now her son's wife, and I saw no need to enlighten her. Thankfully Christian seemed to take the same view, for he raised no objection when she ordered me hither and thither as she'd always done, nor looked askance when I was smartly reprimanded for reciting her favourite poetry too slowly.

I guessed he was preparing himself for India's return, she having departed with her fiancé for a ride around the countryside, and I knew it would be an unhappy meeting. I meant to avoid the confrontation if I possibly could.

But it seemed I should not escape, for when we heard the carriage draw up outside, he stood up and signalled that I should follow him into the drawing room as soon as the poetry reading were finished. I read ever more slowly until Her Ladyship fell asleep in her chair, and then I had no more excuse to linger.

I listened for a moment outside the drawing room door.

'It's nothing serious,' I heard India say. 'It's simply grief at my father's death. And we have had great trouble with Mama's personal maid. The girl is unable to dress hair.'

I dithered foolishly, unable to decide whether I should knock or walk straight in. Then I knocked so timidly that no one heard me, and was obliged at last to throw open the door and announce myself.

Christian was standing by the window with his back to the room, and the other two were seated upon the sofa. None of them turned at my entry, and I perceived Christian to be sorely preoccupied.

I sat down, uncertain and ill at ease, thinking I should say nothing, but should somehow contrive to offer my silent support to my husband.

India stood up, forcing her brother to face her.

'We've been left very much to ourselves since you've been so busy,' she said directly. 'Mama has had to do a great deal on her own. I've naturally had to spend my time making ready my new home . . .'

Christian turned away once more and the Honourable Timothy Harrington spluttered over his cigar.

'We intended to seek medical advice, of course. But with your doctor having left the village, and Her Ladyship indisposed to travel, it was all rather difficult . . .'

Christian swung round to face them.

'Why wasn't I told?' he demanded. 'Why wasn't I sent for?'

I was watching him closely, aware from the cut of his shoulder just how angry he was, and anxious to diffuse any serious disagreement, I risked an opinion.

'The important thing is to get medical help now,' I said quickly. 'We could send for a doctor from Lynn, or we could take Lady Crompton . . .' I stumbled over the title, 'back to London to see a specialist there . . .'

Christian, turned toward the window once more, seemed hardly to have heard me, and it was a moment before I realized that the others did not mean to respond to anything I said, nor indeed, to acknowledge my presence at all.

'I think that might be best,' I stuttered, desperate to cover my embarrassment. 'I would guess it is some depression brought on by bereavement and exacerbated by spending a great deal of time alone . . . If only we had known . . .'

India stared through me, as though I were made of glass.

'Mama would not wish to spend time in your household, my dear Christian,' she said, making clear she were addressing him and not me. 'Such a thought would greatly distress her. She didn't even wish you to attend the wedding. But of course, it was only proper that you should give me away . . . And fortunately Tim was able to prevail upon her . . .'

Tim glanced uncomfortably at his intended.

'We must all make the best of a bad job,' he muttered.

Christian turned back from the window, and I felt my heart leap into my throat.

'What the hell do you mean by that?'

'I say, steady on, old man! Watch your language in front of the ladies . . .'

India walked toward the door.

'There is only one lady present,' she declared icily, 'and she does not intend to tolerate such talk . . .'

Her fiancé jumped to his feet and followed her out, mercifully leaving us alone.

I watched my husband struggle with his temper, and wondered for a wretched moment how I might restrain him from ordering Mr Harrington or his bride out of Crompton Hall. Then to my enormous relief, he held out his hand to me and laughed.

'You are the only lady present,' he murmured, folding me into his arms and kissing my hair. 'And now I shall do what I have long imagined doing . . . I shall take you into my own bed . . . In my own house.'

It was the only night we ever spent together at Crompton Hall. He told me there would be many such nights, and that when India was married and gone, there would be nothing to mar our happiness.

He told me we should have five fine sons, and that they would roam the Crompton estate with Ivy's children, and that my mother and brother would move out of Lavender Cottage and into the Hall with us.

He told me that he had no taste for soldiering and would give up his Army career as soon as his term ended. Then he would become a gentleman farmer and repair all the cottages on the Crompton estate until they were as good as Adam Goodchild's. And when all this was accomplished, I should become a country doctor, tending to the villagers as Dr Harte had done.

'Though I think you will still give them lavender oil,' he laughed.

He told me I should have my portrait painted by the best, the most expensive, artist in the land, and that it would hang in the library in place of India's.

'She can take her portrait with her when she goes,' he said.

He told me he had made a will, and that Crompton Hall would pass to me and my heirs if he should die.

'I shall ask you only to care for Mama,' he said. 'And to make sure that Kitty and Michael continue to receive their income . . . This I know you will do . . .'

I should have been happy at all his promises of love, and to know that I was trusted with his most secret and sacred commissions. And yet I could not be. A terrible melancholy settled upon me as I lay in his arms, and I seemed to scent destruction and death in the very air around me.

'Please don't talk of dying,' I whispered, burying my face in his neck and pulling him close. 'Please let this moment last for ever . . .'

'I don't believe in for ever,' he said gaily, unable to shed his customary light-heartedness even in the shadow of my tears. 'And so, my dearest Alice, we shall content ourselves with now . . .'

*　　*　　*

Spirits and phantoms. Angels and ghosts.

They inhabit this world just as surely as we do ourselves, and we have only to reach out to touch them.

They are potent as the imagination, real as dreams. They live and breathe, and though they are not flesh, they grieve and hope and laugh, just as we.

I did not visit Crompton Hall for many years and when I returned, I found them all still waiting for me.

Those bold Iceni warriors, flitting across the terrace and the lawns, those fighting women with one breast bouncing beside their bows ... And all my own dear ghosts, the living memories of all whom I had loved ...

I'd taken the train to Crompton station, just as I did half a lifetime ago, but this time without my husband beside me. Instead I was accompanied by my niece, making her first solo trip to England and much excited that she was, at last, to visit Crompton village.

Michael came to meet us in his extravagant car, supervising the unloading of the portrait from the guard's van and stowing it into his luggage compartment.

Kathryn was with him, and the two girls fell upon each other with kisses and giggles, always the very best of friends, even though their friendship had been forged by letter, and with an ocean in between them.

'This is a wonderful day!' Michael said, hugging me close. 'I think you will approve what we have done ... But where's Ivy? I thought she, at least, might have come with you ... The champagne is ready and waiting!'

'I think we can do justice to the champagne,' I said bravely. 'Don't you, Eleanor?'

I too had wanted Ivy to come, but she'd been busy with her own celebrations, helping prepare for her grandson's graduation.

But there was more than this, I knew, to her refusal. My sister and I both lost husbands in the Great War, but where my own loss had all but destroyed my life, hers had been the means to freedom. After my mother's death, Ivy vowed she would never set foot in Crompton village again. And she was not the only member of my family to make that selfsame vow . . .

A new road had been built from Crompton to the north, and now I found that we drove along the old perimeter of the beech woods, much reduced in size since Michael had sold so much land to pay for his renovations. To my surprise, I saw that the new road afforded a view of the lake.

'The sedge has never recovered,' Michael said, catching my eye in his driving mirror. 'We've tried everything to cure the blight . . . But nothing works.'

'Is it true?' Eleanor demanded breathlessly. 'That it began to die the day Eugenie was drowned? Do you think if they ever found her body, the sedge would grow back?'

'Of course not,' I said stiffly, ruffled by my niece's forthright manner and annoyed with Kathryn whom I guessed to be the source of this idea. 'That's just superstitious nonsense, and I shall thank you not to mention it again . . .'

Nevertheless, it was true. Many years ago, on the morning of India's wedding, Christian himself had remarked upon the death of the sedge, noting that it first began to wither after the drowning and finally to die after the fruitless draining of the lake . . . But he'd made light of it, saying that we should one day have the debris cleared away . . . 'And throw great boating parties, Alice! And picnics with our sons upon the banks . . .'

Spirits and phantoms. Angels and ghosts.

I had not believed I would ever see the lake, the beech woods nor the Hall again, and I had refused all Michael's entreaties over twenty years or more, welcoming him often to my home in London, but never choosing to visit him at Crompton.

But now I was here, and as we drove past the long vanished lavender fields, I seemed to see again the waving sea of purple-blue, buried just beneath the roots of the golden barley, ready to spring anew at any moment. As though in a vision or a fantasy, or in the eye of a storyteller . . .

Eleanor was excited and impatient, demanding to know

which was Blue Farm, which the pile of blackened stones that had once been Goodchild Manor, and which Lavender Cottage.

'My daddy's old home!' she declared in her impossible accent as we passed my mother's cottage, long since sold from the Crompton estate and belonging now, we were told, to Blue Farm.

'And that ugly old place must be Lavender House!'

'Charlie's son is still there,' Michael informed me, 'but there isn't much to keep him in Crompton . . . And I doubt there'll ever be a trade in lavender again . . .'

'Unless,' said Eleanor earnestly, 'Aunt Alice's ideas become fashionable once more! Oh, gee! That surely can't be Crompton Hall!'

But, indeed, it was, looking as fine as I ever remembered it, the stonework cleaned and patched, the portico rebuilt, the window frames replaced and freshly stained.

'I can't believe it!' I whispered to Michael.

The last time I'd seen it the west wing lay in ruin, weeds sprouted between the flagstones on the terrace, and the avenue of limes hung limp and ragged, with no gardener to see to their pruning, nor foreman to decide which should be felled and which left to prosper. Now the trees waved bright and strong, and the lawns, for so long a veritable wilderness, were clipped and lush, as green as they'd been on the night of India's birthday party.

'Your father would have been proud of you,' I murmured as Michael helped me from the car, 'and so am I . . .'

He tucked my arm into his own and signalled to the girls to bring in the portrait.

'I wouldn't be here if it weren't for you,' he murmured in my ear, 'I would still be a poor orphan boy in the backstreets of Dublin . . .'

I smiled and squeezed his arm, but I knew it wasn't true. Michael Crompton Malone, with his father's flair and his mother's talent, would never have failed to make his mark.

'I trust you haven't heard from Lady Harrington,' I asked as he led me into the hallway I remembered so well, and now that I saw it again, so very fondly. 'She'll be after you if she hears that Crompton Hall has been restored . . .'

He laughed heartily, a sudden poignant reminder of Christian's irrepressible humour.

'She's finally given up! My lawyer hasn't heard a word in three years. It seems Lord Harrington lost much of his fortune after Independence . . . They're finding it hard to keep the Hampshire estate going. They surely wouldn't wish to take on Crompton Hall as well . . .'

His wife had joined us, greeting me as she always did, as though I were her husband's natural mother with every right to her concern and love.

'Oh, you're here on your own!' she exclaimed, kissing me on both cheeks. 'We'd hoped you might persuade him to come with you . . .'

I shook my head.

'I wouldn't even try,' I said.

The girls clattered into the hallway behind us, balancing the portrait between them, Eleanor marvelling at the splendour of the stairway and the carved hall-stand, on which stood a magnificent display of blooms. She bent her head to sniff a flower.

'If this had been my house,' she declared passionately, 'I shouldn't have given it up for anyone . . .'

I didn't know whether she meant me, or India, perhaps, or even Michael himself, who'd pondered many times the wisdom of hanging on to Crompton Hall. But as she spoke, I found myself agreeing, and taking deep satisfaction in the knowledge that through my love for Michael, through adopting him as my own dear son and making him Christian's legitimate heir, I had not lost the house at all . . .

Kathryn was intent upon the portrait, pulling at the string which held its covers in place.

'Where are we going to hang it? Here in the hall, do you think?'

Michael raised an eyebrow at me.

'In the library,' I said steadily. 'That's where it hung originally . . . And where Christian wished my own portrait to hang . . .'

We walked through the hall and into Sir Robin's old lair where I was delighted to see his books, removed to a place of safety once the house fell into disrepair, now dusted down and back upon their shelves.

'Over the mantel,' I said as the covers finally fell away. 'That's where it must go . . .'

We all stood and stared at the painting. I had not looked at it since the day my face was added to it, and I saw now that only the madness of grief had persuaded me to commission such an extraordinary act at all. The painting was unbalanced, and indeed, it could hardly have been otherwise since my artist had been ordered to cram me into the small space behind India . . .

'That's a pretty queer picture!' Eleanor said with her usual directness. 'Whatever made you do it?'

I laughed self-consciously.

'I don't rightly know . . . Except that Christian had wanted my portrait to be done . . . And India would not take her own portrait away with her . . . And although Christian never liked it, to me it had great sentimental value . . .'

I pointed to her face.

'That is my dear friend as I will always remember her, despite everything that happened afterward . . . It seemed somehow right that we should be pictured together . . . As the companions we had always been and the sisters we were briefly to become . . . A representation, I suppose, of how things might have been . . .'

I heard my voice falter then, and Michael moved toward me quickly, putting his arm around my shoulder and declaring that the picture was a fine piece, that it summed up the spirit of Crompton Hall and should always hang above the library mantel. Considering his own vexed dealings with India, this seemed to me a great generosity.

I could not tell any of them that I had once dreamed my own face beside India's in the portrait, nor that for a long time I'd cherished the hope she might one day repent and seek my friendship again . . . That she might come to console me upon the loss of my beloved Christian

. . . Or thank me for my long service to her ailing mother
. . . Or even beg the forgiveness of dear Luke, though,
of course, I would never have revealed any such hope to
him . . .

And neither could I say that I had pondered long and
hard upon the mystery of *heart*, and that for many years
could not understand why hers had failed her, why she
had imagined herself so misused by me, nor why she had
turned so decisively from all she once seemed set to be . . .
Could not understand, that is, until I finally came to see
that the failure of *heart* is no more or less than a failure of
imagination . . . That unless we can imagine the suffering
of others, and take every chance afforded to increase our
compassion, then we shall never experience *heart* and the
world will never be transformed.

'Champagne!' announced Michael's wife ushering us all
from the library. 'Come along now! It's all set out in the
morning room . . .'

'We're celebrating a great deal more than the restoration
of Crompton Hall today,' Michael said mischievously,
winking at his wife. 'We are celebrating the arrival of a
famous person in our midst . . .'

'Who is that?' I asked, surprised, accepting my glass.

'Why it is you!' he laughed, waving a folded copy of *The
Times* under my nose. 'I knew you wouldn't have seen it!
Now we must turn to page seventeen . . .'

Eleanor fell upon the newspaper with a squeal of delight,
rummaging through it while I looked on in mild embarrassment, knowing what was coming for I was not so modest
that I refused to acknowledge my own achievements or to
read reports that praised my own work.

'A most interesting lecture,' Eleanor read aloud, 'on the
subject of 'The Role of the Spirit in the Healing Process'
with a book of the same name to follow shortly!'

She looked up at me in triumph.

'By Doctor Alice Harte!' she said.

I had thought to stay only a night, but was persuaded to

remain for the weekend, and found myself accommodated in the bedroom that had once been India's.

It had not changed at all. The heavy flock curtains still hung at the casement, and the furniture, now repolished and buffed, was only slightly rearranged, the tallboy and the dressing table being transposed. Then, in the bottom drawer of a chest, I found the tapestry quilt I had patched for India's birthday, musty and mothballed, yet still bright and intact. I laid it over the bed, and in a fleeting dissolution of the boundaries between past and present, felt myself to be Alice Harper, personal maid, once more. I sat down before the mirror where India had sat so many times while I brushed her beautiful hair, and as I stared into the glass, I was seized by a curious intimation of other faces, other moments in time, and I wondered about all who would sleep in this room and sit before this mirror.

'It would be nice if this could stay the way it is,' I said pensively to Kathryn, whose room it normally was. 'I think I should like that . . .'

I hardly knew why I said it, except, perhaps, that India's room spoke to me of a time when all my possibilities lay before me, when the course of history might still have been changed . . . Perhaps those other faces, the ones I'd glimpsed behind mine in the mirror, might catch the echo of my hopes and use them to achieve their own . . . Perhaps they might come to know my story.

It was in such fanciful mood that I set off alone for the beech woods next morning, taking the path to the pool where Christian liked to swim, and where I'd used to hide myself in the mallow bushes. I smiled at the memory, and though I was melancholy, I was not mournful, for it seemed to me then that I should surely see him again one day . . . As though the imprint of his nature had been left upon the world, awaiting only the turn of a page to bring it fresh and new to life again . . .

And then, walking back through the kitchen garden and pausing for a moment beside the old fig tree, I sat down on the bench beneath it, and looking up, saw a solitary cluster of green fruit. I reached to pluck it, and it was as I turned again that I seemed to see an unknown figure sitting where I had sat just a moment before . . . A young woman perhaps, although I could not be certain.

Spirits and phantoms. Angels and ghosts. Sometimes if you stand on tiptoe, you can peek into the future . . .

Our little lives may be set into eternity, and all our suffering transformed in the blink of an eye . . . But we shall see and take comfort by one means only.

Imagination, of course.

Chapter Twenty-four

Laurie did all the things she'd never done before at Crompton Hall.

She had a massage with lavender oil. She painted a passable watercolour of the lake and the summerhouse. She tried yoga and tai chi, and though she would not play the glockenspiel, she listened contentedly while others did.

She swam in the pool in the woods, earning the admiration of clients and staff alike who all declared it far too cold.

She learned to meditate, and to visualize her cancer as a virulent underground creature, a rat perhaps, or something alien from a distant galaxy, tunnelling through her sinews.

'What will kill it?' asked Dale Mitchell.

'Captain James T. Kirk,' she replied, 'and the crew of the Starship Enterprise . . . They're in there with their phasers . . . They're after it.'

She delved into the letters stored in rows of great binders in the library, exhuming Crompton history from the past eighty years, alternatively fascinated, sobered and uplifted by what she found.

She went back to the journals, poring over India's pages of philosophical musings, imagining she saw, in the easy embrace of Eastern thought, the seeds of India's eventual decline . . . She read every word that Alice had written, in diaries and in letters and in her book *The Role of the Spirit in the Healing Process*, finding many dull observations about various diseases and their remedies, as well as much complex theorizing about prayer, wishing for more that were purely personal, thinking there seemed to be so much which had never been told . . .

And then, her reading done, she wrote long and late in her own journal, filling its pages with stories of India and Alice, interweaving them with her own.

When she needed air, she walked to the churchyard beyond the woods and laid flowers on Ruth's grave.

She went into the church and found a stone tablet commemorating the lives of Sir Robin and Lady Frances Crompton-Leigh.

She saw Christian's name inscribed on a memorial plaque to the war dead, and wondered if Ivy's husband were mentioned there too.

She sat in the front pew and pictured India's wedding to Timothy Harrington, the cream satin of the gown, the white tulle of the bridal veil, the scarlet and gold of Christian's regimental dress as he gave her away, the scent of camellias, picked that morning by Hardy, drifting down the aisle . . . Which pew had Alice sat in after all? And did she and India ever meet again after that day?

She walked back along the shore of the lake and considered the state of the sedge. It *was* brown and dead-looking, but there were large patches of green in it too, and it was these that showed from the distance of her bedroom window . . . The tale about it withering after the drowning had been exaggerated, she decided . . . But it was still an evocative story, like the one about birds who would no longer sing on the sites of the concentration camps . . .

She picked blackcurrants in the kitchen garden and gathered a few stray figs, standing on the gnarled bench to reach up into the tree. Figs shouldn't be dried, of course, they should be pickled in brandy as Lady Crompton had decreed . . .

She took her harvest into the kitchen and found that the new chef had walked out, so she cooked lentil and pineapple curry for supper, a speciality from the New Leaf, with fig and blackcurrant compote for dessert.

'Are you looking for a job?' Dale asked her wryly. 'This sure beats broccoli and coconut!'

Laurie shook her head.

'No thanks,' she smiled, 'I'm going back to my life . . . Whatever that turns out to be!'

She had not seen Sean again. True to his word, he'd kept out of her way, and for this she was grateful. She didn't know if the final line had been drawn, but for the first time since she'd been told she had cancer – perhaps for the first time in her entire life – she was in no hurry. There would be a working out, one way or another, and whichever, it would be for the best.

Her own fortitude astonished her. It seemed to spring from a deep and hitherto unimagined source, a hidden stream of bubbling, dancing life which watered her dry heart and nourished her spirit.

I am Laurie Davison. I am alive. I may be dead this time next year, but right this moment, I'm alive . . .

'I hope,' said Val warily, 'it isn't another false dawn.'

'Well maybe it is . . . I'm not claiming I've beaten the fear for ever . . . But if I fall again, at least I'll know there's a way back up . . .'

Dale Mitchell showed no such caution.

'Be grateful for each good moment,' he told her. 'Celebrate every day you feel you can beat it . . . Those times will keep you going . . .'

Laurie hesitated.

'Did they keep Ruth going?' she asked him.

He signalled her toward the counselling suite.

'Go on in,' he said, 'and we'll talk about Ruth . . . But first there's something I'd like to show you . . .'

The portrait of India and Alice was back above the mantel.

'I got sick of that ugly old beast,' he said laughing. 'I mean the elephant, not India . . .'

Laurie looked up at the painting, remembering the first time she ever saw it, how odd and unbalanced the composition had seemed, how compelling and beautiful India had appeared . . .

'So Miranda won't be getting it after all?'

He shook his head.

'I knew you didn't approve of me parting with it. And I'd begun to wonder whether Kat would either . . . Although she wouldn't have stopped me. She considers me to have an equal claim on Crompton Hall and all that's in it. I am, after all, related to Alice . . .'

Laurie looked at him quizzically.

'Is it true you use this painting on all your clients? To see how susceptible they are? To prompt their imagination?'

'Oh, it doesn't have to be the painting,' he said easily, 'it can be anything . . . A journal, a book, the lake or the summerhouse . . . The old kitchen, India's room, the attic where Alice slept . . . Or maybe the church, although we have to be careful about the graves. Some people see the Grim Reaper around every corner. They can't bear to think about the people who once lived here and who are now all gone . . .'

He smiled.

'But not you,' he murmured, 'and not Ruth . . .'

Laurie looked away.

'Did Ruth know she was dying?' she asked at last.

'I believe she did, but we never spoke directly of it . . . Instead we talked of the day when we'd be together again. Of how arriving in Heaven must be like coming out in the main terminal at Heathrow. Everyone milling about, wondering where they're supposed to be . . . Looking out for their long-lost folks . . . I told her I'd stand by the British Airways desk, and that I'd be wearing my jeans and my red-checked shirt . . .'

Laurie laughed, despite her discomfort with this vision.

'Do you really believe that?' she asked him tentatively.

'I'm not sure. Some days I do, and others I think it's all garbage . . . But I do know that it gave us both great comfort to imagine we'd see each other again.'

He paused, looking at her carefully, considering his words.

'I also know that the power of prayer sustained Ruth at the end . . . It didn't cure her . . . Just as Alice's prayers failed to bring Christian home safely from the Front . . . And yet I saw myself how it changed the experience of death. She was peaceful. She was happy. Not happy she was dying, but happy that the moment had come in such a calm and consummating way . . .'

Laurie met his gaze.

'And how do you imagine that prayer sustained poor Christian?' she asked quietly because she could not ignore the question. 'I don't suppose he died peacefully . . .'

Dale nodded.

'I don't suppose he did . . . But the purpose and the result of prayer may not always coincide. He was prayed for, yes. And when the moment came, he acted with astonishing courage. I don't know what went through his mind as he ran on to the battlefield, but there's one thing I *do* know . . . Greater love hath no man than that he lay down his life for his friends . . . Maybe prayer, in some mysterious way, achieved that . . .'

Laurie said nothing, struggling with unfamiliar ideas, wondering for one awful moment whether Dale were about to be revealed as a Bible-toting evangelist, out to claim her for the kingdom of God.

He sensed her doubt.

'The practice of prayer isn't linked to any particular religious philosophy,' he said gently. 'Although it can be, of course . . . As it was for Ruth.'

He smiled.

'As indeed it is for many people who come here . . . We've had Buddhists and Pagans and Sufis and Born-Again Christians . . .'

'Is that what Ruth was?' Laurie interrupted, needing to know.

He shook his head.

'Ruth was a lifelong member of the Greek Orthodox Church. They had a lot in common . . . Both very disciplined, very traditional . . . And very beautiful.'

He looked down, and Laurie's heart went out to him, longing for something she might say, knowing there was nothing.

In the end she reached out and took his hand.

'You're doing a great thing here,' she said simply. 'You're giving people purpose and hope.'

'I like to think so,' he replied. 'And I'll keep on while I can . . . But I have to face the fact that we can't survive indefinitely ... We're running out of dough ... We've got the classic problem facing Western medicine. If you're going to give people the treatment they deserve, you need a hell of a lot of money. Some people can afford to pay, but many can't. For every person who benefits from Crompton Hall, there are a hundred others who'll never have the chance ...'

Laurie was shocked.

'What will you do?' she asked.

He shrugged.

'I don't know. Pray, I guess.'

'Will that work?'

He smiled distantly.

'One way or another,' he said.

'I don't know very much about prayer,' Laurie muttered, 'I wish I did ...'

'Well, then,' he said, brightening, 'you must persevere with Alice's book. She's the one with all the theories!'

But of course, it wasn't Alice's theories that Laurie wanted. It was Alice's story.

In her last few days at Crompton Hall, she uncovered the rest of it, Alice's thirty-year marriage to Luke Harte, their work together exploring the pathology of disease, the papers they published about the link between body and mind, the home they shared in Putney ...

As she wandered through the grounds and walked by the lake, with Val and Edie, or sometimes just with Dale himself, she sensed Alice at every step. Where once she had imagined India's ghost stalking the beech woods, now she could see only Alice ... Alice whose story had seemed so unpromising, whose destiny had seemed to be fatally constrained by her circumstance, whose childless state, like Laurie's own, had not proved the defining factor ...

'When I first came to Crompton Hall,' she told Val, 'I thought I was going barmy ... I imagined I knew the place, that I was somehow tuning in to everything that had happened here.'

'It's not barmy,' Val said squarely. 'It's a gift. We could all go mad, you know, having cancer . . . But there has to be some reward. If you start to accept it, and if you believe you can live with it, then you suddenly find yourself moving up a gear . . .'

That's it! I was cruising along in fourth, not even knowing there was a fifth . . . And now I'm in the fast lane, and it's bloody scary . . . But even so, I'm not pulling in . . .

'Maybe we could meet?' Laurie said impulsively. 'After I'm through with my radiotherapy . . . In London? I'll take you to dinner at the New Leaf cafe . . .'

'Yes,' said Val, surprised, 'That would be lovely. Thanks . . .'

Laurie made one final entry in her journal.

Imagine *this*: You spend your whole life doubting the existence of God, and then, against all odds, you find yourself in Heaven.

But when you get there, although it's very swish, streets of gold and pearly thrones, and although there's a right old knees-up, with all your long-departed aunties casting down their crowns, you can't help feeling a bit miffed.

You can't forget all the people you've left behind and how bloody miserable they still are.

You can't stop thinking that it's all been a bit of a cock-up really, that the great feast, jolly though it is, doesn't exactly compensate for ten thousand years of human suffering.

Say, what a swell party this is! Sorry? I was wondering about the Black Death . . . *Oh, do have a smoked salmon canape!* Well, that's fine and dandy, but what about the Holocaust? *Oh, do come and try the sherry trifle!*

You might get quite shirty about it all.

Then imagine that a kindly angel takes you to one side and attempts to explain. *All time is eternally present*, she says. *Nothing is wasted, nothing is lost.*

So, you peep over the parapet of Paradise, and what do you see? *Human experience transformed.* Hitler taking up embroidery and retiring to the countryside. Martin Luther

King dodging the fatal bullet. The World Peace Treaty signed and the hole in the ozone mended. *Whatever you want to see!*

And then you begin to understand. The past is meticulously woven into the fabric of the present, a complex pattern of recurring motifs, so subtle, so intricate, that mostly, you can't even see the join.

And above the past floats the future, a gauze veil haphazardly tacked on to the original material, light enough to let the colours show through. *So that's it!* Everything, everyone, is there for ever, straining to impart their news, imploring you to listen. Not trapped in time, but liberated from it. A great shout of joy escapes your lips. *Jubilate!*

Now imagine *this:* You turn back from the parapet. You can't see over anymore, and you suddenly realize it was all a delusion. No redemption, no salvation. Just a pretty lie designed to help you through the night. All that pain and sorrow for nothing. A right cock-up after all.

You're pretty sick now. You start to think some pretty black thoughts. For example, you start to consider that clinical depression, far from being a disordered condition, is the only truly rational state. You reckon that suicides, far from losing the balance of the mind, have actually achieved it. Remember the Japanese family who jumped off a high-rise building, hand in hand? Or the bloke who wrote the best-seller about painless ways to kill yourself? Heroes, one and all.

But then, imagine *this*: Something happens, now, in the present, in the real world, something both terrible and wonderful, something that alters your perception for good, that makes you see fact and fantasy as strands of the same pattern, each of them vital to the preservation of your sanity, the horror and the hope existing side by side.

Suppose, in short, that you get cancer? That you think you're dying? That you bitch and moan, and then, just when you think it's all over, you see a way through.

What would you do?

Well, you'd want to tell your story, wouldn't you?

*　　*　　*

She woke that last morning to a world unseasonably bright and warm.

She threw off the tapestry quilt and wandered to the window, opening it to let the weak sun kiss her face. She gazed across to the glinting lake with its curious brown-green sedge, reckoning she would take one final walk in the beech woods.

Gloria and Shelley were coming to pick her up, and this time, Laurie knew, she wouldn't be returning to Crompton Hall. Or at least, not as a client. If she came back, it would be because she had something to give. And how good it would be *to give* . . . It seemed to Laurie that her old life had contained far too much taking . . .

She slipped out through the house unseen, guessing that all hands were required for breakfast, walking quickly through the kitchen garden and the orchard, into the woods.

She had no particular route in mind, and she hadn't imagined that anyone else might be about.

But as she neared Christian's pool, she heard voices. Children's voices, thin and high, shrieking in delight.

Spirits and phantoms. Angels and ghosts . . .

Heart pounding, Laurie stepped into the mallow bushes, thinking for one mad moment that her fantasies had taken flesh . . . What children were these? Luke Harte's daughters, perhaps, before the fever epidemic struck . . .

She peered cautiously through the leaves.

Two golden-haired girls were splashing in the pool, and between them, floating on his back, was Sean, laughing as one twin grabbed his leg and the other tickled his stomach.

Laurie drew in her breath. Here, caught in one brief snapshot, was all she had once wanted . . . All she'd dreamed would one day be hers . . .

She watched for another moment, and then, just as Alice Harper had done before her, walked swiftly away from the vision and into her unknown future.

*　　*　　*

Gloria was anxious, still angry with herself for having let Laurie drive to Norfolk.

'Everyone said it was mad . . . Driving straight after a mastectomy . . .'

'I'm okay,' Laurie laughed, hugging her close, 'but I'm very glad you're here to take me home . . .'

Gloria's lip trembled.

'You're really coming home, darling? For good?'

'For good,' Laurie whispered. 'And believe me, it truly feels good . . .'

Gloria uttered a faint sigh of relief, and unable to resist the opportunity, pressed home her advantage.

'You remember my idea for the consulting suite? Above the cafe? Well, I've found the most marvellous homeopath who wants to set up shop right away . . . She told me about a special treatment for cancer . . . It's called Iscador. A derivative of mistletoe, she says . . .'

I took a dilution of mistletoe berries mixed with crushed sprigs of St John's wort into the hospital, and fed it to my mother in surreptitious sips . . .

'Mistletoe?' Laurie echoed thoughtfully. 'Well, fancy that . . . I'd like to hear all about it, of course! And I've got a few ideas myself for your consulting suite. In fact, I can hardly wait to get started . . .'

Shelley raised one painted eyebrow, then let it drop. She had more urgent matters on her mind.

'What happened with Sean?' she whispered as Gloria turned to greet Val. 'Did you see him?'

'Yes. And nothing happened . . .'

'Nothing at all? I can't believe it!'

'Sorry, but it's true . . .'

'Then where's the gorgeous Dale?' demanded Shelley, swallowing her disappointment and looking round the hallway hopefully. 'I need one last look before we finally depart, and I'm sure you do . . .'

He appeared from the counselling suite at just that moment, Californian man, exactly as Laurie had first seen him, in his red-checked shirt and his blue jeans. Ruth surely wouldn't miss him if he turned up at Heaven's terminal today . . .

'I hate to say goodbye,' he said, taking Laurie's hand. 'I sure hope you'll come back and visit?'

She smiled.

'Of course,' she said, 'but in the meantime, here's something to remember me by . . .'

She handed him her journal, complete with all her angry outbursts, and all her stories of India and Alice.

'Keep it with the others,' she said.

'Thank you,' he said surprised, 'I will . . .'

He walked out with them on to the driveway, but then hung back so he might bid her a private goodbye.

'Good luck with your radiotherapy,' he said, 'and everything that comes after . . . You know where I am if you need me . . .'

She hesitated.

'There's something I meant to ask and hardly dared to . . . But I've just been reminded of it, and now I've got to know . . . Alice's mother? How long did she survive? Did she beat her cancer?'

He grinned.

'Nell Harper lived into her seventies, and the cancer never recurred. Whether that was due to Alice, to the kind of tumour she had, to Nature, the Lord Almighty, or simply to her own refusal to lie down and die before she'd had her three score years and ten . . . Well, who knows? But Nell is worth remembering when times get tough . . .'

Laurie looked down.

'There's something you can do when I'm gone,' she murmured, embarrassed and yet still determined to say it. 'You can pray for me . . .'

'Have done since the day you arrived,' he said seriously, fixing her with the deep grey eyes, 'and you can be sure, I'll keep right on . . .'

Unexpectedly, he leaned forward and kissed her quickly on the cheek, dropping his hand upon her shoulder as they walked out to the waiting cars.

'That man is an angel,' Shelley declared the moment

the door was closed, 'and he fancies you! I know he does . . .'

'Control yourself, girl,' Laurie said sternly. 'The man's in grief . . .'

Shelley kicked the engine into life.

'Just think,' she said wickedly, 'how very suitable a widower would be . . . That's really got the first wife problem licked!'

Laurie fought a giggle.

'I didn't hear that, okay?'

Shelley guffawed loudly.

'Oh come on, Laurie . . . I said it at the start . . . Any woman in her right mind would have the pants off Dale Mitchell . . .'

They were driving out through the avenue of limes, Gloria close behind them in Laurie's car, on through the village with its pink and white houses, past Lavender Cottage, Blue Farm, and the waving fields of barley . . .

Thank you, Alice Harper, thank you. I won't ever forget.

'I bet he phones,' said Shelley, 'I bet he comes to see you . . .'

Laurie shook her head absently.

'I wouldn't want him to . . . You don't understand . . .'

'Oh *come on!* Life's too short to hang about . . .'

It was a moment before her own remark registered.

'Oh *shit*, Laurie! Shit, shit, shit! I didn't mean that . . . I'm just playing the fool as usual, trying to kid you out of it . . . God-damn it, life's not short! We're going to live to be ninety, you and me both . . .'

'Take it easy,' Laurie soothed. 'It's okay. It doesn't matter . . .'

They were out on the road that ran past the beech woods, skirting the lake. Laurie shaded her eyes against the glittering water.

'Anyway,' she murmured, 'you're right. Life *is* short . . .'

She turned her gaze from the lake, fixing instead on the road ahead.

She smiled at Shelley.

'Short and sweet,' she said.